The End of

The Works of Robert E. Howard

The End of the Trail
Western Stories

Robert E. Howard

Edited and
with an introduction by
Rusty Burke

University of Nebraska Press
Lincoln

Set in Fred Smeijers' typeface Quadraat by
Keystone Typesetting, Inc.
Book designed by Richard Eckersley.
Printed and bound by Thomson-Shore, Inc.
⊜
Library of Congress Cataloging-in-Publication Data
Howard, Robert Ervin, 1906–1936.
The end of the trail : western stories / Robert E. Howard ;
edited and with an introduction by Rusty Burke.
p. cm. — (The works of Robert E. Howard)
Includes bibliographical references and index.
ISBN 0-8032-2424-9 (cloth: alk. paper)
ISBN 0-8032-7356-8 (pbk. : alk. paper)
1. Western stories. I. Burke, Rusty. II. Title.
PS3515.0842A6 2005e
813'.52—dc22
2004029092

Always the simple, strong men go into the naked lands and fight heroical battles to win and open those lands to civilization. Then comes civilization, mainly characterized by the smooth, the dapper, the bland, the shrewd men who play with business and laws and politics and they gain the profits; they enjoy the fruit of other men's toil, while the real pioneers starve.

Well, they have gone into the night, a vast and silent caravan, with their buckskins and their boots, their spurs and their long rifles, their waggons and their mustangs, their wars and their loves, their brutalities and their chivalries; they have gone to join their old rivals, the wolf, the panther and the Indian, and only a crumbling 'dobe wall, a fading trail, the breath of an old song, remain to mark the roads they travelled. But sometimes when the night wind whispers forgotten tales through the mesquite and the chaparral, it is easy to imagine that once again the tall grass bends to the tread of a ghostly caravan, that the breeze bears the jingle of stirrup and bridle-chain, and that spectral camp-fires are winking far out on the plains.

Robert E. Howard

CONTENTS

Introduction

I'm seriously contemplating devoting all my time and efforts to western writing, abandoning all other forms of work entirely; the older I get the more my thoughts and interests are drawn back over the trails of the past; so much has been written, but there is so much that should be written.
— Robert E. Howard to August W. Derleth, November 28, 1935

The Texas author Robert Ervin Howard (1906–36) is best known for his tales of heroic fantasy featuring such mighty heroes as Conan, Kull, and Solomon Kane. But in the last few years of his too-short life, Howard turned his attention more and more to tales of the West. His most commercially successful westerns were the rollicking tall tales involving Breckinridge Elkins. Appearing in every issue of Action Stories between March 1934 and October 1936, these stories proved so popular that when the editor of Action Stories moved to Argosy, he asked Howard to create another such character for that magazine. "If I can get a series running in Argosy, keep the Elkins series running in Action Stories, now a monthly, and the Buckner J. Grimes yarns in Cowboy Stories, I'll feel justified in devoting practically all my time to the writing of western stories," Howard wrote to H. P. Lovecraft in May 1936, only a month before his death.

But while the humorous western tales were his bread and butter, Howard was showing increasing confidence in his handling of the traditional western, as the stories in this volume will attest. Many critics believe that, given a few years, Howard might have become an important western writer. H. P. Lovecraft, in a memorial tribute to his friend written shortly after Howard's death, stated: "Steeped in the frontier atmosphere, Mr. Howard early became a devotee of its virile Homeric traditions. His knowledge of its history and folkways was profound, and the descriptions and reminiscences contained in his private letters illustrate the eloquence and power with which he would have celebrated it in literature had he lived longer." And in the first collection of Howard's stories, *Skull-Face and Others*, the Arkham House editor and publisher August Derleth said, "He had in him the promise of becoming an important American regionalist, and to that end he had been assimilating the lore and legend, the history and culture patterns of his own corner of Texas with a view to writing of them seriously." In this, Lovecraft and Derleth concur with Howard's own sentiments: "I have always felt that if I ever accomplished anything worthwhile in the literary field, it would be with stories dealing of the central and western frontier."

"I was born," Howard wrote, "in the little ex-cowtown of Peaster, about 45 miles west of Fort Worth, in the winter of 1906, but spent my first summer in lonely Dark Valley among the sparsely settled Palo Pinto hills. From then until I was nine years old I lived in various parts of the state—in a land-boom town on the Staked Plains, near the New Mexican line; in the Western Texas sheep country; in San Antonio; on a ranch in South Texas; in a cattle town on the Oklahoma line, near the old North Texas oil-fields; in the piney woods of East Texas; finally in what later became the Central West Texas oil belt." In 1919 the family finally settled in Cross Plains, in the house where Robert would spend the rest of his life. He held the usual assortment of jobs for a young man in a small town, but he seems to have decided very early on that he would become a writer. In the rough-and-tumble atmosphere in which he grew up, this was a most unusual ambition, and even young Bob's closest friends did not quite understand it.

It seems to me that many writers, by virtue of environments of culture, art and education, slip into writing because of their environments. I became a writer in spite of my environments. Understand, I am not criticizing those environments. They were good, solid and worthy. The fact that they were not inducive to literature and art is nothing in their disfavor. Never the less, it is no light thing to enter into a profession absolutely foreign and alien to the people among which one's lot is cast; a profession which seems as dim and faraway and unreal as the shores of Europe. The people among which I lived—and yet live, mainly—made their living from cotton, wheat, cattle, oil, with the usual percentage of business men and professional men. That is most certainly not in their disfavor. But the idea of a man making his living by writing seemed, in that hardy environment, so fantastic that even today I am sometimes myself assailed by a feeling of unreality. Nevertheless, at the age of fifteen, having never seen a writer, a poet, a publisher or a magazine editor, and having only the vaguest ideas of procedure, I began working on the profession I had chosen.

Howard submitted his first story for professional publication, "Bill Smalley and the Power of the Human Eye," to *Western Story* when he was just fifteen. Although the story is a tale of the North Woods, it is nevertheless interesting that his first professional submission was to a magazine of western fiction. Nor was the tale of the West neglected in the young author's work: his first published stories, " 'Golden Hope' Christmas" and "West Is West," were of this type. The latter is a short, humorous piece about a tenderfoot who stays atop an unrideable bronco only because his gunbelt and lariat get tangled up with the saddle. " 'Golden Hope' Christmas," included herein, shows the clear influence of O. Henry and Bret Harte but stands up well as a charming Christmas fable, and already shows flashes of Howard's later style, particularly in his portrayal of gunman Red Ghallinan. Both stories were published in the December 22, 1922, issue of *The Tattler*, the student newspaper of Brownwood High School, where Howard spent his last year of school. " 'Golden Hope' Christmas" won a ten dollar prize, while "West Is West" was awarded five dollars.

Howard made his first professional sale to *Weird Tales* in 1924, and he concentrated his efforts over the next few years on stories of fantasy and horror, with occasional submissions to *Adventure* and *Argosy*, the two most popular general fiction pulps, and a few other magazines as well. In a listing of his stories made in 1929, he shows one story, now lost, sent to *Western Story* in 1925, but no other westerns until 1928, when he sold "Drums of the Sunset" to his hometown newspaper, *The Cross Plains Review*, for twenty dollars. A traditional western, perhaps showing the influence of such writers as Eugene Manlove Rhodes and Zane Grey, the story features one of Howard's more memorable eccentrics, "Hard Luck" Harper, and also gives us a hint of Howard's love of folk songs, particularly cowboy songs. The story ran as a nine-part serial from November 1928 through

January 1929. Howard later retitled it "Riders of the Sunset" and attempted to sell it to *Argosy* and *Western Story* without success.

By 1929 Howard's professional career was beginning to take off. He was by this time a regular contributor to *Weird Tales*, and he had made a few sales to other magazines, so he began spreading his literary net a bit wider, writing stories in a variety of genres and submitting them to *Argosy*, *Adventure*, *Liberty*, *Ghost Stories*, *True Stories*, and others. He caught on with prize-ring tales for Fiction House's *Fight Stories* and *Action Stories*: the Steve Costigan series would prove one of his most successful. But after one sale each to both *Ghost Stories* and *Argosy*—both boxing stories—he had little success with these other magazines. "The Extermination of Yellow Donory" failed to catch on with *Adventure*, *Argosy*, or *Western Story*, although it is a clever character piece. "The subject of psychology is the one I am mainly interested in these days," Howard had written earlier in describing the stories "The Dream Snake" and "The Shadow Kingdom" as studies in psychology. During the period in which "Yellow Donory" was written, Howard was writing a number of other psychological tales, such as "Crowd-Horror," in which a boxer loses all self-control when he hears the crowd roar, and "The Touch of Death," in which a man sitting in a room with a corpse is overcome by his own fear. In "Yellow Donory" we find Howard's first real foray into a subject that would come to fascinate him: the psychology of the gunman.

"The Judgment of the Desert," another 1929 story unsuccessfully submitted to *Argosy*, is a more traditional western tale that certainly might have found a home a few years later, when the demand for westerns led to a significant increase in the number of western magazines. Here we find the first instance of what would become a staple of Howard's westerns, a less-than-happy ending.

Howard apparently abandoned western writing for a time; in 1930 his interests resided primarily in Irish history and legend, resulting in stories of Irish adventurers such as Turlogh O'Brien and Cormac Mac Art. These stories were an important step toward the later creation of Conan and Howard's histories of the Crusades. In the latter half of the year, however, two men began to turn Howard's thinking back toward western themes. His good friend Tevis Clyde Smith, of Brownwood, Texas, began selling articles about Texas history to newspapers in both Brownwood and Dallas: in researching the articles, Smith had been interviewing old-time pioneers and their descendants, which may have inspired Howard to do the same as his interest in the West grew. In June Howard began corresponding with another notable *Weird Tales* contributor, H. P. Lovecraft, whose interest in the Texan's brief mentions of local lore or legends prompted more discussion of these topics. By January 1931 Howard had submitted an article, "The Ghost of Camp Colorado," to *The Texaco Star*, a magazine published by the oil company that featured occasional historical articles. He also revised and retitled "Drums of the Sunset" in an attempt to sell it; wrote a new story, "A Killer's Debt"; brought his boxing sailor, Steve Costigan, closer to home in "Texas Fists"; and began writing stories for *Weird Tales* using a southwestern setting.

"Gunman's Debt" is the first of what we might call the truly "Howardian" western stories, in that it is much grimmer than his previous work in the form and shares certain characteristics with his heroic fantasy work, particularly in its bleak viewpoint and the cataclysmic violence of its climax. There are no "good guys" in the story: the ostensible "hero," John Kirby, is a gunman and feudist, merely the best among a very bad lot. Howard was fascinated by the psychology of outlaws and feudists: no story better illustrates this than "The Man on the Ground," which appeared in *Weird Tales* in 1933. "One of the main things I like about Farnsworth Wright's magazines," Howard wrote, "is you don't have to make your heroes such utter saints." Wright edited *Weird Tales* and *Oriental Stories* (later *The Magic Carpet Magazine*), through which Howard's grimmest, most somber characters stalked. It is regrettable that Wright did not edit a western magazine, so that Howard might have gone further toward fulfilling his promise in that field. Howard's protagonists did not fit the standard mold for the western hero; as some have pointed out, they would have been more at home on the mean streets of *Black Mask* than in *Western Story*.

Howard had a particular fascination with outlaws, notably John Wesley Hardin and Billy the Kid, and most of his heroes have more than a little outlaw in their nature. Even his heroic fantasy characters—Kull, Conan, Turlogh, Cormac and others—are, at one time or another in their careers, outlaws. Howard was a thoroughgoing populist in his politics, and the outlaw, driven to crime by the depredations of corrupt authorities, is a staple of populist literature. Jesse James, Wes Hardin, and Billy the Kid are the forerunners of those outlaws of Howard's own day, such as Pretty Boy Floyd and John Dillinger, who were seen as heroes by some, particularly the rural poor. Howard's own admiration for Hardin and the Kid, and for other outlaws, shines through his letters to Lovecraft: "Your real gunman was always a man of keen perceptions and a high order of intelligence. It was not merely physical superiority that made such men as Billy the Kid, John Wesley Hardin, John Ringgo and Hendry Brown super-warriors. It was their razor-edged intelligence, their unerring judgment of human nature, and their natural knowledge of human psychology." The influence of such figures may be seen in Howard's Steve Allison (The Sonora Kid), hero of "The Devil's Joker" and "Knife, Bullet and Noose."

Like Howard's contemporary Middle-Eastern adventurer Francis X. Gordon (El Borak), Steve Allison was an early creation who figured in a number of incomplete stories written when Howard was in his teens. In fact, these two characters were teamed up in several such abortive tales. The early Steve Allison, like the early Francis X. Gordon, seems to have been a man of the world, as much at home as a guest in a German castle or a New York hotel as on a ranch or in an Afghan hill village. The later incarnations of these characters would lose the more cultivated side in favor of the man who has "gone native." El Borak found his milieu in the Middle East, while The Sonora Kid found his place along the Texas-Mexico border: both were modeled on the gunmen that Howard admired. Allison was the first to be resurrected when Howard sent "The Devil's Joker" and "Knife, Bullet and Noose" to his new agent, Otis Adelbert Kline, in the late spring of 1933, but Allison did not find the publication success his erstwhile partner met with a year later. The Sonora Kid stories failed to sell during Howard's lifetime.

"Law-Shooters of Cowtown," received by Howard's agent on the same day as the two Sonora Kid stories, also featured a character from an earlier story, this time Grizzly Elkins, the buffalo hunter of "Gunman's Debt." "Law-Shooters" features one of Howard's most graphically brutal fistfights and a scene in which Elkins wades through the lynch mob with an iron bar. Either scene alone was probably enough to sink the story's chances with most editors of western magazines (it's hard to imagine *Western Story* or *Wild West Weekly* printing a line like "Blood and brains spattered in his face"), and to boot, the story also features crooked lawmen, definitely not standard fare for the traditional western. In this regard the story anticipates "Vultures of Wahpeton."

"The phenomenon of an outlaw looting a section under the guise of an officer of the law was not unknown in the early West—as witness Henry Plummer, and some others," Howard wrote to Lovecraft, regarding the plot of his Breckinridge Elkins story "A Gent From Bear Creek," which had just appeared in *Action Stories*. He went on to relate at some length episodes from the beginning and end of Hendry Brown's brief career as marshal of Caldwell, Kansas: the marshal had come to a bad end when he and some accomplices attempted to rob the bank. Not long afterward, he told August Derleth that he had just written a thirty-thousand-word western story in which "my main character was drawn from Hendry Brown." This story was "Vultures of Wahpeton," and Howard called it "one of the best stories I've ever written." He told Derleth he'd written the first draft of the story in two and a half days and expressed doubt that anyone would accept it. Unfortunately, Howard's assessment was correct: although the story is Howard's best nonhumorous western and although the western magazine market was becoming more receptive to grim, violent stories, "Vultures of Wahpeton" had difficulty finding a home. The story's merits are considerable, however: in "Vultures," Howard accomplished for the Western story that which he had already done for the sword-and-sorcery story, in which he had blended the adventure, fantasy, and horror genres. To the western story Howard added the populist sensibility of the hardboiled detective, himself an amalgam of outlaw and policeman ("an agent of law and an outlaw who acts outside the structures of legal authority for the sake of a personal definition of justice," says Richard Slotkin). The critic George Knight wrote, "Doubtless, had Howard lived, his efforts with the Western story could have led him to approach that form with the same tough attitude that characterizes his fantasy. It is interesting to think that he might have taken the Western along a similar line of development as Hammett took the detective tale." As Steve Tompkins pointed out, "Howard had begun doing exactly that: it is not very far at all from Wahpeton to Poisonville, the former Personville of Dashiell Hammett's *Red Harvest*."

Stephen Marcus said, "One of Hammett's obsessive imaginations was the notion of organized crime or gangs taking over an entire society and running it as if it were an ordinary society doing business as usual. . . . It is a world of universal warfare, the war of each against all, and of all against all. The only thing that prevents the criminal ascendancy from turning into permanent tyranny is that the crooks who take over society cannot cooperate with one another, repeatedly fall out with each other, and return to the Hobbesian anarchy out of which they have momentarily arisen." It is easy to imagine why authors such as Hammett and Howard were obsessed with this notion: in many American cities in the 1920s, mobsters corrupted high-ranking officials while warring among themselves. "We are organized," says Sheriff Middleton to Steve Corcoran in "Vultures." "We know who to trust; they don't." But it soon becomes clear that even within the gang no one knows whom to trust. "His hapless deputy McNab," writes Tompkins, "is just one of the characters in 'Vultures' to sense 'that he was beginning to be wound in a web he could not break,' to deem himself 'too tangled in a web of subtlety to know where or how or who to smite.' " The characters might have been modeled on Hendry Brown and on Henry Plummer's "Innocents" gang in 1860s Montana, but they could just as easily have been modeled on Capone's or Luciano's mobs.

This mistrust of everyone, verging on paranoia, harks back to Howard's earliest sword-and-sorcery story, "The Shadow Kingdom," in which King Kull learns that serpent men with the ability to assume the appearance of any human have insinuated themselves into his palace, and that absolutely no one can be trusted. Mistrust of appearances, and in particular mistrust of authority, is a constant theme of Howard's work, another characteristic that would have made him more at home in the hard-boiled detective field than the western, where the good guys wore white hats. Yet Howard "actively detest[ed]" detective stories: "I can scarcely endure to read one, much less write one." Thus he had to bring his hard-boiled sensibility to fields he liked better: heroic adventure and the western. Fearing that no editor of the day would want to publish "Vultures" with its bleak ending, Howard supplied another, happier conclusion as well. The editor of *Smashing Novels*, in December 1936, for some reason chose to publish both endings, calling the darker one "more powerful, dramatically," a judgment with which most would concur.

Shortly before writing "Vultures of Wahpeton" Howard had completed revising an unsold story by another writer, Chandler Whipple (writing as "Robert Enders Allen"). According to Whipple, Howard's agent, Otis Kline, had dropped by to see him when he was working as an editor at Popular Publications, and during the course of the conversation, "asked if he couldn't try to sell something of mine that I had failed to market. I gave him 'The Last Ride.' He told me he thought he could get Bob Howard to turn it into a saleable piece, and I told him to go ahead." It is not known how much of "The Last Ride" is Howard and how much is Whipple, who got top billing when the story was published as "Boot-Hill Payoff" in *Western Aces*.

In early 1936 John F. Byrne, who had been regularly buying Howard's stories for Fiction House since 1929, took over the editorship of *Argosy* and asked Howard to create a series for that magazine along the lines of the Breckinridge Elkins stories that had been appearing in every issue of *Action Stories*. Howard obliged with his tales of Pike Bearfield, but he also took the opportunity to work in some nonhumorous stories as well. The first of these to appear in print was "The Dead Remember," a tale of voodoo vengeance that would have been right at home in *Weird Tales*. That magazine was well over a thousand dollars in arrears to Howard, though, so he was trying other markets first. The last of Howard's five *Argosy* stories to appear was "Vulture's Sanctuary," a more traditional western with a conventional happy ending but with a veritable Conan of a cow-puncher as its hero.

Howard's letters to H. P. Lovecraft and August Derleth contained sometimes lengthy accounts of episodes from Western history or the lives of gunfighters. Some, such as his stories of John Wesley Hardin and Billy the Kid, appear to have derived largely from his reading. "Billy the Kid and the Lincoln County War" (selected for this volume and titled by the editor) shows the influence of Walter Noble Burns's best-selling *The Saga of Billy the Kid* but is told with the passionate intensity characteristic of Howard. "Beyond the Brazos River" (again selected and titled by the editor) seems to come from Howard's interviews with old-time pioneering Texans or their descendants. "In this country," he wrote Derleth, "frontier days were yesterday." In another letter he said:

San Antonio is full of old timers—old law officers, trail drivers, cattlemen, buffalo hunters and pioneers. No better place for a man to go
who wants to get first hand information about the frontier. The lady
who owned the rooms I rented, for instance, was an old pioneer woman
who had lived on a ranch in the very thick of the "wire-cutting war" of
Brown County; and on the street back of her house lived an old gentleman who went up the Chisholm in the '80s, trapped in the Rockies,
helped hunt down Sitting Bull, and was a sheriff in the wild days of
western Kansas. I wish I had time and money to spend about a year
looking up all these old timers in the state and getting their stories.

The title "Beyond the Brazos River" was chosen quite deliberately. This
passage from a 1931 letter seems very clearly to presage the theme of
Howard's Conan story "Beyond the Black River" (the rivers in the story
even begin with the same letters as the Texas rivers, Black/Brazos, Thun-
der/Trinity). Novalyne Price Ellis, who knew Howard well from 1934 to
1936, insisted that "Beyond the Black River" was a Texas story.

"I hope," Howard told Lovecraft, "to some day write a history of the
Southwest that will seem alive and human to the readers, not the dry and
musty stuff one generally finds in chronicles. To me the annals of the land
pulse with blood and life, but whether I can ever transfer this life from my
mind to paper, is a question." Certainly the stories retold in his letters, of
Hardin and Billy, of Bigfoot Wallace and the Marlow boys and others,
show that he could bring blood and life to chronicles: in his retelling the
stories are even more vividly intense than the accounts of participants in
the events. But he was not to get his chance to create an epic of the
Southwest. In June of 1936 his beloved mother sank into her final coma,
and an exhausted, dispirited, and ultimately despondent Robert E. Howard came to the end of his own trail at the age of only thirty. He left behind
a legacy of stories and poems that have continued to be enjoyed by generations of new readers. For all that he wrote during the Great Depression,
there is about his stories something always modern, always meaningful.
And of course, there is always the headlong narrative pace and the explosive action that makes Howard one of the most entertaining writers ever
to spin a yarn.

The End of the Trail

"Golden Hope" Christmas

Red Ghallinan was a gunman. Not a trade to be proud of, perhaps, but Red was proud of it. Proud of his skill with a gun, proud of the notches on the long blue barrels of his heavy .45's. Red was a wiry, medium sized man with a cruel, thin lipped mouth and close-set, shifty eyes. He was bow-legged from much riding, and, with his slouching walk and hard face he was, indeed, an unprepossessing figure. Red's mind and soul were as warped as his exterior. His sinister reputation caused men to strive to avoid offending him but at the same time it cut him off from the fellowship of people. No man, good or bad, cares to chum with a killer. Even the outlaws hated him and feared him too much to admit him to their gang, so he was a lone wolf. But a lone wolf may sometimes be more feared than the whole pack.

Let us not blame Red too much. He was born and reared in an environment of evil. His father and his father's father had been rustlers and gunfighters. Until he was a grown man, Red knew nothing but crime as a legitimate way of making a living and by the time he learned that a man may earn a sufficient livelihood and still remain within the law he was too set in his ways to change. So it was not altogether his fault that he was a gunfighter. Rather, it was the fault of those unscrupulous politicians and mine-owners who hired him to kill their enemies. For that was the way Red lived. He was born a gun-fighter. The killer instinct burned strongly in him – the heritage of Cain. He had never seen the man who surpassed him or even equalled him in the speed of the draw or in swift, straight shooting. These qualities, together with the cold nerve and reckless bravery that goes with red hair, made him much in demand with rich men who had enemies. So he did a large business.

But the fore-van of the law began to come into Idaho and Red saw with hate the first sign of that organization which had driven him out of Texas a few years before – the vigilantes. Red's jobs became fewer and fewer for he feared to kill unless he could make it appear self-defense.

At last it reached a point where Red was faced with the alternative of moving on or going to work. So he rode over to a miner's cabin and announced his intention of buying the miner's claim. The miner, after one skittish glance at Red's guns, sold his claim for fifty dollars, signed the deed, and left the country precipitately.

Red worked the claim for a few days and then quit in disgust. He had not gotten one ounce of gold dust. This was due, partly, to his distaste for work, partly to his ignorance of placer mining, and mostly to the poorness of the claim.

He was standing in the front door of the saloon of the little mining town when the stage-coach drove in and a passenger alit.

He was a well built, frank-appearing young fellow and Red hated him instinctively. Hated him for his cleanness, for his open, honest, pleasant face, because he was everything Red was not.

The newcomer was very friendly and very soon the whole town knew his antecedents. His name was Hal Sharon, a tenderfoot from the east, who had come to Idaho with high hopes of striking a bonanza and going home wealthy. Of course there was a girl in the case, though Hal said little on that point. He had a few hundred dollars and wanted to buy a good claim. At this Red took a new interest in the young man.

Red bought drinks and lauded his claim. Sharon proved singularly trustful. He did not ask to see the claim but took Red's word for it. A trustfulness that would have touched a less hardened man than Red.

One or two men, angered at the deliberate swindle, tried to warn Hal but a cold glance from Red caused them to change their minds. Hal bought Red's claim for five hundred dollars.

He toiled unceasingly all fall and early winter, barely making enough to keep him in food and clothes, while Red lived in the little town and sneered at his uncomplaining efforts.

Christmas was in the air. Everywhere the miners stopped work and came to town to live there until the snow should have melted and the ground thawed out in the spring. Only Hal Sharon stayed at his claim, working on in the cold and snow, spurred on by the thought of riches – and a girl.

It was a little over three weeks until Christmas, when, one cold night, Red Ghallinan sat by the stove in the saloon and listened to the blizzard outside. He thought of Sharon doubtless shivering in his cabin up on the slopes and he sneered. He listened idly to the talk of the miners and cow-punchers who were discussing the coming festivals, a dance and so on.

Christmas meant nothing to Red. Though the one bright spot in his life had been one Christmas years ago when Red was a ragged waif, shivering on the snow covered streets of Kansas City.

He had passed a great church and, attracted by the warmth, had entered timidly. The people had sung "Hark the Herald Angels Sing!" and when the congregation passed out, an old, white-haired woman had seen the boy and had taken him home and fed him and clothed him. Red had lived in her home as one of the family until spring but when the wild geese began to fly north and the trees began to bud, the wanderlust got into the boy's blood and he ran away and came back to his native Texas prairies. But that was years ago and Red never thought of it now.

The door flew open and a furred and muffled figure strode in. It was Sharon – his hands shoved deep in his coat pockets.

Instantly Red was on his feet, hand twisting just above a gun. But Hal took no notice of him. He pushed his way to the bar.

"Boys," he said, "I named my claim the Golden Hope, and it was a true name! Boys, I've struck it rich!"

And he threw a double handful of nuggets and gold-dust on the bar.

On Christmas Eve Red stood in the door of an eating house and watched Sharon coming down the slope, whistling merrily. He had a right to be merry. He was already worth twelve thousand dollars and had not exhausted his claim by half. Red watched with hate in his eyes. Ever since the night Sharon had thrown his first gold on the bar, his hatred of the man had grown. Hal's fortune seemed a personal injury to Red. Had he not worked like a slave on that claim without getting a pound of gold? And here this stranger had come and gotten rich off that same claim! Thousands to him, a measly five hundred to Red. To Red's warped mind this assumed monstrous proportions – an outrage. He hated Sharon as he had never hated a man before. And, since with him to hate was to kill, he

3

determined to kill Hal Sharon. With a curse he reached for a gun when a thought stayed his hand. The Vigilantes! They would get him sure if he killed Sharon openly. A cunning light came to his eyes and he turned and strode away toward the unpretentious boarding-house where he stayed.

Hal Sharon walked into the saloon.

"Seen Ghallinan lately?" he asked.

The bar-tender shook his head.

Hal tossed a bulging buck-skin sack on the bar.

"Give that to him when you see him. It's got about a thousand dollars worth of gold dust in it."

The bar-tender gasped. "What! You giving Red a thousand bucks after he tried to swindle you? Yes, it is safe here. Ain't a galoot in camp would touch anything belonging to that gun-fighter. But say – "

"Well," answered Hal, "I don't think he got enough for his claim; he practically gave it to me. And anyway," he laughed over his shoulder, "it's Christmas!"

CHAPTER II

Morning in the mountains. The highest peaks touched with a delicate pink. The stars paling as the darkness grew grey. Light on the peaks, shadow still in the valleys, as if the paint brush of the Master had but passed lightly over the land, coloring only the highest places, the places nearest to Him. Now the light-legions began to invade the valleys, driving before them the darkness; the light on the peaks grew stronger, the snow beginning to cast back the light. But as yet no sun. The King had sent his couriers before him but he himself had not appeared.

In a certain valley, smoke curled from the chimney of a rude log cabin. High on the hillside, a man gave a grunt of satisfaction. The man lay in a hollow, from which he had scraped the drifted snow. Ever since the first hint of dawn, he had lain there, watching the cabin. A heavy rifle lay beneath his arm.

Down in the valley, the cabin door swung wide and a man stepped out. The watcher on the hill saw that it was the man he had come to kill.

Hal Sharon threw his arms wide and laughed aloud in the sheer joy of living. Up on the hill, Red Ghallinan watched the man over the sights of a

Sharps .50 rifle. For the first time he noticed what a magnificent figure the young man was. Tall, strong, handsome, with the glow of health on his cheek.

For some reason Red was not getting the enjoyment he thought he would. He shook his shoulders impatiently. His finger tightened on the trigger – suddenly Hal broke into song; the words floated clearly to Red.

"Hark the Herald Angels Sing!"

Where had he heard that song before? Then suddenly a mist floated across Red Ghallinan's eyes; the rifle slipped unnoticed from his hands. He drew his hand across his eyes and looked toward the east. There, alone, hung one great star and as he looked, over the shoulder of a great mountain came the great sun.

"Gawd!" gulped Red, "why – it is Christmas!"

Drums of the Sunset

The Wanderer

Now, come all you punchers, and listen to my tale,
When I tell you of troubles on the Chisholm Trail!

Steve Harmer was riding Texas-fashion, slow and easy, one knee hooked over the saddle horn, hat pulled over his brows to shade his face. His lean body swayed rhythmically to the easy gait of his horse.

The trail he was following sloped gradually upward, growing steeper as he continued. Cedars flanked the narrow path, with occasional pinons and junipers. Higher up, these gave place to pines.

Looking back, Steve could see the broad level country he had left, deeply grassed and sparsely treed. Beyond and above, the timbered slopes of the mountains frowned. Peak beyond peak, pinnacle beyond pinnacle they rose, with great undulating slopes between, as if piled by giants.

Suddenly behind the lone rider came the clatter of hoofs. Steve pulled aside to let the horsemen by, but they came to a halt beside him. Steve swept off his broad-brimmed hat.

There were two of the strangers, and one was a girl. To Steve she seemed strangely out of place, somehow, in this primitive setting. She sat her horse in an unfamiliar manner and her whole air was not of the West. She wore an Eastern riding habit – and then Steve forgot her clothes as he looked at her face. A vagrant curl, glinting gold in the sun, fell over her white forehead and from beneath this two soft grey eyes looked at him. Her full lips were half parted –

"Say, you!" a rough voice jarred Steve out of his daydreams.

The girl's companion was as characteristically Western as she was not. He was a heavily built man of middle life, thickly bearded and roughly clad. His features were dark and coarse, and Steve noted the heavy revolver which hung at his hip.

This man spoke in a harsh, abrupt manner.

"Who're you and where do you reckon you're goin'?"

Steve stiffened at the tone. He shot a glance at the girl, who seemed rather pale and frightened.

"My name's Harmer," said he, shortly. "I'm just passin' through."

"Yeah?" the bearded lips parted in a wolfish grin. "I reckon, stranger, you done lost your way – you shoulda took that trail back yonder a ways that branched off to the south."

"I ain't said where I was goin'," Steve responded, nettled. "Maybe I have reason for goin' this way."

"That's what I'm thinkin'," the bearded man answered, and Steve sensed the menacing note in his voice. "But you may have reason for takin' the other trail yet. Nobody lives in these hills, and they don't like strangers! Be warned, young feller, and don't git into somethin' you don't know nothin' about."

And while Steve gaped at him, not understanding, the man flung a curt order to the girl, and they both sped off up the trail, their horses laboring under the stress of quirt and spur. Steve watched in amazement.

"By golly, they don't care how they run their broncs uphill. What do you reckon all that rigamarole meant? Maybe I oughta taken the other trail, at that – golly, that was a pretty girl!"

The riders disappeared on the thickly timbered slope and Steve, after some musing, nudged his steed with his knee and started on.

I'm a goin' West and punch Texas cattle!
Ten dollar horse and forty dollar saddle.

Crack! A sharp report cut through the melody of his lazy song. A flash of fire stabbed from among trees further up the slope. Steve's hat flew from his head, his horse snorted and reared, nearly unseating his rider.

Steve whirled his steed, dropping off on the far side. His gun was in his hand as he peered cautiously across his saddle in the direction from which the shot had come. Silence hovered over the tree-masked mountain side and no motion among the intertwining branches betrayed the presence of the hidden foe.

At last Steve cautiously stepped from behind his horse. Nothing happened. He sheathed his gun, stepped forward and recovered his hat, swearing as he noted the neat hole through the crown.

"Now did that whiskered galoot stop up there some place and sneak back for a crack at me?" he wondered. "Or did he tell somebody else to – or did that somebody else do it on their own idea? And what is the idea? What's up in them hills that they don't want seen? And was this sharpshooter tryin' to kill me or just warn me?"

He shook his head and shrugged his shoulders.

"Anyway," he meditated as he mounted, "I reckon that south trail is the best road, after all."

The south branch, he found, led down instead of up, skirting the base of the incline. He sighted several droves of sheep, and as the sun sank westward, he came upon a small cabin built near a running stream of clear water.

"Hi yah! Git down and set!" greeted the man who came to the door.

He was a small, wizened old fellow, remarkably bald, and he seemed delighted at the opportunity for conversation which Steve's coming afforded. But Steve eyed him with a suspicious glance before he dismounted.

"My name is Steve Harmer," said Steve abruptly. "I'm from Texas and I'm just passin' through. If you hone for me to ride on, just say so and they won't be no need for slingin' lead at me."

"Heh, heh!" laughed the old fellow. "Son, I kin read yore brand! You done fell in with my neighbors of the Sunset Mountains!"

"A tough lookin' hombre and a nice lookin' girl," admitted Steve. "And some fellow who didn't give his name, but just ruined my best hat."

"Light!" commanded the old man. "Light and hobble yore bronc. This ain't no hotel, but maybe you can struggle along with the accommodations. My name is . . . 'Hard Luck Harper,' and I aim to live up to that handle. You ain't by no chance got no corn juice in them saddle bags?"

"No, I ain't," answered Steve, dismounting.

"I was afeard not," sighed the old man. "Hard Luck I be to the end – come in – I smell that deer meat a-burnin'."

After a supper of venison, sourdough bread and coffee, the two sat on the cabin stoop and watched the stars blink out as they talked. The sound of Steve's horse, cropping the luxuriant grass, came to them, and a night breeze wafted the spicy scents of the forest.

"This country is sure different from Texas," said Steve. "I kinda like these mountains, though. I was figurin' on campin' up among 'em tonight, that's why I took that west trail. She goes on to Rifle Pass, don't she?"

"She don't," replied the old man. "Rifle Pass is some south of here and this is the trail to that small but thrivin' metropolis. That trail you was followin' meanders up in them hills and where she goes, nobody knows."

"Why don't they?"

"Fer two reasons. The first is, they's no earthly reason fer a man in his right mind to go up there, and I'll refer you to yore hat fer the second."

"What right has this bird got to bar people from these mountains?"

"I think it must be a thirty-thirty caliber," grinned the old man. "That feller you met was Gila Murken, who lays out to own them mountains, like, and the gal was his niece, I reckon, what come from New York.

"I dunno what Gila's up to. I've knowed him, off and on, fer twenty years, and never knowed nothin' good. I'm his nearest neighbor, now, but I ain't got the slightest idee where his cabin is – up there somewhere." He indicated the gigantic brooding bulk of the Sunset Mountains, black in the starlight.

"Gila's got a couple fellers with him, and now this gal. Nobody else ever goes up that hill trail. The men come up here a year ago."

Steve mused. "An' what do you reckon is his idee for discouragin' visitors?"

The old man shrugged his shoulders and shook his head. "Son, I've wondered myself. He and his pards lives up in them mountains and regular once a week one of 'em rides to Rifle Pass or maybe clean to Stirrup, east. They have nothin' to do with me or anybody else. I've wondered, but, gosh, they ain't a chance!"

"Ain't a chance of what?"

"Steve," said Hard Luck, his lean hand indicating the black vastness of the hills, "somewhere up there amongst them canyons and gorges and cliffs, is a fortune! And sometimes I wonder if Gila Murken ain't found it.

"It's forty year ago that me and Bill Hansen come through this coun-

9

try – first white men in it, so far as I know. I was nothin' but a kid then an' we was buffalo hunters, kinda strayed from the regular course.

"We went up into them hills, Sunset Mountains, the Indians call 'em, and away back somewheres we come into a range of cliffs. Now, it don't look like it'd be that way, lookin' from here, but in among the mountains they's long chains of cliffs, straight up and down, maybe four hundred feet high, clay and rock – mighty treacherous stuff. They's maybe seventeen sets of these cliffs, Ramparts, we call 'em, and they look just alike. Trees along the edge, thick timber at the base. The edges is always crumblin' and startin' landslides and avalanches.

"Me and Bill Hansen come to the front of one of these Ramparts and Bill was lookin' at where the earth of the cliff face had kinda shelved away when he let out a whoop!

"Gold! Reef gold – the blamedest vein I ever see, just lying there right at the surface ready for somebody to work out the ore and cart it off! We dropped our guns and laid into the cliff with our fingernails, diggin' the dirt away. And the vein looked like she went clear to China! Get that, son, reef gold and quartz in the open cliff face.

" 'Bill,' says I, 'we're milyunaires!'

"And just as I said it, somethin' came whistlin' by my cheek and Bill gave one yell and went down on his face with a steel-pointed arrow through him. And before I could move a rifle cracked and somethin' that felt like a red hot hammer hit me in the chest and knocked me flat.

"A war party – they'd stole up on us while we was diggin'. Cheyennes they was, from the north, and they come out and chanted their scalp songs over us. Bill was dead and I lay still, all bloody but conscious, purtendin' I was a stiff, too.

"They scalped Bill and they scalped me – "

Steve gave an exclamation of horror.

"Oh, yes," said Hard Luck tranquilly. "It hurt considerable – fact is, I don't know many things that hurt wuss. But somehow I managed to lie still and not let on like I was alive, though a couple of times I thought I was goin' to let out a whoop in spite of myself."

"Did they scalp you plumb down to the temples?" asked Steve morbidly.

"Naw – the Cheyennes never scalped that way." Hard Luck ran his hand contemplatively over his glistening skull. "They just cut a piece out of the top – purty good sized piece, though – and the rest of the ha'r kinda got discouraged and faded away, after a few years.

"Anyway, they danced and yelled fer awhile an' then they left an' I began to take invoice to see if I was still livin'. I was shot through the chest but by some miracle the ball had gone on through without hitting anything important. I thought, though, I was goin' to bleed to death. But I stuffed the wound with leaves and the webs these large white spiders spin on the low branches of trees. I crawled to a spring which wasn't far away and lay there like a dead man till night, when I came to and lay there thinkin' about my dead friend, and my wounds and the gold I'd never enjoy.

"Then, I got out of my right mind and went crawlin' away through the forest, not knowin' why I did it. I was just like a man that's drunk: I knowed what I was doin' but I didn't know why I was doin' it. I crawled and I crawled and how long I kept on crawlin' I don't know fer I passed clean out, finally, and some buffalo hunters found me out in the level country, miles and miles from where I was wounded. I was ravin' and gibberin' and nearly dead.

"They tended to me and after a long time my wounds healed and I come back to my right mind. And when I did, I thought about the gold and got up a prospectin' party and went back. But seems like I couldn't remember what all happened just before I got laid out. Everything was vague and I couldn't remember what way Bill and me had taken to get to the cliff, and I couldn't remember how it looked. They'd been a lot of landslides, too, and likely everything was changed in looks.

"Anyway, I couldn't find the lost mine of Sunset Mountain, and though I been comin' every so often and explorin' again, for forty years me nor no other livin' man has ever laid eyes on that gold ledge. Some landslide done covered it up, I reckon. Or maybe I just ain't never found the right cliff. I don't know.

"I done give it up. I'm gettin' old. Now I'm runnin' a few sheep and am purty contented. But you know now why they call me Hard Luck."

"And you think that maybe this Murken has found your mine and is workin' it on the sly?"

"Naw, really I don't. T'wouldn't be like Gila Murken to try to conceal the fact – he'd just come out and claim it and dare me to take it away from him. Anyway," the old man continued with a touch of vanity, "no dub like Gila Murken could find somethin' that a old prospector like me has looked fer, fer forty year without findin', nohow."

Silence fell. Steve was aware that the night wind, whispering down from the mountains, carried a strange dim throbbing – a measured, even cadence, haunting and illusive.

"Drums," said Hard Luck, as if divining his thought. "Indian drums; tribe's away back up in the mountains. Nothin' like them that took my scalp. Navajoes, these is, a low class gang that wandered up from the south. The government give 'em a kind of reservation back in the Sunset Mountains. Friendly, I reckon – trade with the whites a little.

"Them drums is been goin' a heap the last few weeks. Still nights you can hear 'em easy; sound travels a long way in this land."

His voice trailed off into silence. Steve gazed westward where the monstrous shadowy peaks rose black against the stars. The night breeze whispered a lonely melody through the cedars and pines. The scent of fresh grass and forest trees was in his nostrils. White stars twinkled above the dark mountains and the memory of a pretty, wistful face floated across Steve's vision. As he grew drowsy, the face seemed nearer and clearer, and always through the mists of his dreams throbbed faintly the Sunset drums.

CHAPTER 2

Mystery

Steve drained his coffee cup and set it down on the rough-hewn table.

"I reckon," said he, "for a young fellow you're a pretty good cook – Hard Luck, I been thinkin'."

"Don't strain yoreself, son. It ain't a good idee startin' in on new things, at this time of yore life – what you been thinkin' about?"

"That mine of yours. I believe, instead of goin' on to Rifle Pass like I was thinkin' of doin', I'll lay over a few days and look for that lost gold ledge."

"Considerin' as I spent the best part of my life huntin' it," said Hard Luck testily, "it's very likely you'll stub yore toes on it the first thing. The Lord knows, I'd like to have you stay here as long as you want. I don't see many people. But they ain't one chance in a hundred of you findin' that mine, and I'm tellin' you, it ain't healthy to ramble around in the Sunsets now, with Gila Murken hatchin' out the Devil only knows what, up there."

"Murken owes me a new hat," said Steve moodily. "And furthermore and besides it's time somebody showed him he ain't runnin' this country. I crave to hunt for that mine. I dreamed about it last night."

"You better forgit that mountain-business and work with me here on my ranch," advised Hard Luck. "I'll give you a job of herdin' sheep."

"Don't get insultin'," said Steve reprovingly. "How far up in them hills can a horse go?"

"You can navigate most of 'em on yore bronc if you take yore time an' let him pick his way. But you better not."

In spite of Hard Luck's warning, Steve rode up the first of the great slopes before the sun had risen high enough for him to feel its heat. It was a beautiful morning; the early sunlight glistened on the leaves of the trees and on the dew on the grass. Above and beyond him rose the slopes, dark green, deepening into purple in the distance. Snow glimmered on some of the higher peaks.

Steve felt a warmth of comfort and good cheer. The fragrance of Hard Luck's coffee and flapjacks was still on his palate, and the resilience of youth sang through his veins. Somewhere up there in the mysterious tree-clad valleys and ridges adventure awaited him, and as Steve rode, the lost mine of the Sunsets was least in his thoughts.

No trail led up the way he took, but his horse picked his route between boulders and cedars, climbing steep slopes as nimbly as a mountain goat. The cedars gave way to pines and occasionally Steve looked down into some small valley, heavily grassed and thickly wooded. The sun was slanting toward the west when he finally pulled up his horse on the crest of a steep incline and looked down.

A wilder and more broken country he had never seen. From his feet the earth sloped steeply down, covered with pines which seemed to cling precariously, to debouch into a sort of plateau. On three sides of this plateau rose the slanting sides of the mountains. The fourth or east side fell away abruptly into cliffs which seemed hundreds of feet high. But what drew Steve's gaze was the plateau itself.

Near the eastern cliffs stood two log cabins. Smoke curled from one, and as Steve watched, a man came out of the door. Even at that distance Steve recognized the fellow whom Hard Luck had designated as Gila Murken.

Steve slipped from the saddle, led his horse back into the pines a short distance and flung the reins over a tree limb. Then he stole back to the crest of the slope. He did not think Murken could see him, hidden as he was among the trees, but he did not care to take any chances. Another man had joined Murken and the two seemed to be engaged in conversation. After awhile they turned and went into the second cabin.

Time passed but they did not emerge. Suddenly Steve's heart leaped strangely. A slim girlish form had come from the cabin out of which the men had come, and the sunshine glinted on golden hair. Steve leaned forward eagerly, wondering why the mere sight of a girl should cause his breath to come quicker.

She walked slowly toward the cliffs and Steve perceived that there was what seemed to be a deep gorge, presumably leading downward. Into this the girl disappeared. Steve now found that the mysterious cabins had lost much of their interest, and presently he went back to his horse, mounted and rode southward, keeping close to the crest of the slopes. At last he attained a position where he could look back at the plateau and get a partial view of the cliffs. He decided that they were some of the Ramparts, spoken of by Hard Luck. They rose steep and bare for four hundred feet, deeply weathered and serrated. Gorges cut deep into them and promontories stood out over the abysses beneath. Great boulders lined the edge of the precipices and the whole face of the cliffs looked unstable and treacherous.

At the foot, tall forest trees masked a rough and broken country. And as he looked Steve saw the girl, a tiny figure in the distance, come out into a clearing. He watched her until she vanished among the trees, and then turned his steed and rode back in the direction from which he had come, though not following the same route. He took his time, riding leisurely.

The sun slanted westward as he came to the lower slopes and looked back to see the rim of the Ramparts jutting below the heights he had left. He had made a vast semicircle and now the cliffs were behind and above him, instead of in front and below.

He went his leisurely way and suddenly he was aware of voices among the cedars in front of him. He slipped from his saddle, dropped the reins to the horse's feet and stole forward. Hidden among the undergrowth, he looked into a small glade where stood two figures – the girl of the cliffs and a tall lanky man.

"No! No!" the girl was saying. "I don't want to have anything to do with you. Go away and let me alone or I'll tell my uncle."

"Haw! Haw!" The man's laugh was loud but mirthless. "Yore uncle and me is too close connected in a business way for him to rile me! I'm tellin' you, this ain't no place for you and you better let me take you away to whar there's people and towns and the like."

"I don't trust you," she answered sullenly.

"Aw, now don't you? Come on – admit you done come down here just to meet me!"

"That's a lie!" the girl cried, stung. "You know I just went for a stroll; I didn't know you were here."

"These mountains ain't no place for a 'stroll.' "

"My uncle won't let me have a horse and ride, unless he's with me. He's afraid I'll run away."

"And wouldn't you?"

"I don't know. I haven't anywhere to go. But I'd about as soon die as stay here much longer."

"Then let me take you away! I'll marry you, if you say so. They's many a gal would jump to take Mark Edwards up on that deal."

"Oh, let me alone! I don't want to marry you, I don't want to go away with you, I don't even want to look at you! If you really want to make a hit with me, go somewhere and shoot yourself!"

Edwards' brow darkened.

"Oh ho, so I ain't good enough for you, my fine lady. Reckon I'll just take a kiss anyhow."

His grimed hands shot and closed on her shoulders. Instantly she clenched a small fist and struck him in the mouth, so that blood trickled from his lips. The blow roused all the slumbering demon in the man.

"Yore a spit-fire," he grunted. "But I 'low I'll tame you."

He pinioned her arms, cursed soulfully as she kicked him on the shins, and crushed her slim form to him. His unshaven lips were seeking hers when Steve impulsively went into action.

He bounded from his covert, gripped the man's shoulder with steely fingers and swung him around, smashing him in the face with his left hand as he did so. Edwards gaped in astonishment, then roared and rushed in blindly, fingers spread to gouge and tear. Steve was not inclined to clinch rough-and-tumble fashion. He dropped his right fist nearly to his ankle and then brought it up in a long sweeping arc that stopped at Edwards's chin. That worthy's head went back as if it were hinged and his body, following the motion, crashed to the leaf-covered earth. He lay as if in slumber, his limbs tossed about in a careless and nonchalant manner. Steve caressed his sore knuckles and glanced at the girl.

"Is – is – is he dead?" she gasped, wide eyed.

"Naw, miss, I'm afraid he ain't," Steve answered regretfully. "He's just listenin' to the cuckoo birds. Shall I tie him up?"

"What for?" she asked reasonably enough. "No, let's go before he comes to."

And she started away hurriedly. Steve got his horse and followed her, overtaking her within a few rods. He walked beside her, leading his steed, his eyes admiringly taking in the proud, erect carriage of her slim figure, and the faint delicate rose-leaf tint of her complection.

"I hope you won't think I'm intrudin' where I got no business," said the Texan apologetically. "But I'm a seein' you to wherever you're goin'. That bird might follow you or you might meet another one like him."

"Thank you," she answered in a rather subdued voice. "You were very kind to help me, Mr. Harmer."

"How'd you know my name?"

"You told my uncle who you were yesterday, don't you remember?"

"Seems like I recollect, now," replied Steve, experiencing a foolish warm thrill that she should remember his name. "But I don't recall you saying what your name was."

"My name is Joan Farrel. I'm staying here with my uncle, Mr. Murken, the man with whom you saw me yesterday."

"And was it him," asked Steve bluntly, "that shot a hole in my hat?"

Her eyes widened; a frightened look was evident in her face.

"No! No!" she whispered. "It couldn't have been him! He and I rode right up on to the cabin after we passed you. I heard the shot but I had no idea anyone was shooting at you."

Steve laughed, rather ashamed of having mentioned it to the girl.

"Aw, it wasn't nothin'. Likely somebody done it for a joke. But right after you-all went on, somebody cracked down on me from the trees up the trail a ways and plumb ruint my hat."

"It must have been Edwards," she said in a frightened voice. "We met him coming down the trail on foot after we'd gotten out of sight of you, and Uncle stopped and said something to him I couldn't hear, before we went on."

"And who is Edwards?"

"He's connected with my uncle's business in some way; I don't know just how. He and a man named Allison camp up there close to our cabin."

"What is your uncle's business?" asked Steve with cool assumption.

She did not seem offended at the question.

"I don't know. He never tells me anything. I'm afraid of him and he don't love me."

Her face was shadowed as if by worry or secret fear. Something was haunting her, Steve thought. Nothing more was said until they had reached the base of the cliffs. Steve glanced up, awed. The great walls hung threateningly over them, starkly and somberly. To his eye the cliffs seemed unstable, ready to crash down upon the forest below at the slightest jar. Great boulders jutted out, half embedded in the clay. The brow of the cliff, fringed with trees, hung out over the concave walls.

From where he stood Steve could see a deep gorge, cut far into the face of the precipice and leading steeply upward. He caught his breath. He had never imagined such a natural stairway. The incline was so precipitous that it seemed it would tax the most sure-footed horse. Boulders rested along the trail that led through it, as if hovering there temporarily, and the high walls on each side darkened the way, looming like a sinister threat.

"My gosh!" said he sincerely. "Do you have to go up that gulch every time you leave your cabin?"

"Yes – or else climb the slopes back of the plateau and make a wide circle, leaving the plateau to the north and coming down the southern ridges. We always go this way. I'm used to climbing it now."

"Must have took a long time for the water to wash that out," said Steve. "I'm new to this mountain country, but it looks to me like if somebody stubbed their toe on a rock, it would start a landslide that would bring the whole thing right down in that canyon."

"I think of that, too," she answered with a slight shudder. "I thank you for what you've done for me. But you mustn't go any further. My uncle is always furious if anyone comes into these mountains."

"What about Edwards?"

"I'll tell my uncle and he'll make him leave me alone." She started to go, then hesitated.

"Listen," said Steve, his heart beating wildly, "I'd like to know you better – will – will you meet me tomorrow somewhere?"

"Yes!" she spoke low and swiftly, then turned and ran lightly up the slope. Steve stood, looking after her, hat in hand.

Night had fallen as Steve Harmer rode back to the ranch of Hard Luck Harper.

> Clouds in the west and a-lookin' like rain,
> And my blamed old slicker's in the wagon again!

he declaimed to the dark blue bowl of the star-flecked sky.

The crisp sharp scent of cedar was in the air and the wind fanned his cheek. He felt his soul grow and expand in the silence and the majesty of the night.

> Woke up one mornin' on the Chisholm Trail –
> Rope in my hand and a cow by the tail!

He drew rein at the cabin stoop and hailed his host hilariously. Old Hard Luck stood in the door and the starlight glinted on the steel in his hand.

"Huh," grunted he suspiciously. "You done finally come back, ain't you? I'd 'bout decided you done met up with Gila Murken and was layin' in a draw somewheres with a thirty-thirty slug through yore innards. Come in and git yore hoofs under the table – I done cooked a couple of steers in hopes of stayin' yore appetite a little."

Steve tended to his horse and then entered the cabin, glancing at the long rifle which the old man had stood up against the cabin wall.

"That was a antique when they fought the Revolution," said Steve. "What's the idea? Are you afraid of Murken?"

"Afeard of Murken? That dub? I got no call to be afeard of him. And don't go slingin' mud at a gun that's dropped more Indians than you ever see. That's a Sharps .50 caliber and when I was younger I could shave a mosquito at two hundred yards with it.

"Naw, it ain't Murken I'm studyin'. Listen!"

Again Steve caught the faint pulsing of the mountain drums.

"Every night they get louder," said Hard Luck. "They say them redskins is plumb peaceful but you can't tell me – the only peaceful Indian I ever see had at least two bullets through his skull. Them drums talks and whispers and they ain't no white man knows what's hatchin' back up in them hills where nobody seldom ever goes. Indian magic! That's what's goin' on, and red magic means red doin's. I've fought 'em from Sonora to the Bad Lands and I know what I'm talkin' about."

"Your nerves is gettin' all euchered up," said Steve, diving into food set before him. "I kinda like to listen to them drums."

"Maybe you'd like to hear 'em when they was dancin' over yore scalp," answered Hard Luck gloomily. "Thar's a town about forty mile northwest of here whar them red devils comes to trade sometimes, 'steader goin' to Rifle Pass, and a fellow come through today from thar and says they must be some strange goin's on up in the Sunsets.

" 'How come?' says I.

" 'Why,' says he, 'them reservation Navajoes has been cartin' down greenbacks to buy their tobaccer and calico and the other day the store-keepers done found the stuff is all counterfeit. They done stopped sellin' to the Indians and sent for a Indian agent to come and investigate. More-over,' says he, 'somebody is sellin' them redskins liquor too.' "

Hard Luck devoted his attention to eating for a few moments and then began again.

"How come them Indians gets any kind of money up in the mountains, much less counterfeit? Reckon they're makin' it theirselves? And who's slippin' them booze? One thing's shore, Hell's to pay when redskins git drunk and the first scalp they'll likely take is the feller's who sold them the booze."

"Yeah?" returned Steve absent-mindedly. His thoughts were elsewhere.

"Did you find the mine?" asked Hard Luck sarcastically.

"What mine?" The Texan stared at his host blankly.

Hard Luck grunted scornfully and pushed back his chair. After awhile silence fell over the cabin, to be broken presently by Steve's voice rising with dolorous enjoyment in the darkness:

And he thought of his home, and his loved ones nigh,
And the cowboys gathered to see him die!

Hard Luck sat up in his bunk and cursed, and hurled a boot.

"For the love of mud, let a old man sleep, willya?"

As Steve drifted off into dreamland, his last thoughts were of gold, but it was not the lost ore of the Sunsets; it was the soft curly gold that framed the charming oval of a soft face. And still through the shimmery hazes of his dreams beat the sinister muttering of the Sunset drums.

CHAPTER 3

The Girl's Story

The dew was still on the mountain grass when Steve rode up the long dim slopes to the glade where he had fought Edwards the day before. He sat down on a log and waited, doubting if she whom he sought would really come.

He sat motionless for nearly an hour, and then he heard a light sure step and she stood before him, framed in the young glow of the morning sun. The beauty of her took Steve's breath and he could only stand, hat in hand, and gape, seeking feebly for words. She came straight to him, smiling, and held out her hand. The touch of her slim firm fingers reassured him and he found his voice.

"Miss Farrel, I plumb forgot yesterday to ask you where you'd rather meet me at, or what time. I come here because I figured you'd remember – I mean, you'd think – aw heck!" he stumbled.

"Yes, that was forgetful of us. I decided that you'd naturally come to the place where you found me yesterday and I came early because – because I was afraid you'd come and not find me here and think I wasn't coming," she finished rather confusedly.

As she spoke her eyes ran approvingly over Steve, noting his six-foot build of lithe manhood and the deep tan of his whimsical face.

"I promised to tell you all I know," said she abruptly, twisting her fingers. She seemed paler and more worried than ever. Steve decided that she had reached the point where she was ready to turn to any man for help, stranger or not. Certainly some deep fear was preying on her.

"You know my name," she said, seating herself on the log and motioning him to sit beside her. "Mr. Murken is my mother's brother. My parents separated when I was very young and I've been living with an aunt in New York state. I'd never been west before, until my aunt died not long ago. Before she died she told me to go to her brother at Rifle Pass and not having anywhere else to go, I did so.

"I'd never seen my uncle and I found him very different from what I had expected. He didn't live at Rifle Pass then, but had moved up in these mountains. I came on up here with a guide and my uncle seemed very much enraged because I had come. He let me stay but I'm very unhappy because I know he don't want me. Yet, when I ask him to let me go, he refuses. He won't even let me go to Rifle Pass unless he is with me, and he won't let me go riding unless he's with me. He says he's afraid I'll run away, yet I know he doesn't love me or really want me here. He's not exactly unkind to me, but he isn't kind either.

"There are two men who stay up there most of the time: Edwards, the man you saw yesterday, and a large black-bearded man named Allison. That one, Allison, looks like a bandit or something, but he is very courteous to me. But Edwards – you saw what he did yesterday and he's forever trying to make love to me when my uncle isn't around. I'm afraid to tell my uncle about it, and I don't know whether he'd do anything, if I did tell him.

"The other two men stay in a smaller cabin a little distance from the one occupied by my uncle and myself, and they won't let me come anywhere near it. My uncle even threatened to whip me if I looked in the windows. I think they must have something hidden there. My uncle locks me in my cabin when they are all at work in the other cabin – whatever they're doing in there.

"Sometimes some Indians come down the western slopes from somewhere away back in the hills, and sometimes my uncle rides away with them. Once a week one of the men loads his saddle bags full of something and rides away to be gone two or three days.

"I don't understand it," she added almost tearfully. "I can't help but believe there's something crooked about it. I'm afraid of Edwards and only a little less afraid of my uncle. I want to get away."

Suddenly she seized his hands impulsively.

"You seem good and kind," she exclaimed. "Won't you help me? I'll pay you – "

"You'll what?" he said explosively.

She flushed.

"I beg your pardon. I should have known better than to make that remark. I know you'll help me just from the goodness of your heart."

Steve's face burned crimson. He fumbled with his hat.

"Sure I'll help you. If you want I'll ride up and get your things – "

She stared at him in amazement.

"I don't want you committing suicide on my account," said she. "You'd get shot if you went within sight of my uncle. No, this is what I want you to do. I've told you my uncle won't let me have a horse, and I certainly can't walk out of these mountains. Can you meet me here early tomorrow morning with an extra horse?"

"Sure I can. But how are you goin' to get your baggage away? Girls is usually got a lot of frills and things."

"I haven't. But anyway, I want to get out of this place if I have to leave my clothes, even, and ride out in a bathing suit. I'll stroll out of the cabin in the morning, casually, come down the gulch and meet you here."

"And then where will you want to go?"

"Any place is as good as the next," she answered rather hopelessly. "I'll have to find some town where I can make my own living. I guess I can teach school or work in an office."

"I wish – " said he impulsively, and then stopped short.

"You wish what?" she asked curiously.

"That them drums would quit whoopin' it up at night," he added desperately, flushing as he realized how close he had been to proposing to a girl he had known only two days. He was surprised at himself; he had spoken on impulse and he wondered at the emotion which had prompted him.

She shivered slightly.

"They frighten me, sometimes. Every night they keep booming, and last night I was restless and every time I awoke I could hear them. They didn't stop until dawn. This was the first time they've kept up all night"

She rose.

"I've stayed as long as I dare. My uncle will get suspicious of me and come looking for me if I'm gone too long."

Steve rose. "I'll go with you as far as the gorge."

Again Steve stood among the thick trees at the foot of the Ramparts and watched the girl go up the gorge, her slim form receding and growing smaller in his sight as she ascended. The gulch lay in everlasting shadow and Steve unconsciously held his breath, as if expecting those grim, towering walls to come crashing down on that slender figure.

Nearly at the upper mouth she turned and waved at him, and he waved back, then turned and made his way back to his horse. He rode carelessly, and with a slack rein, seeming to move in a land of rose-tinted clouds. His heart beat swiftly and his blood sang through his veins.

"I'm in love! I'm in love!" he warbled, wild-eyed, to the indifferent trees. "Oh heck! Oh golly! Oh gosh!"

Suddenly he stopped short. From somewhere further back and high above him came a quick rattle of rifle fire. As he listened another volley cracked out. A vague feeling of apprehension clutched at him. He glanced at the distant rim of the Ramparts. The sounds had seemed to come from that direction. A few straggling shots sounded faintly, then silence fell. What was going on up above those grim cliffs?

"Reckon I ought to go back and see?" he wondered. "Reckon if Murken and his bold boys is slaughterin' each other? Or is it some wanderin' traveler they're greetin'? Aw, likely they're after deer or maybe a mountain lion."

He rode on slowly, but his conscience troubled him. Suddenly a familiar voice hailed him and from the trees in front of him a horseman rode.

"Hi yah!" The rider was Hard Luck Harper. He carried the long Sharps rifle across his saddle bow and his face was set in gloomy lines.

"I done got to worryin' about a brainless maverick like you a-wanderin' around these hills by yoreself with Gila Murken runnin' wild thata-way, and I come to see if you was still in the land of the livin'!"

"And I reckon you're plumb disappointed not to run into a murder or two."

"I don't know so much about them murders," said the old man testily. "Didn't I hear guns a-talkin' up on the Ramparts a little while ago?"

"Likely you did, if you was listenin'."

"Yeah – and people don't go wastin' ammunition fer nothin' up here – look there!"

Hard Luck's finger stabbed upward and Steve, a numbing sense of foreboding gripping his soul, whirled to look. Up over the tree-lined rim of the Ramparts drifted a thin spiral of smoke.

"My Lord, Hard Luck!" gasped Steve. "What's goin' on up there?"

"Shet up!" snarled the old man, raising his rifle. "I hear a horse runnin' hard!"

The wild tattoo of hoofs crashed through the silence and a steed burst through the trees of the upper slope and came plunging down toward them, wild-eyed, nostrils flaring. On its back a crimsoned figure reeled and flopped grotesquely. Steve spurred in front of the frantic flying animal and caught the hanging rein, bringing the bronco to a rearing, plunging halt. The rider slumped forward and pitched to the earth.

"Edwards!" gasped Steve.

The man lay, staring up with blank wide eyes. Blood trickled from his lips and the front of his shirt was soaked in red. Hard Luck and Steve bent over him. At the first glance it was evident that he was dying.

"Edwards!" exclaimed Hard Luck. "What's happened? Who shot you? And whar's yore pards and the gal?"

"Dead!" Edwards' unshaven lips writhed redly and his voice was a croak.

"Daid!" Hard Luck's voice broke shrilly. "Who done it?"

"Them Navajoes!" the voice sank to a ghastly whisper as blood rose to the pallid lips.

"I told you!" gibbered Hard Luck. "I knowed them drums meant deviltry! I knowed it!"

"Shut up, can't you?" snarled Steve, torn by his emotions. He gripped the dying man's shoulder with unconsciously brutal force and shook him desperately.

"Edwards," he begged, "you're goin' over the ridge – can't you tell us how it was before you go? Did you see Murken and his niece die?"

"Yes – it – was – like – this," the man began laboriously. "I was – all set to go – to Rifle Pass – had my bronc loaded – Murken and Allison was out near – the corral – the gal was – in the cabin. All to once – the west slopes began to shower lead. Murken went down – at the first fire. Allison was hit—and I got a slug through me. Then a gang – of Navajoes come ridin' down – the slopes – drunk and blood crazy.

"I got to my bronc – and started ridin' and – they drilled me – a couple of times from behind. Lookin' back I saw – Allison standin' in the cabin door with – both guns goin' and the gal – crouchin' behind him. Then the whole mob – of red devils – rushed in and I saw – the knives flashin' and drippin' as – I come into – the gulch."

Steve crouched, frozen and horror struck. It seemed that his heart had crumbled to ashes. The taste of dust was in his mouth.

"Any of 'em chasin' you, Edwards?" asked Hard Luck. The old Indian fighter was in his element now; he had sloughed off his attitude of lazy good nature and his eyes were hard and cold as steel.

"Maybe – don't know" the wounded man muttered. "All our fault – Murken would give 'em whiskey. Warned him. They found out – the money – he was given' 'em – was no good."

The voice broke suddenly as a red tide gushed to Edwards' lips. He lurched up on his elbows, then toppled back and lay still.

Hard Luck grunted. He stepped over to Edwards' horse which stood trembling, and cut open the saddlebags. He nodded.

"No more'n I expected."

Steve was rising slowly, mechanically wiping his hands on a wisp of grass. His face was white, his eyes staring.

"She's dead!" he whispered. "She's dead!"

Hard Luck, gazing at him, felt a pang in his heart. The scene brought back so poignantly the old bloody days of Indian warfare when men had seen their loved ones struck down by knife and arrow.

"Son," said he, solemnly, "I never expected to see such a sight as this again."

The Texan gave him a glance of agony, then his eyes blazed with a wild and terrible light.

"They killed her!" he screamed, beating his forehead with his clenched fists. "And by God, I'll kill 'em all! I'll kill – kill – "

His gun was swinging in his hand as he plunged toward his horse.

Hard Luck sprang forward and caught him, holding him with a wiry strength that was astounding for his age. He ignored the savage protests and curses, dodged a blow of the gun barrel which the half-crazed Texan aimed at his face, and pinioned Steve's arms. The youth's frenzied passion went as suddenly as it had come, leaving him sobbing and shaken.

"Son," said Hard Luck calmly, "cool down. I reckon you don't want to lift them Navajo scalps any more'n I do, and before this game's done, we're goin' to send more'n one of 'em over the ridge. But if you go gallopin' up after 'em wide open thataway, you'll never git the chance to even the score, fer they'll drill you before you even see 'em. Listen to me, I've fought 'em from Sonora to the Bad Lands and I know what I'm talkin' about. Git on yore bronc. We can't do nothin' more fer Edwards and we got work to do elsewhar. He said Allison and Murken and the gal was daid. I reckon Murken and Allison is gone over the ridge all right, but he didn't rightly see 'em bump off the gal, and I'll bet my hat she's alive right now."

Steve nodded shortly. He seemed to have aged years in the last few minutes. The easygoing young cowpuncher was gone, and in his place stood a cold steel fighting man of the old Texas blood. His hand was as steady as a rock, as he sheathed his pistol and swung into the saddle.

"I'm followin' your lead, Hard Luck," said he briefly. "All I ask is for you to get me within shootin' and stabbin' distance of them devils."

The old man grinned wolfishly.

"Son, yore wants is simple and soon satisfied; follow me!"

CHAPTER 4

A Trail of Blood

Steve and Hard Luck rode slowly and warily up the tree-covered slopes which led to the foot of the Ramparts. Silence hung over the mountain forest like a deathly fog. Hard Luck's keen old eyes roved incessantly, ferreting out the shadows, seeking for sign of something unnatural, something which was not as it should be, to betray the hidden assassins. He talked in a low, guarded tone. It was dangerous but he wished to divert Steve's mind as much as possible.

"Steve, I done looked in Edwards' saddle bags, and what you reckon I found? A whole stack of greenbacks, tens, twenties, fifties and hundreds, done up in bundles! It's money he's been packin' out to Rifle Pass. Whar you reckon he got it?"

Steve did not reply nor did the old man expect an answer. The Texan's eyes were riveted on the frowning buttresses of the Ramparts, which now loomed over them. As they came under the brow of the cliffs, the smoke they had seen further away was no longer visible.

"Reckon they didn't chase Edwards none," muttered Hard Luck. "Leastways they ain't no sign of any horses followin' his. There's his tracks, alone. These Navajoes is naturally desert Indians, anyhow, and they're 'bout as much outa place in the mountains as a white man from the plains. They can't hold a candle to me, anyhow."

They had halted in a thick clump of trees at the foot of the Ramparts and the mouth of the steep defile was visible in front of them.

"That's a bad place," muttered Hard Luck. "I been up that gulch before Gila built his cabins up on the plateau. Steve, we kin come at them Navajoes, supposin' they're still up on there, by two ways. We kin circle to the south, climb up the mountain-sides and come down the west slopes or we kin take a chance an' ride right up the gulch. That's a lot quicker, of course, pervidin' we ain't shot or mashed by fallin' rocks afore we git to the top."

"Let's take it on the run," urged Steve, quivering with impatience. "It'll take more'n bullets and rocks to stop me now."

"All right," said Hard Luck, reining his horse out of the trees, "here goes!"

Of that wild ride up the gorge Steve never remembered very much. The memory was always like a nightmare, in which he saw dark walls flash past, heard the endless clatter of hoofs and the rattle of dislodged stones. Nothing seemed real except the pistol he clutched in his right hand and the laboring steed who plunged and reeled beneath him, driven headlong up the slope with spurs that raked the panting sides.

Then they burst into the open and saw the plateau spread wide and silent before them, with smoldering masses of coals where the cabins and corrals should have stood. They rode up slowly. The tracks of horses led away up into the hills to the west and there was no sign of life.

Dreading what he might see, Steve looked. Down close to where the corral had been lay the body of Gila Murken. Lying partly in the coals that marked the remnants of the larger cabin, was the corpse of a large dark-faced man who had once worn a heavy beard, though now beard and hair were mostly scorched off. There was no sign of the girl.

"Do you – do you think she burned in the cabin, Hard Luck?"

"Naw, I know she didn't fer the reason that if she hada, they'd be some charred bones. They done rode off with her."

Steve felt a curious all-gone feeling, as if the realization that Joan was alive was too great a joy for the human brain to stand. Even though he knew that she must be in a fearful plight, at least she was living.

"Look it the stiffs," said Hard Luck admiringly. "There's whar Allison made his last stand – at the cabin door, protectin' the gal, I reckon. This Allison seemed to be a mighty hard hombre but I reckon he had a streak of the man in him. Stranger in these parts to all but Murken."

Four Navajoes lay face down in front of the white man's body. They were clad only in dirty trousers and blankets flung about their shoulders. They were stone dead.

"Trail of blood from whar the corral was," said Hard Luck. "They caught him in the open and shot him up afore he could git to the cabin, I figure. Down there at the corral Murken died. The way I read it, Allison made a break and got to the cabin whar the gal was. Then they surged in on him and he killed these four devils and went over the ridge hisself."

Steve bent over the grim spectacle and then straightened.

"Thought I knowed him. Allison – Texas man he was. A real bad hombre down on the border. Got run outa El Paso for gun-runnin' into Mexico."

"He shore made a game stand fer his last fight."

"Texas breed," said Steve grimly.

"I reckon all the good battlers ain't in Texas," said Hard Luck testily. "Not denyin' he put up a man-sized fight. Now then, look. Trails of fourteen horses goin' west – five carryin' weight, the rest bare – tell by the way the hoofs sink in, of course. All the horses missin' out of the corral, four dead Indians here. That means they wan't but a small party of 'em. Figurin' one of the horses is bein' rid by the gal, I guess we got only four redskins to deal with. Small war party scoutin' in front of the tribe, I

28

imagine, if the whole tribe's on the war path. Now they're lightin' back into the hills with the gal, the broncs they took from the corral, and the horses of their dead tribesmen – which stopped Allison's bullets. Best thing fer us to do is follow and try to catch up with 'em afore they git back to the rest of their gang."

"Then, let's go," exclaimed Steve, trembling with impatience. "I'm nearly crazy standin' here doin' nothin'."

Hard Luck glanced at the steeds, saw that they had recovered from the terrific strain of the flying climb, and nodded. As they rode past the embers of the smaller cabin, he drew rein for an instant.

"Steve, what's them things?"

Steve looked sombrely at the charred and burnt machines which lay among the smoking ruins.

"Stamps and presses and steel dies," said he. "Counterfeit machines. And look at the greenbacks."

Fragments of green paper littered the earth as if they had been torn and flung about in anger or mockery.

"Murken and Edwards and Allison was counterfeiters, then. Huh! No wonder they didn't want anybody snoopin' around. That's why Murken wouldn't let the gal go – afeard she knew too much."

They started on again at a brisk trot and Hard Luck ruminated.

"Mighta known it when they come up here a year ago. Reckon Edwards went to Rifle Pass every week, or some other nearby place, and put the false bills in circulation. Musta had an agent. And they give money to the Indians, too, to keep their mouths shet, and give 'em whiskey. And the Indians found they'd been given money which was no good. And bein' all fired up with Murken's bad whiskey, they just bust loose."

"If so be we find Joan," said Steve somberly, "say nothin' about her uncle bein' a crook."

"Sure."

Their steeds were mounting the western slopes, up which went the trail of the marauders. They crossed the ridge, went down the western incline and struck a short expanse of comparatively level country.

"Listen at the drums!" muttered Hard Luck. "Gettin' nearer. The whole tribe must be on the march."

The drums were talking loud and clear from somewhere in the vastness in front of them and Steve seemed to catch in their rumble an evil note of sinister triumph.

Then the two riders were electrified by a burst of wild and ferocious yells from the heavily timbered levels to the west, in the direction they were going. Flying hoofs beat out a thundering tattoo and a horse raced into sight running hard and low, with a slim white figure lying close along his neck. Behind came four hideous painted demons, spurring and yelling.

"Joan!" The word burst from Steve's lips in a great shout and he spurred forward. Simultaneously he heard the crash of Hard Luck's buffalo gun and saw the foremost redskin topple earthward, his steed sweeping past with an empty saddle. The girl whirled up beside him, her arms reaching for him.

"Steve!" Her cry was like the wail of a lost child.

"Ride for the plateau and make it down through the gulch!" he shouted, wheeling aside to let her pass. "Go!"

Then he swung back to meet the oncoming attackers. The surprize had been as much theirs as the white men's. They had not expected to be followed so soon, and when they had burst through the trees, the sight of the two white men had momentarily stunned them with the unexpectedness of it. However, the remaining three came on with desperate courage and the white men closed in to meet them.

Hard Luck's single shot rifle was empty, but he held it in his left hand, guiding his steed with his knees, while he drew a long knife with his free hand. Steve spurred in, silent and grim, holding his fire until the first of the attackers was almost breast to breast with him. Then, as the rifle stock in the red hands went up, Steve shot him twice through his painted face and saw the fierce eyes go blank before the body slumped from the saddle. At the same instant Hard Luck's horse crashed against the bronc of another Indian and the lighter mustang reeled to the shock. The redskin's thrusting blade glanced from the empty rifle barrel and the knife in Hard Luck's right hand whipped in, just under the heart.

The lone survivor wheeled his mustang as if to flee, then pivoted back with an inhuman scream and fired point-blank into Steve's face, so closely that the powder burned his cheek. Without stopping to marvel at the miracle by which the lead had missed, Steve gripped the rifle barrel and wrenched.

White man and Indian tumbled from the saddles, close-locked, and there, writhing and struggling in the dust, the Texan killed his man, beating out his brains with the pistol barrel.

"Hustle!" yelled Hard Luck. "The whole blame tribe is just over that rise not a half a mile away, if I'm to jedge by the sounds of them riding-drums!"

Steve mounted without a backward glance at the losers of that grim red game who lay so stark and motionless. Then he saw the girl, sitting her horse not a hundred yards away, and he cursed in fright. He and Hard Luck swept up beside her and he exclaimed:

"Joan, why didn't you ride on, like I told you?"

"I couldn't run away and leave you!" she sobbed; her face was deathly white, her eyes wide with horror.

"Hustle, blast it!" yelled Hard Luck, kicking her horse. "Git movin'! Do you love birds wanta git all our scalps lifted?"

Over the thundering of the flying hoofs, as they raced eastward, she cried:

"They were taking me somewhere – back to their tribe, maybe – but I worked my hands loose and dashed away on the horse I was riding. Oh, oh, the horrors I've seen today! I'll die, I know I will."

"Not so long as me and brainless here has a drop of blood to let out," grunted Hard Luck, misunderstanding her.

They topped the crest which sloped down to the plateau and Joan averted her face.

"Good thing scalpin's gone outa fashion with the Navajoes," grunted Hard Luck under his breath, "or she'd see wuss than she's already saw."

They raced across the plateau and swung up to the upper mouth of the gulch. There Hard Luck halted.

"Take a little rest and let the horses git their wind. The Indians ain't in sight yit and we kin see 'em clean across the plateau. With this start and our horses rested, we shore ought to make a clean gitaway. Now, Miss Joan, don't you look at – at them cabins what's burned. What's done is done and can't be undid. This game ain't over by a long shot and what we want to do is to think how to save us what's alive. Them that's dead is past hurtin'."

"But it is all so horrible," she sobbed, drooping forward in her saddle. Steve drew up beside her and put a supporting arm about her slim waist. He was heart-torn with pity for her, and the realization that he loved her so deeply and so terribly.

"Shots!" she whimpered. "All at once – like an earthquake! The air seemed full of flying lead! I ran to the cabin door just as Allison came reeling up all bloody and terrible. He pushed me back in the cabin and stood in the door with a pistol in each hand. They came sweeping up like painted fiends, yelling and chanting.

"Allison gave a great laugh and shot one of them out of his saddle and roared: 'Texas breed, curse you!' And he stood up straight in the doorway with his long guns blazing until they had shot him through and through again and again, and he died on his feet." She sobbed on Steve's shoulder.

"Sho, Miss," said Hard Luck huskily. "Don't you worry none about Allison; I don't reckon he woulda wanted to go out any other way. All any of us kin ask is to go out with our boots on and empty guns smokin' in our hands."

"Then they dragged me out and bound my wrists," she continued listlessly, "and set me on a horse. They turned the mustangs out of the corral and then set the corral on fire and the cabins too, dancing and yelling like fiends. I don't remember just what all did happen. It seems like a terrible dream."

She passed a slim hand wearily across her eyes.

"I must have fainted, then. I came to myself and the horse I was on was being led through the forest together with the horses from the corral and the mustangs whose riders Allison had killed. Somehow I managed to work my hands loose, then I kicked the horse with my heels and he bolted back the way we had come."

"Look sharp!" said Hard Luck suddenly, rising in his saddle. "There they come!"

The crest of the western slopes was fringed with war-bonnets. Across the plateau came the discordant rattle of the drums.

CHAPTER 5

Thundering Cliffs

"Easy all!" said Hard Luck. "We got plenty start and we got to pick our way, goin' down here. A stumble might start a regular avalanche. I've seen such things happen in the Sunsets. Easy all!"

They were riding down the boulder-strewn trail which led through the defile. It was hard to ride with a tight rein and at a slow gait with the noise of those red drums growing louder every moment, and the knowledge that the red killers were even now racing down the western slopes.

The going was hard and tricky. Sometimes the loose shale gave way under the hoofs, and sometimes the slope was so steep that the horses reared back on their haunches and slid and scrambled. Again Steve found time to wonder how Joan found courage to go up and down this gorge almost every day. Back on the plateau, now, he could hear the yells of the pursuers and the echoes shuddered eerily down the gorge. Joan was pale, but she handled her mount coolly.

"Nearly at the bottom," said Hard Luck, after what seemed an age. "Risk a little sprint, now."

The horses leaped out at the loosening of the reins and crashed out onto the slopes in a shower of flying shale and loose dirt. "Good business – " said Hard Luck – and then his horse stumbled and went to its knees, throwing him heavily.

Steve and the girl halted their mounts, sprang from the saddle. Hard Luck was up in an instant cursing.

"My horse is lame – go on and leave me!"

"No!" snarled Steve. "We can both ride on mine."

He whirled to his steed; up on the plateau crashed an aimless volley as if fired into the air. Steve's horse snorted and reared – the Texan's clutching hand missed the rein and the bronco wheeled and galloped away into the forest. Steve stood aghast, frozen at this disaster.

"Go on!" yelled Hard Luck. "Blast you, git on with the gal and dust it outta here!"

"Get on your horse!" Steve whirled to the girl. "Get on and go!"

"I won't!" she cried. "I won't ride off and leave you two here to die! I'll stay and die with you!"

"Oh, my Lord!" said Steve, cursing feminine stubbornness and lack of logic. "Grab her horse, Hard Luck. I'll put her on by main force and – "

"Too late!" said Hard Luck with a bitter laugh. "There they come!"

Far up at the upper end of the defile a horseman was silhouetted against the sky like a bronze statue. A moment he sat his horse motionless and in that moment Hard Luck threw the old buffalo gun to his shoulder. At the reverberating crash the Indian flung his arms wildly and toppled headlong, to tumble down the gorge with a loose flinging of his limbs. Hard Luck laughed as a wolf snarls and the riderless horse was jostled aside by flying steeds as the upper mouth of the defile filled with wild riders.

"Git back to the trees," yelled Hard Luck, leading the race from the cliff's base, reloading as he ran. "Guess we kin make a last stand, anyway!"

Steve, sighting over his pistol barrel as he crouched over the girl, gasped as he saw the Navajoes come plunging down the long gulch. They were racing down-slope with such speed that their horses reeled to their knees again and again, recovering balance in a flying cloud of shale and sand. Rocks dislodged by the flashing hoofs rattled down in a rain. The whole gorge was crowded with racing horsemen. Then –

"I knowed it!" yelled Hard Luck, smiting his thigh with a clenched fist.

High up the gulch a horse had stumbled, hurtling against a great boulder. The concussion had jarred the huge rock loose from its precarious base and now it came rumbling down the slope, sweeping horses and men before it. It struck other boulders and tore them loose; the gorge was full of frantic plunging steeds whose riders sought vainly to escape the avalanche they had started. Horses went down screaming as only dying horses can scream, a wild babble of yells arose, and then the whole earth seemed to rock.

Jarred by the landslide, the overhanging walls reeled and shattered and came thundering down into the gorge, wiping out the insects which struggled there, blocking and closing the defile forever. Boulders and pieces of cliff weighing countless tons shelved off and came sliding down. The awed watchers among the trees rose silently, unspeaking. The air seemed full of flying stones, hurled out by the shattering fall of the great rocks. And one of these stones through some whim of chance came curving down through the trees and struck Hard Luck Harper just over the eye. He dropped like a log.

Steve, still feeling stunned, as if his brain had been numbed by the crash and the roar of the falling cliffs, knelt beside him. Hard Luck's eyes flickered open and he sat up.

"Kids," said he solemnly, "that was a terrible and awesome sight! I've seen a lot of hard things in my day and I ain't no Indian lover, but it got me to see a whole tribe of fighting men git wiped out that way. But I knowed as shore as they started racing down that gulch, it'd happen."

He glanced down idly at the stone which had struck him, started, stooped and took it up in his hand. Steve had turned to the girl, who, the reaction having set in, was sobbing weakly, her face hidden in her hands. The Texan put his arms about her hesitantly.

"Joan," said he, "you ain't never said nothin' and I ain't never said nothin' but I reckon it hasn't took words to show how I love you."

"Steve – " broke in Hard Luck excitedly.

"Shut up!" roared Steve, glaring at him. "Can't you see I'm busy?"

Hard Luck shrugged his shoulders and approached the great heap of broken stone and earth, from which loose shale was still spilling in a wide stream down the slight incline at the foot of the cliffs.

"Joan," went Steve, "as I was sayin' when that old buzzard interrupted, I love you, and – and – and if you feel just a little that way towards me, let me take care of you!"

For answer she stretched out her arms to him.

"Joan kid," he murmured, drawing her cheek down on his bosom and stroking her hair with an awkward, gentle hand, "reckon I can't offer you much. I'm just a wanderin' cowhand – "

"You ain't!" an arrogant voice broke in. Steve looked up to see Hard Luck standing over them. The old man held the stone which had knocked him down, while with the other hand he twirled his long drooping mustache. A strange air was evident about him – he seemed struggling to maintain an urbane and casual manner, yet he was apparently about to burst with pride and self-importance.

35

"You ain't no wanderin' cowboy," he repeated. "You'll never punch another cow as long as you live. Yore one fourth owner of the Sunset Lode Mine, the blamedest vein of ore ever discovered!"

The two stared at him.

"Gaze on this yer dornick!" said Hard Luck. "Note the sparkles in it and the general appearance which sets it plumb apart from the ordinary rock! And now look yonder!"

He pointed dramatically at a portion of the cliff face which had been uncovered by the slide.

"Quartz!" he exulted. "The widest, deepest quartz vein I ever see! Gold you can mighta near work out with yore fingers, by golly! I done figured it out – after I wandered away and got found by them buffalo hunters, a slide come and covered the lode up. That's why I couldn't never find it again. Now this slide comes along, forty year later, and uncovers it, slick as you please!

"Very just and proper, too. Indians euchered me outa my mine the first time and now Indians has give it back to me. I guess I cancel the debt of that lifted ha'r.

"Now listen to me and don't talk back. One fourth of this mine belongs to me by right of discovery. One fourth goes to any relatives of Bill Hansen's which might be living. For the other two fourths, I'm makin' you two equal partners. How's that?"

Steve silently gripped the old man's hand, too full for speech. Hard Luck took the young Texan's arm and laid it about Joan's shoulders.

"Git to yore love makin' and don't interrupt a man what's tryin' to figure out how to spend a million!" said he loftily.

"Joan, girl," said Steve softly, "what are you cryin' about? It's easy to forget horrors when you're young. You're wealthy now, we're goin' to be married just as soon as we can – and the drums of Sunset Mountains will never beat again."

"I guess I'm just happy," she answered, lifting her lips to his.

"He first come in the money, and he spent it just as free!
"He always drank good liquor wherever he might be!"

So sang Hard Luck Harper from the depths of his satisfaction.

The Extermination of Yellow Donory

Fate works in a manner unreasonable and paradoxical; men are driven by desperation to plunge headlong into the depths they have spent their lives trying to avoid or escape. There is on record the suicide of a man who, rather than fight a duel in which he had an even chance of surviving, chose the certain path and shot himself the night before. . . .

"All my life," wailed Joey Donory, "I been a scringin', scrawlin', whimperin', gutless *yellow coward!*"

He paused as if for response, but none was forthcoming. The wind sighed mournfully and monotonously outside his shack; except for this noise there was silence. Which is not surprizing, considering that Joey was entirely alone. Nor was his aloneness surprizing, for Joey was raving in his way, and he raved only in solitude. Never had he been known to express a deep emotion in public, or lift his voice with undue feeling. In the presence of strangers or unfriendly acquaintances he maintained a dumb and prayerful silence; even among his few friends he was not garrulous. And the reason thereof cut him to the marrow. Even now he raised voice and spoke bitterly on the subject.

"Yah! I ain't even got the guts to talk back at 'em. They kick me around and make wisecracks and razz me till the world turns blue, an' never a comeback I got. An' it gets worse, the older I get, 'cause a grown man ain't 'sposed to take things like a kid does. Whata break I get!"

Maudlin tears gathered in his bleared and reddened eyes as he reached uncertainly for the ominously dark bottle which stood at his elbow. This he shook anxiously, showing some slight relief when a sensuous and throaty gurgle came from within. The relief was brief, however. He drank long and sadly, then began his rambling monologue again, which monologue was becoming rather incoherent.

Joey Donory was not an imposing man. He was young but he did not look it, nor did his manner suggest it. He was short and wiry with a slight stoop, a long neck, and a sun-wrinkled melancholy face set off by long drooping whiskers. Those whiskers were his solitary pride. All else was bitterness. Born and bred in an environment where most men were large and imposing, his lack of size was bad enough, but his handicaps were more than physical.

"An' it ain't so much me bein' thataway. Most of the real bad hombres wasn't so big. Lookit Billy the Kid; no bigger'n what I be. 'Tain't tallness and 'tain't beef. It's what ya got in ya, an' I just ain't got it. Why'nt I? How'n thunder 'd I know? Lackin' the necessary heft fur fist fightin' I oughter be a wildcat with knives an' guns, but knives gimme the creeps an' the feel of a gat upsets my belly. I should oughta stayed on th' ole man's ranch up on the Sour Water Range where folks knowed me an' where I coulda kept outa their way.

"An' lookit me, too," his voice rose, embittered, for, just as many lonely men do, Joey was in the habit of talking aloud to himself. "Look here at me, top hand and first class miner, 'spite uh my size! How many those big hams can make that brag? How many fellers runnin' loose, cow punch an' miner too?

"An' kin I keep a job anywheres? Like hell I kin! Some big ham starts bullyraggin' me till I up and clear, or else I lose my nerve so bad and fall down on the work so bad, I get th' ole can. Me, what outghta be drawin' as good wages 's any man in the Copper Basin country. An' now what'm I goin' do? Broke – no way uh gettin' any money – outa grub – an' that dam' Bull Groker ridin' me till the world turns blue an' I can't even keep a job dish-washin' f' fear he'll come in an' poke me in the jaw just to be comic. Wish I had the guts to give 'm the works – f' I's a man I'd shoot 'm s' fulla holes he'd look lika open windy.

"Today he slaps me on th' back s' hard I spill my liquor all over m' shirt front n' 'en, 'Haw! Haw!' he laughs, 'Haw! Haw! Haw!' th' big ham!"

Again the bottle for which Joey had spent his last dollar was tilted upward and Joey's mumbling profanity and self-pity merged with sounds indicative of liquid refreshments.

The bottle bumped on the table. Joey, prone though he was to exaggerate his troubles, a failing characteristic of those to whom life has been over-rough, was really in desperate circumstances. He was, as he had said, broke, and though there were plenty of jobs for such as he, a barrier stood in the way. Any job he took would entail coming into daily contact with large, rough and ready men. He shuddered and became nauseated. Physical fear was more than a fault of his; it was a black incubus, a monstrous cancer, born in him and nurtured by fear and a realization and contempt of himself. And it was growing with the years. He knew unreasoning fear of arrogant men and bullies, and always among any gang of men there is a bully – maybe a nasty-minded tyrant, maybe a blatant jackass who is at heart good-natured – but a bully just the same. From job to job Joey flitted until he was broken – a mass of quivering nerves – about ready for the psychopathic ward.

"Never, in all m' fool life, have I did one blame thing which could possibly be called courageous! All m' life. When I was a kid, I didn't mind – never kept no job over four months – when they started ridin' me I started ridin' for new ranges. Good thing I learned up to bein' top hand on m' ole man's ranch 'fore I started driftin'. Minin', that come natural. I picked her up easy, workin' in short snatches. 'f I'd had eddication I'd a been uh minin' engineer. Used to when I'd quit uh job, I'd not worry – go get 'nother 'un. Stummick's turned on that. Los' what little nerve I ever did have."

Joey laid his head on his arms and wept. What seems trivial to others is the pure essence of Hell to the sufferer, and the incubus of realized cowardice is the worst that haunts manhood. From that orgy of weakness and tears, Joey Donory rose with an iron resolve crystallizing in his liquor-muddled brain. He had reached the state in which even the most trivial discomforts loom monstrously and with deathly portent. And Joey's troubles were not trivial.

"Better t' be dead than t' be yellow!" he muttered, a light of almost feral desperation growing in his weak reddened eyes. "'f I thought it'd get better – but I've been thinkin' that fur twenty-five years an' it gets worse. T'morrow I won't have the nerve – got to decide tonight. Already decided – goin' kill m' fool self!"

He paused and looked around with a sort of dreary triumph, aware that he had made a statement dramatic and fraught with dire portent.

"Goin' kill m'self," he repeated. "Then they'll see!"

He felt suddenly invested with a deep, dark significance. Somberly, and with a brooding majesty slightly affected by a wobbling walk, he crossed the room and, after some uncertain fumbling, jerked open a drawer. A cold blue glitter of steel winked up at him. Joey Donory's soul shrivelled within him. He covered his face with his hands and reeled away.

"Oh, m' Gawd," he groaned, tears of humiliation and helpless fury flooding his eyes. "I ain't even got th' guts to bump m'self off!"

He raised his head, hopelessly. The night wind blew drearily, and faint on its whisper came the far off blare of a tinny talking machine. The noise conjured up a mental picture of the Elite Saloon, that dive of iniquity where men talked loud, drank hard and died suddenly. Out of the depths of self-abasement and alcohol, an idea fantastic and paradoxical was born. Joey Donory turned cold at the mere conception of that idea, but he was past the borderline of desperation.

"They say Demon Darts hit town today," he whispered to himself, cold sweat beading his brow.

The merriment in the Elite was in full swing. Men reeled, shouted and swung the shrill-voiced ladies of the resort, but man or woman, drunk or sober, they were all careful to leave clear a generous space near the end of the bar. In the center of this forbidden spot, throned in somber regality and crowned with a brooding and sinister aloofness, stood Demon Darts in all his glory. Your true killer is ever the actor, the perfect showman.

This particular gunman was almost a legend in the Copper Basin country, though he had never before honored the locality with his presence. For that matter, he was almost traditional all over the West. Lurid and terrible were the tales of his deeds, and no one, looking at the great dark bulk of him, and at the sinister, lined face with the narrow, cold, merciless eyes glittering beneath the heavy black brows, could doubt that there was a large measure of truth in most of those tales.

All the local bad hombres were silent and subdued. Even – nay, and especially – Bull Groker, the burly miner who ruled supreme over the Copper Basin fighting men, had seen fit to make an early and unobtrusive exit. He breathed a frank sigh as the saloon doors swung shut behind him, guided by his careful hand; and at that moment a smaller figure heaved up suddenly in the gloom and a set of thin steely fingers clutched his arm with a nervous grip.

"Donory!" said Groker with disapproval. "Ain't I tell you early in the evenin' not to come foolin' 'round where they's men?"

"Is Demon Darts in there?" hissed Joey, unheeding.

The unexpectedness of the question almost rendered Groker speechless, and he could only find words as follows: "Uh, yeah, why, uh, yeah, he is, but whata you want – "

Joey had already pushed past him, and Groker, burned up with curiosity to know what the most arrant coward in the country wanted with the most notorious killer, followed him. Joey had not been in the Copper Basin many months, but even so he had endured enough at the hands of Bull to assure that worthy of the smaller man's lack of courage. Now he noted that Joey was white-faced and was shaking as if in the grip of a chill.

In an element rude and elemental where human passions are frank and blatant, shocks and surprizes may be expected. Jars unexpected and sudden had come to the hardened sinners who frequented the Elite, but it is safe to say that never were they so jolted out of their cynic callousness than that night. The unexpected frightens, and it was with a sudden icy chill of real horror that the drinkers, dancers and gamblers heard a sudden voice blat: *"Demon Darts! He's the shrinkin' vi'let I'm lookin' fur!"*

Dancing, drinking, gambling stopped as if the participants had all been struck dead. A cocktail shaker slipped from a nerveless hand and crashed on the floor like the crack of Doom. There in the doorway, with his arms still wide spread holding apart the swinging doors, and with his mouth still gaping from yelling those frightful words, stood Joey Donory.

Joey Donory had yelled at Demon Darts. Strong men held their breaths and waited for the skies to fall. The watchers blanched, fearful lest the insulted gunman include all present in the sweeping doom which must inevitably mow down the lunatic in the doorway.

As for Darts, he had jerked about at the sound of the voice, his hand shooting to the big black gun at his hip; but he had not drawn and now he stood eyeing the intruder somberly. To the horrified watchers that stare was an assurance of sudden death in its most grisly form, but a close observer would have noted not a little amazement and bewilderment in the killer's icy eyes. Not in years had any man addressed Demon Darts thus. The not inconsiderable few who had called with the intention of giving him a one-way ticket to the next world had been either wary and subtle or blazing and passionate, but one and all had accorded him the respect due him. Yet here this shrimp – that made it more sinister. Darts did not know Joey. Had the maniac been a giant it would have been easier to understand, for notwithstanding the time-honored adage that Colonel Colt makes all men equal, few people really believe it, and still are prone to think that a blazing gun is more effective in the hand of a big powerful man than in the hand of, say, one of Joey's proportions.

Now Donory strode forward and the people gave back as if he were a leper. He saw all eyes turn from him to the man who stood alone at the bar and with a sinking feeling he knew it was the killer. The sight chilled him to the marrow but he was wild with drink, with desperation engendered by a lifetime of humiliation, and to a lesser extent, by the dramatics of the moment. Even in this deadly hour he was aware of the intense stares and they went to his head. Always Joey Donory had craved to be the center of attraction. Now he was It with a vengeance and as he had burned all his bridges, he would make the most of the moment.

He walked up to the silent and somber Darts and eyed him insolently.

"D-Demon Da-arts!" he sneered, unable to keep his voice from shaking a little or the cold sweat from beading his brow. "A hell of a gunman *you* are, you lousy tramp!"

A sudden and really painful gurgling gasp escaped the onlookers. Joey instinctively shut his eyes and awaited the end. But in a couple of seconds he realized that he was still alive and his eyes jerked open – wide. Darts had not even drawn; he was eyeing the smaller man with a strange expression growing in his eyes. Darts moved quickly but he did not think quickly. However, an idea was fermenting in his skull.

He spoke for the first time: "Ya tired uh livin', feller? Don't ya know I'm just as liable to plug ya as look at ya?"

The audience shivered in an ecstasy of anticipatory fright.

Joey was getting shaky. It was not courage but a sort of insanity that was keeping him up, and his knees began to rattle. He wanted to get this over with before he lost all his nerve and broke down. Of course, suicide was his object. Badgering Darts to make the gunman kill him. A quick ending ("They don't have time ta suffer when they stop my lead," the killer had boasted), a way out without using his own hand, courage for which he lacked – moreover, the empty honor of leaving a certain glamor about his taking off, as the man who had baited the terrible Demon Darts.

And now Darts seemed inclined to prolong the agony and Joey went wild. Maybe the Demon thought so little of him that he would not even waste powder on him!

"Go on!" he shouted. "Shoot me, why don't ya?" He tore open his shirt and crowded forward almost against the staring gunman; his voice broke in a great sob sounded like fury to the crowd. "Ya always bragged yore victims didn't kick after ya pulled the trigger! Go on, if ya got the guts of a louse!"

"Listen here!" said Darts in a strange, strangled voice. "You got no call to be pickin' a fight with me. I ain't never even seen you before!"

The feeling was growing. This fellow was some terrible gunfighter, so terrible that even Demon Darts would be no match for him. Else how would he dare the Demon? He must know he had a cinch, to thus face Darts empty-handed and goad him to wrath. What was the cinch? Gunmen planted in the crowd? T.N.T. under the floor? Derringers up his sleeves and inhuman skill at using them? Cold sweat began to appear on the brow of Demon Darts. He was far from being a coward, but this was ghastly! This fellow knew he had him – Darts – in a triple cinch, somehow! There is nothing so numbing as the experience of a man who has for years been used to frightened respect, and is suddenly confronted with someone who not only seems to hold no fear of him, but to actually be contemptuous of him. The higher a man values his own prowess, the higher he is likely to value the untested prowess of a scornful foe. Most gunmen are high-strung – human panthers – a panther is a terrible fighter, but the flutter of a girl's handkerchief will sometimes stampede him. Demon Darts began to shake like a leaf. His hand fell limply from his belt.

"Don't you go pickin' no fight wi' me," he said thickly and with some difficulty. "I got no quarrel wi' you. Le's – le's have a drink an' forget it."

Joey scarcely knew what the man was saying. All he knew was that this nightmare was being prolonged. He went temporarily crazy.

"You ain't nothin' but a big false alarm!" he screamed, seeking wildly for insults which would sting this man out of what Joey thought to be a contemptuous indifference. "You big tramp, I ain't even got a pocket knife and you got on two guns! Yo're yellow! Yo're a lousy, yellow, low-down thievin' coyote that ain't got the guts to drill a man only in the back – "

He stopped for breath, perceiving as though through a fog that Demon Darts, blue about the lips and ghastly as to eye, said nothing. Entirely distraught, Joey slapped his face with resounding force. At that, Darts ducked wildly and gave a strangled cry.

"Ya ain't goin' to force me into no one-sided slaughter-fight, ya cold-blooded murderer!" he screamed. "If ya kill me, ya gotta do it – *now!*"

And reeling like a man blind-drunk, he crowded past Joey and ran blunderingly to the doors, plunging through them into the night – to be seen no more in the Copper Basin country.

Silence lay like a black pall over the Elite Saloon. Joey, dazed, entirely incapable of coherent thought, moved mechanically and without conscious volition toward the door. He could not yet realize what had happened. Men and women cowered back from him, horror mirrored in their eyes.

At the side of the door stood Bull Groker, and this worthy croaked hoarsely like a frog as Joey neared him. The dreary portent of the noise drew Joey's lackluster gaze and Groker made infantile and futile motions with his feet as though he would flee but could not. Then with a heroic effort he said, after several gagging false starts:

"M-m-m-mister D-D-Donory, b-be ya goin' to drill me?"

"Me?" said Joey in a mechanical but ghostly whisper. "Naw – I come here to see Demon Darts – it's him I wants."

"He's in Californy by this time," said Groker with a vast whimpering sigh of prayerful relief. "Mister Donory, I wanta thank ya for not havin' killed me. I know I been kinda offensive at times, but ya knowed it was just my friendly hearty way. I'll take care not to do it no more. Will ya not be sore at me, Mister Donory?"

"No!" whispered Joey, still in a daze.

"L-l-lemme shake yore hand, please sir, Mister Donory," gulped Groker, almost weeping with relief; he shook Joey's limp hand with awe, but his instincts were all for kissing it. Then he moved away to the bar, looking back over his shoulder and walking with stiff, automaton-like steps. The other men in the place stood staring spellbound. As yet they were incapable of thought.

As Joey opened the doors to depart, someone touched him respectfully on the shoulder. He turned to meet the admiring gaze of one of the wealthiest mine owners in the Copper Basin country.

"Mister Donory, I've been wanting to meet a man like you for a long time; a man all fire and steel, but with perfect control of himself! You're just the man to handle some big deals I'm planning. I've had a lot of trouble with the men lately but under you, they'll be lambs. You'll pardon me if I say this was a big surprise. I should have known, though, that you have too much self-control, that you're too big to fool with such small calibers as Bull Groker and the like. Like all real gunmen, you were just waiting for a fellow who was more on your level, weren't you?"

"Er-ya-ump – " gurgled Donory, staring wildly.

"Sure you were. And, Mister Donory," the last in a low confidential voice, "don't think I'm intruding, but why do you have it in for Darts?"

"I ain't – I don't – " began Joey, finding partially coherent speech.

"The true old type of Western gunfighter," said the mining magnate admiringly. "You fellows don't have to have a grudge – it's just to see who is the best man!" He slapped Joey rather timidly on the shoulder, evidently much awed at the new-risen celebrity. "You come around – no, I'll come around to your shack tomorrow and we'll talk business."

"Ahh-uh-ayeah – " garbled Joey. "Uh-uh-goo-goo-night – "

"Goodnight, Mister Donory!" came the respectful chorus from the entire crowd.

Donory drifted out into the darkness, walking like a man in a trance.

"Strange nuts, these real gunfighters," said the magnate to the wan and pallid crowd. "Cold as ice – yet he was a flaming firebrand when he was calling Darts."

"Gimme a drink," said a cowboy suddenly. "By Judas, I kin hardly believe it yet. Say, fellers, this here is somethin' ya kin tell yore grand-chillern. That ya saw Demon Darts take water an' back down – take a cussin' an' a rap in th' pan, an' run like a jackrabbit. Believe me, it's Mister Donory from now on out with me. Who ya reckon he is, anyhow?"

"Lord knows – " "Tex Slade, maybe – " "Gotta string of killin's nine mile long, I bet!" "Anyway, Darts shore knowed him – " "Yeah, he plumb turned blue when Donory come in – " "An who'da thought it, him bein'

45

so mild like – " "Them mild ones is the real bad 'uns – " Thus the saloon buzzed with semi-hysterical conversation.

Back at his shack the situation was beginning to dawn on Joey.

"By golly!" yammered that hero wildly. "I plumb bluffed the liver outa Darts, not intendin' to, an' he took it on the lam!"

Joey was shaking as from an ague.

"Musta been clean outa my head! Thank the Lord I'm still alive. An' now, by golly, I got a reputation that I'll never have to defend an' which nobody'll question 'cause Darts is such a bloody devil. I went out to get exterminated – " A slow grin overspread his homely countenance which of late years had known few grins. "By golly, they was a killin', 'cause right there Yellow Donory was exterminated an' in his place now is *Mister* Donory – what I care if I ain't really brave? Long's people remember tonight, no man'll dare start anything with me! An' here'm I, *Mister* Donory, with a man's job I kin keep at last, an' a man's rightful respect."

The Judgment of the Desert

CHAPTER I

"The Left Barrel – "

Somewhere a Mexican was singing to the drowsy accompaniment of a guitar. The sound came clearly to Stan Brannigan as he picked his way along the narrow, unpaved, and unlighted street, and the unfamiliar words reminded him forcibly that he was a long way from home and in a foreign land, where no one either knew or cared that he was alive.

It was late; late even for this wild border village where revelry and debauchery lasted until the stars began to pale, as a general rule. Most of the adobe houses along the one street were dark and silent, and only from one, a more pretentious frame building, lights streamed and voices mingled with the click of roulette wheels. Stan paused a moment in front of the doors, which were closed, hesitated, then started on. As he did so, voices were raised in fierce altercation inside the saloon, there sounded a rush of feet and the sudden crack of a pistol.

Stan whirled as the doors crashed open. Etched in the flood of lamp-light from the bar, a figure reeled across the sill and pitched headlong out into the street. Stan sprang forward, knelt and lifted the man's head, noting that the victim was a white-bearded old man.

"Any way I can help you?"

The old man's breath was coming in terrible rattling gasps; his with-ered fingers gripped Stan's wrists like claws. He opened his mouth and a trickle of blood stained his beard.

"My hut – " he gasped, fighting hard for a moment's life, "my – gun – the – left – barrel – "

The form went limp in Stan's arms, then stiffened. The young man eased the corpse to the earth and rose, mechanically cleansing his blood-stained hands. He was then aware that quite a crowd had gathered; they

47

had evidently come out of the saloon, and now they stood back and whispered among themselves.

Standing above the dead man was a huge, powerfully built man, and to him Stan's gaze was drawn as by a magnet. This man was tall and broad, with stooping shoulders and gnarly arms, but it was his face which drew Stan's attention. If ever a face was stamped with evil and hate, it was this man's. His lips writhed in a snarl, and from under heavy black brows, his eyes blazed, gleaming with a sort of magnetic savagery. Stan's gaze traveled down to the pistol in the fellow's right hand.

"Dead?" the word was jerked out, more an assertion than a question.

"Yes," Stan nodded.

"Tried to hold up my joint," the other said slowly, his eyes glaring into Stan's as though in challenge. "I plugged him."

Stan made no reply, but from somewhere among the knot of Mexicans and white men who looked on, there came a short sardonic laugh. The head of the killer came up with a jerk, and his eyes flamed with a new and sinister light as they roved vainly for the laughter. Then those eyes came back to Stan.

"He say anything before he croaked?" the killer asked harshly.

Stan hesitated. He could not have told just what instinct prompted him to lie; but under the burning intensity of those savage eyes, he felt somehow that the truth had better be withheld.

"No," he answered briefly, "he didn't say anything."

The killer scanned his face with an almost painful intensity, then grudgingly holstered his gun, and said a few abrupt words in Spanish. A couple of Mexicans lifted the body of the old man and carried it back into the saloon. Stan hesitated, and then turned away. He had not taken four steps when he was aware that he was being accompanied. His sudden companion was a man of medium height, wiry and incredibly broad-shouldered and long-armed. In the light which streamed from the open saloon door, Stan saw that he was clad in worn cowboy garb, with two guns hung low at his hips. His face was hard and brown as an Indian, his eyes narrow and piercing. Then the doors slammed and the man was only a shadowy figure at his side, indistinct in the pale starlight.

Stan, undecided, said nothing, and the pair strode along for awhile in silence; then –

48

"That old boy, pard," said the stranger softly, "shore got a rough deal."

"Yeah?" Stan's voice was noncommittal.

"Yeah, he did. He wasn't tryin' to hold up no joint. That fellow, Hansen, and him had a row; Hansen started for him, he started for the door, and Hansen shot him in the back."

Stan gave an involuntary exclamation of horror and anger.

"Easy!" whispered the other. "They may be somebody within hearin'."

"But how can a thing like that happen, with all those fellows lookin' on?" asked Stan angrily.

His companion laughed shortly. "You ain't in the U.S.A. now. You're in Old Mexico, and a particular tough part of Mexico at that. Right here in Sangre Del Diablo anything can happen – and quite often does. The old idee of 'might's right' goes over great here, and that fellow Hansen just now happens to be the might. He owns that saloon and is the real ruler of the whole village. As for the onlookers, the only onlooker while ago in the saloon that wasn't Hansen's man, hand and heart, was me. What's your name and what you doin' across the border?"

"In the first place," said Stan, nettled, "it ain't any of your business."

"Shore," the other returned amiably, "that's always understood. You say it's none of my business, and I agrees. Now, that being settled, who are you and what you doin' here?"

Stan laughed, half irritated, half amused.

"I haven't anything to hide," he said. "My name's Stan Brannigan, and I've been punchin' cows across the line in Arizona. I come across the border just to see what I could find – for fun and adventure, like – but so far I've found nothin' but chile con carne, tortillas, and lukewarm beer."

"You ain't been goin' to the right joints – most of these fellows keeps ice for the beer – but as for findin' nothin' – hell! You've busted right into the middle of the wildest and most dangerous adventure you ever heard of. My name is – er, that is, you can call me Spike. I'm Texas born, original, and I'm in Sangre Del Diablo on business. And that business concerns the old codger that just stopped Hansen's lead.

"Wait!" As they had walked, Spike had casually steered Stan toward the edge of the tiny village, and now they stood on the edge of the desert, dotted darkly in the starlight by cactus and a few straggling mesquites. Behind them loomed the black bulks of the adobe houses.

"Let's sit down a minute," suggested Spike. "This is a lot better'n talkin' in a house where fellers can git behind doors and listen to yore secrets. Now, then, pard, me and you are due for a great break! Luck's flyin' our way with all wings spread – but it all rests with you."

"What rests with me?"

"Whether the good luck keeps flyin' or settles on our shoulder."

"I don't get you at all," said Stan, bewildered. "What you mean?"

"It hinges," said Spike mysteriously, "on what old Sour Sanson said before he died, to you."

"Didn't you hear me tell Hansen he didn't say nothin'?"

"Be reasonable," said Spike imperturbably, lighting a cigarette. "You'd naturally lie to Hansen; somethin' about him what inspires falsehood in anybody. The average bird not only feels inclined to lie to Hansen instinctively, but also to steal from him, slander him – if it could be did – and poke him in the jaw. Hansen's that kind of a bird. Shootin' him oughta come under the head of public improvements. But anyway, let's git down to facts. I don't know no more'n Hansen does, what old Sour said when he was dyin', but I do know that a feller like Sour will say somethin' before he dies, no matter how much lead he's got in him. With all the mystery that they was hangin' over him, it ain't right or decent to suppose that he kicked out without saying *nothin'*."

Stan remained silent.

"I'll give you the lowdown," said Spike, puffing at his cigarette, "and then it'll be up to you whether you talk or not.

"Back several years ago when old Pancho Villa was raisin' Cain in these parts, they was a very wealthy old Mexican which lived in Spain. This Mex had been run outa the country by the Federal government, but had managed to take mosta his private fortune along. He went into business in Spain, so I been told, and the more he thought about the deal he'd got, the worse it burned him up. He musta gone clean cuckoo. Anyway, he finally got together a terrible lot of money and sent it from Spain to Mexico. It was intended for Pancho Villa. 'Take this gold,' the old Mex wrote, 'and fight the Federals till Hades freezes,' or somethin' like that.

"But the gold never got to Villa – who coulda sure used it about that time. Some say his own men to whom it was delivered double-crossed him, some say a passel of Yaquis hopped 'em and scuppered the lot; anyway, the gold disappeared and no man's ever seen or heard of it since, unless – "

"Unless what?"

"Unless it's old Sour Sanson! Now wait; this old galoot's a old time prospector. Been roamin' the deserts of Texas, Arizona, California, and Mexico for gosh knows how long. Never made a real strike yet. But wait! A few weeks ago, old Sour blows into Sangre Del Diablo with gold – plenty of it. He says he's struck it back in the hills, but won't say where, not even when he's drunk. But it don't sound right, nor look right. The gold's all in one hunk, and a lot of fellers, who knows gold too, decides that it's been melted down. See? Right away they remember Villa's gold, lost or stolen somewhere in these parts. This is what Hansen and several others thinks, includin' me: that the gold was hid long ago and the hiders was killed and never come back to git it. Then old Sour stumbles onto the hidin' place, but is afeard to pack it all out at once. So he melts some of the coins down, see, and pretends it's virgin lode. Heck, he couldn'ta got away with that with anybody – anybody could see the stuff had been melted.

"Hansen and his gang gits after the old boy and after tryin' kindness and coaxin' and gittin' him drunk – all of which fails – they git rough. Tonight, Hansen grabs the old man and tried to make him talk, and you know what happened. Sanson broke away and run, but Hansen, crazy with rage, got him.

"I happened to be there – drifted up from Sonora a few days ago, havin' had wind of this 'gold strike.' Now you know all I know. If you know any more, I'd be glad to hear from you. You know, we'd make a fine pair to go after that gold – you couldn't hope to git it by yourself."

"Alright," said Stan thoughtfully, "I'll tell you. The old man said: 'My hut – my gun – the left barrel.' Maybe you can make somethin' out of that. I can't see no reason to it."

"Me neither," confessed Spike, "but we'll investigate. 'My hut': that's old Sour's hut across on the other side of town. 'My gun': he usually packs a queer old muzzle loadin' pistol, but he wasn't wearin' it tonight. 'The left barrel': maybe he's got the gold hid in a barrel of flour! Let's go."

CHAPTER II

The Face at the Window

"Light that candle," said Spike. "Maybe Hansen sent spies to foller you, and maybe people might git suspicious if they see a dead man's hut all lit up. But the village as a whole is asleep and don't know old Sour's dead, and anyway we got to have a light to work by."

Stan complied, glancing curiously about him at the squalid adobe hut that had housed the murdered Sour Sanson. A bunk, a rude chair and table, an open fireplace, a packsaddle, and a few mining tools met his gaze. The candle guttered on the table and dripped hot tallow ceaselessly.

"Understand Hansen had the hut searched before now, while Sour was drunk," said Spike. "Anyhow, we'll do a better job. Tear it apart if necessary."

"What are you expectin' to find?"

"I dunno. But I bet my hand that Sour's last words referred to the gold, somehow."

Stan looked intently at his companion, taking in again the low hung gun, the quick nervous motions of the hands, and, above all, the cold steel intensity of the narrow eyes.

"Say, who are you anyhow?" Stan asked bluntly. "And what are you?"

"As for who I am," said Spike stolidly, bending down to examine the bunk, "one name's as good as another, south of the border. As for what I am, I'm just only merely nothin' but a wanderin' cowpuncher, mild and peaceful, with the hankerin's and instincks of a prospector."

Stan stood idly in the center of the room while Spike prowled about, gouging into holes and breaking furniture. His eyes, roaming about, centered on a belt hanging from a nail driven into the wall. From this belt hung a long black holster holding a pistol of antique and curious design. The old prospector's last words in his mind, Stan crossed the room and lifted the gun from its scabbard. It was an old muzzleloader of European manufacture, ornately carved and scrolled on stock, lock and barrel –

Stan started, remembering. The gun was double-barreled, and the percussion cap was missing on the nipple of the left barrel.

He drew forth the tiny ramrod from its groove beneath the twin barrels and, turning the screw on the end, inserted it into the muzzle. He felt something that might or might not be a charge, twisted carefully, felt the screw catch, and withdrew the rod.

Transfixed by the screw was a wadded up piece of very thin leather. He unfolded it; drawn in faint red lines was a map of some sort, with words laboriously scrawled beneath.

"Spike!" he exclaimed, but Spike was already at his side, his eyes blazing.

"A map!" the other exclaimed. "A map where the gold's hid! I knowed it! And look! The old man writ it out plain – the Canon Los Infernos in the mountains of – "

Looking over Spike's shoulder, Stan cried out sharply and suddenly. Framed in the one window was a face, swarthy and evil – a Mexican whose eyes gleamed with hate and avarice as he glared at the map in Spike's hand. Only for an instant did Stan see the face before it vanished – only the merest fraction of a second, but in that instant Spike whirled, drew, and fired. It seemed he did it all in one motion, with a volcanic quickness which stunned and bewildered his companion.

While Stan still stood in amazement, Spike leaped to the door and slid through. Stan came to himself and leaped after him, but at the threshold he met Spike returning.

"Got away," snarled the Texan. "Missed him. Not far though." And he tossed a tall sombrero on the floor. Stan noted the hole in the crown.

"For a peaceful cowpuncher," said Stan slowly, "you sure unleathered your gun in a hurry. I just caught a glance of him as he ducked, yet you managed to draw and shoot at him so quick he didn't have time to get his hat out of the way."

"Oh, I been practicin' with guns a good deal," said Spike, a slight shadow of seeming annoyance crossing his dark features. "Forgit it; here's the map. It says plain that the gold's hid in Hell's Canyon up in the mountains south of here. The hardest part is before us. That Mex was bound to been one of Hansen's men. We got to git outa here before the whole gang descends on us. They's miles and bare desert and a lot of terrible rough mountains between here and the canyon we wants. Right now we'll beat it out to my camp at the edge of town. It ain't so long till daylight, and they's no time to sleep now. We gotta be away out on the desert by sunup. Come on."

"Still and all," persisted Stan as they left the hut, "that speed of yours is sure a revelation. Nobody could have done it no quicker, not even that famous border badman, Mike O'Mara."

"Don't mention that bloody devil to me," snarled Spike. "Le's git goin'."

CHAPTER III

Fruit of the Desert

The swiftly mounting sun blinded Stan Brannigan as its blazing rays beat back from the alkali sand. He hitched at his belt and cursed softly. He was inured to desert travel, but this beat any desert he had ever seen for heat and drought; besides, he was feeling the effect of last night's loss of sleep.

He glanced at Spike, slumped in his saddle and swaying easily with the motion of his plodding mount. A slouchy but effective rider. The heat beat down on Stan, and he cursed himself for allowing a stranger to inveigle him into a wild-goose chase. He fumed at the time they were making, though he realized that it would be suicide to attempt any faster pace, considering the distance they must traverse.

They had left the little village of Sangre Del Diablo just before the utter blackness that precedes dawn. Four horses made up their string: their mounts, one pack horse loaded with as much economy as was possible, and a spare mount. They had one pick, one shovel, their weapons, canteens, and a supply of food, which, with proper use, would last them until their return.

Now the sun was high in the heavens, and Stan continually looked back, always expecting to sight the cloud of dust which would announce a band of pursuers.

"I ain't expectin' a fight yet," said Spike, as Stan spoke to him. "Hansen knows we got the map now, and if I'm any judge, he'd rather wait till we get the gold and then try to take it away from us. Anyway, I figure he'll let us lead him to the gold – if he can – before he looms on the scene. Still, he's got no idea which way we went. We sneaked out so cautious like, I don't think no one saw us. Maybe he can track us, and maybe he can't. This sand shifts pretty fast. Anyhow, I ain't worryin' about him till I see him – and maybe not then. Only one of that gang that's really dangerous. That's Yaqui Slade; not a Injun but a bad white man. Real gunfighter. Hansen? Bah. Harder to whip than a buffalo in rough-and-tumble, but slow as mud with a gun."

"Then he ought to be easy for you," said Stan slowly.

Spike spat in the sand and did not reply. Stan gazed at the great bulk of mountains looming far away in the heat laden sky. Heat waves shimmered between, making them seem vague and illusive. But even at that distance, Stan could tell that those craggy heights were barren and terrible. They seemed fraught with menace, brooding there like prehistoric monsters, evil things of another age.

"One mountain spring I know," said Spike, following his companion's gaze. "It's kind of a freak. You don't find much water in them hills. Right in the mouth of Canon Los Infernos, too. Blame lucky and convenient for us."

A long silence followed, broken only by the creak of sweaty leather and the scruff of the horses' hooves through the sand. Stan wiped the sweat from his brow. Spike slumped further into his saddle, swaying with such perfect rhythm in accord to his mount's motions that he seemed part of the animal.

They did not stop for a midday meal. The grip of the gold lust had its talons on Spike, and the spirit had entered Stan's blood to a certain extent.

"How much money did that old Mex send Villa?" asked Stan.

"A million dollars, they say."

"Applesauce! In gold? It'd take a train to carry that much gold."

"I ain't sayin' how it was packed," answered Spike. "But the story has it a million dollars. If we find it, we'll pack out what we can, and hide the rest in a different place."

The sun passed the zenith and slanted westward, but with scant abatement of the heat which curled the leather of the saddles.

"We been easy on the horses," said Spike, as the sun began to set, "but they got to rest and have a little water. We'll unsaddle 'em and wait till the moon sets. That ain't so terrible long, but long enough for 'em to rest and us to eat a little. Then we'll move on and rest again about daylight."

"Alright," Stan answered. Again a silence fell as the stars blinked out. The two men rode on through the pallid light of the young moon like phantoms; like the last men alive in a dead world. The sands glinted silver, shading into blackness. The cactus reared up like stunted giants, silent and brooding.

They halted, threw off packs and saddles, watered the horses from the canteens and sat down to eat, rest, and smoke. They said little. Stan was weary and not inclined to conversation. His mind dallied with the thought of the treasure, but he was unable to become enthusiastic. It seemed too much like a dream, too unreal. Real life consisted, to Stan Brannigan, of hard, heartbreaking toil: riding through all kinds of weather, hot and cold; sweating in the dust and fury of the roundup; branding, roping – he sighed. No, a million dollars in gold was too good to be true. He glanced at his companion.

Spike's eyes gleamed in the glow of his cigarette. He seemed darkly brooding, drawn apart from human fellowship. Something about him set him apart; even though he was friendly and jovial, Stan sensed that there was a barrier of reserve between them. Again the younger man wondered – who was this steely-eyed man who called himself Spike?

Stan yawned and stretched, humming to keep himself awake. An old border ballad came to his lips:

Mike O'Mara rode up from Sonora,
    Packin' a forty-five gun;
He met a Texas ranger,
    And says, "Good mornin', stranger,
Yore work on earth is done."

Spike made a fierce, passionate gesture, as if stung out of his calm.

"Can't you lay off that bird?" His tone was vibrant with a strange passion. "What you wanta keep draggin' up the name of – of O'Mara?"

"Why," said Stan, puzzled, "anybody's likely to sing that song; it ain't been but a few years since O'Mara was raisin' Cain on the border down around Tiajuana, and further down in Sonora."

"Let him rest," said Spike harshly. "Mike O'Mara's dead and gone; he'll never come back. Forgit him. Let the world forgit him."

"What you got against him?" asked Stan curiously.

"That's neither here nor there. Lay down and git some sleep. I'll wake you when the moon sets."

"Ain't you sleepy?"

"Naw – git to sleep. As for O'Mara, I'll just say this, and I don't want to ever hear the swine mentioned again: he killed one man too many – the last man he shot down in cold blood. Git to sleep now."

Stan spread his blanket and dropped into a dreamless sleep, from which it seemed he was awakened in a few minutes by a hand on his shoulder.

"Le's git on the move," Spike was saying. "Moon's down and it's time we was travellin'."

A few minutes of fumbling at cinches and bridles and then they moved out across a darkened desert which pulsed blackly beneath the stars. Stan, rubbing the clinging sleep out of his eyes, stared ahead at the vague black bulk of the mountains. They seemed no nearer.

At the first tint of dawn they again halted for awhile, then moved on again. The sun was coming up over the desert like a red shield of flame. The sands throbbed crimson, like a shallow sea of blood, and through those red shadows, Stan saw a figure stumbling.

"Look, Spike!"

"I see him," rapped the other, quickening his mount's pace. "Some feller that's lost his bronc and got lost. Hey!"

Stan added his voice to Spike's stentorian shout, and at the sound the distant figure wavered about uncertainly, started toward them at a weak stumbling gait.

"A boy," said Spike, reaching for his canteen. "Just a kid – no, by Judas, it's a girl!"

Stan cried out; the slim figure had pitched headlong in the sand and lay still. They hastened forward, dismounted beside the still form. Stan lifted her gently in his arms and, tilting his canteen, let a thin stream of water trickle through the parched and blistered lips. Spike fanned the fainted girl with his hat, and presently she opened her eyes, stared wildly about her, then clutched at the canteen with the piteous cry of a famished animal.

"Easy, sister, easy," cautioned Stan gently. "Don't drink too fast; it ain't good for you."

The girl looked up at him uncertainly, and Stan squirmed uneasily from the glance of her large deep eyes. She was a slim little figure, dressed in a khaki shirt and riding breeches, and the slouch hat had fallen from her head, revealing a mass of unruly golden curls. Her eyes were a soft gray, shaded by long dark lashes, and though her full red lips were blistered and her delicate cheeks burned brown by the sun, Stan realized in a panic that this was the most beautiful girl he had ever met.

"Class here," he thought dazedly. "Looks and blood, too. High class family, I betcha a nickel. What's she doin' wanderin' around here?"

"Let me have some more water, please," she begged, and Stan put the canteen to her lips, again cautioning her to drink slowly.

At last she sat up, replaced her hat, and drew her hand dazedly across her brow.

"Where am I?" she asked like a lost child.

"In the desert between Sangre Del Diablo and the Infernos Mountains." She shook her head wearily.

"That doesn't mean anything to me. I rode and rode and rode, till my horse gave out almost. Then when I dismounted to rest him, he got away from me. I've been wandering – all night, it seems."

"Lucky we found you when we did. A few hours of this sun would have about finished you. We'll take you back to – "

"Stan!" Spike broke in harshly, speaking for the first time. He was standing beside his horse and a black look was on his face – a worried, angry expression.

"Stan, we can't take her back! We got to go on!"

"But we can't leave her here, Spike!"

"She can go with us. Anyway, we can't go back till we've done what we started to do. I tell you, this is our only chance."

"But, Spike – " began Stan uncertainly and somewhat angrily.

"Oh, don't send me back!" the girl's cry was as sharp as a wounded bird's. "No, no!" she caught Stan's arm and clung desperately to him. "Take me with you – or leave me here where you found me – anything – but don't, please don't, take me back! I'd rather die here!"

"Alright," Stan was rather appalled at the desperation in her tone and her face. "We got a long dangerous journey in front of us, but if you won't go back, it's a cinch you can't stay here."

"Get her on the spare bronc," Spike said shortly. "Let's git movin'. We got no time to waste. Hansen's on our track right now, like as not, and we can't fight his gang out in the open. We *got* to git in the mountains before they catch up with us."

Stan helped the girl on the horse, but his heart smote him as he thought of the perils which faced them, and to which she would necessarily be exposed if she accompanied them. But evidently from her manner a worse peril lay behind her, and letting her go seemed the only way out.

They took up their journey again in silence. Spike's manner had changed. His air of lazy good nature had dropped from him. Stan heard him curse beneath his breath as he glanced at the girl, and several times he shook his head, either in pity or anger.

As for the girl, she said nothing, neither asked their names nor, when Stan introduced himself and Spike, did she volunteer her own, except to say briefly: "You may call me Joan." She was evidently at the point of nervous collapse from fatigue and mental strain of some sort, but she bore up bravely and uttered no word of complaint, even when the increasing heat made her sway in her saddle. Stan watched and pitied her suffering from the depths of his heart, but he realized their desperate need for covering miles. There was no time to stop – and in this blazing wilderness, no refuge from the merciless sun if they should stop. Somehow the fearful day wore on, and as the sun rocked down the west, the first cactus-covered slopes of the foothills rose in front of them.

As darkness fell, Spike drew rein.

"Here we camp," he said harshly. "Horses had a hard day. We all got to be fresh when we tackle them mountains tomorrer. We'll rest here all night and start out early in the mornin'. I think we've got enough start on Hansen for that. Anyway, we'll keep a lookout all night."

Stan realized that Spike, with his burning urge for the gold, would have gladly pushed on through the night, and he felt more warmly toward the strange man as he knew that it was because of the girl that Spike had decided to wait until morning.

Joan was so exhausted that she had to be lifted from her saddle, and she crumpled in Stan's arms in a state of collapse. He made a pillow for her with his blankets and bathed her forehead and face, using as much water for the purpose as he dared. Their canteens were getting low, and they might not find the spring of which Spike had spoken. Joan submitted meekly and silently to his care, and Stan experienced a foolish protective glow in his bosom. He was glad to care for her, and he began to feel a tingling about his heart which, he decided with a sigh, must be the beginnings of this love stuff he had heard and read so much about.

They supped sparingly on water and the cooked food which they had brought along, not daring to light a fire lest the light betray them to possible pursuers. Afterward, the men smoked cigarettes and the girl sat in silence, watching the stars. Suddenly she spoke, and her voice was hard and bitter.

"I suppose you wonder why I ran away from somewhere?"

"Miss, it ain't any of our business," answered Stan.

"But I'll tell you," she cried with a swift passionate gesture. "I'm a member of a party of tourists who are camped back there across the border. There's a man there whom I hate – yesterday my father told me that I had to marry this man. My family was going to make me – you don't know my family. They've been making me do things I didn't want to do all my life. That night I saddled a horse and ran away. I rode straight across the border, and kept riding.

"Oh, I know it was the act of a fool. I didn't stop to think. I *couldn't* think. I was nearly crazy. I knew if I stayed my family would force me into marrying him – and I hate him. I hate him!"

Stan did not doubt this statement. Her eyes blazed and her small hands clinched into tiny fists.

"I guess you think I'm a fool and bad, too," she said savagely.

"I reckon we don't," said Stan, but she gave no heed.

"I'll never go back and marry a man I hate," she said slowly. "I don't know who you men are and I don't care. I don't know where you're going or what you intend to do about me. And I don't care. I've always done what the family wanted me to do – now the family can go to hell!"

"You're workin' yourself into a unnecessary passion," said Stan calmly. "We're just a couple of hard-workin' decent cowpunchers, and you're as safe with us as you'd be anywhere, as far as we're concerned. After we finish our job, we got to take you back to your family. But if I'm any judge of parents, they'll be so blame glad to get you back, they won't want you to do nothin' you don't want to do. Now you better git some sleep so as to be fresh in the mornin'."

CHAPTER IV

Hell's Canyon

Sunrise found the wanderers toiling up the cactus-grown slopes that marked the lower reaches of the Infernos Mountains. As they mounted, the way grew rougher and more barren. The soil grew thinner, less sandy, even more arid, and the cactus thinned out. The sun beat back insufferably from the bare rocks which pulsed in the heat. Stan wondered if this illusive treasure were worth all this trouble, but the light in Spike's cold eyes grew in ferocious intensity. The horses suffered, and the humans suffered more. No word of complaint came from any of them, but even Spike snarled beneath his breath as the mounting sun hurled all its power upon their unprotected heads.

The higher they climbed, the wilder and more rugged grew the hills.

"The hills of Hell!" thought Stan dizzily – an appropriate name. Not men but demons surely flung up this waste of waterless Purgatory, this range of burning soil and baked rock where even cactus would not grow. The Hills of Hell – again and again this phrase beat on Stan's brain, keeping time with the stumbling clink of the horses' hoofs.

Mid-afternoon found them riding through a terrific maze of plateaus and gorges, overshadowed by great black crags and overhanging ledges. Here there was no breath of air and even in the shadow of the crags the heat was terrible.

"Spike," said Stan, "they better be a million in gold – after all we've went through."

Spike nodded shortly. He had scarcely spoken since the girl joined them, and Stan sensed that he bitterly resented her presence, though his attitude toward her was impersonally polite. If Joan felt this, she gave no sign of it.

At nightfall they pushed on through a nightmarish chaos of ghostly crags and distorted cliffs, which, silvered by the moon, took on goblin shapes and fantastic designs.

The moon had not yet set, but it hovered on the western rim when Spike drew rein at the broad mouth of a canyon, and pointed.

"Here's Canon Los Infernos – and there's the spring."

"You're all wet," Stan was weary and skeptical. "There's no water in these hills."

"Yes, they is. I told you it was a freak. Right over yonder under them overhangin' rocks. It bubbles outa the earth right by the side of a boulder that you could build a hotel on. Just a small spring. But now we can drink all we want to."

They could and did. Even Spike, burning with impatience, realized the futility of a treasure hunt by starlight, and they ate, fed and watered the horses, and sank down beside the spring, thankful for the opportunity to rest and drink.

Stan lighted a cigarette and puffed with deep satisfaction.

"Nothin' to it," said he. "Takes a heap of discomfort to make a man appreciate a few hours of ease. And believe me, this country's plumb full of discomforts."

"I've seen worse," muttered Spike.

"Maybe I have too, but I don't remember where. How do you like the border, Miss Joan?"

"I hate it," her eyes flashed in the gloom. "My only brother – the only one of my family who ever showed any consideration for me – died in one of these vile border towns, years ago when I was just a child. Killed in a gambling hall in Tiajuana."

"What was his name?" Spike's voice rasped the stillness.

"Tom Kirby; he was murdered by a desperado named Mike O'Mara."

Stan shot a swift glance at Spike. The man sat as if frozen; the cigarette had fallen from his lips, the color had drained from his face, and his hands clinched until the nails sank into the palms. Then, muttering something about seeing to the horses, he rose and lurched away into the gloom, moving like a drunken man. Stan shook his head in puzzlement. What connection was there between his strange friend and the desperado who some years since had blazed meteor-like along the wild border, leaving a name that had become almost a myth, surrounded by bloody legends?

Suddenly Spike appeared again, looming up like a carven image, indistinct in the shadows.

"You all better git to sleep," he said. "I'll watch a while, then wake you up, Stan, and we'll take time about. Miss Joan – I – uh – you – yore brother was the last man Mike O'Mara killed, and he regretted it all of his life. It was right after that that O'Mara died, and he suffered plenty, if it'll help you to know that."

Then before the girl could speak, he had faded into the shadows again.

The night passed uneventfully. At dawn, Spike and Stan were poring over the map.

Stan read aloud the scrawling characters of old Sour Sanson: "This here is the map of the gold I found. Twenty paces from the boulder marked on the map, in the face of the cliff."

Spike bent over the faint tracery on the leather. "Here's the boulder he marked. Must be away up the canyon. Let's fill the canteens, saddle up and be gittin' along. When – or if – we find the mazuma we'll leave the canyon by another route; longer way but more apt to dodge Hansen and his men. By golly, I can't understand why they ain't hove in sight. We musta slipped clean away from 'em. I hope so."

"I thought you was kinda honin' for a tussle with 'em."

"I was, till the girl joined us. That makes things different."

Steve nodded. Spike's attitude had changed strangely toward Joan. There was a gentle, almost tender note in his voice when he spoke to her, and he was careful to see that she got various small considerations, which before he had neglected.

The sun was high in the heavens when they reached the place marked on the dead prospector's map. It was a wild rugged region, boulder-strewn and overhung by threatening crags.

"This here must be the boulder," said Spike, indicating a huge rock which rose not far from the face of the cliff that towered above the floor of the canyon. Stan felt his pulse quicken. Maybe there was something to the tale of the gold! Spike, on the other hand, seemed to have lost much of his fire. He was cold and calculating, and Stan felt that this change was largely a result of the girl – why, he could not say.

"Before we start huntin'," said Spike, "we'll let Miss Joan sit in the shadow of this rock where it's not so hot, while we climb that bluff there and take a look around. We can see a long way from there."

Joan sat patiently watching, while her two protectors struggled up the steep slope in the glare of the pitiless sun. Stan was sweat-soaked and sun-blinded long before they reached the top; his chest heaved with the exertion and his knees trembled, but Spike showed no particular distress.

"You must be made outa iron," said Stan, half in envy, half in irritation.

"I been livin' in this country a long time," Spike answered absently, drawing a pair of binoculars from a case.

"Look here; we're a long ways above the canyon wall proper, and most of the crags; we can see clean back to the mouth of it where the spring is, and a lot further – say!" his body stiffened as he glared through the lens, then he handed them to Stan.

"Focus back beyond the canyon mouth some ways."

Stan gazed and presently he saw six tiny figures swim into view. He caught only a glimpse, then they vanished into a deep defile.

"Six men on horseback!"

"Yeah!" Spike rapped. "We gotta work fast. Hansen and his bullies, of course. Blame good thing we clumb up here. They're away back there where the goin's terrible hard. I reckon they're trailin' us, but I believe we got time to git the gold – if it's there – and git out before they arrive. Take 'em hours to git here at the rate they're goin'."

They hastened down the slopes recklessly, tearing clothing and risking broken bones. Saying nothing to Joan about what they had seen, they went to work.

"Twenty paces to the face of the cliff." Spike stepped them off and attacked the cliff with a kind of fierce savagery. A few blows of his pick and a crumbling of loose rocks revealed one large rock, apparently blocking some sort of an aperture. Stan stepped forward, but Spike shoved him away and, digging his fingers into the dirt beside the rock, gripped the edge and exerted all his strength. The sweat flowed from his bronzed features, blood trickled from under his fingernails, but he still jerked and heaved. Then suddenly the stone gave way, precipitating him to the earth in a tiny avalanche of dirt and pebbles. Stan gave an exclamation. A small cave was revealed, and in this cave stood a rotting sack through whose crumbling sides bulged a stream of glinting gold!

Stan gaped in bewilderment. His brain reeled. After all, he had never really expected to find the treasure.

"Holy jumpin' Jerusalem!" he gasped, finding his voice. "It's true! Great Moses, Spike, it's true!"

Spike scrambled up, his eyes blazing.

"True!" he snorted. "You ack like you didn't believe! Git the slack outa yore jaw and bring me them saddlebags. We got no time to waste."

Joan had left her shade and was standing there, her eyes wide as she gazed upon the crumbling sack with its shimmering treasure.

"Spanish coins!" she exclaimed. "There must be thousands of dollars! Now I understand why you men came here."

"Hustle with them bags," snarled Spike. "Yeah, this is why, Miss, and what's more, you're goin' to share in it. Now, shut up; we ain't got time to talk."

"No million here by a long shot," said Stan as they scooped the coins into the bag.

"Lucky for us," rapped Spike. "We couldn't carry out a million in gold and we likely wouldn't want to leave it. No time to count it – but they's thousands of dollars here. We can pack it all by throwin' away everything but just what we need. I can walk, if necessary."

"Wonder how old Sour found it?" Stan was working fast and talking faster.

"No tellin'. Them old prospectors is always slammin' a pick into the cliff or somewhere. It's a cinch he took some of the gold, and fixed the place back like it was. Come on, the bags is full. Throw away everything but the water and enough food for one meal. We gotta starve if necessary, but we gotta git out! By golly, with the gold and the girl too, we'll be lucky if we ever see the border!"

CHAPTER V

The Coming of Hansen

Loose shale shifted and clinked beneath the hoofs of the horses. Stan gazed up at the narrow walls of the defile down which they were riding and strove to correlate his thoughts. Within the last two hours things had happened with such amazing quickness that he was almost dizzy. The sight of their pursuers, the finding of the gold, the flight. Above all, the gold! The sudden transition from poverty to wealth is enough to stun any man. Stan could scarcely believe, but the bulging saddlebags which swung on each side of the pack horse and at his own saddle were proof indisputable.

They were traversing a narrow gorge which led away from Hell's Canyon at right angles.

"Got only about a half hour start of Hansen now," Spike had said. "Chances are that our horses are fresher though, and our only chance is to dodge in and out among all these canyons and gorges, and try to lose 'em. They don't know the country like I do."

So they rode, and when Stan glanced at the trim little figure ahead of him, riding between himself and Spike, he felt a gnawing apprehension that drowned all thought of the gold. Hansen would stop at nothing, he knew. Still, Hansen had yet to catch them, and even if he did, the matter was not decided – though Stan realized that six to two was terrific odds.

They rode and the sun slanted westward. They had made so many turns and twists that Stan was already lost. He could not have retraced his steps to the canyon where they found the gold, without Spike's guidance, though he felt that he could, if necessary, find a way through the mountains to the desert.

"We gotta make all the time we can," said Spike, "so we'll have a good start when we hit the desert. On the straightaway run, that's when we'll catch hell. Once Hansen sees us, he'll kill every horse they got to catch us. We can't kill our horses and we can't let him git in sight of us. So you see what we're up against. And, Stan," his voice dropped low and became a trifle diffident, "if I don't make it through, see that the kid gits my share, will yuh?"

"You mean Joan?"

"Yeah."

"Sure. But we'll make it alright."

"I dunno," muttered the Texan. "Somehow I feel like I'll never see the line; last night I dreamed about Tom Kirby."

"Joan's brother that got killed? Was he a friend of yours?"

"He musta been," Spike said with a bitterness that startled Stan, and the subject was dropped.

The sun sank westward, but still the heat waves shimmered and danced with mocking life.

"I been thinkin'," began Stan suddenly. "This money now: have we got any real right to it, Spike?"

"Why not?" Spike exclaimed passionately. "Ain't we gone through hell to get it? It's ours by right of discovery. The old Mex sent it to Villa; old Sour found it – Sour's dead and so is Villa, and none of 'em left any heirs, so far as I know. Likely the old Mex is dead, too. No, sir! This here money is ours!"

Stan subsided. The sun was beginning to set and they were riding through a broad, low-walled defile. Spike drew rein.

"We got to stop awhile. Another hour's ride will git us out onto the desert where we can't stop. This is risky, but the best chance we got. We ain't heard or seen a thing of Hansen. We got to rest and water the horses for the long pull tonight. We'll rest here awhile."

They unsaddled and placed the packs, saddlebags, and saddles close to the canyon wall.

"I'll go back a ways and watch," said Spike. "I'll go back past that bend in the canyon; from there I can see 'em comin' a long way. If you hear shots, mount and ride!"

Stan cried out in protest. "And leave you there to fight Hansen by yourself? A great chance! If they heave in sight, you flag it back to camp, and we'll all take it on the run."

Spike merely nodded and strode away up the canyon.

"Who is he?" asked Joan curiously, as she stretched out on the blanket Stan spread for her, grateful for the chance to rest.

"You know as much as I do," answered Stan. "He's a fine fellow, but I don't know what his real name is."

Joan sighed in pure weariness. Stan's heart smote him as he looked at her, as if he were responsible for her exhaustion. Her pretty face was drawn and haggard, her skin dark and sunburned, her eyes burned darkly as if they had sunk into their sockets.

"This has been a terrible trip for you, kid," he said gently. "And I'm afraid the worst ain't over yet."

"I'm not worrying," she answered. "It's not the suffering of the journey – I can stand that. It's what is waiting for me back north of the border."

67

"Don't let that worry you," Stan said. "I dunno how old you are; you're mighty young but I know you're past eighteen. Nobody can make you marry somebody when you're of age, that way. An' now you ain't dependent on nobody because you're wealthy, same as us."

"You don't mean you're going to share your gold with me?" she cried.

"Sure I do; ain't you gone through as much as we have? And didn't you hear Spike say you was to share equal? Sure."

To his utter horror, tears gathered in the deep gray eyes, and her lip trembled.

"Oh, forgoshsakes!" he wailed contritely. "What I done now?"

"N-nothing," she gulped. "You're so good to me I can't help crying. Since my brother Tom was killed, I haven't been used to much kindness. You two men have treated me just as if I were a queen; you've been so courteous and kind to me – I can't help crying because I'm happy."

Stan sighed in relief, though his bewilderment was not abated.

"Dames is sure queer critters," he thought. "They squall when they're sad and squall when they're glad. But this girl is a mighty nice little kid."

The sun was setting in a wallow of red behind the canyon wall. The last rays emblazoned the red clay bluffs and the barren rocks, lending illusion and enchantment. The cliffs seemed banded with bloody fire, and the deepening sky above was a great copper bowl.

"You know," said Stan, "I was just thinking: what a lucky chance it was we come on to you. If Spike and me hadn't been gold huntin', and if we hadn't found you right early in the mornin' – "

His full attention was fastened on his listener; simultaneously he heard a foot crunch in the shale, and the girl's eyes flared wide with terror. Stan whirled and came up with a bound, cursing himself for his negligence. As in a dream he saw, with one fleeting glance, the heavy features of Hansen, the dark sombre face of Slade – even as he turned, he drew and fired full at Hansen. But the man was slightly behind the others. A stocky fellow between them reeled and fell, and before Stan could pull the trigger again, Slade's pistol spat. Stan felt a terrible blow on the side of his head; there was a blinding blaze of fire, then the light went out and he knew no more.

CHAPTER VI

"O'Mara Pays His Debts!"

Slowly Stan drifted back to life. His head throbbed unbearably and when he sought to lift his hands to his wound, he was unable to do so. He realized then that he was bound hand and foot, so closely that the circulation of his blood was almost cut off, and his limbs were numb. There was a great deal of dried blood on his head and face, but the wound seemed to have ceased bleeding.

A strange radiance leaped and flickered in front of him, and he saw that this was a camp fire. About this fire sat several figures. He saw the huge bulk of Hansen, the lean, Indian-like figure of Yaqui Slade, La Costa, the Frenchman – all bad men whom he recognized from Spike's descriptions. Also, there was a Mexican and a tall man in riding clothes. This man was a stranger to Stan and evidently to the rest. There was an air of wealth about him; the manner of one to whom life has been good. He was handsome in an arrogant sort of way and, gazing at him, Stan hated him more than Hansen, for some reason. Across from this man, white under her tan, and staring-eyed, sat Joan Kirby.

She cried out when she saw Stan's eyes were open, and tried to rise to come to him, but Hansen reached out a restraining hand.

"No you don't, sister; you stay where you're at."

"But he needs attention," she begged. "He needs water – and you wouldn't let me bandage his wound, you beast!"

"You'll git nowhere callin' me names," said Hansen stolidly. "As for attention, he'll git that quicker'n he wants it, I reckon."

"Say listen," broke in Slade, "here's us sittin' around this fire like a passel of fools with this bird's pard runnin' loose. What's to prevent him pickin' us off at a distance?"

"He ain't got no rifle. We're here in the angle of the canyon wall, and the only way he can git to us is to show hisself right in front of us. I hope he does do that. But he won't. I betcha that bird's on his way to the border right now."

"I dunno," muttered Slade. "He looks like a bad hombre to me. Some place I've seen him, but I can't remember where."

"Keep an eye out for him, anyhow. And now," turning toward Stan, "maybe our little friend here would like to know how come us to git the drop on him – before he kicks out.

"I'll tell you, feller, and when I git through tellin', you'll see Bad Hansen ain't to be fooled with. My Mex come back on the run after your pard had shot at him and missed, and told me you birds had found a map in old Sour's hut.

"You stole a march on me, I admit. When I finally found where Spike had been camped, you was already a long time gone. But some Mexes had seen you leave, and they said you'd headed for the mountains. Knowin' old Sour had been up in the Hell Mountains before he come back with that gold. I put two and two together and we sot out after you.

"Alright. After coverin' considerable many miles, we run onto this feller," indicating the stranger, "Mr. Harmer. Lookin' for a runaway girl, he was."

Stan saw Joan shudder, and he cursed.

"You're the swine they was goin' to make her marry, huh? If I could get my hands free, I'd teach you to persecute a helpless girl, you – "

"No use ravin', Brannigan," said Hansen, with a grin. "I'd be glad to untie you just to see the fight, if I could afford to. But they's too much at stake. We got the gold now, and I ain't goin' to risk it.

"Alright. Mr. Harmer's Mexican guide had found by the tracks that a girl had joined the party we was trackin'. So I give Mr. Harmer the lay of the land, and he agreed to throw in with us. We pushed our horses hard and made for Hell's Canyon. The Mex figured that you birds would head there first, no matter where else you was goin', because the only spring in these mountains is there."

"Maybe you thought we didn't know about the spring. We didn't, but the Mex did. We wasn't many hours behind you when you found the gold, and you hadn't more'n got outa sight when we rode up to where you found it. We didn't waste no time there. The Mex, he knows these hills better'n your pard knows 'em, and we ain't had no trouble at all in follerin' you. We been keepin' just behind you all the way, stayin' outa sight and lettin' you wear your broncs down. We figured it'd be better to let you pack the gold as far as possible 'cause the load is so hard on the horses.

"The Mex knew just about which way you'd take leavin' Hell's Canyon and gittin' outa the mountains, so we didn't have to stay in sight of you to keep track of you. Then we was watchin' when you stopped, with high power glasses from back yonder. We saw your pard go up to the bend of the canyon to watch, and so we took a pasear around and come in from another side. Right down yonder a ways is a gorge comin' into this canyon that I bet even your pard don't know about. And you was so interested in the girl, you didn't hear us comin'.

"Oh, we've took you good and plenty all the way," Hansen concluded, with a hard, satisfied laugh.

"Anyway," Stan snarled, "I settled one of you."

"Yep," agreed Hansen, "you shore wound Shorty's clock. But it saved my life, so I ain't kickin'. Somebody's always got to die in the gettin' of a treasure like this, and I'd rather it'd been Shorty than me.

"And a treasure that don't cost some lives ain't no good," he continued, more to himself than to his listeners. "This 'un's shore been baptized in blood. I don't know how many men got killed in the gettin' and hidin' of it, but old Sour Sanson died for it, Shorty died for it, you're goin' to die for it, and yore pard, too, if he's got the guts to come and fight for it.

"A kind of a pity Slade's lead didn't kill you right off the bat. But he had to shoot over La Costa's shoulder, and shoot quick, so the bullet just grazed yore skull and knocked you out for a while. I ain't decided just how we'll finish you."

"Shoot and be damned," Stan snarled, though his flesh crawled. "You ain't got the guts to kill a man les'n you shoot him in the back."

"Hard words, Brannigan," said Hansen imperturbably. "But I understand how you feel. I'd like to feel the same way if I was in yore place. But I don't hold no grudge. We got the gold and the girl – "

"I beg your pardon, Mr. Hansen," broke in Harmer, with the crisp accent of the Easterner. "I have the girl."

"My mistake, Mr. Harmer," Hansen bowed politely, but Stan sensed a ponderous mockery in the man's courtesy.

"Enough of this talk," broke in La Costa. "Let us divide the gold like you said, Hansen."

"No hurry," said Hansen. "I'm kind of hopin' Spike will show up and git bumped off. And I'm inclined to rest. Ain't we done agreed to wait till mornin' to start back to Sangre Del Diablo? Then what's the hurry? We can divide the gold any time."

A silence fell. Hansen gazed into the fire, his huge hairy hands on his knees. The keen eyes of Slade roved the shadows outside the circle of firelight. The Mexican shifted and muttered, uneasily. The glance of the Easterner, Harmer, roved between Hansen and the girl. As for Joan, she sat with her hands clasped, and never lifted her eyes except to look at Stan. Beneath her tan, her face was white, and her eyes were filled with a horror that made Stan writhe. A wave of insane fury and desperation rose redly in his brain, and he strove vainly against his bonds. Where in God's name was Spike?

As if divining his thoughts, Hansen spoke:

"Guess yore pard feels plenty like a fool, Brannigan. While he was settin' there by the bend, we come down on you from the other way. We'd a gone after him, too, only we figured when he heered the shots, he'd come runnin'. But he didn't; too slick, I guess."

Another silence fell. The moon was obscured by clouds, a rare thing. The firelight made the further gloom seem deeper. Somewhere out there Spike was lurking; what did he mean to do? Had he deserted his friends – Stan dismissed the thought.

A tension was in the air. Stan knew that some sort of a climax was approaching; he read it in the fright of the girl, in the dark somberness of Slade's face, in the meaning glances Hansen stole at Joan.

Harmer evidently sensed this also, for suddenly he rose abruptly.

"I think that Joan and I will move on," he said, and spoke to the Mexican.

Hansen shot a few terse words to the guide, and he sank back again.

"No hurry," said Hansen, his gleaming eyes belying his lazy tone. "The girl's worn out; you'd be a fool to start this time of night."

"I'm beginning to think I'd be a fool to stay here," said Harmer bluntly. "There's no reason why we should continue in each other's company. We each have what we were looking for. I have the girl who is engaged to marry me; you have the gold. That's fair enough."

"Maybe, maybe," said Hansen. "I know yore a wealthy man, Harmer, and the money's nothin' to you. Alright," the giant seemed to tense, and his air of good nature fell from him, "you want the girl – *have you thought that maybe I want her too?*"

Harmer stood stock still for a moment as these words penetrated his consciousness; then, with an oath, he jerked open his coat and tore out a revolver.

And even as he did so, Hansen shot him – once through the head and twice through the body as he fell. The Easterner crumpled, spinning clear around as he toppled in a sort of staggering arc that carried him outside the circle of firelight. He never moved after he struck the earth. The thundering reverberations of the shots roared through the canyon, echoing and re-echoing. Joan cried out in horror and covered her eyes.

" 'Nother one marked up agin the gold," said Hansen, with a brutal laugh. "Though you might say as how this bird died for a dame instead of money. Mighty cheap thing to die for, says I. I've killed men before over women, but I'd a sight rather git killed over gold than over a girl. There, there, kid, don't look so frightened; I know from the things you said to Harmer when we first caught you that you hadn't no love for him. I've saved you from marryin' him, and, after all, I'm the better man – you'll git used to me – or maybe it's Brannigan you love."

"It is!" she retorted, lifting her head defiantly.

"Say, listen," broke in Slade harshly. "Enough of this stuff. We got to do somethin' about this feller Spike – "

Even as he spoke – as if his words had materialized the man – Spike stood before them. There had been no sound, or else no one had heard his stealthy approach. One moment there was no one there, the next instant Spike was crouching in the firelit shadows, both guns roaring death at the three men about the fire.

At the first crackle of the volley, Hansen went to his knees, spurting blood, but clawing for his gun; La Costa toppled over and lay without moving; Slade, hard hit, staggered, but even in that split second, drew and began firing pointblank, his shots mingling with the booming of Spike's guns. At that range, neither of them could miss; Stan plainly heard the smack of the bullets. Spike's knees were buckling, his shirt front was a crimson stain. The gun slid from Slade's nerveless hand and he crumpled, dying on his feet.

Spike dropped an empty, smoking gun and groped blindly for the angle of the canyon wall, for support. Hansen, on his knees, had found his gun at last and now, gripping it with both hands, he shot Spike through the chest as Slade fell. Spike reeled; then, leaning against the wall at his back, steadied himself and sent his last bullet through Hansen's brain.

A deathly silence followed the inferno of battle; a silence that stunned. Joan had fainted. Spike, dripping blood at every step, lurched over to where Stan lay bound; he moved slowly, uncertainly, like a man in a dream, and his breath came in rattling gasps.

He dropped to his knees beside Stan and cut him loose; then, as Stan worked his numb arms, Spike slipped to the earth and lay prostrate. Stan lifted his head.

"Spike, old boy," he almost sobbed, "are yuh hurt bad?"

"Shot all to pieces, Stan," the voice came almost in a whisper. "That Slade, I knowed he was bad; the others woulda been easy. I'd a come – before – but – I – wanted – to take – 'em off guard. Slipped up – while – Hansen – was – killin' – Harmer.

"Joan – see – she – gits – my share. I'm glad – in a way – that this happened. I feel better – dyin' – now. I partly paid my debt – to her. Years ago – I killed her brother – Tom Kirby. I'm Mike O'Mara – the killer. Found after – Tom Kirby – died – I'd killed – an innocent man. Broke me – up. They thought – O'Mara wandered away – and died – in the desert. I didn't. I – changed – my name – left – that part of – the country. Kirby's face – haunted me. Couldn't stand – the thought – or the name – of Mike O'Mara. Glad I can – die – in some peace, now. Tell 'em – O'Mara – always – paid – his – debts!"

His laboring voice trailed away into silence. Stan felt the body go limp in his arms. He lifted his face to the stars which were blinking through the clouds.

"Gunman or not, Mike O'Mara," he said huskily, "you were a man! If your heart was black, your soul was white, and if you can hear me, up among them stars where you've gone, know, Mike O'Mara, that you've more'n made up for your sins."

Gunman's Debt

John Kirby suddenly straightened in his saddle, and his whole body went taut as he stared after the figure which had just vanished around the corner of a horse-pen. There was a tantalizing familiarity about that figure, but his glimpse had been so brief he was unable to place it. He turned his glance away to the cluster of houses that marked San Juan, a huddle of raw board houses breaking the monotony of the prairie. Crude, primitive in its newness, it was a smaller counterpart of other prairie towns he had seen. But the rails had not yet reached it, nor the trail herds that came up the long road men called the Chisholm.

Three saloons, one of which included a dance hall and another a gambling dive, stables, a jail, a store or so, a double row of unpainted board houses, a livery stable, corrals, that made up the village men now called San Juan.

Kirby turned into the stable. He was a hard-bodied man, somewhat above medium height, darkened by the sun and winds of many dim trails. The scabbard at his right hip hung low, and the butt that jutted from it was worn smooth from much handling. Something in the man's steely gaze set him apart from the general run of the cowboys who rode up the trail yearly in increasing hordes.

Kirby left his horse at the stable, and emerging, halted in response to a gesture from a thick-bodied man, dark faced, who wore a silver-plated star on his dingy shirt.

"I'm Bill Rogers, the marshal of San Juan," said he. "This is my deputy, Jackson," jerking a thumb at a nondescript-looking individual who accompanied him. "Just hit town?"

"Yeah; my name's Kirby; I was ridin' with a trail herd headin' for Ellsworth, and turned off this way, havin' business in San Juan."

"You'll have to hand over that gun to me," said Rogers, apologetically. "We got a law against wearin' guns in town. When you start to leave, come around to my office and I'll give it back to you. That's it, down there in the front part of the jail."

Kirby hesitated instinctively. It was no light matter to ask a man of his caliber to disarm himself. Then he shrugged his shoulders. This was not the Texas border country, where each clump of chaparral might conceal a feudist enemy. He had no enemies in Kansas, to the best of his knowledge. One man had come up the trail whom he would have to kill if he met, but that man was dead. Unbuckling his gun-belt, he handed it to the marshal. Rogers grunted what might have been thanks or an expression of relief, and hurried away, the scabbarded sixshooter swinging from his hand, trailed by his silent deputy.

Kirby felt his empty thigh curiously, aware of a strange unrest at the absence of the familiar weight there. Then with a shrug, he strode up the dusty street toward a saloon, in which a light had just sprung up against the gathering darkness. The town seemed quiet, in contrast with those towns that had already received the rails and become shipping centers for the Texas herds. Only a few figures passed along the street, vague in the deepening dusk.

Kirby entered the saloon, which was really a dance hall provided with a bar. It was the biggest building in town, and really elaborate for a village of that size. It boasted two stories, the second floor being occupied by the girls who worked in the establishment. San Juan expected an eventual boom.

Voices rose in altercation from within: a feminine voice, strident with anger, holding a hint of hysteria, and a deeper voice, masculine, and slightly alcoholic.

"Aw, leave me alone, Joan. I told you I was through. Get away from me."

"You can't throw me down like this!" the voice broke in a sob that sounded more like rage than grief. "You can't! I won't – "

There was the sound of an open-handed blow, and a shriek.

"Now will you lemme 'lone?"

"You filthy breed!" the woman was screaming like a virago. "Throw me over and knock me around, will you? Damn you, Jack Corlan, you won't live to see the sun come up again!"

"Aw, shut up!" The swinging doors opened as Kirby reached a hand for them, and a lithe figure lurched through, brushing against the cowboy: a slender, darkly handsome youngster, whose aquiline features bore more than a suggesion of Indian blood. Beyond him, in the saloon, Kirby saw the woman, a supple, black-haired girl in the costume of the dancing halls. Abruptly she ceased her shrill tirade, turned and fled up the stair, sobbing. Kirby's eyes narrowed; not at the violence of the scene, but at the holstered gun he had noted swinging at the man's hip. Why had he not been disarmed, if the law required it?

The dance hall was empty, save for one bartender, and the slender figure mounting the stair. The night rush had not begun – if there ever was one in San Juan. Kirby leaned on the bar and ordered whiskey; the barkeep began polishing the bar with a cloth. He worked with a preoccupied air, but Kirby, who missed little of what went on about him, noted that the man was watching him sidewise, and was moving further away from him all the time, toward the other end of the bar.

Booted feet stamped on the threshold, and the door was flung open. Natural alertness made Kirby turn; and he froze, his whiskey glass half lifted. A dozen steps away stood a big, black-bearded man, leering at him. This man stood on wide braced legs, his thumbs hooked into his sagging belt, just above the jutting butts of his pistols.

"Jim Garfield!" Kirby hissed the name, in a voice so low as to be scarcely audible.

"Yeah, Jim Garfield!" jeered the bearded man, his whiskers bristling in a savage grin. "Your old friend! Aintcha glad to see me, Kirby?"

"I thought you was dead," growled Kirby. "Your old man said you were."

"That was the idee!" Garfield showed yellowed teeth as his grin broadened, grew more venomous. "I wanted you damned Kirbys to think that. I come up here on business that concerned you all, and I didn't want nothin' known about it. I thought you was trailin' me when Red Donaldson here brought me word you had rode into town; but I reckon it's just one of them there coincidences!" He guffawed loudly.

Kirby looked beyond him at a tall lean man whose cold eyes contrasted with his flaming mop of hair.

"So it was you I saw duck behind that corral. I thought I knew you."

"So we arranged a welcome committee," Garfield spread his legs wider and seemed to hug himself with glee. "Before we give you the keys to the city, though, I want to tell you why I come up here. See them boys there?" He indicated half a dozen men clustering behind him – men whose sinister profession was stamped on their features. "Them boys work for me now, Kirby. I've done hired 'em. They're ridin' back to Texas with me when I go, them and maybe a dozen more. When they get through with the Kirbys – " again he guffawed, but there was no mirth in the laughter, only a saw-edged threat.

Kirby said nothing, but he was white under his bronze. For a dozen years merciless feud had waged between the Kirbys and the Garfields, down there on the lower reaches of the Rio Grande. Ambushes in the brush had followed on the heels of terrible gun-battles in the streets of little border towns. The original reason for the feud was immaterial. At last the Kirbys had seemed to triumph. But now John Kirby stood face to face with a threat that bade fair to wipe his very name off the earth in blood. He knew the type of the men who stood behind Jim Garfield: barroom gladiators, two gun men, cowtown killers, who slew for pay, and sold their guns to the highest bidder. It was these that Jim Garfield planned to loose on Kirby's unsuspecting kin. John Kirby felt suddenly sick, and his skin was beaded with cold sweat.

Garfield perceived this. "Hey, John, what you sweatin' about? Don't you like your licker?" He guffawed at his own humor, then suddenly went hard and grim as steel. "I got somethin' that'll fix it," he muttered, his eyes beginning to burn like coals of blue fire. He drew his gun and cocked it, and took deliberate aim at Kirby's breast. Behind him his henchmen likewise drew. Kirby stood frozen with fury, helplessness, and the horror of dying like a sheep. His hand twitched at his empty hip. Where in God's name was the marshal? Why had he, John Kirby, been disarmed, when every outlaw that rode up the trail was allowed to swagger through the streets armed to the teeth? In unnatural clarity he saw the whole scene: the booted figures, guns in hand, the dark faces leering at him, the girl at the head of the stair above, leaning over the railing, frozen with dreadful fascination. The one lamp that lighted the place hung just above her, and bathed her features in its light. All this John Kirby saw without exactly realizing that he saw it. His whole consciousness was focussed on that

78

burly, menacing figure that half crouched before him, head bent down, squinting along the dull blue barrel.

"Just takin' toll now, John," mumbled Garfield. "You remember my brother Joe you killed in Zapata? You're goin' to meet him right away – "

Crash! The lamp splintered; Garfield, startled, yelped and fired blindly. Kirby heard the bullet smash into the bar close by. But he was already moving. Galvanized into frantic action, he raced down along the bar, wheeled and dived headfirst through a window, limned faintly in the blackness. Behind him guns banged wildly in the dark, men yelled, and the bull-like voice of Jim Garfield dominated the clamor, intolerable with blood lust and primitive disappointment.

Scrambling up, Kirby ran around the corner of the building. Just as he did, he caromed into a dark figure which was emerging from a back door. He caught at it savagely, checked his grip as his fingers encountered flesh too soft for a man.

"Don't!" a voice gurgled. "It's only me – Joan!"

"Who the devil's Joan?" he demanded.

"Joan Laree!" There was haste and urgency in the tone. "I smashed the lamp – saved your life!"

"Oh, you're the girl that was on the stair!" muttered Kirby.

"Yes – but don't stop. Come on!"

She seized his hand and pulled him away from the building. He followed. He was bewildered, and a stranger in the town. She had aided him already; there was no reason to distrust her.

She led him out on the bald prairie that ran up the very back stoops of San Juan. Behind them the clamor increased as a light was lit. Doors crashed as vengeful men ran out into the street. Kirby cursed his lack of weapons beneath his breath. He was not used to flight. The girl panted, urged him to increased efforts. He saw her goal – a shack a short distance from any other house. They reached it, and she fumbled at the door, opened it, and beckoned him in. He stepped into the darkness and she followed and threw something – a cloak perhaps, over the one window. She pushed the door shut, which creaked on thick leather hinges. There was the scratch of a match, and her face was limned in its yellow glow as she lighted a coal oil lamp. Kirby gazed at her, fascinated. She reminded him of a young panther – slim, supple, youthful. Her black hair caught burnished glints in the lamplight. Her dark eyes glowed. She raked back her locks with a nervous hand as she faced him.

"Why did you do this?" he demanded. "They'll skin you for breakin' that lamp."

"They weren't noticing me," she answered scornfully. "They don't know I did it. Why did Jim Garfield want to kill you? Why did you come here?"

"I came here to see a friend of mine I heard was tendin' bar," he answered. "Bill Donnelly; know him?"

"I did know him," she answered. "He's dead."

"Somebody shoot him?" Kirby's grey eyes narrowed.

"No," she laughed hardly. "He shot himself – in the back. Quite a few men have committed suicide that way. Those that wouldn't take orders from Captain Blanton."

"Who's he?"

"He owns this town. Never mind. It isn't a good idea to talk about Blanton, even when nobody's listening. Sit down. Don't worry. Nobody'll think of you coming here. This is my shack. I sleep here when I get fed up with the racket at the Silver Boot."

"If I could get hold of a gun I wouldn't need to bother you," he muttered, seating himself on a raw-hide bottomed chair.

"I'll get you a gun," she promised, seating herself on the opposite side of the rough hewn table. She cupped her chin in her hands, rested her elbows on the table, and stared closely at him.

"There's a feud between you and Jim Garfield?"

"You heard what he said."

"He'd have killed you if it hadn't been for me."

He assented, but stirred restlessly; he had learned that such a remark from a woman generally preceded a demand for services of some kind.

"Would you do something for me?" she asked bluntly.

"Anything in reason," he answered warily.

"I want a man killed!"

His head snapped up angrily, just that blunt, naked statement, as if he were a hired gunman, a thug ready to do murder for a price.

"What man?" he asked, controlling his resentment.

"Jack Corlan. He passed you as you came into the Silver Boot. The dirty half-breed – " Her white hands clenched convulsively.

"Didn't look like he had that much Indian in him to me," said Kirby.

"Well, he's got Cheyenne blood, anyway," she said sullenly; "his father was white, and he's been raised white, but – well, that's got nothing to do with it. He's done me dirt. I was fool enough to think I loved him. He threw me over for another woman. Then he cursed me and hit me. You saw him hit me. I want you to kill him."

Revulsion swept over John Kirby and he rose, picking up his hat.

"I shore appreciate what all you've done for me, Miss," he drawled. "I wish I could do somethin' for you some time."

She sprang up, white.

"You mean you won't help me?"

"I mean I'll catch this fellow and beat him to a pulp," said Kirby. "But I'm not killin' a man that never harmed me, just because a jealous woman wants me to. I'm not that low."

"Low!" she sneered. "Who are you to talk of being low? I know you. I've heard of you. You're a gunman, a killer! You've killed half a dozen men in your life."

"I live in a land where men have to fight," he answered somberly. "If I wasn't quick with a gun, I wouldn't have lived to get grown. But I never killed a man that wasn't threatenin' my life, or the lives of my kin. If I saw you bein' threatened by a man, I'd blow his light out. But I don't consider that there's sufficient cause to kill the man you mentioned."

She was livid and shaking with fury; she gasped and panted.

"You fool! I'll tell Garfield where you're hiding!"

"Surely you didn't think I'd stay here?" he retorted. "I'm leavin'; I thank you for what you did tonight, and I aim to repay you some time, but in a decent way."

He turned away; and with a cry of ungovernable fury, she caught up a pistol from the table, threw it down with both hands. He whirled just in time to hear the crack of the shot, and to get the lead on the side of the head instead of the back. He did not feel the impact, but the light went out like the snuffing of a candle.

John Kirby regained consciousness slowly, but with perfect realization of where he was and what had occurred. The oil lamp still burned on the table. The shack was empty except for himself; the door stood open a crack. He gripped the table and reeled up, sick, weak and dizzy. He lifted a hand to his scalp, discovered a ragged tear. The bullet had grazed him. He cursed, holding on to the table. His head throbbed, and his movements had started the wound bleeding afresh. The heat of the oil lamp nauseated him. He reeled to the door, threw it open and passed out into the starlit night. Walking sent waves of agony through his bruised brain. He weaved around the corner of the house, blind and dizzy. Suddenly his stumbling feet met empty air and he plunged downward to strike the earth with sickening force.

The jolt brought the blood down his face in streams, but cleared his head. He shook himself and sat up, seeing more clearly. He realized that he had fallen into a ravine at the back of the house. That ravine, he believed, was the same one that meandered around one end of the town, skirting the back of the building which served as a jail. He started to pull himself up, then halted as voices reached him. Somebody was approaching the shack. He recognized a clear feminine voice.

"I tell you, I don't know how he got in my shack! He was there when I opened the door. He jumped for me, and I screamed and shot him. I lit the lamp and saw he was the fellow that was in the Silver Boot."

"Blast it, gal," that was Jim Garfield's plaint, "if you've robbed me of the pleasure of killin' John Kirby – "

"I don't know whether he's dead or not! I shot him in the head. He was still breathing when I left. I ran to the Silver Boot as fast as I could – "

"Alright, alright," that was a deeper, unfamiliar voice which carried a tone of command. "Here's the shack; get your guns ready; if he isn't dead he might be laying for us – here, McVey, open the door."

Almost instantly followed a yelp of animal disappointment.

"He ain't here!"

The deep voice broke in. "Joan, are you lying to us?"

Red Donaldson cut in. "You drop that tone, Captain Blanton. I don't like it. No, she ain't lyin'. See that blood on the floor? And there's the mark of bloody fingers on that table. He was here alright, but I reckon he come to and left."

Garfield broke into violent profanity.

"Well, we'll find him," assured Blanton. "Get out of here, you fellows, and scatter through town. He can't have gone far, if he's wounded. Go to the stable first, and see if his horse is still there. Joan, go with them; get back to the Silver Boot and tend to the customers. That's where you belong, anyway."

"Captain Blanton," it was Red Donaldson's voice, dangerously silky, "if I was you, I'd be more polite to a lady. Come on, Miss Laree, I'll see you back safe."

Boots clumped away, and Kirby, momentarily expecting a search of the ravine, heard Blanton, still in the shack, say: "Corlan, what are you doing here? I thought I told you fellows – "

"I don't care what you told them fools!" the voice rose with the petulancy of intoxication. "I ain't your dog to order around. I do more work than any of your men, and you treat me like a dog. I rode fifty miles between midnight last night and this noon, and you know what I did before I made that ride!"

"Shut up, you fool!" exclaimed Blanton.

"I won't shut up unless you give me some more money!" shouted Corlan. "I'm the only man that can do your dirty work in that direction, because any other man of yours would lose his scalp if he tried it! You can't treat me like you treat the rest! I want more money!"

"I'd have given you more if you'd asked for it with some decency," snapped Blanton. "But you can't bulldoze me, Corlan. Not another cent tonight."

"No?" mouthed the inebriated one. "Suppose I tell what I know? Oh, I ain't talkin' about Bill Donnelly. Everybody knows I killed him for you, and nobody cares. I'm talkin' about Grizzly Elkins. What do you think them buffalo hunters would do if – "

"You cursed fool!" There was fear and blood-lust too in Blanton's voice, and then came the sound of a heavy blow, the stumbling fall of a heavy body. Corlan mouthed a shrieking curse: "I'll kill you!" Then there was the reverberating report of a .45. Kirby glared at the tiny square of light that was the window, wishing he could see through the solid walls.

Then came Blanton's voice: "You've killed him!"

"Well," it was Garfield speaking, "if I hadn't drilled him, he'd have got you. You know how them Indians and breeds is when they're drunk.

Come on; leave him lay; we'll send some of the boys after him. Let's get out and look in that gully."

Electrified, Kirby began to grope his way along the winding bank. The floor of the ravine was narrow, but fairly even, and he made good time. Evidently Garfield and Blanton had halted to indulge in some other discussion or argument. He heard Blanton say: "Garfield, I don't like the idea of your taking so many of my men down into Texas to fight out your feud. We have too good a thing of it here."

"Well," answered Garfield, "I like your idee of rakin' in the trail herds and controllin' the buffalo hide trade, and all, but money ain't everything. We've went over that before."

"And another thing," grated Blanton; "that fellow Donaldson is too brash. I don't like him."

"Oh, he's stuck on the Laree gal," replied Garfield. "Red's a good sort."

"He'll be a dead man if he don't watch his step," ground Blanton. "I don't have to endure the insolence of your companions, just because I have to put up with your society – "

"You bet you have to put up with me!" exclaimed Garfield. "You needn't to be so high and mighty. I know you was with the Cullen Baker gang in Arkansas – "

"Shut up, curse you!" exclaimed Blanton.

"Well," said Garfield, "the Federal Government paid ten thousand dollars for Baker's body at Little Rock, in '69, and it's my understandin' that there's a equal sum on *your* head, provided they ever catch you. You're safe, after all these years, that is if somebody – like me, for instance – don't bring up the matter to the government. Or if somethin' was to happen to me, my brother Bill's got a letter down in Texas I writ him, tellin' him what to do."

"You've got me in a cleft stick," muttered Blanton. "Say no more about it. You have no cause to complain; you'll be rich as I am, if you'll deal square with me." Then they left the shack.

Stumbling and groping along the ravine, Kirby suddenly realized that the building that loomed up against the stars was the jail. A light was burning there, and Kirby crawled out of the ravine, stole around the corner and looked in through the window. In the small room which was separated from the cells – now empty – by iron bars, and which served as marshal's office, the deputy Jackson was sprawled in a chair, reading what looked like a paper back novel. Kirby's eager gaze rested on a familiar object glinting dully on a table. His gun!

He slipped around the corner of the house, then crying out incoherently, he threw open the door and staggered in. Jackson bounced out of his chair like a jumping jack, a gun flashing into his hand. Then he gaped stupidly, evidently not recognizing Kirby; the cowboy's features were masked with half-dried blood, he was dusty and disheveled.

"What in hell – "

"I've been robbed!" gasped Kirby. "Somebody slugged me back of a saloon and robbed me – call the marshal – "

He reeled and fell against the table. Jackson glared at him, his six-shooter hanging limp.

"Robbed?" he mouthed. "Slugged? Who done it?"

"I dunno; I couldn't see him," mumbled Kirby, slumping further over the table.

"Well what do you want me to do?"

"I want you to drop that gun and reach high!" snapped Kirby coming up with his gun cocked in his hand. Jackson's mouth flew open; his pistol thumped on the floor; his hands went up like a puppet's on a string.

Kirby caught up a bunch of keys from the table.

"Into that cell! Hustle!"

"You can't do this!" mouthed Jackson, obeying with automaton-like steps. "I'm a law – you can't do this!"

Kirby grunted and snapped the lock. Jackson grabbed the bars and glared wildly through them; his "You can't do this!" came faintly to Kirby's ears as he hurried out on the street.

The cowboy glided into the shadows of the houses. It was later than he had supposed. All lights were out in the dwellings; only the saloons were illuminated. Staying in the shadows he approached the stable, when he heard the pounding of hoofs down the road. The rider came into sight, in the light streaming across the street from the saloons – a big man on a reeling horse. He pulled up before the Buffalo Horn, and fell, rather than descended, from his saddle. He was surrounded by a crowd which streamed out of the bars. Excited voices rose in a babble, over which the stranger's voice dominated – a bull's bellow, gasping and panting.

"Plumb wiped out," Kirby heard him say. "Old Yeller Tail's braves – dunno hardly how I got clear – been ridin' and hidin' for a night and a day, and this night – gimme a drink, dammit!"

He was half-carried, half-guided into the bar; as he passed through the door, Kirby got a glimpse of him – a burly giant clad in buckskins; somebody addressed him as Elkins.

The cowboy turned away and hurried to the stable. His instinct caused him to glide around behind and peek through a knot hole. Three men, with Winchesters across their knees, squatted in the stall where his horse was confined. They chewed tobacco, spat and conversed in low monotones.

"I don't believe that puncher's goin' to show up," quoth one. "I bet he's stole a horse and lit a shuck."

"Well, we stay here till mornin', anyhow," answered another. "Say, didn't Joan Laree carry on when she saw Jack Corlan?"

"Yeah," said the other, "she was plenty sweet on him. Doggone, that was a dirty trick – shootin' a man through the winder that way. He must have been aimin' at Garfield, don't you reckon?"

"Well," opined the first speaker, "he'll be aimin' for Glory at the end of a rope if the boys catch him. Bringin' his Texas feuds up here and killin' Jack Corlan just for nothin'. Dern him!"

"I liked Jack," said another. "He was all white, even if he did have Injun blood in him."

"Yes, he was!" snorted another in disgust. "You mutts make me sick; just because a man's croaked, you got to make him out a saint. Corlan was a yellow dog and you know it; he'd sell his soul for a drink to the highest bidder."

Voices rose in fresh squabbling as Kirby turned and moved silently away, bewildered. It became evident to him that Garfield and Blanton had accused him of Corlan's murder. After all, they were the only witnesses.

He stood, hesitant. They were taking no chances of his escaping. Doubtless every horse in town would be well guarded. And if he did not get away at once, it would be too late. When daylight came, they would find him, wherever he hid. The bare prairie offered no hiding place. If he started on foot, it would be suicide. And it was imperative that he ride south, to warn his kin of the impending doom. But was it? He was galvanized by a sudden realization. If Jim Garfield died, the gunmen would never ride south. Better that he finished Garfield here and now. If he died in the attempt – well, his was the fanatical clan spirit of the Scotch-Irish Southwesterner. He was willing to sacrifice his life for the good of his family, if need be.

He took half a dozen steps, then a dim form rose in the shadow. Instantly he covered it, his finger quivering on the trigger; then he saw it was a woman; dark eyes, reflecting the starlight, looked levelly at him.

"Joan Laree!" he hissed. "What are you doin' here?"

"I've been waiting here," she answered in a low voice. "I thought you would come for your horse. I wanted to tell you he was being guarded, but you came from the other end of the stables."

"But why – ?" he was uneasy and suspicious.

"I wanted to thank you!" she whispered. "You – you killed him, after all!"

"No, I didn't!" he protested. "I – "

"Oh, they told me!" she exclaimed. "I saw him – and the broken window through which your bullet came. Garfield said you were aiming at him – but I don't care. I'm sorry I shot you. I owe you a debt."

"My God, this is awful." He shuddered slightly in revulsion. "What kind of a woman are you, anyhow? I tell you, though, I didn't – "

"Don't talk," she murmured. "We'll be overheard; men are looking for you everywhere. Come with me; trust me once more."

He hesitated, with a feeling of being caught in a web of fantasy and illusion. This part of it was like a dream; the rest, the violence of men, the trickery, the murder, he could understand; but this strange, beautiful, evil woman moved through the skeins of the pattern like a cryptic phantom, inscrutable, inexplicable. He realized that he was in her power; a scream would fetch a horde of armed men. He must trust her, or pretend to trust her; she spoke of a debt; perhaps she really sought to pay the grisly debt she seemed to consider she owed him. He looked at her as at a being more and yet less than human; he was repelled by her strange, bloody nature, yet drawn powerfully by her beauty. Like a rabbit hypnotized by a snake, he followed her.

There was a hint of dawn in the air. It was the darkness that precedes dawn. Not a light burned in San Juan. Even the saloons were dark. She led him behind the houses, and as they went, he was impelled to ask: "Who was that fellow who rode into town an hour or so ago, yellin'?"

"Grizzly Elkins, the buffalo hunter," she answered. "His outfit was one that Captain Blanton grub-staked. They'd gotten a load of hides, and sent them on into San Juan with Blanton's drivers. The wagons got here yesterday morning. Elkins and his men stayed in camp to get another load; the wagons were to return with supplies, and get the other hides. But after the wagons left, a band of Comanches swooped down on the hunters and killed them all except Elkins. They couldn't kill him. He's a brute of a man. Here's the place."

She fumbled at a door, opened it, and stepped inside into total darkness. With her lips close to his ear, she whispered: "I'll hide you here until I can steal you a horse."

"Alright," he grunted. "A fast horse for a getaway – but I'm goin' to kill Jim Garfield before I leave here, whether I get away or not."

She led him across a room, groping in the dark, to another door.

"In here," she whispered. He entered, and she shut the door. He stood for a few moments in the dark, thinking she had entered with him. He spoke to her. There was no answer. Somewhere he heard an outside door close softly. In a panic he turned to the door. His hands slid over it, he thrust strongly against it. It was solid oak that might balk a bull; and it was bolted on the other side. There was no lock to blow off. Turning, he stumbled about the room, groping for other doors. He found neither doors nor windows. But he discovered one thing; the room was built of square-cut logs; the only log hut in San Juan; doubtless it had been at one time used for a jail. There was no bursting out of it. He was trapped. A wave of frantic fury swept over him. Trapped, after all the warnings he had had! Dawn begin to steal through the cracks between the logs.

He stood upright, in the middle of the floor, waiting. Nor did he have to wait. A door was thrown up, boots stamped on the dirt floor, and voices he knew and hated boomed.

"In that room," said Joan, her voice cold and deadly as steel.

"You was mistook once tonight," rumbled Jim Garfield. "You sure he's in there?"

"Sure, he's in there." She lifted her voice and it was like the slash of a keen knife edge. "Open the door, Kirby! Here are friends of yours!"

The cowboy made no reply.

"What's this all about, anyway?" complained a bull-like voice that Kirby recognized as that of Grizzly Elkins.

"We have a criminal trapped in that room, Elkins," answered Blanton; "that is, if this girl isn't lying."

"I'm not lying," she answered. "He's in there. I led him here, telling him I was going to help him. He killed the man I loved."

And inside the silent room, John Kirby shook his head in bewilderment at the everlasting paradox that was woman; she had tried to kill him because he refused to kill the man who had jilted her; now she trapped him to his doom, because she thought he had killed that man. It was fantastic, impossible, yet it was the truth.

"Yes, he killed Jack Corlan," said Blanton. "Killed your friend, Bill Donnelly, too."

"He did?" It was a roar of wrath. "Why, the low-down hound! I'll go in and drag him out myself!"

"No, wait!" Blanton lifted his voice. "Kirby, are you coming out and surrender?"

Kirby made no reply.

"Aw, hell!" snorted McVey; "le's bust it down." He threw the bolt, hurled his shoulder against the door. Kirby shot at the sound. The heavy bullet splintered through the oak, and McVey cried out and fell heavily. An answering volley sent lead ripping through the panels, but Kirby was flattened out against the wall, out of range.

"Get back there, you dern fools!" bellowed Jim Garfield. "You don't know that hombre like I do. Aw, shut up!" This last to the groaning McVey; "man with no more sense'n what you got oughta be shot."

"Well, what are we goin' to do?" demanded another voice – that of Hopkins. "He can't get out without runnin' into our lead – but no more can we get in at him. Le's burn his out."

"No, you won't," exclaimed Blanton. "This cabin is my property, and it's too close to the saloons. Start a fire here and the whole town might go."

"Water, for God's sake, Captain, get me some water!" moaned McVey.

"Shut up," snarled Blanton; "we can't help you, laying right in front of that door; want to get us killed? Crawl out of range if you want help."

"I can't crawl!" sobbed McVey. "My back's broke. For God's sake, somebody, get me some water!"

"You don't need water," snapped Blanton. "Go ahead and die, can't you?"

"That ain't no way to talk to a dyin' man, Cap'n," protested Grizzly Elkins. He raised his voice: "Hey, Kirby, I'm goin' to haul McVey away from that door! I ain't got no gun, and I ain't makin' no move at you till I get McVey out of the way. If you want to shoot me through the door, shoot and be damned!"

With which defiance the burly buffalo hunter rolled forward on his moccasined feet, grasped the dying man and lugged him over by the wall. Kirby did not fire. Elkins laid McVey down, and drawing a whiskey flask from his pocket, put it to the man's lips.

"You're crazy, risking your life for a fool like that," sneered Blanton.

McVey's glazing eyes flamed with a brief fire and he hitched himself painfully on his elbow. "Fool?" he cried, his voice breaking in a sob of pain and hysteria. "That's the thanks a man gets for doin' your dirty work! You wouldn't give me a drink of water when I'm dyin'! You damn' blood-sucker, you take everything a man's got, and give him nothin'. I hope Kirby kills you, too, just like you killed Jack Corlan!"

"*What!*" It was a scream from Joan Laree. She sprang forward, caught the dying man in a frantic grasp. "What are you talking about? Kirby killed Jack Corlan!"

"He didn't, neither!" The gasp was growing fainter. "Corlan owed me money and was goin' to get it from Blanton and pay me; when Blanton sent us off, I sneaked back. I heered 'em arguing, and a shot. It come from inside the shack, not from the outside. Either Blanton or Garfield killed Corlan."

Blood welled from his lips, his head sank back. Joan Laree started up, a mad woman. She rushed at Blanton, beating frantically on his breast with her clenched fist, screaming: "You lied! You killed Jack! You killed him! You devil! You killed him!"

Garfield squirmed guiltily and said nothing. Blanton, face contorted with anger, caught her wrist and slung her away from him.

"Well, what of it?" he snarled. "What does it matter who sent the dirty breed to hell? What are you going to do about it?"

"I'll show you!" she screamed, whirling on the gaping Grizzly Elkins. "You want to know why Yellow Tail knew where to find your camp?" she shrieked.

"Shut up!" roared Blanton. "Don't listen to her, Elkins; she's mad as a hare!"

"I'm not!" she screamed, terrifying in her frenzy. "Corlan talked to me before he left San Juan the other day! He talked after he came back, yesterday. He'd been to the Cheyenne camp! He was a friend with old Yellow Tail, because he was kin to the chief, on the Indian side! He betrayed you, Elkins, and set the Indians on to you – "

"What?" roared the giant hunter, electrified.

"She lies!" screamed Blanton, livid.

"I don't lie!" she cried. "Blanton did this so he'd own all the hides you'd shipped into San Juan! They amount to a small fortune, and they're his if you were all blotted out! It's part of his plan – cows, hides, land – he means to steal all – "

There was a crashing report, a burst of flame and smoke. Joan staggered, catching at her breast. Blanton ran out of the door, the gun smoking in his hand. The girl slid to her knees, holding out one hand toward the petrified hunter in agonized appeal.

"Believe me!" she gasped. "Blanton betrayed you – had your friends murdered – "

She sank sidewise and lay still. And suddenly the buckskin-clad giant exploded into a deafening roar. His hand swept to his hip and up, with a broad glimmer of steel. Garfield yelped and fired pointblank, but the great body was in motion with a blur of quickness, induced by coiled steel muscles. Garfield missed as Elkins bounded into the air and the hunter's butcher knife was sheathed to the hilt in Hopkins' breast. Ashley plunged frantically away from the threat of that dripping blade, and caromed into Garfield, staggering him, and making his second bullet fly wild. And then a new factor entered the brawl.

The door flew open and framed in the opening stood John Kirby, his gun burning red. Ashley dropped; Sterling shot once, missed, and sank to his knees, shot through the belly and breast, vainly groping for his left hand gun. Garfield yelled and fired, and Kirby's hat leaped from his head. The next instant Garfield howled as a bullet ripped along his ribs, and turning, fled from the cabin. As he went through the door, Elkins' knife, hurled with vengeful force, flashed by his head and sank deep into the log jamb. Spouting blood, Garfield ran across the street into the Silver Boot.

Kirby came out into the room, reloading his empty gun. The place was like a shambles. Elkins, snorting like a buffalo, blood trickling from a nicked ear, tugged his knife out of the wood, and turned to Kirby: "No use in us scrappin'. Come on; out this way!"

Kirby made no reply; chance had made allies of them, and it was useless to waste words. They ran out a side door, darted across the space that lay between the cabin and the next house. From across the street Winchesters cracked and bullets whined past. Then they reached the house and flung themselves inside. They were met by a frightened woman who sobbed: "Oh my God, what kind of goin's on is these: We'll all be murdered! Here I am, tryin' to run a respectable boardin' house – "

"You better pike it out the back door, Mizz Richards," boomed Elkins. "We got to use your house for a spell, and they's liable to be some lead floatin' around in the air. Gwan, beat it, before they start shootin' into here. I'll pay you for whatever damage is done."

A .45-90 slug, ripping its way through the thin wall, was more convincing than the buffalo hunter's eloquence. Mrs. Richards gave vent to shrill lamentations and scurried out the back door and across the prairie as if the Sioux were on her trail.

"This here's my room," grunted Elkins, kicking open a door; "here, grab this!" He thrust a Winchester repeater into Kirby's willing hands, and himself picked up a Sharps .50 – one of the single shot buffalo guns used by the hunters. "Now we'll fix 'em. These walls won't stop bullets, but neither'll theirs."

Crouching each at a separate window, the fighters gazed slit-eyed across the street. No one was in sight; the town might have been deserted; but every now and then, belying the thought, there sounded the vicious crack of a rifle, a wisp of smoke curled upward, and there was the splintering impact of lead on wood.

"Garfield's in the Silver Boot," muttered Kirby, squinting along the Winchester barrel. "Don't know how many men there are in there with him. I just caught a glimpse of Blanton. He's in the Big Chief bar; seems to be just one gun speakin' there."

"Nobody in there but the bartender," said Elkins, "and I know him; he'd high tail it the minute the shootin' started." He pressed the trigger and the thundering crash of the heavy gun was answered by an angry yelp from the Silver Boot.

A puff of smoke jetted from a window in the Big Chief, and a bullet ploughed across the sill, showering Elkins with splinters. Kirby answered the shot, but without success. Blanton was alone in the saloon. Four rifles were cracking over in the Silver Boot, and feminine shrieks of protest from the second floor told that the dancing girls had awakened and were not enjoying the sport.

"Wish these walls was logs," grumbled Elkins. "Damn this high falutin' style of board houses. Wouldn't stop bird shot. Le's make a break back to the cabin."

"Wait!" exclaimed Kirby. "Who's that ridin' down the street? By God, it's Red Donaldson!"

He threw up his rifle and fired, and with the crack of the shot, the red-haired gunman shot from the saddle, and ran into the cabin. Kirby cursed.

Then there sounded a cry from inside the cabin so poignant that the gunfire stopped. Donaldson ran madly into the open, and something about him halted Kirby's finger.

"Who killed her?" Red was shrieking. "Joan Laree! She's shot! Who did it? Who did it?"

A disheveled head stuck out of an upstairs window of the Silver Boot, and the owner shrilled: "Blanton did it! I heard the shot and saw him run out with a gun in his hand, just before all the shooting started – "

She yelped and vanished as a bullet from the Big Chief smashed the window above her head.

Red Donaldson yelled bloodthirstily, whipped out his gun and charged recklessly across the street, eyes glaring. Even as he mounted the low porch in front of the saloon, a shotgun thundered inside and the blast knocked him down, to lie writhing in the dirt. At that Jim Garfield yelled vengefully.

"By God, Blanton!" he howled. "You can't kill my friends that way!"

93

As reckless as Donaldson had been, he charged out of the Silver Boot, shotgun in hand. He yelped in exultation as he got a view of his former companion through a window, dropped to one knee and threw the shotgun to his shoulder – and at that instant a sixshooter cracked in the doorway behind him and the bullet smashed between his shoulders. He bellowed like a wounded bull, his shotgun futilely blasting the air. He fell writhing, half-raised himself and sent the contents of the second barrel roaring through the doorway out of which he had just come. A howl told that some of the pellets were fleshed.

Kirby fired at the glimpse through a window, and a man crashed down heavily across the sill and lay there twitching. He missed Elkins, then saw him. The buffalo hunter, while the attention of the fighters was held by the killing of Garfield, had slipped out of the boarding house, run down the street, dashed recklessly across, and gained the back of the Silver Boot. Kirby got a glimpse of him, running, stooped, like a great bear, grotesque in his swiftness, a flaming mass of rubbish in his hands.

Soon smoke began to rise. Elkins yelled in primitive exultation, ran hither and yon, ducking the slugs, firing the buildings. First the girls, then the men ran from the Silver Boot. Kirby let them go. The fight was taken out of them. They forked their mustangs and headed out of town on the run. The Big Chief began to blaze, and Blanton charged out. Kirby fired and saw him stagger, but he came on, a shotgun in his hands. Elkins was before him, charging him recklessly with his knife. The shotgun went up, covered the hairy giant. Behind Blanton the tattered shape that was Red Donaldson moved, life still in it. A gun came up, wavered, exploded. Blanton staggered to the impact of the lead in his back, and his charge went wild. Elkins covered the distance between them in one long bound and drove his knife to the hilt in Blanton's breast.

San Juan was burning; smoke mounted in the morning sky; together Elkins and Kirby rode southward.

The Man on the Ground

Cal Reynolds shifted his tobacco quid to the other side of his mouth as he squinted down the dull blue barrel of his Winchester. His jaws worked methodically, their movement ceasing as he found his bead. He froze into rigid immobility; then his finger hooked on the trigger. The crack of the shot sent the echoes rattling among the hills, and like a louder echo came an answering shot. Reynolds flinched down, flattening his rangy body against the earth, swearing softly. A gray flake jumped from one of the rocks near his head, the ricocheting bullet whining off into space. Reynolds involuntarily shivered. The sound was as deadly as the singing of an unseen rattler.

He raised himself gingerly high enough to peer out between the rocks in front of him. Separated from his refuge by a broad level grown with mesquite-grass and prickly-pear, rose a tangle of boulders similar to that behind which he crouched. From among these boulders floated a thin wisp of whitish smoke. Reynolds's keen eyes, trained to sun-scorched distances, detected a small circle of dully gleaming blue steel among the rocks. That ring was the muzzle of a rifle, and Reynolds well knew who lay behind that muzzle.

The feud between Cal Reynolds and Esau Brill had been long, for a Texas feud. Up in the Kentucky mountains family wars may straggle on for generations, but the geographical conditions and human temperament of the Southwest were not conducive to long-drawn-out hostilities. There feuds were generally concluded with appalling suddenness and finality. The stage was a saloon, the streets of a little cow-town, or the open range. Sniping from the laurel was exchanged for the close-range thundering of six-shooters and sawed-off shotguns which decided matters quickly, one way or the other.

The case of Cal Reynolds and Esau Brill was somewhat out of the ordinary. In the first place, the feud concerned only themselves. Neither friends nor relatives were drawn into it. No one, including the partici-pants, knew just how it started. Cal Reynolds merely knew that he had hated Esau Brill most of his life, and that Brill reciprocated. Once as youths they had clashed with the violence and intensity of rival young catamounts. From that encounter Reynolds carried away a knife scar across the edge of his ribs, and Brill a permanently impaired eye. It had decided nothing. They had fought to a bloody, gasping deadlock, and neither had felt any desire to "shake hands and make up." That is a hypocrisy developed in civilization, where men have no stomach for fighting to the death. After a man has felt his adversary's knife grate against his bones, his adversary's thumb gouging at his eyes, his adver-sary's boot-heels stamped into his mouth, he is scarcely inclined to for-give and forget, regardless of the original merits of the argument.

So Reynolds and Brill carried their mutual hatred into manhood, and as cowpunchers riding for rival ranches, it followed that they found opportunities to carry on their private war. Reynolds rustled cattle from Brill's boss, and Brill returned the compliment. Each raged at the other's tactics, and considered himself justified in eliminating his enemy in any way that he could. Brill caught Reynolds without his gun one night in a saloon at Cow Wells, and only an ignominious flight out the back way, with bullets barking at his heels, saved the Reynolds scalp.

Again Reynolds, lying in the chaparral, neatly knocked his enemy out of his saddle at five hundred yards with a .30-30 slug, and, but for the inopportune appearance of a line-rider, the feud would have ended there, Reynolds deciding, in the face of this witness, to forego his original intention of leaving his covert and hammering out the wounded man's brains with his rifle butt.

Brill recovered from his wound, having the vitality of a longhorn bull, in common with all his sun-leathered iron-thewed breed, and as soon as he was on his feet, he came gunning for the man who had waylaid him.

Now after these onsets and skirmishes, the enemies faced each other at good rifle range, among the lonely hills where interruption was unlikely.

For more than an hour they had lain among the rocks, shooting at each hint of movement. Neither had scored a hit, though the .30-30's whistled perilously close.

In each of Reynolds's temples a tiny pulse hammered maddeningly. The sun beat down on him and his shirt was soaked with sweat. Gnats swarmed about his head, getting into his eyes, and he cursed venomously. His wet hair was plastered to his scalp; his eyes burned with the glare of the sun, and the rifle barrel was hot to his calloused hand. His right leg was growing numb and he shifted it cautiously, cursing at the jingle of the spur, though he knew Brill could not hear. All his discomfort added fuel to the fire of his wrath. Without process of conscious reasoning, he attributed all his suffering to his enemy. The sun beat dazingly on his sombrero, and his thoughts were slightly addled. It was hotter than the hearthstone of hell among those bare rocks. His dry tongue caressed his baked lips.

Through the muddle of his brain burned his hatred of Esau Brill. It had become more than an emotion: it was an obsession, a monstrous incubus. When he flinched from the whip-crack of Brill's rifle, it was not from fear of death, but because the thought of dying at the hands of his foe was an intolerable horror that made his brain rock with red frenzy. He would have thrown his life away recklessly, if by so doing he could have sent Brill into eternity just three seconds ahead of himself.

He did not analyze these feelings. Men who live by their hands have little time for self-analysis. He was no more aware of the quality of his hate for Esau Brill than he was consciously aware of his hands and feet. It was part of him, and more than part: it enveloped him, engulfed him; his mind and body were no more than its material manifestations. He *was* the hate; it was the whole soul and spirit of him. Unhampered by the stagnant and enervating shackles of sophistication and intellectuality, his instincts rose sheer from the naked primitive. And from them crystallized an almost tangible abstraction – a hate too strong for even death to destroy; a hate powerful enough to embody itself in itself, without the aid or the necessity of material substance.

For perhaps a quarter of an hour neither rifle had spoken. Instinct with death as rattlesnakes coiled among the rocks soaking up poison from the sun's rays, the feudists lay each waiting his chance, playing the game of endurance until the taut nerves of one or the other should snap.

It was Esau Brill who broke. Not that his collapse took the form of any wild madness or nervous explosion. The wary instincts of the wild were too strong in him for that. But suddenly, with a screamed curse, he hitched up on his elbow and fired blindly at the tangle of stones which concealed his enemy. Only the upper part of his arm and the corner of his blue-shirted shoulder were for an instant visible. That was enough. In that flash-second Cal Reynolds jerked the trigger, and a frightful yell told him his bullet had found its mark. And at the animal pain in that yell, reason and lifelong instincts were swept away by an insane flood of terrible joy. He did not whoop exultantly and spring to his feet; but his teeth bared in a wolfish grin and he involuntarily raised his head. Waking instinct jerked him down again. It was chance that undid him. Even as he ducked back, Brill's answering shot cracked.

Cal Reynolds did not hear it, because, simultaneously with the sound, something exploded in his skull, plunging him into utter blackness, shot briefly with red sparks.

The blackness was only momentary. Cal Reynolds glared wildly around, realizing with a frenzied shock that he was lying in the open. The impact of the shot had sent him rolling from among the rocks, and in that quick instant he realized that it had not been a direct hit. Chance had sent the bullet glancing from a stone, apparently to flick his scalp in passing. That was not so important. What was important was that he was lying out in full view, where Esau Brill could fill him full of lead. A wild glance showed his rifle lying close by. It had fallen across a stone and lay with the stock against the ground, the barrel slanting upward. Another glance showed his enemy standing upright among the stones that had concealed him.

In that one glance Cal Reynolds took in the details of the tall, rangy figure: the stained trousers sagging with the weight of the holstered six-shooter, the legs tucked into the worn leather boots; the streak of crimson on the shoulder of the blue shirt, which was plastered to the wearer's body with sweat; the tousled black hair, from which perspiration was pouring down the unshaven face. He caught the glint of yellow tobacco-stained teeth shining in a savage grin. Smoke still drifted from the rifle in Brill's hands.

These familiar and hated details stood out in startling clarity during the fleeting instant while Reynolds struggled madly against the unseen chains which seemed to hold him to the earth. Even as he thought of the paralysis a glancing blow on the head might induce, something seemed to snap and he rolled free. Rolled is hardly the word: he seemed almost to dart to the rifle that lay across the rock, so light his limbs felt.

Dropping behind the stone he seized the weapon. He did not even have to lift it. As it lay it bore directly on the man who was now approaching.

His hand was momentarily halted by Esau Brill's strange behavior. Instead of firing or leaping back into cover the man came straight on, his rifle in the crook of his arm, that damnable leer still on his unshaven lips. Was he mad? Could he not see that his enemy was up again, raging with life, and with a cocked rifle aimed at his heart? Brill seemed not to be looking at him, but to one side, at the spot where Reynolds had just been lying.

Without seeking further for the explanation of his foe's actions, Cal Reynolds pulled the trigger. With the vicious spang of the report a blue shred leaped from Brill's broad breast. He staggered back, his mouth flying open. And the look on his face froze Reynolds again. Esau Brill came of a breed which fights to its last gasp. Nothing was more certain than that he would go down pulling the trigger blindly until the last red vestige of life left him. Yet the ferocious triumph was wiped from his face with the crack of the shot, to be replaced by an awful expression of dazed surprize. He made no move to lift his rifle, which slipped from his grasp, nor did he clutch at his wound. Throwing out his hands in a strange, stunned, helpless way, he reeled backward on slowly buckling legs, his features frozen into a mask of stupid amazement that made his watcher shiver with its cosmic horror.

Through the opened lips gushed a tide of blood, dyeing the damp shirt. And like a tree that sways and rushes suddenly earthward, Esau Brill crashed down among the mesquite-grass and lay motionless.

Cal Reynolds rose, leaving the rifle where it lay. The rolling grass-grown hills swam misty and indistinct to his gaze. Even the sky and the blazing sun had a hazy unreal aspect. But a savage content was in his soul. The long feud was over at last, and whether he had taken his death-wound or not, he had sent Esau Brill to blaze the trail to hell ahead of him.

Then he started violently as his gaze wandered to the spot where he had rolled after being hit. He glared; were his eyes playing him tricks?

Yonder in the grass Esau Brill lay dead – yet only a few feet away stretched another body.

Rigid with surprize, Reynolds glared at the rangy figure, slumped grotesquely beside the rocks. It lay partly on its side, as if flung there by some blind convulsion, the arms outstretched, the fingers crooked as if blindly clutching. The short-cropped sandy hair was splashed with blood, and from a ghastly hole in the temple the brains were oozing. From a corner of the mouth seeped a thin trickle of tobacco juice to stain the dusty neck-cloth.

And as he gazed, an awful familiarity made itself evident. He knew the feel of those shiny leather wrist-bands; he knew with fearful certainty whose hands had buckled that gun-belt; the tang of that tobacco juice was still on his palate.

In one brief destroying instant he knew he was looking down at his own lifeless body. And with the knowledge came true oblivion.

The Sand-Hills' Crest

Here where the post-oaks crown the ridge, and the dreary sand-drifts lie,
I'll sit in the tangle of chaparral till my enemy passes by –
Till the shotgun speaks beneath my hand to my enemy passing by.

  (My grandfather came from Tennessee,
  And a fine blue broadcloth coat wore he –
  In a ragged, torn shirt I wait
  For my enemy passing by.)

The drouth burned up the wheat I sowed, my gaunt scrub-cattle died,
Because the winter pasture failed, and the last branch-water dried.
The young corn withered where it stood in the field on the bare hill-side.

I had one horse to work my land – one horse, and he was lame;
I hid my still in the shinnery where no one ever came.
I hid it deep in the thickets; the corn was from my own bin,
The laws would never have found it, but my neighbor turned me in.
For an old spite I'd clean forgot, my neighbor turned me in.

  (When my grandfather was a lad,
  A hundred slaves his father had;
  He clothed them better than I am clad.
  They were sleek and fat and prime,
  I've been hungry many a time.
  They fed full, child, man and wife;
  I've been hungry most of my life.)

I found a man to go my bond – he knows that I won't run;
I've never been forty miles from home; the drouth starved all my steers.

The Sand-Hills' Crest

The sinking sun is shining on the barrel of my gun.
They'd try me in the county court and give me seven years.

Seven years behind the bars because they found my still;
He showed it to the snooping laws, the man I'm going to kill.
Then they'll give me Life or the Chair, according to the judge's will,
Death's not so damned hard to a man that's lived all his life on a post-
    oak hill.

   (When my grandfather first came West
   Was never a fence on the prairie's breast,
   There was land to choose, and he chose the best,
   But it slipped through his fingers, like the rest,
   Driving his sons to the sand-hills' crest.)

The post-oaks stand up dull and brown against the tawny sky;
I hate them like I hate the man who'll soon be passing by;
At fifty feet I can not miss, I'm going to watch him die.
Die like the dirty dog he is, where the drifted sand-beds lie.

The Devil's Joker

The Sonora Kid hated snakes with an obsessional hatred that embraced all species, venomous or harmless. Big Bill Harrigan was a practical joker whose sense of humor sometimes ran away with his judgment. Otherwise he would never have played the joke he did on the Sonora Kid in the Antelope Saloon. He could not have realized the full extent of the Kid's fear and loathing for reptiles. At any rate, he approached the lean young cowpuncher, with a wink at the crowd, accosted him jovially – and tossed a chicken snake over his arm. The Kid, at the sight and touch of that wriggling horror, recoiled with a frantic yell that set the crowd off in a thunder of riotous mirth. And the Kid went temporarily crazy. White and blazing with unreasoning, instinctive mad fury, he drew and shot Big Bill Harrigan in the stomach. Big Bill's roar of laughter broke short in a grunt of agony and he crashed to the floor.

The general mirth was cut off just as suddenly. The Kid, almost as stunned by his action as were the rest, was the first to recover himself. His other gun flashed from its scabbard, and both muzzles trained on the numbed crowd, as the killer backed to the door, face white and eyes blazing.

"Keep back!" he snarled. "Don't move, none of you! Keep your hands up!"

"You can't get away with this, Kid!" It was Sheriff John MacFarlane, a tall, stalwart man, and utterly fearless. "It's cold-blooded murder, and you know it! Harrigan ain't even got a gun – "

"Shut up!" snarled the Kid. "Right or wrong, the noose ain't wove for me, yet. Don't none of you move, if you don't wanta get your guts blown out!"

"I'll get you!" raved MacFarlane. "I'll follow you clean to Hell – "

With a snarl, the Kid bounded through the door, out of the square of light and into the darkness by the hitching-racks. So quickly he moved that he was in the saddle and wheeling his tall bay away, even as the first figures framed themselves in the doorway, baffled by the darkness, and wary of a shot from it. As the Kid whirled away, he crashed a volley into the earth among the hoofs of the horses at the rack, that sent them plunging and screaming and breaking loose in frantic terror.

Shots spat red in the dark behind him as he fled, and the night crackled with shouts and curses as the vengeful men sought to catch and quell frantic steeds. By the time the first pursuers were spurring on the trail of the fugitive, the drum of his horse's hoofs had vanished in the night.

They did not catch the Sonora Kid that night, or the next, nor for the many days and nights that he kept the trail, putting much country between him and the memory and friends of Big Bill Harrigan. He knew John MacFarlane's threat had been no idle one. The Sheriff had his own ideas of justice, and he had never failed to make good his promise to any man, law-breaker or not. The Kid knew MacFarlane would follow him; would follow him across state lines, even into Mexico, if necessary. And the Kid did not want to meet him. He was not afraid of MacFarlane; young as the Kid was, his name was mentioned with respect in that wild hill country southwest of the Pecos, from which he had come to MacFarlane's country. But the Kid did not wish to kill the Sheriff; he knew MacFarlane was a good man. He knew his own action had seemed the act of a cold-blooded murderer. MacFarlane had never objected to a fair fight. But this, the Kid admitted, had been murder. Harrigan had been wearing no gun; he had stood empty-handed and laughing when the Kid's .45 knocked him down. The Kid swore with sick regret and fury. He knew how he must appear in the sight of those who saw it. They could not understand that shock and fright of a fear that had haunted him since babyhood had made him momentarily loco. They would not – they could not – believe him if he said that he did not realize what he was doing when he shot jovial, good-natured Harrigan.

And because, rightly or wrongly, the Kid was human enough to desire not to decorate the end of a rope, he put days and nights of hard riding between him and the scene of the shooting.

It was not by chance that he rode into the camp of Black Jim Buckley, dusty and worn from sleeplessness and the grind of that long trek.

Buckley greeted him without any appearance of surprise.

"Glad to see you, Kid. I been wonderin' how long it'd be before you started ridin' outlaw trails. Man of your talents got no business herdin' cows for a dollar a day. We can use you."

Frank Reynolds and Dick Brill were with Buckley – veteran outlaws, gunfighters with an awesome list of dead, men hard and tough and dangerous as the mountain-land that bred them. They readily welcomed the Kid on Buckley's say-so; there was no question of friendship or trust. They were a wolf-pack, banded together for mutual protection, wary of each other as of the rest of the world. These men were untamed, not amenable to the rules governing the mass of humanity. While they lived, they lived hard, violently, ruthlessly taking what they wished; when they died it would be in their boots, with their guns blazing, no more asking quarter than they had given it.

"I knew the Kid on the Pecos," said Buckley easily. "Call him his regular name of Steve Allison back there. Never heard of him pullin' no rustlin' or stick-up jobs, but he was almighty quick with his shootin' irons. You-all have heard of him."

His companions nodded without changing expression. The Kid's reputation was a dangerous thing to him, making it hard for him to live an ordinary life. Already famed as a gunfighter, with several killings behind him, the natural thing was for him to either turn law-enforcer or law-breaker. Circumstances had forced him into the latter course. It was impossible for a gunman to live the life of an ordinary cowhand.

"Got a job in mind down Rio Juan way," said Buckley. "Been kinda waitin', hopin' another good man would ride in. You couldn't come at a better time."

"Cattle or railroad?" demanded the Kid.

"Mine payroll. Hard for three men to work it. Need a man that ain't known so well. You was made for the part. Look here – "

On the hard earth, with the point of his stockman's knife, Buckley scratched a map, pointing out salient details as he unfolded his plan with a clarity and logic that showed why he was famed as the greatest of his profession. The three faces bent over his work, keen, alert, with almost wolf-like keenness that set them apart from other men. This keenness was no less apparent in the Kid's features than in the grimmer, more hardened faces of his companions.

"Tomorrow we ride down to meet Shorty and get the rest of the details," said Buckley. "You stay here and watch the cabin. Don't want nobody to get a peek at you till we spring the trick. Anybody see you with us, it'd spoil the whole deal."

After his companions had fallen asleep in their bunks, the Kid still sat silent and immobile before the dying fire, his chin propped on his bronzed fist. He seemed to glimpse the implacable hand of Fate driving him inexorably on to a life of crime. All his killings except the last had seemed necessary to him; at least they had been in fair fights. But because of them he had moved on continually, always restless and turbulent, yet always avoiding the actual state of outlawry by narrow margins. Now this latest twist of Fate had plunged him into it, and in a paroxysm of reasonless rage against the whims of Chance, he determined to play out the hand Life had dealt him to its red finish. If he were destined to ride the outlaw trail, then he would be no half-hearted weakling, but would carry himself in such a way that men would remember him longer for his crimes than they had remembered him for an honorable life. It was with a sort of bitter satisfaction that the Kid at last sought his bunk.

At dawn, Buckley and the others rode away, to their meeting with the mysterious Shorty – probably a treacherous employee of the mining company they intended looting. The Kid believed he knew why Buckley took both the others; the bandit chief was afraid to leave one of them alone with him. Reynolds and Brill were jealous of their lethal fame. The Kid was quick-tempered. Without the modifying presence of Buckley, a quarrel between Allison and either of the others was too likely a prospect to risk. Buckley wanted his full force for the job in hand. Afterwards – well, that was another matter. The Kid realized that sooner or later he would be drawn into a quarrel, to test his nerve, or because of some gunman's quick-triggered vanity.

Alone, the time dragged slowly. The Kid's restless nature abhorred idleness. His thoughts stung him. If he had any liquor he would have gotten blind drunk. He kept thinking of Big Bill Harrigan slumping to the floor. None of his other killings had ever worried him; but those men had died with their guns in their hands. Big Bill's belt had been empty. The Kid swore sickly and resumed his panther-like pacing of the cabin.

Toward sundown he heard the noise of approaching hoofs. Quick suspicion flashed across his mind, as he recognized it as the sound of a single horse. He went quickly to the leather-hinged door and threw it open, just in time to see a tall horseman on a tired black stallion ride into the clearing. It was Sheriff John MacFarlane.

At the sight, all other emotions were swept from the Kid's brain by a surge of red fury, the rage of a cornered thing.

"So you've hunted me down, you damned bloodhound!" he yelled.

"Wait, Kid – " shouted MacFarlane; then reading the unreasoning killer's lust in the Kid's glaring eyes, he snatched at his gun. Even as it cleared the leather, the Kid's .45 roared. MacFarlane's hat flew from his head and he pitched from the saddle and lay still in an oozing pool of blood, and his horse reared and bolted.

The Kid came forward, cursing, his pistol smoking in his hand. He kicked the prostrate form in a paroxysm of resentment, then bent closer to examine his enemy. MacFarlane was still living. The Kid discovered that his bullet had ploughed through the Sheriff's scalp, instead of going through the skull. He could not tell if the skull were fractured. He stood above the senseless man, an image of bewilderment.

If he had killed his enemy, the matter would have been at an end. But he could not put his gun to the senseless man's head and finish him. The Kid did not reach this conclusion by an elaborate method of reasoning on morals and ethics. It was a part of him, just as his blinding speed with a gun was part of him. He could not murder in cold blood like that; nor could he leave the man there to die without attention.

At last, swearing heartily, he lifted the limp form and lugged it into the cabin. MacFarlane was taller and heavier than the wiry Kid, but the task was accomplished, and the Sheriff laid on a bunk in the back room of the cabin. The Kid set to work cleansing and dressing the wound, with skill acquired in many such tasks. MacFarlane began to show some signs of returning consciousness, and the bandaging was just completed when the Kid heard horses outside, and the sound of familiar voices. Recognizing them, he did not leave his work, and had just completed the bandages when Buckley stalked in, followed by his companions. They halted short at the sight of the man in the bunk.

"What the hell, Kid," said Buckley softly. "What's the deal?"

"Fellow followed me from the Antelope," Allison answered briefly. "Said he would. Reckon he came alone. I creased him."

"Reckon that's middlin' pore shootin', Kid," murmured Frank Reynolds.

The Kid took no notice of the remark. MacFarlane groaned and stirred, and Buckley leaned forward to peer into the wounded man's face.

"Well, I'll be damned," he murmured. "This here's a visitor I shore never expected to receive like this. Reckon you know who this is, Kid?"

"Reckon I do," returned the other.

"Then why'n hell are you so polite with him?" demanded Brill. "If you know him, why didn't you put another bullet in him and finish him?"

Icy lights flickered in the Kid's steely gray eyes.

"Reckon that's my business, Brill," he returned slowly. No need to try to tell them that he couldn't leave even a wounded enemy to die; needless as to tell the crowd in the Antelope that the touch of a fangless snake could drive a man momentarily loco.

"Drop it boys," requested Buckley. "No use in wranglin' amongst ourselves. The Kid done a good job when he dropped this coyote. Everybody makes a mistake now and then. I savvy how you feel, Kid. You ain't been in the business long enough to realize that a fellow like this is just pizen to us, and don't deserve mercy no more'n a copperhead snake. You reckon this Sheriff would tend to you and bandage you up after he shot you, les'n it was to save you for the gallows or the pen?"

"Don't make no difference whether he would or not, Buckley," the Kid answered. "That ain't the point at all. If I'd killed him the first crack, it'd been alright. But I wouldn't let an egg-suckin' hound lay and die without doin' somethin' for him."

"That's alright, Kid," answered Buckley soothingly. "You don't have to. You done what you felt was your duty. Now you just leave the rest to me. You don't even have to watch, if you don't wanta. Just go out and turn our hosses into the corral, and when you get back, everything'll be o.k."

The Kid scowled.

"What you mean, Buckley?"

"Why, hell!" broke in Dick Brill. "Are you so damned innocent, Kid? This here's John MacFarlane; you think we're goin' to let him live?"

"You mean you're goin' to murder him?" ejaculated the Kid, aghast.

"That's a hard way of puttin' it, Kid," protested Buckley. "We just aim to see that he don't get in our way no more. I got my personal reasons, outside of the matter of ordinary safety precautions."

"He's comin' to," said Reynolds.

The Kid turned to see the Sheriff's eyes flicker open. They were dazed. He muttered incoherently. The Kid bent and put a canteen of water to his lips. The wounded man drank mechanically.

"Kid," said Buckley, "come out into the cabin and we'll get all this straight."

The Kid was the last to leave the back room. He closed the door after him.

"What you figgerin' on doin' with this rat, Kid?" asked Buckley.

"Why, tend to him till he's dead or well," answered Allison.

Brill swore beneath his breath. Buckley shook his head.

"Are you crazy, Kid? We got to dust outa here pronto. Everything's set down at Rio Juan. We won't be ridin' back this way."

"Then you'll ride without me," the Kid answered doggedly.

"You mean you'll throw us over, pass up the job?" Buckley's voice was soft. "You mean you'll let us down, for this bloodhound that's been trailin' you?"

"I mean I ain't no murderer!" exclaimed the goaded Kid. "I can't kill a man after I've knocked him out. I can't leave him to die. I can't let him be murdered. Any of them things would be just like blowin' his brains out after I shot him down. I got no love for this hombre. But it ain't a matter of like or dislike."

"This fellow killed my brother," Buckley's voice was softer yet, but lights were beginning to glimmer in his eyes.

"And you can look him up and kill him after he gets on his feet. It ain't nothin' to me. But you ain't massacrin' him like a sheep."

"Kid," breathed Buckley "you've showed your hand; now I'm showin' mine. You can't let us down and get away with it. This coyote of the law don't leave this shack alive. Take it or leave it; if you leave it, you got to say your say with gun-smoke."

There was an instant of tense silence, like a tick of Eternity in which Time seemed to stand still, and the night held its breath. In that brief space the Kid knew that he faced his supreme test. He saw the faces of his former companions, frozen into hard masks, in which their eyes burned with a wolfish light. Like a flicker of lightning, his hand snapped to his gun.

Buckley moved with equal speed. Their guns crashed together. The Kid reeled back against the wall, his six-shooter falling from his numb fingers. Buckley dropped, the whole top of his head torn off. On the heels of the double report came the thunder of the guns of Brill and Reynolds. Even as he reeled, the Kid's left-hand gun was spurting smoke and flame. He rocked and jerked to the impact of lead, but he kept his feet. Reynolds was down, shot through the neck and belly. Brill, roaring like a bull and spouting blood, charged with a staggering rush, shooting as he came. He tripped over Buckley's prostrate form, and as he fell, the Kid shot him straight through the heart.

The silence that followed the brief deadly thunder was appalling. The Kid lurched away from the wall. The cabin with its staring dead men and shreds of drifting smoke swam before his blurred sight. His whole right side seemed dead, and his left leg refused to balance his weight. Suddenly the floor seemed to rush up and strike him heavily. In the confused mist which engulfed him, he seemed to hear John MacFarlane calling to him, as if from a vast distance.

A little later he looked dizzily into MacFarlane's face. The big sheriff was pale and his words seemed strange.

"Hang on, Kid; I ain't much of a sawbones, but I'm goin' to do the best I can."

"Lay off me, or I'll blow your head off," snarled the Kid groggily. "I ain't askin' no favors from you. I thought you was about dead."

"Just knocked out," answered MacFarlane. "I came to and heard everything that went on out here. My God, Kid, you're shot to pieces – broken shoulder-bone, bullets in your thigh, breast, right arm – you realize you've just killed the three worst gunfighters in the State? And you done it for me. You got to get well, Kid – you got to."

"So you can see me kick in a noose?" snarled the Kid. "Don't you put no bandages on me. If I got to cash, I'll cash like a gent. I wasn't born to be hanged."

"You got it all wrong, Kid," answered MacFarlane. "Get this straight –

I wasn't trailin' you to arrest you. I was huntin' you to put you right. The law ain't lookin' for you. Harrigan ain't dead. He ain't even hurt."

The Kid laughed unpleasantly.

"No? Don't lie, MacFarlane. I shot him plumb in the belly."

"I know you did, but listen: Big Bill wasn't wearin' no gun-belt, you remember. Well, he had his six-shooter under his shirt, inside his waistband. Your bullet just flattened out against the cylinder of his gun. It knocked him down and took all the wind outa him and bruised his belly somethin' fierce, but otherwise it didn't hurt him none. He don't hold no grudge. I got to thinkin' about it, and decided you just didn't think what you was doin'. Now I know it. Now get your mind to thinkin' about gettin' over these wounds."

"I'll do it, alright," grunted the Kid, concealing his joy with the instinct of his breed. "Gotta redeem myself – I shoot Harrigan and I shoot you, and you both live to tell about it. Got to do somethin' to persuade people I ain't such a poor shot as all that."

MacFarlane, knowing the Kid's kind, laughed.

Knife, Bullet and Noose

Steve Allison, also known as the Sonora Kid, was standing alone at the Gold Dust Bar when Johnny Elkins entered, glanced furtively at the bartender, and leaned close to Allison's elbow. Out of the corner of his mouth he muttered: "Steve, they're out to get you."

The Kid showed no sign that he had heard. He was a wiry young man, slightly above medium height, slim, but strong as a cougar. His skin was burned dark by the sun and winds of many dim trails, and from under the broad rim of his hat, his eyes glinted grey as chilled steel. Except for those eyes he might have been but one more of the army of cowpunchers that rode up the Chisholm yearly; but low on his hips hung two ivory-butted guns, and the worn leather of their scabbards proclaimed that their presence was no mere matter of display.

The Kid emptied his glass before he answered, softly.

"Who's out to get me?"

"Grizzly Gullin!" Elkins shot an uneasy glance toward the door as he whispered the formidable name. "The town's full of buffalo hunters, and they're on the prod. They ain't talkin' much, but I got wind of who they're stalkin', and it's you!"

The Kid rang a coin on the bar, scooped up his change and turned away. Elkins rolled after him, trying to match his friend's long stride. Elkins was freckled, bow-legged, and of negligible stature. They emerged from the saloon and tramped along the dusty street for some yards before either spoke.

"Dawggone you, Kid," panted Elkins. "You make me plumb mad. I tell you, somebody in this cowtown is primin' them shaggy-hided hunters with bad licker and devilishness."

"Who?"

"How'm I goin' to know? But that blame' Mike Connolly ain't got no love for you, since you took some of the boys away from him that he was goin' to lock up when we was up here last year. You know he was a buffalo hunter too, once. Them fellows stand in together. They can pot you cold, and he won't turn a finger."

"Nobody asks him to turn a finger," retorted Allison with the quick flash of vanity that characterized the gunfighter. "I don't need no buffalo-skinnin' cowtown marshal to shoo a gang of bushy-headed hunters off of me."

"Le's ride," urged Elkins. "What are you waitin' on? The boys pulled out yesterday."

"Well," answered Allison, "you know we brought in the biggest herd that's come to this town this year. We sold to R. J. Blaine, the new cattle-buyer, and we kind of caught him flatfooted. He didn't have enough ready cash to pay for the herd in full. He give me enough to pay off the boys, though, and sent to Abilene for more. It may get here today. Yesterday I sent the boys down the trail. They'd blowed in most of their money, and with all these buffalo hunters that's swarmin' in to town, I was afraid they'd get into a ruckus. So I told 'em to head south, and I'd wait for the money and catch up with 'em by the time they hit the Arkansas."

"Old man Donnelly is so blame sot in his ways he's a plumb pest sometimes," grumbled Elkins. "Why couldn't Blaine send him a draft or somethin'?"

"Donnelly don't trust banks," answered the Kid. "You know that. He keeps his money in a big safe in the ranch house, and he always wants his trail boss to bring the money for the cows in big bills."

"Which is plumb nice for the trail boss," snarled Elkins. "It ain't enough to haze four thousand mossy horns from the lower Rio Grande clean to Kansas; his pore damn' sucker of a trail boss has got to risk his life totin' the cash money all the way back. Why, Hell, Steve, at twenty dollars a head, that wad'll make a roll that'd choke a mule. Every outlaw between here and Laredo will be gunnin' for yore hide."

"I'm goin' to see Blaine now," answered the Kid abruptly. "But money or not, I ain't dustin' out till I've had a show-down with Gullin. He can't say he run me out of town."

He turned aside into the unpainted board building that served as dwelling place and office for the town's leading business man.

Blaine greeted him cordially as he entered. The cattle buyer was a big man, well-fed and well-dressed. If not typical, he was a good representation of one of the many types following the steel ribbons westward across the Kansas plains, where, at the magic touch of the steel, new towns blossomed overnight, creating fresh markets for the cattle that rolled up in endless waves from the south. Shrewd, ambitious, and with a better education than most, the man was the dominating factor in this new-grown town, which hoped to rival and eclipse the older cowtowns of Abilene, Newton and Wichita. Blaine had been a gambler in Nevada mining camps before the westward drive of the rails had started the big cattle boom. Though he wore no weapon openly, men said that in his gambling days no faro-dealer in the west was his equal in gun-skill.

"I guess I know what you're after, Allison," Blaine laughed. "Well, it's here. Came in this morning." Reaching into his ponderous safe he laid a bulky roll of bills on the table. "Count 'em," he requested. The Kid shook his head.

"I'll take your word for it." He drew a black leather bag from his pocket, stuffed the bills into it, and made the draw string fast. The whole made a package of no small bulk.

"You mean to tote all that money down the trail with you?" Blaine demanded.

"Clean to the Tomahawk ranch house," grinned the Kid. "Old man Donnelly won't have it no other way."

"You're taking a big risk," said Blaine bluntly. "Why don't you let me give you a draft for the amount on the First National Bank of Kansas City?"

"The old man don't do business with no banks," replied the Kid. "He likes his money where he can lay hands on it all the time."

"Well, that's his business and yours," answered the cattle buyer. "The tally record and the bill of sale we fixed up the other day, but suppose you sign this receipt, just as a matter of form. It shows I've paid you the money in due form and proper amount."

The Kid signed the receipt, and Blaine, as he folded the paper for placing it in safe-keeping, remarked: "I understand your vaqueros pulled out yesterday."

"Yeah, that's right."

"That means you'll be riding alone part of the way," protested Blaine. "And with all that money – "

"Aw, I'll be alright, I reckon," answered the Kid. Because he was naturally reticent, he did not add that he would be accompanied by Johnny Elkins, a former Tomahawk hand who had remained in Kansas since the drive of the last year, and now, wearied of the northern range, was riding south with his old friend.

"I reckon the trail will be a lot safer than town, maybe," said Allison; "so I'm goin' to leave this money with you for safe-keepin' for awhile. I got some business to 'tend to. I'll call for it sudden-like, maybe, late tonight, or early in the mornin'. If I don't call at all – well, I can trust you to see it gets to old man Donnelly eventually."

As he strode from Blaine's office, his spurs jingling in the dust, a ragged individual sidled up to him and said: "Grizzly Gullin and the boys want to know if you got guts enough to come down to the Buffalo Hump."

"Go back and tell 'em I'll be there," as softly answered the Kid.

The fellow hurried away in the deepening dusk, and the Kid went swiftly to his hotel, thence to a livery stable. Presently he again came up the street, but this time astride a wiry mustang. The cowtown was awake and going full blast. Tinny pianos blared from dance halls, boot heels stamped on the board walks, saloon doors swung violently, and the yipping of hilarious revelers was punctuated by the shrill laughter of women, and the occasional crack of pistols. The trail riders were celebrating, releasing the nervous energy stored up on that grinding thousand-mile trek.

There was nothing restrained, softened or refined about the scene. All was primitive, wild, raw as the naked boards of the houses that stood up gaunt and unadorned against the prairie stars.

Mike Connolly and his deputies stalked from dance hall to dance hall, glared into every saloon, into every gambling dive. They maintained order at pistol point, and they had no love for the lean bronzed riders who hazed the herds up the trail men called the Chisholm.

There were, indeed, hard characters among these riders. It was a hard life, that bred hard men. At first the trail drivers came seeking only a peaceful market. Fighting their way through hostile lands swarming with

Indians and white outlaws, they expected to find rest, safety and the means of enjoyment in the Kansas towns. But the cowtowns soon swarmed with gamblers, crooks, professional killers, parasites that follow every boom, whether of gold, silver, oil or cattle. An unsophisticated cowboy found the dangers of the trail less than the dangers of the boom-towns.

They began to ride up the trails with their guns strapped down, ready for trouble, ready to fight Indians and outlaws on the trail, gamblers and marshals in the towns. Gunfighters, formerly limited mainly to officers and gamblers, began to be found in the ranks of the cowboys. Of this breed was Steve Allison, and it was because of this that old John Donnelly had chosen him for his trail boss.

The Kid tied his horse to the hitching rack by the Buffalo Hump, and strode lightly toward the square of golden light that marked the doorway. Inside glasses crashed, oaths and boisterous laughter crackled, and a voice roared:

> It wuz on a starry night, in the month of July,
> They robbed the Danville train;
> It wuz two of the Younger boys what opened the safe,
> And toted the gold away!

A shadowy form bulked up before the Kid, and even as his right hand gun slid silently from its scabbard, Johnny Elkins' voice hissed: "Steve, are you locoed?"

Johnny's fingers gripped the Kid's arm, and Allison felt the youngster trembling in his excitement. His face was a pale blur in the dim light.

"Don't go in there, Steve!" his voice thrummed with urgency.

"Who-all's in there?" asked the Kid softly.

"Every damn' buff-hunter in town! Grizzly Gullin's been ravin' and swearin' he'll cut out yore heart and eat it raw. I tell you, Steve, they know it 'uz you that killed Bill Galt, and they craves yore scalp."

"Well, they can have it if they got the guts to take it," said the Kid without passion.

"But you know their way," protested Johnny. "If you go in there and get into a fight with Gullin they'll shoot you in the back. Somebody'll shoot out the light, and in the scramble nobody'll know who done it – or give a damn."

"I know." None knew the tricks of the cowtown ruffians better than the Kid. "That's the way some of these tinhorns got Joe Ord, trail boss for the Triple L, last month. Robbed him, too, I reckon. Leastways, he'd been paid for the cows he brung up the trail, and they never found the money. But that was gamblers, not hunters."

"What's the difference?"

"None, as far as stoppin' a bullet goes," grinned the Kid. "But listen here, Johnny – " His voice sank lower, and Elkins listened intently. He shook his head and swore dubiously, but when the Kid turned and strode toward the lamp-lit doorway, the bowlegged puncher rolled after him.

As the kid framed himself in the door, the clamor within ceased suddenly. The fellow who had been singing, or rather bellowing, broke short his lament for Jesse James, and wheeled like a great bear toward the doorway.

Allison's quick gaze swept over the saloon. It was thronged with buffalo hunters, to which the establishment catered. Besides the bartenders, there was but one man there not a hunter – the marshal, Mike Connolly, a broad built man, with a hard immobile face, and a heavy gun strapped low on either hip.

The hunters were all big men, many of them clad in buckskin and Indian moccasins. All were burned dark as Indians, and they wore their hair long. Living an incredibly primitive life, they were hard and ferocious as red savages, and infinitely more dangerous. Hairy, burly, fierce, their eyes gleamed in the lamp light, their hands hovered near the great butcher knives in their belts.

In the midst of the room stood one who loomed above the rest – a great, shaggy brute who looked more like a bear than a man: Grizzly Gullin. This man gave a roar as Allison entered, and rolled toward him, small eyes blazing, thick hairy hands working as if to tear out his enemy's throat.

"What you doin' here, Allison?" His voice filled the saloon, and almost seemed to make the one kerosene lamp flicker.

"Heard you all craved to meet me, Gullin," the Kid answered tranquilly. His eyes never exactly left Gullin's hairy face, but they darted sidelong glances that took in all the room.

Gullin rumbled like an enraged bull. His shaggy head wagged from side to side, his hairy hands moved back and forth, without actually reaching toward a weapon. Like most of the other hunters he wore a gun, but it was with the long broad-bladed butcher knife strapped high on his left side, hilt forward, that he was deadly.

"You killed Bill Galt!" he roared, and the crowd behind him rumbled menacingly.

"Yeah, I did," admitted the Kid.

Gullin's face grew black; his veins swelled; he teetered forward on his moccasined feet as if about to hurl himself bodily at his enemy.

"You admit it!" he yelled. "You killed him in cold blood – "

"I shot him in a fair fight," snarled the Kid, his eyes suddenly icy. "Last year he stampeded a herd of Tomahawk cattle just out of pure cussedness – run a herd of buffalo into 'em. They went over a bluff by the hundreds, and took one of the hands with 'em. He was smashed to a pulp. When we come up the trail this year, I met Bill Galt on the Canadian, and I blew his light out. But he had an even break."

"You're a liar!" bellowed Gullin. "You shot him in the back. A man heard you braggin' about it, and told us. You murdered Bill and let him lay there like he was a dog."

"I wouldn't have let a dog lay," answered the Kid with bitter scorn. "When I rode off Galt was buzzard meat and I didn't feel no call to cover him up. But I didn't shoot him in the back."

"You can't lie out of it!" howled Gullin, brandishing his huge fists.

The Kid cast a quick look at the hemming faces, dark with passion, the straining bodies. It was something more than the old feud of cowpuncher and buffalo-hunter. Mike Connolly stood back, aloof, silent.

"Well, why don't you start the ball rollin'?" demanded the Kid, half crouching, hands hovering above his gun butts.

"'Cause we ain't murderers like you," sneered Gullin. "Connolly there is goin' to see fair play. You're a gunman; you got guts enough to fight with a man's weepons?"

"Meanin' a butcher knife? Gullin, there ain't no weapon I'm afraid to meet you with!"

"Alright!" yelled the hunter, tearing off his gun belt and tossing it to Mike Connolly. "You ain't wearin' no knife; git him one, Joe."

The bartender ducked down into an assortment of lethal weapons pawned to him at various times, in return for drinks, by impecunious customers, and laid half a dozen knives on the plank bar.

The Kid, drawing both his guns, handed them to Johnny Elkins, who casually backed toward the door. Allison, after a brief inspection, took up a knife with a heavy hilt and a narrow, comparatively short blade – a weapon of unmistakable Spanish make.

The hunters had drawn back around the walls, leaving a space clear. The Kid had no illusions about what was to follow. He knew his own reputation; knew that the whole affair was a trap, planned to get his deadly guns out of his hands. If Gullin's knife failed, it would be a bullet in the cowboy's back. The Kid stamped in the sawdust as if trying the footing, moving near an open window as he did so. Then he turned and indicated that he was ready.

Gullin ripped out his knife and charged like the bear for which he was named. For all his bulk he was quick as a cat. His moccasin-shod feet were adapted to the work at hand. Opposing was the Kid, much inferior in bulk, wearing high-heeled boots unfitted for quick work on the sawdust-strewn floor. The knife in his hand looked small compared to the great scimitar-curved blade of Gullin. What the hunters overlooked, or did not know, was that Allison was raised in a land swarming with Mexican knife-fighters.

The Kid, facing that roaring, hurtling bulk, knew that if they came to hand-grips, he was lost. He had seen Gullin, his shoulder broken by a cowboy's bullet, leap like a huge cat through the air and drive the knife, with his left hand, through his enemy's heart.

Gullin roared and charged; the Kid's hand went back and snapped out. The Spanish knife flashed through the lamp-light like a beam of blue lightning, and thudded against Gullin's breast – the hilt quivered under his heart. The giant stopped short, staggered. His mouth gaped and blood gushed from it. He pitched headlong –

As Gullin fell, the Kid's hand whipped inside his shirt and out again, gripping a double-barreled derringer. Even as it caught the lamp light, it cracked twice. A hunter lifting a cocked sixshooter crumpled, and the lamp shattered, casting a shower of blazing oil.

In the darkness bedlam broke loose. There were wild shots, stampeding of feet, splintering of chairs and tables, curses, yells, and Mike Connolly's stentorian voice demanding a light.

The Kid had wheeled, even as the room was plunged in darkness, and dived headlong through the nearby window. He hit on his feet, catlike, and raced toward the hitching rack. A form loomed up before him, and even as he instinctively menaced it with the empty derringer, he recognized it.

"Johnny! Got my guns?"

Two familiar smooth butts were shoved into his eager hands.

"I beat it as soon as everybody was watchin' you all," Johnny spluttered with excitement. "You nailed him, Steve? By the good golly – "

"Get your cayuse and hit the trail, Johnny," ordered Allison, swinging up on his horse. "Dust it out of town and wait for me at that creek crossin' three miles south of town. I'm goin' after the money Blaine's holdin' for me. Vamoose!"

A few minutes later the Kid dropped reins over his horse's head and slid up to the lighted window inside which he saw Richard J. Blaine busily engaged in writing. At the Kid's hiss he looked up, gaped, and started violently. The Kid pushed the partly open window up the rest of the way, and climbed in.

"I ain't hardly got no time to go around to the door," he apologized. "If you'll give me the money, I'll be makin' tracks."

Blaine rose, still confused, hastily crumpling up the sheet on which he had been writing, and thrusting it into his pocket. He turned toward his safe, which stood open, and inside which Allison could see the black leather bag, then turned back, as if struck by a sudden thought.

"Any trouble?"

"No trouble; just a bunch of fool buffalo hunters."

"Oh!" The cattle buyer seemed to be regaining some of his composure. The color came back to his face.

"You startled the devil out of me, coming through that window. What about those hunters?"

"They took it ill because I killed that stampedin' side-winder Bill Galt," answered the Kid. "I don't know how they found out. I ain't told nobody in this town except you and Johnny Elkins. Reckon some of my outfit must have talked. Not that I give a damn. But I don't go around braggin' about the coyotes I have to shoot. They sure planned to get me cold – " in a few words he related what happened at the Buffalo Hump. "Now I reckon they'll try lynch-law," he concluded. "They'll swear I murdered somebody."

"Oh, I guess not," laughed Blaine. "Bed down here till mornin'."

"Not a chance; I'm dustin' now."

"Well, have a drink before you go," urged Blaine.

"I ain't hardly got time." The Kid was listening for sounds of pursuit. It was quite possible the maddened hunters might trail him. And he knew that Mike Connolly would give him no protection against the mob.

"Oh, a few minutes won't make any difference," laughed Blaine. "Wait, I'll get the liquor."

Frontier courtesy precluded a refusal. Blaine passed into an adjoining room, and the Kid heard him fumbling about. The Kid stood in the center of the office-room, nervous, alert, and because it was his nature to observe everything, he noticed a ball of paper crumpled on the floor, ink-stained – evidently part of a letter Blaine had spoiled and discarded. He would have paid no attention to it, but suddenly he saw his own name scrawled upon it.

Quickly he bent and secured it. Smoothing out the crumpled sheet, he read. It was a letter addressed to John Donnelly, and it said: "Your trail boss Allison was killed in a barroom brawl. I had paid him for the cows, and have a receipt, signed by him. However, the money was not found on his body. Marshal Connolly verifies that fact. He had been gambling heavily, I understand, and he must have used your money after he ran out of his own. It's too bad, but – "

The door opened and Blaine stood framed in it, whiskey bottle and glasses in hand. He saw the paper in the Kid's fingers, and he went livid.

The bottle and glasses fell to the floor with a shattering crash. Blaine's hand darted under his coat and out, just as the Texan's .45 cleared leather. The shots crashed like a double reverberation – but it was the .45 that thundered first. The window behind Allison shattered, and Blaine tumbled to the floor, to lie in a widening pool of dark crimson.

The Kid snatched the bulky black leather pouch from the opened safe, and stuffed it into his shirt as he ran from the room. He forked his mustang and headed south at a run. Behind him sounded the mingled clamor of cowtown night life, mixed now with an increasing, ominous roar – the bellow of the manhunt. The Kid grinned hardly – knife, bullet, noose – all had failed that night; as well as the sinister plotting of the last man in Kansas Allison would have dreamed of suspecting.

Johnny Elkins was waiting for him at the appointed place, and together they took the trail that ran southward for a thousand miles.

"Well?" Johnny wriggled impatiently. Allison explained in a few words.

"I see it all now. Blaine figgered on gettin' cows and money too. He held up the pay for the herd, so as to get me in town alone, so he thought. He worked them hunters up to get me. He had the receipt to prove that he'd paid me the dough. Then if I got killed, and the money not on me – Right at the last he tried to keep me there, till the mob found me, I reckon."

"But he couldn't know you'd leave the dough with him for safe-keepin'," objected Johnny.

"Well, it was a natural thing to do. And if I hadn't, I reckon Connolly would have took it off me, after I was killed in the Buffalo Hump. He was Blaine's man. That must have been how and why Joe Ord got his."

"And everybody figgered Blaine was such a big man," meditated Johnny.

"Well," answered Allison, "a few more big herds grabbed for nothin', and I reckon he would have been a big man; but big or little, it's all the same to a .45."

Which comment embraced the full philosophy of the gunfighter.

Law-Shooters of Cowtown

Clamor of cowtown nights . . . boot heels stamping on sawdust-strewn floors . . . thunder of flying hoofs down the dusty street . . . yipping of the lean trail drivers, reeling in the saddle, hilarious after the thousand-mile trek . . . cracking of pistols, smash of glasses, flutter of cards on the tables . . . oaths, songs, laughter in all the teeming saloons and dance halls, louder yet in the plank-barred Silver Boot.

Grizzly Elkins slapped a twenty dollar gold piece down on the monte game. Elkins stood out, even in that throng of tall men. He was hairy as a bear, burly and powerful as a bear. Burned dark as an Indian, he wore the buckskins and moccasins of an earlier day. His shoulders were broad and thick as those of an ox. One of the army of buffalo hunters wandering between the Pecos and the upper Missouri, he was as much a part of that wild land as one of the beasts he hunted.

He leaned over the table with the men about him, watching the play of the cards. He grunted explosively as he saw the winning card come up.

The dealer's narrow white hand raked up the coins.

"Wait there, you!" Grizzly Elkins's voice was a roar that filled the saloon. "Gimme my change. I bet just five outer that twenty piece."

The dealer looked up with a sneer on his thin lips. He was Jim Kirby, gambler and gunman, his metal proven in many a game of chance – both with cards and with sixshooters.

"I never give change," he retorted. "If you don't want to bet your wad, don't lay it on my board. I've got no time for pikers."

Elkins' small eyes blazed.

"Why, you dirty thief – !" His bellow brought the men at the bar around as on a pivot.

Kirby's hand darted like the head of a snake to his scabbard; but Elkins, for all his bulk, moved quick as a great cat. With a berserk bellow he ripped out his butcher knife and hurled himself recklessly across the table. The great blade flashed blue in the lamplight and plunged to the hilt in the gambler's breast, as the table tilted and buckled beneath the headlong impact. The explosion of Kirby's gun nearly deafened the hunter, the flash of powder stinging and blackening his neck and beard. Out of the tangle of chairs, limbs, and broken wood, Elkins heaved up like a bear out of a trap, roaring and brandishing his knife, red to the hilt. Under his feet Kirby lay still and white in a broadening pool of crimson.

For an instant Elkins rocked on his straddling legs, glaring about him, shaggy head jutting truculently, knife lifted. Then with a yell he turned and ran for the door. A clamor broke out about and behind him, as a pack bays the fleeing wolf. Jim Kirby had been popular with the scum of the cowtowns.

"Stop him!" "Grab him!" "Shoot him!" "He murdered Kirby, the son of a – "

Another stride would carry the fugitive through the door and into the night, but in the square of light outside, a tall, lean figure loomed suddenly – Buck Chisom, the marshal's gunfighting deputy. He heard the yells and acted with the steel-trap comprehension of his breed.

Elkins halted short; his thick arm shot back – but before it could snap forward in the motion that could nail a man to a tree with the thrown knife, Chisom's hand, moving too quick for the sight to follow, came up with a gleam of blue steel. A jet of flame ripped the night. Elkins jerked spasmodically; he swayed backward, then pitched on his face, his fingers relaxing about the bloody hilt of his butcher knife.

When the buffalo hunter regained consciousness, his first sensation was a dizzy pain in his head. His next was an astonishment that he was alive, after having been shot by Buck Chisom at such deadly close range. He lifted his hand tentatively to his scalp and discovered it was crusted with dried blood, with which his bushy hair was likewise clotted. He swore. The bullet had merely creased his scalp, knocking him senseless. Evidently the light directly behind his target had dazzled Chisom. That his captor had not bothered to bandage his wound, Elkins did not resent, or even think about. Born and bred on the frontier, living a life incredibly primitive, the buffalo hunter had all the tough stoicism of the wild, and its contempt for pain and injury.

He was lying on a rude wooden bunk, which was scantily covered with a ragged blanket. He sat up, swearing, and instinctively reaching for the butcher knife he always wore strapped high on his left side, hilt forward. The sheath was empty, as he might have known it would be.

As he glared about him, a mocking laugh caused him to bristle truculently. He was where he would have expected to be – in the jail. It was a one-room building, made of undressed logs, with one door and one window. The window was barred, but even without the bars, it was too small to have accommodated Elkins' bull shoulders. There were two bunks, and on the other sat the man who had laughed.

Elkins glared at him with scant favor. He knew him: a fellow named Richards, a lean, black haired, shifty eyed cowboy.

"Well, how you like it, fellow?" this customer greeted the discomfited plainsman.

"How would I like it, you bow-legged hedgehog?" roared Elkins. Attuned to the wide spaces and the winds of the great plains, the buffalo hunter's voice was always a roar. "Just wait'll I get my hands on that blamed marshal and his gun-throwin' deperty! I'll scour the street with their blasted carcasses!"

"Talk's cheap," sneered Richards.

"What you doin', takin' up for them rats?" demanded Elkins. "Didn't they throw you in?"

"For drunk and disorderly conduck, yes," admitted the other. "But I ain't no derned murderer."

"Who is?" rumbled Elkins, bristling instantly.

"You murdered Jim Kirby."

"You're a liar. I killed him like I would any other varmint. And when I get out of this den, I'm a-goin' to commit some more necessary homicides."

"When you git out," predicted Richards vindictively, "you're goin' to be decoratin' a tree limb at the end of a rope. Listen!"

Elkins stiffened abruptly. The night wind carried the various sounds of the cowtown – but it carried another sound: the swelling, awesome roar of maddened men. The hunter knew what it meant.

"They's enough rats in this town to hang me if they could get me," he snarled; "but I reckon the marshal will handle 'em."

"Well," Richards leered as if at a secret jest, "I wouldn't rely too much on Joel Rogers if I was you – nor Buck Chisom neither."

Elkins wheeled suddenly. He seemed to fill the place, not only with his great bulk, but with his somber and ferocious personality.

"What you mean?" he demanded.

"That's all right," grinned Richards. "What I know, well, I know it; and what you don't know won't hurt you none – not after tonight!"

"You damned rat!" roared Elkins, eyes a-flame, beard a-bristle; "you'll tell me right now what you're a-hintin' at!"

As he rushed like a maddened bull at the cowboy, the latter leaped from his bunk and met the hurtling giant with a smash that spattered blood from his mouth. Elkins replied with a bloodthirsty yell, and bent the lanky puncher double with a mallet-like blow to the belly, and then they grappled and went to the floor together.

Richards lacked the buffalo hunter's bulk, but he was equally tall, and as hard and rangy as a timber wolf. Neither knew anything about scientific wrestling or boxing, but both were products of the frontier, and their style of fighting was as primitive and instinctive as that of a pair of grizzlies.

Kicking, biting, tearing, gouging, mauling, they rolled back and forth across the floor, smashing into the bunks and caroming against the walls. Rearing upright again, they slugged with primordial abandon, oblivious to the growing roar of the mob, to everything but the lust to obliterate each other. There was no attempt at defense; each blow was driven with the power and will to destroy.

Reeling back from a bear-like smash that tore his ear from his head and left it hanging by a shred of flesh, Richards kicked savagely at Elkins' groin. The plainsman caught his ankle and wrenched sideways. Richards went down with a crash, and Elkins's moccasin heel caught him squarely in the mouth, splintering his teeth.

With an inhuman yell the hunter leaped on the fallen man, driving his knee into Richards's midriff; then seizing the man's throat, he began to hammer his head against the log wall with a fury that would quickly have put the cowboy beyond human aid.

"Wait!" gasped the victim. He was a sorry sight, with one eye closed, an ear mangled, face skinned, blood streaming from smashed nose and torn lips. "I'll tell you – "

"Then hustle!" panted Elkins, spitting out the fragments of a broken tooth. Blood trickled down the hunter's beard, and his buckskin shirt was ripped open, revealing his great hairy chest which heaved from his exertions. "Hustle! I hear that derned mob." His big hands maintained their vise-like grip on his victim's neck.

"I had a bottle about a quarter full of whiskey on me when I come in here," mumbled Richards. "I drunk it and laid down on the bunk to sleep, and whilst I was layin' there, I woke up and heered Rogers and Chisom talkin'. They seen the empty bottle and thought I was dead drunk. They throwed you in here, and Rogers said tonight was as good a night as any to pull what they aimed to pull. He said he'd planned to set a house on fire, and do it whilst everybody was at the fire, but he said he knowed a mob was gatherin' on account of Jim Kirby, he had so many friends, and people would turn out to a lynchin' even better'n they would to a fire, so tonight was the night. And Chisom said yes."

"But what they plannin' to do?" roared Elkins bewilderedly.

"Rob the bank!" answered Richards. "I heered 'em talk about it."

"But they're laws!" protested Elkins.

"I don't care. I knowed Chisom in Nevada. Regular outlaw then, and I guess he ain't changed none. Who knows anything about Rogers? Ain't no tellin' what he was before he come here."

Elkins realized the truth of this statement. In the cowtowns officers were likely to be chosen for their gun-skill, and no questions asked about their previous life. Hendry Brown came straight from Billy the Kid's gang to the office of marshal of Caldwell; John Wesley Hardin, with a price on his head in Texas, was deputy sheriff in Abilene.

The buffalo hunter sprang up, brought back to a realization of his own predicament by a clamor that surged up and around the jail. He heard the sound of many feet running up the hard-packed road, a mingled thunder of shouts and oaths. There is no sound on earth so terrifying as the roar of a mob bent on the destruction of a fellow man. Richards, though he was not the one menaced, turned white and cowered back on one of the bunks.

Elkins snorted, much as a wicked old bull might snort in defiance. His beard bristled, his eyes flamed. A stride took him to the window and he gripped one of the long, thick bars in both his hands. Outside, men surged around the building, gun butts hammered on the door. Strident yells cut the night. Pistols cracked, and lead thudded into the door, bringing a yell of agonized protest from Richards, who was trying to compress himself into as small a space as possible. Elkins yelled back in wordless defiance. He braced his feet; his muscles cracked and bulged; the veins in his temples swelled. An explosive grunt burst from him, as the bar gave way at one end, and was torn out bodily. Another heave, and it was free in his hands.

He wheeled to the door, now groaning and bending inward beneath a terrific assault – he knew the mobsters had a log that they were using as a battering ram.

The door splintered inward, and for an instant he glared into the convulsed faces of the lynchers that ringed the doorway in the light of flickering torches – gamblers, bar-men, gunmen – tinhorns, thieves, criminals – not an honest cowboy or hunter among them.

An instant all stood frozen as he faced them, an awesome figure, tousled, blood-stained, gigantic, with his blazing eyes and iron bludgeon – then with a roar he hurtled through the broken door and crashed into the thick of them.

Yells of fury rose deafeningly, mingled with howls of pain and fear. Torches waved wildly and went out. Guns cracked futilely. In that melee, no man could use a pistol effectively. And in the midst of them Grizzly Elkins ravened like a blood-mad bear among sheep. Swinging the heavy bar like a club, he felt skulls cave in and bones snap beneath its impact. Blood and brains spattered in his face; the taste of blood was in his mouth. Men swarmed and eddied about him in the darkness; bodies caromed against him, wild blows fanned him, or glanced from his arms and shoulders. A better aimed or more lucky stroke crashed full on his head, filling his eyes with sparks of fire, and his brain with momentary numbness. A blindly driven knife broke its point on his broad belt buckle, and the jagged shard tore his buckskin and gashed his side raggedly.

Hands clawed at him, booted feet stamped about him. He tore, slugged, and ripped his way through a seething, surging sea of gasping, screaming, cursing humanity, ruthlessly smashing out right and left. Driving like a crazed bull, he plunged through the bewildered throng, leaving a wake of writhing, bloody figures to mark his progress. A dimly seen hand jammed a gun-muzzle full into his belly, but even as he caught his breath, the hammer snapped on an empty chamber, and the next instant the iron bludgeon fell and the unknown gunman crumpled.

Over his fallen form Elkins leaped, stampeding for the darkness. Behind him the crowd surged and eddied, screaming, cursing, not yet aware that their prey had escaped them. Blows were still struck blindly, pistols banged in the dark.

Reaching the first of the houses that lined the straggling street, a short distance from the isolated jail, Elkins darted behind them, and keeping to the darkness, gained the hitching rack of the Silver Boot. No one was in sight; even the barmen and the loafers had gone to watch the lynching. His bay horse stood as he had left it.

"Blast 'em!" swore Elkins, swinging into the saddle, "reckon they'd of left my hoss here to starve, dern 'em!"

He wheeled his mount, then hesitated, remembering what Richards had said of Joel Rogers and his gunfanning deputy. He did not doubt its truth. The time could not be riper for a bank robbery. In it reposed thousands of dollars, belonging to the cattle buyers, ready for the herds that would soon be drifting up the Chisholm Trail. Elkins had no love for the buyers or the trail drivers; the animosity between the buffalo hunters and the cattle men was a living issue. But the marshal and his deputy had done him an injury, left him as a bait to the raving mob; and in Elkins' primitive code, a wrong unavenged was an unpaid debt. He reined his bay around and rode swiftly toward the bank.

He approached the building from the back. Like all things in that rude town on the western prairies, which had never seen steel rails until the past few months, it was crude – merely a plank structure, unpainted. Inside a wooden grille cut the building in half, and near the back wall stood a heavy iron safe which served as vault. No regular watchman was hired; guarding the bank was part of the duties of the marshal and his deputies.

Elkins halted behind the bank, threw the reins over his horse's head, and drew from its saddle-scabbard the heavy single shot Sharps .50 caliber buffalo rifle. He had no sixshooter, and his knife was gone. Silently as a panther he approached the back door, ordinarily kept bolted. Now it stood partly open, and nearby Elkins saw a couple of horses standing in the deep shadow of the building. The thieves intended a quick getaway. A light showed through the crack of the door. A small candle on the floor lighted the figures of Joel Rogers and Buck Chisom. They were bending over the safe, and as Elkins looked, he saw Rogers strike a match and put it to the end of a fuse.

"We got to jump quick now, Buck," the marshal hissed. "They's enough of that stuff to blow us clean out – "

At that instant Elkins plunged through the door, threw down his big rifle and roared, "Han's up, you all!"

Both men cursed, wheeled and came erect simultaneously. Rogers' hand lurched to his scabbard. The roar of the big Sharps was deafening; a gush of smoke filled the place, through which Elkins saw Rogers sway and fall, his head a gory travesty. At that range the heavy slug had torn off the whole top of his skull.

Through the swirling smoke Elkins saw Buck Chisom's hand dip like a flash and come up with a long sixshooter. Helplessly he stood, the empty rifle in his hands for the flashing second it took to transpire – then, even as the gunman's blue barrel leveled – behind Chisom belched a cataclysmic detonation, the whole building rocked drunkenly; there was a terrible, blinding flash, the rending crash of tortured metal, the air was full of singing fragments, and something hit Elkins with a paralyzing impact.

Half conscious, he found himself lying out in the dust behind the bank, with a heavy weight pinning him down. This weight was Buck Chisom, whether dead or unconscious, the buffalo hunter did not stop to determine. Groggily he realized that the fuse lit by Rogers just before he ordered the men to surrender had exploded the charge meant to blow the safe. And he realized that an explosion terrific enough to catapult Chisom against him and hurl them both through the door, would have been heard for miles. People would be coming on the run to investigate, and he did not care to be found there.

Thrusting aside the limp figure of the gunfighting deputy, the hunter staggered up and whistled shrilly. His horse had bolted with the others, but obedient to its long training, it came galloping back, its reins streaming. On the great plains of the buffalo, a man's life depended on his horse. Elkins swung into the saddle and headed south.

"Get along, Andrew Jackson; I don't crave no words with the people of this here town. I've saved their dern' bank, or anyways, the money in it, and I've done rid 'em of a couple of law-shootin' thieves, but I don't reckon I'll try to explain. Things moves too fast for me in town, anyway. It's us for the Nations, where nobody but Comanches yearns for our scalps."

The Last Ride
With Robert Enders Allen (Chandler Whipple)

CHAPTER I

The Laramies Ride

Five men were riding down the winding road that led to San Leon, and one was singing, in a flat, toneless monotone:

Early in the mornin' in the month of May,
Brady came down on the mornin' train,
Brady came down on the Shinin' Star,
And he shot Mr. Duncan in behind the bar!

"Shut up! Shut up!" It was the youngest of the riders who ripped out like that. A lanky, tow-headed kid, with a touch of pallor under his tan, and a rebellious smolder in his hot eyes.

The biggest man of the five grinned.

"Bucky's nervous," he jeered genially. "You don't want to be no derned bandit, do you, Bucky?"

The youngest glowered at him.

"That welt on yore jaw ought to answer that, Jim," he growled.

"You fit like a catamount," agreed Big Jim placidly. "I thought we'd never git you on yore cayuse and started for San Leon, without knockin' you in the head. 'Bout the only way you show yo're a Laramie, Bucky, is in the handlin' of yore fists."

"T'ain't no honor to be a Laramie," flared Bucky. "You and Luke and Tom and Hank has dragged the name through slime. For the last three years you been worse'n a pack of starvin' lobos – stealin' cattle and horses; robbin' folks – why, the country's near ruint. And now yo're headin' to San Leon to put on the final touch – robbin' the Cattlemen's

Bank, when you know dern well the help the ranchmen got from that bank's been all that kept 'em on their feet. Old Man Brown's stretched hisself nigh to the bustin' p'int to help folks."

He gulped and fought back tears that betrayed his extreme youth. His brothers grinned tolerantly. "It's the last time," he informed them bitterly. "You won't git me into no raid again!"

"It's the last time for all of us," said Big Jim, biting off a cud of tobacco. "We're through after this job. We'll live like honest men in Mexico."

"Serve you right if a posse caught us and hanged us all," said Bucky viciously.

"Not a chance." Big Jim's placidity was unruffled. "Nobody but us knows the trail that follows the secret waterholes acrost the desert. No posse'd dare to foller us. Once out of town and headed south for the border, and the devil hisself couldn't catch us."

"I wonder if anybody'll ever stumble onto our secret hide-out up in the Los Diablos Mountains," mused Hank.

"I doubt it. Too well hid. Like the desert trail, nobody but us knows them mountain trails. It shore served us well. Think of all the steers and horses we've hid there, and drove through the mountains to Mexico! And the times we've laid up there laughin' in our sleeves as the posse chased around a circle."

Bucky muttered something under his breath; he retained no fond memories of that hidden lair high up in the barren Diablos. Three years before, he had reluctantly followed his brothers into it from the little ranch in the foothills where Old Man Laramie and his wife had worn away their lives in futile work. The old life, when their parents lived and had held their wild sons in check, had been drab and hard, but had lacked the bitterness he had known when cooking and tending house for his brothers in that hidden den from which they had ravaged the countryside. Four good men gone bad – mighty bad.

San Leon lay as if slumbering in the desert heat as the five brothers rode up to the doors of the Cattlemen's Bank. None noted their coming; the Red Lode saloon, favorite rendezvous for the masculine element of San Leon, stood at the other end of the town, and out of sight around a slight bend in the street.

No words were passed; each man knew his part beforehand. The three elder Laramies slid lithely out of their saddles, throwing their reins to Bucky and Luke, the second youngest. They strode into the bank with a soft jingle of spurs and creak of leather, closing the door behind them.

Luke's face was impassive as an image's as he dragged leisurely on a cigarette, though his eyes gleamed between slitted lids. But Bucky sweated and shivered, twisting nervously in his saddle. By some twist of destiny, one son had inherited all the honesty that was his parents' to transmit. He had kept his hands clean. Now, in spite of himself, he was scarred with their brand.

He started convulsively as a gun crashed inside the bank; like an echo came another reverberation.

Luke's Colt was in his hand, and he snatched one foot clear of the stirrup, then feet pounded toward the street and the door burst open to emit the three outlaws. They carried bulging canvas sacks, and Hank's sleeve was crimson.

"Ride like hell!" grunted Big Jim, forking his roan. "Old Brown throwed down on Hank. Old fool! I had to salivate him permanent."

And like hell it was they rode, straight down the street toward the desert, yelling and firing as they went. They thundered past houses from which startled individuals peered bewilderedly, past stores where leathery-faced storekeepers were dragging forth blue-barreled scatter-guns. They swept through the futile rain of lead that poured from the excited and befuddled crowd in front of the Red Lode, and whirled on toward the desert that stretched south of San Leon.

But not quite to the desert. For as they rounded the last bend in the twisting street and came abreast of the last house in the village, they were confronted by the gray-bearded figure of old "Pop" Anders, sheriff of San Leon County. The old man's gnarled right hand rested on the ancient single-action Colt on his thigh; his left was lifted in a seemingly futile command to halt.

Big Jim cursed and sawed back on the reins, and the big roan slid to a halt.

"Git outa the way, Pop!" roared Big Jim. "We don't want to hurt you."

The old warrior's eyes blazed with righteous wrath.

"Robbed the bank this time, eh?" he said in cold fury, his eyes on the canvas sacks. "Likely spilt blood, too. Good thing Frank Laramie died before he could know what skunks his boys turned out to be. You ain't content to steal our stock till we're nigh bankrupt; you got to rob our bank and take what little money we got left for a new start. Why, you damned human sidewinders!" the old man shrieked, his control snapping suddenly. "Ain't there nothin' that's too low-down for you to do?"

Behind them sounded the pound of running feet and a scattering banging of guns. The crowd from the Red Lode was closing in.

"You've wasted our time long enough, old man!" roared Luke, jabbing in the spurs and sending his horse rearing and plunging toward the indomitable figure. "Git outa the way, or – "

The old single-action jumped free in the gnarled hand. Two shots roared together, and Luke's sombrero went skyrocketing from his head. But the old sheriff fell face forward in the dust with a bullet through his heart, and the Laramie gang swept on into the desert, feeding their dust to their hurriedly mounted and disheartened pursuers.

Only young Buck Laramie looked back, to see the door of the last house fly open, and a pig-tailed girl run out to the still figure in the street. It was the sheriff's daughter, Judy. She and Buck had gone to the same school in the old days before the Laramies hit the wolf-trail. Buck had always been her champion. Now she went down on her knees in the dust beside her father's body, seeking frantically for a spark of life where there was none.

A red film blazed before Buck Laramie's eyes as he turned his livid face toward his brothers.

"Hell," Luke was fretting, "I didn't aim to salivate him permanent. The old lobo woulda hung every one of us if he could of – but just the same I didn't aim to kill him."

Something snapped in Bucky's brain.

"You didn't aim to kill him!" he shrieked. "No, but you did! Yo're all a pack of low-down sidewinders just like he said! They ain't nothin' too dirty for you!" He brandished his clenched fists in the extremity of his passion. "You filthy scum!" he sobbed. "When I'm growed up I'm comin' back here and make up for ever' dollar you've stole, ever' life you've took. I'll do it if they hang me for tryin', s'help me!"

His brothers did not reply. They did not look at him. Big Jim hummed flatly and absently

Some say he shot him with a thirty-eight,
Some say he shot him with a forty-one;
But I say he shot him with a forty-four,
For I saw him as he lay on the barroom floor.

Bucky subsided, slumped in his saddle and rode dismally on. San Leon and the old life lay behind them all. Somewhere south of the hazy horizon the desert stretched into Mexico where lay their future destiny. And his destiny was inextricably interwoven with that of his brothers. He was an outlaw, too, now, and he must stay with the clan to the end of their last ride.

Some guiding angel must have caused Buck Laramie to lean forward to pat the head of his tired sorrel, for at that instant a bullet ripped through his hat-brim, instead of his head.

It came as a startling surprise, but his reaction was instant. He leaped from his horse and dove for the protection of a sand bank as a second bullet spurted dust at his heels. Then he was under cover, peering warily out, Colt in hand.

The tip of a white sombrero showed above a rim of sand, two hundred yards in front of him. Laramie blazed away at it, though knowing as he pulled the trigger that the range was too long and the target too small for six-gun accuracy. Nevertheless, the hat-top vanished.

"Takin' no chances," muttered Laramie. "Now who in hell is he? Here I am a good hour's ride from San Leon, and folks pottin' at me already. Looks bad for what I'm aimin' to do. Reckon it's somebody that knows me, after all these years?"

He could not believe it possible that anyone would recognize the lanky, half-grown boy of six years ago in the bronzed, range-hardened man who was returning to San Leon to keep the vow he had made as his clan rode southward with two dead men and a looted bank behind them.

The sun was burning hot, and the sand felt like an oven beneath Laramie. His canteen was slung to his saddle, and his horse was out of his reach, drooping under a scrubby mesquite. The other fellow would eventually work around to a point where his rifle would out-range Laramie's six-gun – or he might shoot the horse and leave Buck afoot in the desert.

The instant his attacker's next shot sang past his refuge, he was up and away in a stooping, weaving run to the next sand hill, to the right and slightly forward of his original position. He wanted to get in close quarters with his unknown enemy.

He wriggled from cover to cover, and sprinted in short dashes over narrow strips of open ground, taking advantage of every rock, cactus-bed, and sand-bank, with lead hissing and spitting at him all the way. The hidden gunman had guessed his purpose, and obviously had no desire for a close-range fight. He was slinging lead every time Laramie showed an inch of flesh, cloth, or leather, and Buck counted the shots. He was within striking distance of the sand rim when he believed the fellow's rifle was empty.

Springing recklessly to his feet he charged straight at his hidden enemy, his six-gun blazing. He had miscalculated about the rifle, for a bullet tore through the slack of his shirt. But then the Winchester was silent, and Laramie was raking the rim with such a barrage of lead that the gunman evidently dared not lift himself high enough to line the sights of a six-gun.

But a pistol was something that must be reckoned with, and as he spent his last bullet, Laramie dived behind a rise of sand and began desperately to jam cartridges into his empty gun. He had failed to cross the sand rim in that rush, but another try would gain it – unless hot lead cut him down on the way. Drum of hoofs reached his ears suddenly and glaring over his shelter he saw a pinto pony beyond the sand rim heading in the direction of San Leon. Its rider wore a white sombrero.

"Damn!" Laramie slammed the cylinder in place and sent a slug winging after the rapidly receding horseman. But he did not repeat the shot. The fellow was already out of range.

"Reckon the work was gettin' too close for him," he ruminated as he trudged back to his horse. "Hell, maybe he didn't want me to get a good look at him. But why? Nobody in these parts would be shy about shootin' at a Laramie, if they knew him as such. But who'd know I *was* a Laramie?"

He swung up into the saddle, then absently slapped his saddle bags and the faint clinking that resulted soothed him. Those bags were loaded with fifty thousand dollars in gold eagles, and every penny was meant for the people of San Leon.

"It'll help pay the debt the Laramies owe for the money the boys stole," he confided to the uninterested sorrel. "How I'm goin' to pay back for the men they killed is more'n I can figure out. But I'll try."

The money represented all he had accumulated from the sale of the Laramie stock and holdings in Mexico – holdings bought with money stolen from San Leon. It was his by right of inheritance, for he was the last of the Laramies. Big Jim, Tom, Hank, Luke, all had found trail's end in that lawless country south of the Border. As they had lived, so had they died, facing their killers, with smoking guns in their hands. They had tried to live straight in Mexico, but the wild blood was still there. Fate had dealt their hands, and Buck looked upon it all as a slate wiped clean, a record closed – with the exception of Luke's fate.

That memory vaguely troubled him now, as he rode toward San Leon to pay the debts his brothers contracted.

"Folks said Luke drew first," he muttered. "But it wasn't like him to pick a barroom fight. Funny the fellow that killed him cleared out so quick, if it was a fair fight."

He dismissed the old problem and reviewed the recent attack upon himself.

"If he knowed I was a Laramie, it might have been anybody. But how could he know? Joel Waters wouldn't talk."

No, Joel Waters wouldn't talk; and Joel Waters, old time friend of Laramie's father, long ago, and owner of the Boxed W ranch, was the only man who knew Buck Laramie was returning to San Leon.

"San Leon at last, cayuse," he murmured as he topped the last desert sand hill that sloped down to the town. "Last time I seen it was under circumstances most – what the devil!"

He started and stiffened as a rattle of gunfire burst on his ears. Battle in San Leon? He urged his weary steed down the hill. Two minutes later history was repeating itself.

CHAPTER II

Owl-Hoot Ghosts

As Buck Laramie galloped into San Leon, a sight met his eyes which jerked him back to a day six years gone. For tearing down the street came six wild riders, yelling and shooting. In the lead rode one, who, with his huge frame and careless ease, might have been Big Jim Laramie come back to life again. Behind them the crowd at the Red Lode, roused to befuddled life, was shooting just as wildly and ineffectively as on that other day when hot lead raked San Leon. There was but one man to bar the bandits' path – one man who stood, legs braced wide, guns drawn, in the roadway before the last house in San Leon. So old Pop Anders had stood, that other day, and there was something about this man to remind Laramie of the old sheriff, though he was much younger. In a flash of recognition Laramie knew him – Bob Anders, son of Luke's victim. He, too, wore a silver star.

This time Laramie did not stand helplessly by to see a sheriff slaughtered. With the swiftness born of six hard years below the border, he made his decision and acted. Gravel spurted as the sorrel threw back his head against the sawing bit and came to a sliding stop, and all in one motion Laramie was out of the saddle and on his feet beside the sheriff – half crouching and his six-gun cocked and pointed. This time two would meet the charge, not one.

Laramie saw that masks hid the faces of the riders as they swept down, and contempt stabbed through him. No Laramie ever wore a mask. His Colt vibrated as he thumbed the hammer. Beside him the young sheriff's guns were spitting smoke and lead.

The clumped group split apart at that blast. One man, who wore a Mexican sash instead of a belt, slumped in his saddle clawing for the horn. Another with his right arm flopping broken at his side was fighting his pain-maddened beast which had stopped a slug intended for its rider.

The big man who had led the charge grabbed the fellow with the sash as he started to slide limply from his saddle, and dragged him across his own bow. He bolted across the roadside and plunged into a dry wash. The others followed him. The man with the broken arm abandoned his own crazed mount and grabbed the reins of the riderless horse. Beasts and men, they slid over the rim and out of sight in a cloud of dust.

Anders yelled and started across the road on the run, but Laramie jerked him back.

'They're covered," he grunted, sending his sorrel galloping to a safe place with a slap on the rump. "We got to get out of sight, *pronto!*"

The sheriff's good judgment overcame his excitement then, and he wheeled and darted for the house, yelping: "Follow me, stranger!"

"Bullets whined after them from the gulch as the outlaws began their stand. The door opened inward before Anders's outstretched hand touched it, and he plunged through without checking his stride. Lead smacked the jambs and splinters flew as Laramie ducked after Anders. He collided with something soft and yielding that gasped and tumbled to the floor under the impact. Glaring wildly down Laramie found himself face to face with a vision of feminine loveliness that took his breath away, even in that instant. With a horrified gasp he plunged to his feet and lifted the girl after him. His all-embracing gaze took her in from tousled blond hair to whipcord breeches and high-heeled riding boots. She seemed too bewildered to speak.

"Sorry, miss," he stuttered. "I hope y'ain't hurt, I was – I was – " The smash of a window pane and the whine of a bullet cut short his floundering apologies. He snatched the girl out of line of the window and in an instant was crouching beside it himself, throwing lead across the road toward the smoke wisps.

Anders had barred the door and grabbed a Winchester from a rack on the wall.

"Duck into a back room, Judy," he ordered, kneeling at the window on the other side of the door. "Partner, I don't know you – " he punctuated his remarks with rapid shots, " – but I'm plenty grateful."

"Hilton's the name," mumbled Laramie, squinting along his six-gun barrel. "Friends call me Buck – damn!"

His bullet had harmlessly knocked dust on the gulch rim, and his pistol was empty. As he groped for cartridges he felt a Winchester pushed into his hand, and, startled, turned his head to stare full into the disturbingly beautiful face of Judy Anders. She had not obeyed her brother's order, but had taken a loaded rifle from the rack and brought it to Laramie, crossing the room on hands and knees to keep below the line of fire. Laramie almost forgot the men across the road as he stared into her deep clear eyes, now glowing with excitement. In dizzy fascination he admired the peach-bloom of her cheeks, her red, parted lips.

"Th – thank you, miss!" he stammered. "I needed that smoke-wagon right smart. And excuse my language. I didn't know you was still in the room – "

He ducked convulsively as a bullet ripped across the sill, throwing splinters like a buzz-saw. Shoving the Winchester out of the window he set to work. But his mind was still addled. And he was remembering a pitifully still figure sprawled in the dust of that very road, and a pig-tailed child on her knees beside it. The child was no longer a child, but a beautiful woman; and he – he was still a Laramie, and the brother of the man who killed her father.

"Judy!" There was passion in Bob Anders' voice. "Will you get out of here? There! Somebody's callin' at the back door. Go let 'em in. And stay back there, will you!"

This time she obeyed, and a few seconds later half a dozen pairs of boots clomped into the room, as some men from the Red Lode who had slipped around through a back route to the besieged cabin, entered.

"They was after the bank, of course," announced one of them. "They didn't git nothin' though, dern 'em. Ely Harrison started slingin' lead the minute he seen them masks comin' in the door. He didn't hit nobody, and by good luck the lead they throwed at him didn't connect, but they pulled out in a hurry. Harrison shore s'prised me. I never thought much of him before now, but he showed he was ready to fight for his money, and our'n."

"Same outfit, of course," grunted the sheriff, peering warily through the jagged shards of the splintered window-pane.

"Sure. The damn' Laramies again. Big Jim leadin', as usual."

Buck Laramie jumped convulsively, doubting the evidence of his ears. He twisted his head to stare at the men.

"You think it's the Laramies out there?" Buck's brain felt a bit numb. These mental jolts were coming too fast for him.

"Sure," grunted Anders. "Couldn't be nobody else. They was gone for six years – where, nobody knowed. But a few weeks back they showed up again and started their old deviltry, worse than ever."

"Killed his old man right out there in front of his house," grunted one of the men, selecting a rifle from the rack. The others were firing carefully through the windows, and the men in the gulch were replying in kind. The room was full of drifting smoke.

"But I've heard of 'em," Laramie protested. "They was all killed down in Old Mexico."

"Couldn't be," declared the sheriff, lining his sights. "These are the old gang all right. They've put up warnin's signed with the Laramie name. Even been heard singin' that old song they used to always sing about King Brady. Got a hide-out up in the Los Diablos, too, just like they did before. Same one, of course. I ain't managed to find it yet, but – " His voice was drowned in the roar of his .45-70.

"Well, I'll be a hammer-headed jackass," muttered Laramie under his breath. "Of all the – "

His profane meditations were broken into suddenly as one of the men bawled: "Shootin's slowed down over there! What you reckon it means?"

"Means they're aimin' to sneak out of that wash at the other end and hightail it into the desert," snapped Anders. "I ought to have thought about that before, but things has been happenin' so fast. You *hombres* stay here and keep smokin' the wash so they can't bolt out on this side. I'm goin' to circle around and block 'em from the desert."

"I'm with you," growled Laramie. "I want to see what's behind them masks."

They ducked out the back way and began to cut a wide circle which should bring them to the outer edge of the wash. It was difficult going and frequently they had to crawl on their hands and knees to take advantage of every clump of cactus and greasewood.

"Gettin' purty close," muttered Laramie, lifting his head. "What I'm wonderin' is, why ain't they already bolted for the desert? Nothin' to stop 'em."

"I figger they wanted to get me if they could, before they lit out," answered Anders. "I believe I been snoopin' around in the Diablos too close to suit 'em. Look out! They've seen us!"

Both men ducked as a steady line of flame spurts rimmed the edge of the wash. They flattened down behind their scanty cover and bullets cut up puffs of sand within inches of them.

"This is a pickle!" gritted Anders, vainly trying to locate a human head to shoot at. "If we back up, we back into sight, and if we go forward we'll get perforated."

"And if we stay here the result's the same," returned Laramie. "Greasewood don't stop lead. We got to summon reinforcements." And lifting his voice in a stentorian yell that carried far, he whooped: "Come on, boys! Rush 'em from that side! They can't shoot two ways at once!"

They could not see the cabin from where they lay, but a burst of shouts and shots told them his yell had been heard. Guns began to bang up the wash and Laramie and Anders recklessly leaped to their feet and rushed down the slight slope that led to the edge of the gulch, shooting as they went.

They might have been riddled before they had gone a dozen steps, but the outlaws had recognized the truth of Laramie's statement. They couldn't shoot two ways at once, and they feared to be trapped in the gulch with attackers on each side. A few hurried shots buzzed about the ears of the charging men, and then outlaws burst into view at the end of the wash farthest from town, mounted and spurring hard, the big leader still carrying a limp figure across his saddle.

Cursing fervently, the sheriff ran after them, blazing away with both six-shooters, and Laramie followed him. The fleeing men were shooting backward as they rode, and the roar of six-guns and Winchesters was deafening. One of the men reeled in his saddle and caught at his shoulder, dyed suddenly red.

Laramie's longer legs carried him past the sheriff, but he did not run far. As the outlaws pulled out of range, toward the desert and the Diablos, he slowed to a walk and began reloading his gun.

"Let's round up the men, Bob," he called. "We'll follow 'em. I know the water-holes – "

He stopped short with a gasp. Ten yards behind him Bob Anders, a crimson stream dyeing the side of his head, was sinking to the desert floor.

Laramie started back on a run just as the men from the cabin burst into view. In their lead rode a man on a pinto – and Buck Laramie knew that pinto.

"Git him!" howled the white-hatted rider. "He shot Bob Anders in the back! I seen him! *He's a Laramie!*"

Laramie stopped dead in his tracks. The accusation was like a bombshell exploding in his face. That was the man who had tried to drygulch him an hour or so before – same pinto, same white Stetson – but he was a total stranger to Laramie. How in the devil did *he* know of Buck's identity, and what was the reason for his enmity?

Laramie had no time to try to figure it out now. For the excited townsmen, too crazy with excitement to stop and think, seeing only their young sheriff stretched in his blood, and hearing the frantic accusation of one of their fellows, set up a roar and started blazing away at the man they believed was a murderer.

Out of the frying pan into the fire – the naked desert was behind him, and his horse was still standing behind the Anders cabin – with that mob between him and that cabin.

But any attempt at explanation would be fatal. Nobody would listen. Laramie saw a break for him in the fact that only his accuser was mounted, and probably didn't know he had a horse behind the cabin, and would try to reach it. The others were too excited to think anything. They were simply slinging lead, so befuddled with the mob impulse they were not even aiming – which is all that saved Laramie in the few seconds in which he stood bewildered and uncertain.

He ducked for the dry wash, running almost at a right angle with his attackers. The only man capable of intercepting him was White-Hat, who was bearing down on him, shooting from the saddle with a Winchester.

Laramie wheeled, and as he wheeled a bullet ripped through his Stetson and stirred his hair in passing. White-Hat was determined to have his life, he thought, as his own six-gun spat flame. White-Hat flinched sidewise and dropped his rifle. Laramie took the last few yards in his stride and dived out of sight in the wash.

He saw White-Hat spurring out of range too energetically to be badly wounded, and he believed his bullet had merely knocked the gun out of the fellow's hands. The others had spread out and were coming down the slope at a run, burning powder as they came.

Laramie did not want to kill any of those men. They were law-abiding citizens acting under a misapprehension. So he emptied his gun over their heads and was gratified to see them precipitately take to cover. Then without pausing to reload, he ducked low and ran for the opposite end of the wash, which ran on an angle that would bring him near the cabin.

The men who had halted their charge broke cover and came on again, unaware of his flight, and hoping to get him while his gun was empty. They supposed he intended making a stand at their end of the wash.

By the time they had discovered their mistake and were pumping lead down the gully, Laramie was out at the other end and racing across the road toward the cabin. He ducked around the corner with lead nipping at his ears and vaulted into the saddle of the sorrel – and cursed his luck as Judy Anders ran out the rear door, her eyes wide with fright.

"What's happened?" she cried. "Where's Bob?"

"No time to pow-wow," panted Laramie. "Bob's been hurt. Don't know how bad. I got to ride, because – "

He was interrupted by shouts from the other side of the cabin.

"Look out, Judy!" one man yelled. "Stay under cover! He shot Bob in the back!"

Reacting to the shout without conscious thought, Judy sprang to seize his reins.

Laramie jerked the sorrel aside and evaded her grasp. "It's a lie!" he yelled with heat. "I ain't got time to explain. Hope Bob ain't hurt bad."

Then he was away, crouching low in his saddle with bullets pinging past him; it seemed he'd been hearing lead whistle all day; he was getting sick of that particular noise. He looked back once. Behind the cabin Judy Anders was bending over a limp form that the men had carried in from the desert. Now she was down on her knees in the dust beside that limp body, searching for a spark of life.

Laramie cursed sickly. History was indeed repeating itself that day in San Leon.

For a time Laramie rode eastward, skirting the desert, and glad of a breathing spell. The sorrel had profited by its rest behind the Anders' cabin, and was fairly fresh. Laramie had a good lead on the pursuers he knew would be hot on his trail as soon as they could get to their horses, but he headed east instead of north, the direction in which lay his real goal – the Boxed W ranch. He did not expect to be able to throw them off his scent entirely, but he did hope to confuse them and gain a little time.

It was imperative that he see his one friend in San Leon County – Joel

Waters. Maybe Joel Waters could unriddle some of the tangle. Who were the men masquerading as Laramies?

He had been forging eastward for perhaps an hour when, looking backward from a steep rise, he saw a column of riders approaching some two miles away through a cloud of dust that meant haste. That would be the posse following his trail – and that meant that the sheriff was dead or still senseless.

Laramie wheeled down the slope on the other side and headed north, hunting hard ground that would not betray a pony's hoof-print.

CHAPTER III

Trigger Debt

Dusk was fast settling when he rode into the yard of the Boxed W. He was glad of the darkness, for he had feared that some of Waters' punchers might have been in San Leon that day, and seen him. But he rode up to the porch without having encountered anyone, and saw the man he was hunting sitting there, pulling at a corn-cob pipe.

Waters rose and came forward with his hand outstretched as Laramie swung from the saddle.

"You've growed," said the old man. "I'd never knowed you if I hadn't been expectin' you. You don't favor yore brothers none. Look a lot like yore dad did at yore age, though. You've pushed yore cayuse hard," he added, with a piercing glance at the sweat-plastered flanks of the sorrel.

"Yeah." There was bitter humor in Laramie's reply. "I just got through shootin' me a sheriff."

Waters jerked the pipe from his mouth. He looked stunned.

"What?"

"All you got to do is ask the upright citizens of San Leon that's trailin' me like a lobo wolf," returned Laramie with a mirthless grin. And tersely and concisely he told the old rancher what had happened in San Leon and on the desert.

Waters listened in silence, puffing smoke slowly.

"It's bad," he muttered, when Laramie had finished. "Damned bad –

well, about all I can do right now is to feed you. Put yore cayuse in the corral."

"Rather hide him near the house, if I could," said Laramie. "That posse is liable to hit my sign and trail me here any time. I want to be ready to ride."

"Blacksmith shop behind the house," grunted Waters. "Come on."

Laramie followed the old man to the shop, leading the sorrel. While he was removing the bridle and loosening the cinch, Waters brought hay and filled an old log-trough. When Laramie followed him back to the house, the younger man carried the saddle bags over his arm. Their gentle clink no longer soothed him; too many obstacles to distributing them were rising in his path.

"I just finished eatin' before you come," grunted Waters. "Plenty left."

"Hop Sing still cookin' for you?"

"Yeah."

"Ain't you ever goin' to get married?" chaffed Laramie.

"Shore," grunted the old man, chewing his pipe stem. "I just got to have time to decide what type of woman'd make me the best wife."

Laramie grinned. Waters was well past sixty, and had been giving that reply to chaffing about his matrimonial prospects as far back as Buck could remember.

Hop Sing remembered Laramie and greeted him warmly. The old Chinaman had cooked for Waters for many years. Laramie could trust him as far as he could trust Waters himself.

The old man sat gripping his cold pipe between his teeth as Laramie disposed of a steak, eggs, beans and potatoes and tamped it down with a man-sized chunk of apple pie.

"Yo're follerin' blind trails," he said slowly. "Mebbe I can help you."

"Maybe. Do you have any idea who the gent on the showy pinto might be?"

"Not many such paints in these parts. What'd the man look like?"

"Well, I didn't get a close range look at him, of course. From what I saw he looked to be short, thick-set, and he wore a short beard and a mustache so big it plumb ambushed his pan."

147

"Why, hell!" snorted Waters. "That's bound to be Mart Rawley! He rides a flashy pinto, and he's got the biggest set of whiskers in San Leon."

"Who's he?"

"Owns the Red Lode. Come here about six months ago and bought it off of old Charlie Ross."

"Well, that don't help none," growled Laramie, finishing his coffee and reaching for the makings. He paused suddenly, lighted match lifted. "Say, did this hombre ride up from Mexico?"

"He come in from the east. Of course, he could have come from Mexico, at that; he'd have circled the desert. Nobody but you Laramies ever hit straight across it. He ain't said he come from Mexico original; and he ain't said he ain't."

Laramie meditated in silence, and then asked: "What about this new gang that calls theirselves Laramies?"

"Plain coyotes," snarled the old man. "Us San Leon folks was just gittin' on our feet again after the wreck yore brothers made out of us, when this outfit hit the country. They've robbed and stole and looted till most of us are right back where we was six years ago. They've done more damage in a few weeks than yore brothers did in three years.

"I ain't been so bad hit as some, because I've got the toughest, straightest-shootin' crew of punchers in the county; but most of the cowmen around San Leon are mortgaged to the hilt, and stand to lose their outfits if they git looted any more. Ely Harrison – he's president of the bank now, since yore brothers killed Old Man Brown – Ely's been good about takin' mortgages and handin' out money, but he cain't go on doin' it forever."

"Does everybody figure they're the Laramies?"

"Why not? They send letters to the cowmen sayin' they'll wipe out their whole outfit if they don't deliver 'em so many hundred head of beef stock, and they sign them letters with the Laramie name. They're hidin' out in the Diablos like you all did; they's always the same number in the gang; and they can make a get-away through the desert, which nobody but the Laramies ever did.

"Of course, they wear masks, which the Laramies never did, but that's a minor item; customs change, so to speak. I'd have believed they was the genuine Laramies myself, only for a couple of reasons – one bein' you'd wrote me in your letter that you was the only Laramie left. You didn't give no details." The old man's voice was questioning.

"Man's reputation always follows him," grunted Buck. "A barroom gladiator got Jim. Hank got that gunfighter the next week, but was shot up so hisself he died. Tom joined the revolutionaries and the *rurales* cornered him in a dry wash. Took 'em ten hours and three dead men to get him. Luke – " He hesitated and scowled slightly.

"Luke was killed in a barroom brawl in Santa Maria, by a two-gun fighter called Killer Rawlins. They said Luke reached first, but Rawlins beat him to it. I don't know. Rawlins skipped that night. I've always believed that Luke got a dirty deal, some way. He was the best one of the boys. If I ever meet Rawlins – " Involuntarily his hand moved toward the worn butt of his Colt. Then he shrugged his shoulders, and said: "You said there was two reasons why you knowed these coyotes wasn't Laramies; what's t'other'n?"

"They work different," growled the old man. "Yore brothers was bad, but white men, just the same. They killed prompt, but they killed clean. These rats ain't content with just stealin' our stock. They burn down ranch houses and pizen water-holes like a tribe of cussed Apaches. Jim Bannerman of the Lazy B didn't leave 'em two hundred of steers in a draw like they demanded in one of them letters. A couple of days later we found nothin' but smokin' ruins at the Lazy B, with Jim's body burned up inside and all his punchers dead or shot up."

Buck's face was gray beneath its tan. His fist knotted on the gunbutt.

"The devil!" he choked, in a voice little above a whisper. "And the Laramies are gettin' the blame! I thought my brothers dragged the name low – but these devils are haulin' it right down into hell. Joel Waters, listen to me! I come back here to pay back money my brothers stole from San Leon; I'm stayin' to pay a bigger debt. The desert's big, but it ain't big enough for a Laramie and the rats that wears his name. If I don't wipe that gang of rattlers off the earth they can have my name, because I won't need it no more."

"The Laramies owe a debt to San Leon," agreed old Joel, filling his pipe. "Cleanin' out that snake-den is the best way I know of payin' it."

Some time later Laramie rose at last and ground his cigarette butt under his heel.

"We've about talked out our wampum. From all I can see, everything points to this Mart Rawley bein' connected with the gang, somehow. He must have been the one that shot Bob Anders. He was ahead of the other fellows; they couldn't see him for a rise in the ground. They wouldn't have seen him shoot Anders. He might have been aimin' at me; or he might have just wanted Anders out of the way.

"Anyway, I'm headin' for the Diablos tonight. I know yo're willin' to hide me here, but you can help me more if nobody suspects yo're helpin' me, yet.

"I'm leavin' these saddle-bags with you. If I don't come back out of the Diablos, you'll know what to do with the money. So long."

They shook hands, and old Joel said: "So long, Buck. I'll take care of the money. If they git crowdin' you too close, duck back here. And if you need help in the hills, try to git word back to me. I can still draw a bead with a Winchester, and I've got a gang of hard-ridin' waddies to back my play."

"I ain't forgettin', Joel."

Laramie turned toward the door. Absorbed in his thoughts, he forgot for an instant that he was a hunted man, and relaxed his vigilance. As he stepped out onto the veranda he did not stop to think that he was thrown into bold relief by the light behind him.

As his boot-heel hit the porch yellow flame lanced the darkness and he heard the whine of a bullet that fanned him as it passed. He leapt back, slamming the door, wheeled, and halted in dismay to see Joel Waters sinking to the door. The old man, standing directly behind Laramie, had stopped the slug meant for his guest.

With his heart in his mouth Laramie dropped beside his friend. "Where'd it get you, Joel?" he choked.

"Low down, through the leg," grunted Waters, already sitting up and whipping his bandanna around his leg for a tourniquet. "Nothin' to worry about. You better git goin'."

Laramie took the bandanna and began knotting it tightly, ignoring a hail from without.

"Come out with yore hands up, Laramie!" a rough voice shouted. "You can't fight a whole posse. We got you cornered!"

"Beat it, Buck!" snapped Waters, pulling away his friend's hands. "They must have left their horses and sneaked up on foot. Sneak out the back way before they surround the house, fork yore cayuse and burn the breeze. That's Mart Rawley talkin', and I reckon it was him that shot. He aims to git you before you have time to ask questions or answer any. Even if you went out there with yore hands up, he'd kill you. Git goin', dern you!"

"All right!" Laramie jumped up as Hop Sing came out of the kitchen, almond eyes wide and a cleaver in his hand. "Tell 'em I held a gun on you and made you feed me. T'ain't time for 'em to know we're friends, not yet."

The next instant he was gliding into the back part of the house and slipping through a window into the outer darkness. He heard somebody swearing at Rawley for firing before the rest had taken up their positions, and he heard other voices and noises that indicated the posse was scattering out to surround the house.

He ran for the blacksmith shop, and, groping in the dark, tightened the cinch on the sorrel and slipped on the bridle. He worked fast, but before Laramie could lead the horse outside he heard a jingle of spurs and the sound of footsteps.

Laramie swung into the saddle, ducked his head low to avoid the lintel of the door, and struck in the spurs. The sorrel hurtled through the door like a thunderbolt. A startled yell rang out, a man jumped frantically out of the way, tripped over his spurs and fell flat on his back, discharging his Winchester in the general direction of the Big Dipper. The sorrel and its rider went past him like a thundering shadow to be swallowed in the darkness. Wild yells answered the passionate blasphemy of the fallen man, and guns spurted red as their owners fired blindly after the receding hoofbeats. But before the possemen could untangle themselves from their bewilderment and find their mounts, the echoes of flying hoofs had died away and night hid the fugitive's trail. Buck Laramie was far away, riding to the Diablos.

CHAPTER IV

Sidewinder Ramrod

Midnight found Laramie deep in the Diablos. He halted, tethered the sorrel, and spread his blankets at the foot of a low cliff. Night was not the time to venture further along the rock-strewn paths and treacherous precipices of the Diablos. He slept fitfully, his slumber disturbed by dreams of a girl kneeling beside a wounded man.

With the first gray of dawn he was riding familiar trails that would lead him to the cabin in the hidden canyon that he knew so well, the old hideout of his gang, where he believed he would find the new band which was terrorizing the country. The hideout had but one entrance – a rock-walled tunnel. How the fake gang could have learned of the place Laramie could not know.

The hideout was in a great bowl, on all sides of which rose walls of jumbled rock, impassable to a horseman. It was possible to climb the cliffs near the entrance of the tunnel, which, if the fake gang were following the customs of the real Laramies, would be guarded.

Half an hour after sunrise found him making his way on foot toward the canyon entrance. His horse he had left concealed among the rocks at a safe distance, and lariat in hand he crept along behind rocks and scrub growth toward the old river bed that formed the canyon. Presently, gazing through the underbrush that masked his approach, he saw, half hidden by a rock, a man in a tattered brown shirt who sat at the mouth of the canyon entrance, his hat pulled low over his eyes, and a Winchester across his knees.

Evidently a belief in the security of the hideout made the sentry careless. Laramie had the drop on him; but to use his advantage incurred the possibility of a shot that would warn those inside the canyon and spoil his plans. So he retreated to a point where he would not be directly in the line of the guard's vision, if the man roused, and began working his way to a spot a few hundred yards to the left, where, as he knew of old, he could climb to the rim of the canyon.

In a few moments he had clambered up to a point from which he could glimpse the booted feet of the guard sticking from behind the rock. Laramie's flesh crawled at the thought of being picked off with a rifle bullet like a fly off a wall, if the guard looked his way.

But the boots did not move, he dislodged no stones large enough to make an alarming noise, and presently, panting and sweating, he heaved himself over the crest of the rim and lay on his belly gazing down into the canyon below him.

As he looked down into the bowl which had once been like a prison to him, bitterness of memory was mingled with a brief, sick longing for his dead brothers; after all, they were his brothers, and had been kind to him in their rough way.

The cabin below him had in no wise changed in the passing of the years. Smoke was pouring out of the chimney, and in the corral at the back, horses were milling about in an attempt to escape the ropes of two men who were seeking saddle mounts for the day.

Shaking out his lariat, Laramie crept along the canyon rim until he reached a spot where a stunted tree clung to the very edge. To this tree he made fast the rope, knotted it at intervals for handholds, and threw the other end over the cliff. It hung fifteen feet short of the bottom, but that was near enough.

As he went down it, with a knee hooked about the thin strand to take some of the strain off his hands, he grinned thinly as he remembered how he had used this descent long ago when he wanted to dodge Big Jim who was waiting at the entrance to give him a licking. His face hardened.

"Wish he was here with me now. We'd mop up these rats by ourselves."

Dangling at the end of the rope at arm's length he dropped, narrowly missing a heap of jagged rocks, and lit in the sand on his feet, going to his all-fours from the impact.

Bending low, sometimes on hands and knees, he headed circuitously for the cabin, keeping it between himself and the men in the corral. To his own wonderment he reached the cabin without hearing any alarm sounded. Maybe the occupants, if there were any in the canyon beside the men he had seen, had gone out the back way to the corral. He hoped so.

Cautiously he raised his head over a window sill and peered inside. He could see no one in the big room that constituted the front part of the cabin. Behind this room, he knew, were a bunkroom and kitchen, and the back door was in the kitchen. There might be men in those backrooms; but he was willing to take the chance. He wanted to get in there and find a place where he could hide and spy.

The door was not locked; he pushed it open gently and stepped inside with a cat-like tread, Colt poked ahead of him.

"Stick 'em up!" Before he could complete the convulsive movement prompted by these unexpected words, he felt the barrel of a six-gun jammed hard against his backbone. He froze – opened his fingers and let his gun crash to the floor. There was nothing else for it.

The door to the bunkroom swung open and two men came out with drawn guns and triumphant leers on their unshaven faces. A third emerged from the kitchen. All were strangers to Laramie. He ventured to twist his head to look at his captor, and saw a big-boned, powerful man with a scarred face, grinning exultantly.

"That was easy," rumbled one of the others, a tall, heavily built ruffian whose figure looked somehow familiar. Laramie eyed him closely.

"So yo're 'Big Jim'," he said.

The big man scowled, but Scarface laughed.

"Yeah! With a mask on nobody can tell the difference. You ain't so slick, for a Laramie. I seen you sneakin' through the bresh ten minutes ago, and we been watchin' you ever since. I seen you aimed to come in and make yoreself to home, so I app'inted myself a welcome committee of one – behind the door. You couldn't see me from the winder. Hey, you Joe!" he raised his voice pompously. "Gimme a piece of rope. Mister Laramie's goin' to stay with us for a spell."

Scarface shoved the bound Laramie into an old Morris chair that stood near the kitchen door. Laramie remembered that chair well; the brothers had brought it with them when they left their ranch home in the foothills.

He was trying to catch a nebulous memory that had something to do with that chair, when steps sounded in the bunkroom and "Jim" entered, accompanied by two others. One was an ordinary sort of criminal, slouchy, brutal faced and unshaven. The other was of an entirely different type. He was elderly and pale-faced, but that face was bleak and flinty. He did not seem range-bred like the others. Save for his high-heeled riding boots, he was dressed in town clothes, though the well-worn butt of a .45 jutted from a holster at his thigh.

Scarface hooked thumbs in belt and rocked back on his heels with an air of huge satisfaction. His big voice boomed in the cabin.

"Mister Harrison, I takes pleasure in makin' you acquainted with Mister Buck Laramie, the last of a family of honest horse-thieves, what's rode all the way from Mexico just to horn in on our play. And Mister Laramie, since you ain't long for this weary world, I'm likewise honored to inter-juice you to Mister Ely Harrison, high man of our outfit and president of the Cattlemen's Bank of San Leon!"

Scarface had an eye for dramatics in his crude way. He bowed grotesquely, sweeping the floor with his Stetson and grinning gleefully at the astounded glare with which his prisoner greeted his introduction.

Harrison was less pleased.

"That tongue of yours wags too loose, Braxton," he snarled.

Scarface lapsed into injured silence, and Laramie found his tongue.

"Ely Harrison!" he said slowly. "Head of the gang – the pieces of this puzzle's beginnin' to fit. So you generously helps out the ranchers yore coyotes ruins – not forgettin' to grab a healthy mortgage while doin' it. And you was a hero and shot it out with the terrible bandits when they come for yore bank; only nobody gets hurt on either side."

Unconsciously he leaned further back in the Morris chair – and a lightning jolt of memory hit him just behind the ear. He stifled an involuntary grunt, and his fingers, hidden by his body from the eyes of his captors, began fumbling between the cushions of the chair.

He had remembered his jackknife, a beautiful implement, and the pride of his boyhood, stolen from him and hidden by his brother Tom, for a joke, a few days before they started for Mexico. Tom had forgotten all about it, and Buck had been too proud to beg him for it. But Tom had remembered, months later, in Mexico; had bought Buck a duplicate of the first knife, and told him that he had hidden the original between the cushions of the old Morris chair.

Laramie's heart almost choked him. It seemed too good to be true, this ace in the hole. Yet there was no reason to suppose anybody had found and removed the knife. His doubts were set at rest as his fingers encountered a smooth, hard object. It was not until that moment that he realized that Ely Harrison was speaking to him. He gathered his wits and concentrated on the man's rasping voice, while his hidden fingers fumbled with the knife, trying to open it.

" – damned unhealthy for a man to try to block my game," Harrison was saying harshly. "Why didn't you mind your own business?"

"How do you know I come here just to spoil yore game?" murmured Laramie absently.

"Then why did you come here?" Harrison's gaze was clouded with a sort of ferocious uncertainty. "Just how much did you know about our outfit before today? Did you know I was the leader of the gang?"

"Guess," suggested Laramie. The knife was open at last. He jammed the handle deep between the cushions and the chair-back, wedging it securely. The tendons along his wrists ached. It had been hard work, manipulating the knife with his cramped fingers, able to move just so far. His steady voice did not change in tone as he worked. "I was kind of ashamed of my name till I seen how much lower a man could go than my brothers ever went. They was hard men, but they was white, at least. Usin' my name to torture and murder behind my back plumb upsets me. Maybe I didn't come to San Leon just to spoil yore game; but maybe I decided to spoil it after I seen some of the hands you dealt."

"You'll spoil our game!" Harrison sneered. "Fat chance you've got of spoiling anybody's game. But you've got only yourself to blame. In another month I'd have owned every ranch within thirty miles of San Leon."

"So that's the idea, huh?" murmured Laramie, leaning forward to expectorate, and dragging his wrists hard across the knife-edge. He felt one strand part, and as he leaned back and repeated the movement, another gave way and the edge bit into his flesh. If he could sever one more strand, he would make his break.

"Just how much did you know about our outfit before you came here?" demanded Harrison again, his persistence betraying his apprehension on that point. "How much did you tell Joel Waters?"

"None of yore derned business," Laramie snapped, his nerves getting on edge with the approach of the crisis.

"You'd better talk," snarled Harrison. "I've got men here who'd think nothing of shoving your feet in the fire to roast. Not that it matters. We're all set anyway. Got ready when we heard you'd ridden in. It just means we move tonight instead of a month later. But if you can prove to me that you haven't told anybody that I'm the real leader of the gang – well, we can carry out our original plans, and you'll save your life. We might even let you join the outfit."

"Join the – do you see any snake-scales on me?" flared Laramie, fiercely expanding his arm muscles. Another strand parted and the cords fell away from his wrists.

"Why you – " Murderous passion burst all bounds as Harrison lurched forward, his fist lifted. And Laramie shot from the chair like a steel spring released, catching them all flat-footed, paralyzed by the unexpectedness of the move.

One hand ripped Harrison's Colt from its scabbard. The other knotted into a fist that smashed hard in the banker's face and knocked him headlong into the midst of the men who stood behind him.

"Reach for the ceilin', you yellow-bellied polecats!" snarled Laramie, livid with fury and savage purpose; his cocked .45 menaced them all. "Reach! I'm dealin' this hand!"

CHAPTER V

First Blood

For an instant the scene held – then Scarface made a convulsive movement to duck behind the chair.

"Back up!" yelped Laramie, swinging his gun directly on him, and backing toward the door. But the tall outlaw who had impersonated Big Jim had recovered from the daze of his surprise. Even as Laramie's pistol muzzle moved in its short arc toward Braxton, the tall one's had flashed like the stroke of a snake's head to his gun. It cleared leather just as Laramie's .45 banged.

Laramie felt hot wind fan his cheek, but the tall outlaw was sagging back and down, dying on his feet and grimly pulling trigger as he went. A hot welt burned across Laramie's left thigh, and another slug ripped up splinters near his feet. Harrison had dived behind the Morris chair and Laramie's vengeful bullet smashed into the wall behind him.

It all happened so quickly that the others had barely unleathered their irons as he reached the threshold. He fired at Braxton, saw the scar-faced one drop his gun with a howl, saw "Big Jim" sprawl on the floor, done with impersonation and outlawry forever, and then he was slamming the door from the outside, wincing involuntarily as bullets smashed through the panels and whined about him.

His long legs flung him across the kitchen and he catapulted through the outer door. He collided head-on with the two men he had seen in the corral. All three went into the dust in a heap. One, even in falling, jammed his six-gun into Buck's belly and pulled trigger without stopping to see who it was. The hammer clicked on an empty chamber. Laramie, flesh crawling with the narrowness of his escape, crashed his gun barrel down on the other's head and sprang up, kicking free of the second man whom he recognized as Mart Rawley, he of the white Stetson and flashy pinto.

Rawley's gun had been knocked out of his hand in the collision. With a yelp the drygulcher scuttled around the corner of the cabin on hands and knees. Laramie did not stop for him. He had seen the one thing that might save him – a horse, saddled and bridled, tied to the corral fence.

He heard the furious stamp of boots behind him. Harrison's voice screamed commands as his enemies streamed out of the house and started pouring lead after him. Then a dozen long leaps carried him spraddle-legged to the startled mustang. With one movement he had ripped loose the tether and swung aboard. Over his shoulder he saw the men spreading out to head him off in the dash they expected him to make toward the head of the canyon. Then he wrenched the cayuse around and spurred through the corral gate which the outlaws had left half open.

In an instant Laramie was the center of a milling whirlpool of maddened horses as he yelled, fired in the air, and lashed them with the quirt hanging from the horn.

"Close the gate!" shrieked Harrison. One of the men ran to obey the command, but as he did, the snorting beasts came thundering through. Only a frantic leap backward saved him from being trampled to death under the maddened horses.

His companions yelped and ran for the protection of the cabin, firing blindly into the dust cloud that rose as the herd pounded past. Then Laramie was dashing through the scattering horde and drawing out of six-gun range, while his enemies howled like wolves behind him.

"Git along, cayuse!" yelled Laramie, drunk with the exhilaration of the hazard. "We done better'n I hoped! They got to round up their broncs before they hit my trail, and that's goin' to take time!"

Thought of the guard waiting at the canyon entrance did not sober him.

"Only way out is through the tunnel. Maybe he thinks the shootin' was just a family affair, and won't drill a gent ridin' from *inside* the canyon. Anyway, cayuse, we takes it on the run."

A Winchester banged from the mouth of the tunnel and the bullet cut the air past his ear.

"Pull up!" yelled a voice, but there was hesitancy in the tone. Doubtless the first shot had been a warning, and the sentry was puzzled. Laramie gave no heed; he ducked low and jammed in the spurs. He could see the rifle now, the blue muzzle resting on a boulder, and the ragged crown of a hat behind it. Even as he saw it, flame spurted from the blue ring. Laramie's horse stumbled in its headlong stride as lead ploughed through the fleshy part of its shoulder. That stumble saved Laramie's life for it lurched him out of the path of the next slug. His own six-gun roared.

The bullet smashed on the rock beside the rifle muzzle. Dazed and half-blinded by splinters of stone, the outlaw reeled back into the open, and fired without aim. The Winchester flamed almost in Laramie's face. Then his answering slug knocked the guard down as if he had been hit with a hammer. The Winchester flew out of his hands as he rolled on the ground. Laramie jerked the half-frantic mustang back on its haunches and dived out of the saddle to grab for the rifle.

"Damn!" It had struck the sharp edge of a rock as it fell. The lock was bent and the weapon useless. He cast it aside disgustedly, wheeled toward his horse, and then halted to stare down at the man he had shot. The fellow had hauled himself to a half-sitting position. His face was pallid, and blood oozed from a round hole in his shirt bosom. He was dying. Suddenly revulsion shook Laramie as he saw his victim was hardly more than a boy. His berserk excitement faded.

"Laramie!" gasped the youth. "You must be Buck Laramie!"

"Yeah," admitted Laramie. "Anything – anything I can do?"

The boy grinned in spite of his pain.

"Thought so. Nobody but a Laramie could ride so reckless and shoot so straight. Seems funny – bein' plugged by a Laramie after worshippin' 'em most of my life."

"What?" ejaculated Laramie.

"I always wanted to be like 'em," gasped the youth. "Nobody could ride and shoot and fight like them. That's why I j'ined up with these polecats. They said they was startin' up a gang that was to be just like the Laramies. But they ain't; they're a passel of dirty coyotes. Once I started in with 'em, though, I had to stick."

Laramie said nothing. It was appalling to think that a young life had been so warped, and at last destroyed, by the evil example of his brothers.

"You better go, and raise a posse if yo're aimin' to git them rats," the boy said. "They's goin' to be hell to pay tonight."

"How's that?" questioned Laramie, remembering Harrison's remarks about something planned for the night.

"You got 'em scared," murmured the boy. "Harrison's scared you might have told Joel Waters he was boss-man of the gang. That's why he come here last night. They'd aimed to keep stealin' for another month. Old Harrison woulda had most all the ranches around here by then, foreclosin' mortgages.

"When Mart Rawley failed to git you, old Harrison sent out word for the boys to git together here today. They figgered on huntin' you down, if the posse from San Leon hadn't already got you. If they found out you didn't know nothin' and hadn't told nobody nothin', they just aimed to kill you and go on like they'd planned from the first. But if they didn't git you, or found you'd talked, they aimed to make their big cleanup tonight, and then ride."

"What's that?" asked Laramie.

"They're goin' down tonight and burn Joel Waters' ranch buildings, and the sheriff's, and some of the other big ones. They'll drive all the cattle off to Mexico over the old Laramie trail. Then old Harrison'll divide the loot and the gang will scatter. If he finds you ain't spilled the works about him bein' the top man, he'll stay on in San Leon. That was his idee from the start – ruin the ranchers, buy up their outfits cheap and be king of San Leon."

"How many men's he got?"

"'Tween twenty-five and thirty," panted the youth. He was going fast. He choked, and a trickle of blood began at the corner of his mouth. "I

ought not to be squealin', maybe; t'ain't the Laramie way. But I wouldn't
to nobody but a Laramie. You didn't see near all of 'em. Two died on the
way back from San Leon, yesterday. They left 'em out in the desert. The
rest ain't got back from drivin' cattle to Mexico, but they'll be on hand by
noon today."

Laramie was silent, reckoning on the force he could put in the field.
Waters' punchers were all he could be sure of – six or seven men at the
most, not counting the wounded Waters. The odds were stacking up.

"Got a smoke?" the youth asked weakly. Laramie rolled a cigarette,
placed it between the blue lips and held a match. Looking back down the
canyon, Laramie saw men saddling mounts. Precious time was passing;
but he was loath to leave the dying lad.

"Git goin'," muttered the boy uneasily. "You got a tough job ahead of
you – honest men and thieves both agen you – but I'm bettin' on the
Laramies – the real ones – " He seemed wandering in his mind. He began
to sing in a ghastly whisper the song that Laramie could never hear
without a shudder.

When Brady died they planted him deep,
Put a bottle of whisky at his head and feet,
Folded his arms across his breast,
And said: "King Brady's gone to his rest!"

The crimson trickle became a sudden spurt; the youth's voice trailed
into silence. The cigarette slipped from his lips. He went limp and lay
still, through forever with the wolf-trail.

Laramie rose heavily and groped for his horse, trembling in the shade
of the rock. He tore the blanket rolled behind the saddle and covered the
still figure. Another debt to be marked up against the Laramies.

He swung aboard and galloped through the tunnel to where his own
horse was waiting – a faster mount than the cayuse he was riding. As he
shifted mounts he heard shouts behind him, knew that his pursuers had
halted at the body, knew the halt would be brief.

Without looking back, he hit the straightest trail he knew that led
toward the ranch of Joel Waters.

CHAPTER VI

"String Him Up!"

It was nearly noon when Laramie pulled up his sweating bronc at the porch of the Boxed W ranchhouse. There were no punchers in sight. Hop Sing opened the door.

"Where's Waters?" rapped out Laramie.

"Solly!" Hop Sing beamed on the younger man. "He gone to town to see doctluh and get leg fixed. Slim Jones dlive him in in buckbload. He be back tonight."

"Damn!" groaned Laramie. He saw his plan being knocked into a cocked hat. That plan had been to lead a band of men straight to the outlaws' hideout and bottle them up in their stronghold before they could scatter out over the range in their planned raid. The Boxed W punchers would not follow a stranger without their boss's orders, and only Waters could convince the bellicose citizens of San Leon that Laramie was on the level. Time was flying and every minute counted.

There was only one risky course left open. He swung on his tiring horse and reined away on the road for San Leon.

He met no one on the road, for which he was thankful. When he drew up on the outskirts of the town his horse was drawing laboring breaths. He knew the animal would be useless in case he had to dust out of town with a posse on his heels.

Laramie knew of a back alley that led to the doctor's office, and by which he hoped to make it unseen. He dismounted and headed down the alley, leading the gelding by the reins.

He sighted the little adobe shack where the town's one physician lived and worked, when a jingle of spurs behind him caused him to jerk his head in time to see a man passing the end of the alley. It was Mart Rawley, and Laramie ducked behind his horse, cursing his luck. Rawley must have been prowling around the town, expecting him, and watching for him. His yell instantly split the lazy silence.

"Laramie!" howled Rawley. "Laramie's back! Hey Bill, Lon! Joe! Everybody! Laramie's in town again! This way!"

Laramie forked his mustang and spurred it into a lumbering run for the main street. Lead was singing down the alley as Laramie burst into Main Street, and saw Joel Waters sitting in a chair on the porch of the doctor's shack.

"Get all the men you can rustle and head for the Diablos!" he yelled at the astonished ranchman. "I'll leave a trail for you to follow. I found the gang at the old hide-out – and they're comin' out tonight for a big cleanup!"

Then he was off again, his clattering hoofs drowning Waters' voice as he shouted after the rider. Men were yelling and .45s banging. Ahorse and afoot they came at him, shooting as they ran. The dull, terrifying mob-roar rose, pierced with yells of: "String him up!" "He shot Bob Anders in the back!"

His way to open country was blocked, and his horse was exhausted. With a snarl Laramie wheeled and rode to the right for a narrow alley that did not seem to be blocked. It led between two buildings to a side-street, and was not wide enough for a horse to pass through. Maybe that was the reason it had been left unguarded. Laramie reached it, threw himself from his saddle and dived into the narrow mouth.

For an instant his mount, standing with drooping head in the opening, masked his master from bullets, though Laramie had not intended sacrificing his horse for his own hide. Laramie had run half the length of the alley before someone reached out gingerly, grasped the reins and jerked the horse away. Laramie half turned, without pausing in his run, and fired high and harmlessly back down the alley. The whistle of lead kept the alley clear until he bolted out the other end.

There, blocking his way in the side-street, stood a figure beside a black racing horse. Laramie's gun came up – then he stopped short, mouth open in amazement. It was Judy Anders who stood beside the black horse.

Before he could speak she sprang forward and thrust the reins in his hand.

"Take him and go! He's fast!"

"Why – what?" Laramie sputtered, his thinking processes in a muddle.

The mere sight of Judy Anders had that effect upon him. Hope flamed in him. Did her helping him mean – then reason returned and he took the gift the gods had given him without stopping for question. As he grabbed the horn and swung up he managed: "I sure thank you kindly, miss – "

"Don't thank me," Judy Anders retorted curtly; her color was high, but her red lips were sulky. "You're a Laramie and ought to be hung, but you fought beside Bob yesterday when he needed help. The Anderses pay their debts. Will you go?"

A nervous stamp of her little foot emphasized the request. The advice was good. Three of the townsmen appeared with lifted guns around a corner of a nearby building. They hesitated as they saw the girl near him, but began maneuvering for a clear shot at him without endangering her.

"See Joel Waters, at the doctor' office!" he yelled to her, and was off for the open country, riding like an Apache, and not at all sure that she understood him. Men howled and guns crashed behind him, and maddened citizens ran cursing for their mounts, too crazy-mad to notice the girl who shrieked vainly at them, unheeding her waving arms.

"Stop! Stop! Wait! Listen to me!" Deaf to her cries they streamed past her, ahorse and afoot, and burst out into the open. The mounted men spurred their horses savagely after the figure that was swiftly dwindling in the distance.

Judy dashed aside an angry tear and declaimed her opinion of men in general, and the citizens of San Leon in particular, in terms more expressive than lady-like.

"What's the matter?" It was Joel Waters, limping out of the alley, supported by the doctor. The old man seemed stunned by the rapidity of events. "What in the devil's all this mean? Where's Buck?"

She pointed. "There he goes, with all the idiots in San Leon after him."

"Not all the idiots," Waters corrected "I'm still here. Dern it, the boy must be crazy, comin' here. I yelled myself deef at them fools, but they wouldn't listen – "

"They wouldn't listen to me, either!" cried Judy despairingly. "But they won't catch him – ever, on that black of mine. And maybe when they come limping back, they'll be cooled down enough to hear the truth. If they won't listen to me, they will to Bob!"

"To Bob?" exclaimed the doctor. "Has he come out of his daze? I was just getting ready to come over and see him again, when Joel came in for his leg to be dressed."

"Bob came out of it just a little while ago. He told me it wasn't Laramie who shot him. He's still groggy and uncertain as to just what happened. He doesn't know who it was who shot him, but he knows it wasn't Buck Laramie. The last thing he remembers was Laramie running some little distance ahead of him. The bullet came from behind. He thinks a stray slug from the men behind them hit him."

"I don't believe it was a stray," grunted Waters, his eyes beginning to glitter. "I got a dern good idee who shot Bob. I'm goin' to talk – "

"Better not bother Bob too much right now," interrupted the doctor. "I'll go over there – "

"Better go in a hurry if you want to catch Bob at home," the girl said grimly. "He was pulling on his boots and yelling for our cook to bring him his gun-belt when I left!"

"What? Why, he mustn't get up yet!" The doctor transferred Waters' arm from his shoulder to that of the girl, and hurried away toward the house where Bob Anders was supposed to be convalescing.

"Why did Buck come back here?" Judy wailed to Waters.

"From what he hollered at me as he lighted past, I reckon he's found somethin' up in the Diablos. He come for help. Probably went to my ranch first, and findin' me not there, risked his neck comin' on here. Said send men after him, to foller signs he'd leave. I relayed that there information on to Slim Jones, my foreman. Doc lent Slim a horse, and Slim's high-tailin' it for the Boxed W right now to round up my waddies and hit the trail. As soon as these San Leon snake-hunters has ruint their cayuses chasin' that black streak of light you give Buck, they'll be pullin' back into town. This time, I bet they'll listen."

"I'm glad he didn't shoot Bob," she murmured. "But why – why did he come back here in the first place?"

"He come to pay a debt he figgered he owed in behalf of his no-account brothers. His saddle bags is full of gold he aims to give back to the citizens of this here ongrateful town. What's the matter?"

For his fair companion had uttered a startled exclamation.

"N-nothing, only – only I didn't know it was that way! Then Buck never robbed or stole, like his brothers?"

"Course he didn't!" snapped the old man irascibly. "Think I'd kept on bein' his friend all his life, if he had? Buck ain't to blame for what his brothers did. He's straight and he's always been straight."

"But he was with them, when – when – "

"I know." Waters' voice was gentler. "But he didn't shoot yore dad. That was Luke. And Buck was with 'em only because they made him. He wasn't nothin' but a kid."

She did not reply and old Waters, noting the soft, new light glowing in her eyes, the faint, wistful smile that curved her lips, wisely said nothing.

In the meantime the subject of their discussion was proving the worth of the sleek piece of horseflesh under him. He grinned as he saw the distance between him and his pursuers widen, thrilled to the marvel of the horse between his knees as any good horseman would. In half an hour he could no longer see the men who hunted him.

He pulled the black to an easier, swinging gait that would eat up the miles for long hours on end, and headed for the Diablos. But the desperate move he was making was not dominating his thoughts. He was mulling over a new puzzle; the problem of why Judy Anders had come to his aid. Considering her parting words, she didn't have much use for him. If Bob had survived his wound, and asserted Laramie's innocence, why were the citizens so hot for his blood? If not – would Judy Anders willingly aid a man she thought shot her brother? He thrilled at the memory of her, standing there with the horse that saved his life. If only he weren't a Laramie – How beautiful she was.

CHAPTER VII

Bottled Up

A good three hours before sundown Laramie was in the foothills of the Diablos. In another hour, by dint of reckless riding over trails that were inches in width, which even he ordinarily would have shunned, he came in sight of the entrance to the hide-out. He had left signs farther down the trail to indicate, not the way he had come, but the best way for Waters' punchers to follow him.

Once more he dismounted some distance from the tunnel and stole cautiously forward. There would be a new sentry at the entrance, and Laramie's first job must be to dispose of him silently.

He was halfway to the tunnel when he glimpsed the guard, sitting several yards from the mouth, near a clump of bushes. It was the scarfaced fellow Harrison had called Braxton, and he seemed wide-awake.

Falling back on Indian tactics, acquired from the Yaquis in Mexico, Laramie began a stealthy, and necessarily slow, advance on the guard, swinging in a circle that would bring him behind the man. He crept up to within a dozen feet.

Braxton was getting restless. He shifted his position, craning his neck as he stared suspiciously about him. Laramie believed he had heard, but not yet located, faint sounds made in Laramie's progress. In another instant he would turn his head and stare full at the bushes which afforded the attacker scanty cover.

Gathering a handful of pebbles, Laramie rose stealthily to his knees and threw them over the guard's head. They hit with a loud clatter some yards beyond the man. Braxton started to his feet with an oath. He glared in the direction of the sound with his Winchester half lifted, neck craned. At the same instant Laramie leaped for him with his six-gun raised like a club.

Scarface wheeled, and his eyes flared in amazement. He jerked the rifle around, but Laramie struck it aside with his left hand, and brought down his pistol barrel crushingly on the man's head. Braxton went to his knees like a felled ox; slumped full-length and lay still.

Laramie ripped off belts and neckerchief from the senseless figure; bound and gagged his captive securely. He appropriated his pistol, rifle and spare cartridges, then dragged him away from the tunnel mouth and shoved him in among a cluster of rocks and bushes, effectually concealing him from the casual glance.

"Won the first trick, by thunder!" grunted Laramie. "And now for the next deal!"

The success of that deal depended on whether or not all the outlaws of Harrison's band were in the hide-out. Mart Rawley was probably outside, yet; maybe still back in San Leon. But Laramie knew he must take the chance that all the other outlaws *were* inside.

He glanced up to a ledge overhanging the tunnel mouth, where stood precariously balanced the huge boulder that had given him his idea for bottling up the canyon.

"Cork for my bottle!" muttered Laramie. "All I need now's a lever."

A broken tree limb sufficed for that, and a few moments later he had climbed to the ledge and was at work on the boulder. A moment's panic assailed him as he feared its base was too deeply imbedded for him to move it. But under his fierce efforts he felt the great mass give at last. A few minutes more of back-breaking effort, another heave that made the veins bulge on his temples – and the boulder started toppling, crashed over the ledge and thundered down into the tunnel entrance. It jammed there, almost filling the space.

He swarmed down the wall and began wedging smaller rocks and brush in the apertures between the boulder and the tunnel sides. The only way his enemies could get out now was by climbing the canyon walls, a feat he considered practically impossible, or by laboriously picking out the stones he had jammed in place, and squeezing a way through a hole between the boulder and the tunnel wall. And neither method would be a cinch, with a resolute cowpuncher slinging lead at everything that moved.

Laramie estimated that his whole task had taken about half an hour. Slinging Braxton's rifle over his shoulder he clambered up the cliffs. At the spot on the canyon rim where he had spied upon the hide-out that morning, he forted himself by the simple procedure of crouching behind a fair-sized rock, with the Winchester and pistols handy at his elbows. He had scarcely taken his position when he saw a mob of riders breaking away from the corral behind the cabin. As he had figured, the gang was getting away to an early start for its activities of the night.

He counted twenty-five of them; and the very sun that glinted on polished gun hammers and silver conchas seemed to reflect violence and evil deeds.

"Four hundred yards," muttered Laramie, squinting along the blue rifle barrel. "Three fifty – three hundred – now I opens the ball!"

At the ping of the shot dust spurted in front of the horses' hoofs, and the riders scattered like quail, with startled yells.

"Drop them shootin' irons and hi'st yore hands!" roared Laramie. "Tunnel's corked up and you can't get out!"

His answer came in a vengeful hail of bullets, spattering along the canyon rim for yards in either direction. He had not expected any other reply. His shout had been more for rhetorical effect than anything else. But there was nothing theatrical about his second shot, which knocked a man out of his saddle. The fellow never moved after he hit the ground.

The outlaws converged toward the tunnel entrance, firing as they rode, aiming at Laramie's aerie, which they had finally located. Laramie replied in kind. A mustang smitten by a slug meant for his rider rolled to the ground and broke his rider's leg under him. A squat raider howled profanely as a slug ploughed through his breast muscles.

The half a dozen men in the lead jammed into the tunnel and found that Laramie had informed them truthfully. Their yells reached a crescendo of fury. The others slid from their horses and took cover behind the rocks that littered the edges of the canyon, dragging the wounded men with them.

From a rush and a dash the fight settled to a slow, deadly grind, with nobody taking any rash chances. Having located his tiny fort, they concentrated their fire on the spot of the rim he occupied. A storm of bullets drove him to cover behind the breastworks, and became exceedingly irksome.

He had not seen either Rawley or Harrison. Rawley, he hoped, was still in San Leon, but the absence of Harrison worried him. Had he, too, gone to San Leon? If so, there was every chance that he might get clean away, even if his band was wiped out. There was another chance, that he or Rawley, or both of them, might return to the hide-out and attack him from the rear. He cursed himself for not having divulged the true identity of the gang's leader to Judy Anders; but he always seemed addled when talking to her.

The ammunition supply of the outlaws seemed incxhaustible. He knew at least six men were in the tunnel, and he heard them cursing and shouting, their voices muffled. He found himself confronted by a quandary that seemed to admit of no solution. If he did not discourage them, they would be breaking through the blocked tunnel and potting him from the rear. But to effect this discouragement meant leaving his point of vantage, and giving the men below a chance to climb the canyon wall. He did not believe this could be done, but he did not know what additions to the fortress had been made by the new occupants. They might have chiselled out handholds at some point on the wall. Well, he'd have to look at the tunnel.

"Six-guns against rifles, if this keeps up much longer," he muttered, working his way over the ledges. "Cartridges most gone. Why the devil don't Joel's men show up? I can't keep these hombres hemmed up for ever – damn!"

His arm thrust his six-gun out as he yelped. Stones and brush had been worked out at one place in the tunnel-mouth, and the head and shoulders of a man appeared. At the crash of Laramie's Colt the fellow howled and vanished. Laramie crouched, glaring; they would try it again, soon. If he was not there to give them lead-argument, the whole gang would be squeezing out of the tunnel in no time.

He could not get back to the rim, and leave the tunnel unguarded; yet there was always the possibility of somebody climbing the canyon wall.

Had he but known it, his fears were justified. For while he crouched on the ledge, glaring down at the tunnel-mouth, down in the canyon a man was wriggling toward a certain point of the cliff, where his keen eyes had discerned something dangling. He had discovered Laramie's rope, hanging from the stunted tree on the rim. Cautiously he lifted himself out of the tall grass, ready to duck back in an instant, then as no shot came from the canyon rim, he scuttled like a rabbit toward the wall.

Kicking off his boots and slinging his rifle on his back, he began swarming, ape-like, up the almost sheer wall. His outstretched arm grasped the lower end of the rope, just as the others in the canyon saw what he was doing, and opened a furious fire on the rim to cover his activities. The outlaw on the rope swore luridly, and went up with amazing agility, his flesh crawling with the momentary expectation of a bullet in his back.

The renewed firing had just the effect on Laramie that the climber had feared it would have – it drew him back to his breastwork. It was not until he was crouching behind his breastwork that it occurred to him that the volleys might have been intended to draw him away from the tunnel. So he spared only a limited glance over the rocks, for the bullets were winging so close that he dared not lift his head high. He did not see the man on the rope cover the last few feet in a scrambling rush, and haul himself over the rim, unslinging his rifle as he did so.

Laramie turned and headed back for the ledge whence he could see the opening. And as he did so, he brought himself into full view of the outlaw who was standing upright on the rim, by the stunted tree.

The whip-like crack of his Winchester reached Laramie an instant after he felt a numbing impact in his left shoulder. The shock of the blow knocked him off his feet, and his head hit hard against a rock. Even as he fell he heard the crashing of brush down the trail, and his last, hopeless thought was that Rawley and Harrison were returning. Then the impact of his head against the rock knocked all thought into a stunned blank.

CHAPTER VIII

Boot-hill Talk

An outlaw came scrambling out of the tunnel with desperate haste, followed by another and another. One crouched, rifle in hand, glaring up at the wall, while the others tore away the smaller stones, and aided by those inside, rolled the boulder out of the entrance. Three men ran out of the tunnel and joined them.

Their firing roused Buck Laramie. He blinked and glared, then oriented himself. He saw five riders sweeping toward the tunnel, and six outlaws who had rushed out while he was unconscious, falling back into it for shelter; and he recognized the leader of the newcomers as Slim Jones, Joel Waters' foreman. The old man had not failed him.

"Take cover, you fools!" Laramie yelled wildly, unheard in the din.

But the reckless punchers came straight on and ran into a blast of lead poured from the tunnel mouth into which the outlaws had disappeared. One of the waddies saved his life by a leap from the saddle as his horse fell with a bullet through its brain, and another man threw wide his arms and pitched on his head, dead before he hit the pebbles.

Then only did Slim and his wild crew swerve their horses out of line and fall back to cover. Laramie remembered the slug that had felled him, and turned to scan the canyon rim. He saw the man by the stunted tree, then; the fellow was helping one of his companions up the same route he had taken, and evidently thought that his shot had settled Laramie, as he was making no effort at concealment. Laramie lifted his rifle and pulled the trigger – and the hammer fell with an empty click. He had no more rifle cartridges. Below him the punchers were futilely firing at the tunnel entrance, and the outlaws within were wisely holding their fire until they could see something to shoot at.

Laramie crawled along a few feet to put himself out of range of the rifleman on the rim, then shouted: "Slim! Swing wide of that trail and come up here with yore men!"

He was understood, for presently Slim and the three surviving punchers came crawling over the tangle of rocks, having necessarily abandoned their horses.

" 'Bout time you was gettin' here," grunted Laramie. "Gimme some .30-30s."

A handful of cartridges were shoved into his eager fingers.

"We come as soon as we could," said Slim. "Had to ride to the ranch to round up these snake-hunters."

"Where's Waters?"

"I left him in San Leon, cussin' a blue streak because he couldn't get nobody to listen to him. Folks got no more sense'n cattle; just as easy to stampede and as hard to git millin' once they bust loose."

"What about Bob Anders?"

"Doctor said he was just creased; was just fixin' to go over there when me and Joel come into town and he had to wait and dress Joel's leg. Hadn't come to hisself, last time the doc was there."

Laramie breathed a sigh of relief. At least Bob Anders was going to live, even if he hadn't been able to name the man who shot him. Soon Judy would know the truth. Laramie snapped into action.

"Unless Waters sends us more men, we're licked. Tunnel's cleared and men climbin' the cliff."

"You're shot!" Jones pointed to Laramie's shirt shoulder, soaked with blood.

"Forget it!" snapped Laramie. "Well, gimme that bandanna – " and while he knotted it into a crude bandage, he talked rapidly. "Three of you *hombres* stay here and watch that tunnel. Don't let nobody out, d'you hear? Me and Slim are goin' to circle around and argy with the gents climbin' the cliffs. Come on, Slim."

It was rough climbing, and Laramie's shoulder burned like fire, with a dull throbbing that told him the lead was pressing near a bone. But he set his teeth and crawled over the rough rocks, keeping out of sight of the men in the canyon below, until they had reached a point beyond his tiny fort on the rim, and that much closer to the stunted tree.

They had kept below the crest and had not been sighted by the outlaws on the rim, who had been engrossed in knotting a second rope, brought up by the second man, to the end of the lariat tied to the tree. This had been dropped down the wall again, and now another outlaw was hanging to the rope and being drawn straight up the cliff like a water bucket by his two friends above.

Slim and Laramie fired almost simultaneously. Slim's bullet burned the fingers of the man clinging to the lariat. He howled and let go the rope and fell fifteen feet to the canyon floor. Laramie winged one of the men on the cliff, but it did not affect his speed as he raced after his companion in a flight for cover. Bullets whizzed up from the canyon as the men below spotted Laramie and his companion. They ducked back, but relentlessly piled lead after the men fleeing along the rim of the cliff.

These worthies made no attempt to make a stand. They knew the lone defender had received reinforcements and they were not stopping to learn in what force. Laramie and Slim caught fleeting glimpses of the fugitives as they headed out through the hills.

"Let 'em go," grunted Laramie. "Be no more trouble from that quarter, and I bet them rannies won't try to climb that rope no more. Come on; I hear guns talkin' back at the tunnel."

Laramie and his companion reached the punchers on the ledge in time to see three horsemen streaking it down the trail, with lead humming after them. Three more figures lay sprawled about the mouth of the tunnel.

"They busted out on horseback," grunted one of the men, kneeling and aiming after the fleeing men. "Come so fast we couldn't stop 'em all – uh."

His shot punctuated his remarks, and one of the fleeing horsemen swayed in his saddle. One of the others seemed to be wounded, as the three ducked into the trees and out of sight.

"Three more hit the trail," grunted Slim.

"Not them," predicted Laramie. "They was bound to see us – know they ain't but five of us. They won't go far; they'll be sneakin' back to pot us in the back when their pards start bustin' out again."

"No racket in the tunnel now."

"They're layin' low for a spell. Too damn risky now. They didn't have but six horses in the tunnel. They got to catch more and bring'em to the tunnel before they can make the rush.

"They'll wait till dark, and then we can't stop 'em from gettin' their cayuses into the tunnel. We can't stop 'em from tearin' out at this end, neither, unless we got more men. Slim, climb back up on the rim and lay down behind them rocks I stacked up. Watch that rope so nobody climbs it; we got to cut that, soon's it gets dark. And don't let no horses be brought into the tunnel, if you can help it."

Slim crawled away, and a few moments later his rifle began banging, and he yelled wrathfully: "They're already at it!"

"Listen!" ejaculated Laramie suddenly.

Down the trail, out of sight among the trees sounded a thundering of hoofs, yells and shots.

The shots ceased, then after a pause, the hoofs swept on, and a crowd of men burst into view.

"Yippee!" whooped one of the punchers bounding into the air and swinging his hat. "Reinforcements, b'golly! It's a regular army!"

"Looks like all San Leon was there!" bellowed another. "Hey, boys, don't git in line with that tunnel mouth! Spread out along the trail – who's them three fellers they got tied to their saddles?"

"The three snakes that broke loose from the tunnel!" yelped the third cowboy. "They scooped 'em in as they come! Looks like everybody's there. There's Charlie Ross, and Jim Watkins, the mayor, and Lon Evans, Mart Rawley's bartender – reckon he didn't know his boss was a crook – and by golly, look who's leadin' 'em!"

"*Bob Anders!*" ejaculated Laramie, staring at the pale-faced, but erect figure who, with bandaged head, rode ahead of the thirty or forty men who came clattering up the trail and swung wide through the brush to avoid the grim tunnel mouth. Anders saw him and waved his hand, and a deep yell of approbation rose from the men behind the sheriff. Laramie sighed deeply. A few hours ago these same men wanted to hang him.

Rifles were spitting from the tunnel, and the riders swung from their horses and began to take up positions on each side of the trail, as Anders took in the situation at a glance and snapped his orders. Rifles began to speak in answer to the shots of the outlaws. Laramie came clambering down the cliff to grasp Anders' outstretched hand.

"I came to just about the time you hit town today, Laramie," he said. "Was just tellin' Judy it couldn't been you that shot me, when all that hell busted loose and Judy run to help you out if she could. Time I could get my clothes on, and out-argy the doctor, and get on the streets, you was gone with these addle-heads chasin' you. We had to wait till they give up the chase and come back, and then me and Judy and Joel Waters lit into 'em. Time we got through talkin' they was plumb whipped down and achin' to take a hand in yore game."

"I owe you all a lot, especially your sister. Where's Rawley?" Laramie asked.

"We thought he was with us when we lit out after you," the sheriff answered. "But when we started back we missed him."

"Look out!" yelled Slim on the rim above them, pumping lead frantically. "They're rushin' for the tunnel on horses! Blame it, why ain't somebody up here with me? I can't stop 'em all – "

Evidently the gang inside the canyon had been whipped to desperation by the arrival of the reinforcements, for they came thundering through the tunnel laying down a barrage of lead as they came. It was sheer madness. They ran full into a blast of lead that piled screaming horses and writhing men in a red shambles. The survivors staggered back into the tunnel.

Struck by a sudden thought, Laramie groped among the bushes and hauled out the guard, Braxton, still bound and gagged. The fellow was conscious and glared balefully at his captor. Laramie tore the gag off, and demanded: "Where's Harrison and Rawley?"

"Rawley rode for San Leon after you got away from us this mornin'," growled Braxton sullenly. "Harrison's gone, got scared and pulled out. I dunno where he went."

"Yo're lyin'," accused Laramie.

"What'd you ast me for, if you know so much?" sneered Braxton, and lapsed in stubborn, hill-country silence, which Laramie knew nothing would break, so long as the man chose to hold his tongue.

"You mean Harrison's in on this, Buck?" the sheriff exclaimed. "Joel told me about Rawley."

"In on it!" Laramie laughed grimly. "Harrison is the kingpin, and Rawley is his chief side-winder. I ain't seen neither Harrison nor Rawley since I got here. Be just like them rats to double-cross their own men, and run off with the loot they've already got.

"But we still got this nest to clean out, and here's my idea. Them that's still alive in the canyon are denned up in or near the tunnel. Nobody nigh the cabin. If four or five of us can hole up in there, we'll have 'em from both sides. We'll tie some lariats together, and some of us will go down the walls and get in the cabin. We'll scatter men along the rim to see none of 'em climb out, and we'll leave plenty men here to hold the tunnel if they try that again – which they will, as soon as it begins to get dark, if we don't scuttle 'em first."

"You oughta been a general, cowboy. Me and Slim and a couple of my Bar X boys'll go for the cabin. You better stay here; yore shoulder ain't fit for tight-rope work and such."

"She's my hand," growled Laramie. "I started dealin' her and I aim to set in till the last pot's raked in."

"Yo're the dealer," acquiesced Anders. "Let's go."

Ten minutes later found the party of five clustered on the canyon rim. The sun had not yet set beyond the peaks, but the canyon below was in shadow. The spot Laramie had chosen for descent was some distance beyond the stunted tree. The rim there was higher, the wall even more precipitous. It had the advantage, however, of an outjut of rock that would partially serve to mask the descent of a man on a lariat from the view of the men lurking about the head of the canyon.

If anyone saw the descent of the five invaders, there was no sign to show they had been discovered. Man after man they slid down the dangling rope and crouched at the foot, Winchesters ready. Laramie came last, clinging with one hand and gritting his teeth against the pain of his wounded shoulder. Then began the advance on the cabin.

That slow, tortuous crawl cross the canyon floor seemed endless. Laramie counted the seconds, fearful that they would be seen, fearful that night would shut down before they were forted. The western rim of the canyon seemed crested with golden fire, contrasting with the blue shadows floating beneath it. He sighed gustily as they reached their goal, with still enough light for their purpose.

The cabin doors were shut, the windows closely shuttered.

"Let's go!" Anders had one hand on the door, drawn Colt in the other.

"Wait," grunted Laramie. "I stuck my head into a loop here once already today. You all stay here while I take a *pasear* around to the back and look things over from that side. Don't go in till you hear me holler."

Then Laramie was sneaking around the cabin, Indian-fashion, gun in hand. He was little more than half the distance to the back when he was paralyzed to hear a voice inside the cabin call out: "All clear!"

Before he could move or shout a warning, he heard Anders answer: "Comin', Buck!" Then the front door slammed, and there was the sound of a sliding bolt, a yell of dismay from the Bar X men. With sick fury Laramie realized that somebody lurking inside the cabin had heard him giving his instructions and imitated his voice to trick the sheriff into entering. Confirmation came instantly, in a familiar voice – the voice of Ely Harrison!

"Now we can make terms, gentlemen!" shouted the banker, his voice rasping with ferocious exultation. "We've got your sheriff in a wolf-trap with hot lead teeth! You can give us road-belts to Mexico, or he'll be deader than hell in three minutes!"

CHAPTER IX

Killer Unmasked

Laramie was charging for the rear of the house before the triumphant shout ended. Anders would never agree to buying freedom for that gang to save his own life; and Laramie knew that whatever truce might be agreed upon, Harrison would never let the sheriff live.

The same thought motivated the savage attack of Slim Jones and the Bar X men on the front door; but that door happened to be of unusual strength. Nothing short of a log battering ram could smash it. The rear door was of ordinary thin paneling.

Bracing his good right shoulder to the shock, Laramie rammed his full charging weight against the rear door. It crashed inward and he catapulted into the room gun-first.

He had a fleeting glimpse of a swarthy Mexican wheeling from the doorway that led into the main room, and then he ducked and jerked the trigger as a knife sang past his head. The roar of the .45 shook the narrow room and the knife thrower hit the planks and lay twitching.

With a lunging stride Laramie was through the door, into the main room. He caught a glimpse of men standing momentarily frozen, glaring up from their work of tying Bob Anders to a chair – Ely Harrison, another Mexican, and Mart Rawley.

For an infinitesimal tick of time the scene held – then blurred with gunsmoke as the .45s roared death across the narrow confines. Hot lead was a coal of hell burning its way through the flesh of Laramie's already wounded shoulder. Bob Anders lurched out of the chair, rolling clumsily toward the wall. The room was a mad welter of sound and smoke in the last light of gathering dusk.

Laramie half rolled behind the partial cover of a cast iron stove, drawing his second gun. The Mexican fled to the bunk-room, howling, his broken left arm flopping. Mart Rawley backed after him at a stumbling run, shooting as he went; crouched inside the door he glared, awaiting his chance. But Harrison, already badly wounded, had gone berserk.

Disdaining cover, or touched with madness, he came storming across the room, shooting as he came, spattering blood at every step. His eyes flamed through the drifting fog of smoke like those of a rabid wolf.

Laramie raised himself to his full height and faced him. Searing lead whined past his ear, jerked at his shirt, stung his thigh; but his own gun was burning red and Harrison was swaying in his stride like a bull which feels the matador's steel. His last shot flamed almost in Laramie's face, and then at close range a bullet split the cold heart of the devil of San Leon, and the greed and ambitions of Ely Harrison were over.

Laramie, with one loaded cartridge left in his last gun, leaned back against the wall out of range of the bunkroom.

"Come on out, Rawley," he called. "Harrison's dead. Yore game's played out."

The hidden gunman spat like an infuriated cat.

"No, my game ain't played out!" he yelled in a voice edged with blood-madness. "Not till I've wiped you out, you mangy stray. But before I kill you, I want you to know that you ain't the first Laramie I've sent to hell! I'd of thought you'd knowed me, in spite of these whiskers. I'm Rawlins, you fool! Killer Rawlins, that plugged yore horse-thief brother Luke in Santa Maria!"

"Rawlins!" snarled Laramie, suddenly white. "No wonder you knowed me!"

"Yes, Rawlins!" howled the gunman. "I'm the one that made friends with Luke Laramie and got him drunk till he told me all about this hide-out and the trails across the desert. Then I picked a fight with Luke when he was too drunk to stand, and killed him to keep his mouth shut! And what you goin' to do about it?"

"I'm going to kill you, you hell-buzzard!" gritted Laramie, lurching away from the wall as Rawlins came frothing through the door, with both guns blazing. Laramie fired once from the hip. His last bullet ripped through Killer Rawlins' warped brain. Laramie looked down on him as he died, with his spurred heels drumming a death-march on the floor.

Frantic feet behind him brought him around to see a livid, swarthy face convulsed with fear and hate, a brown arm lifting a razor-edged knife. He had forgotten the Mexican. He threw up his empty pistol to guard the downward sweep of the sharp blade, then once more the blast of a six-gun shook the room. Jose Martinez of Chihuahua lifted one scream of invocation and blasphemy at some forgotten Aztec god, as his soul went speeding its way to hell.

Laramie turned and stared stupidly through the smoke-blurred dusk at a tall, slim figure holding a smoking gun. Others were pouring in through the kitchen. So brief had been the desperate fight that the men who had raced around the house at the first bellow of the guns, had just reached the scene. Laramie shook his head dazedly.

"Slim!" he muttered. "See if Bob's hurt!"

"Not me!" The sheriff answered for himself, struggling up to a sitting posture by the wall. "I fell outa the chair and rolled outa line when the lead started singin'. Cut me loose, somebody."

"Cut him loose, Slim," mumbled Laramie. "I'm kinda dizzy."

Stark silence followed the roar of the six-guns, silence that hurt Buck Laramie's ear-drums. Like a man in a daze he staggered to a chair and sank down heavily upon it. Scarcely knowing what he did he found himself muttering the words of a song he hated:

When the folks heard that Brady was dead,
They all turned out, all dressed in red;
Marched down the street a-singin' a song;
'Brady's gone to hell with his Stetson on!'

He was hardly aware when Bob Anders came and cut his blood-soaked shirt away and washed his wounds, dressing them as best he could with strips torn from his own shirt, and whisky from a jug found on the table. The bite of the alcohol roused Laramie from the daze that enveloped him, and a deep swig of the same medicine cleared his dizzy head.

Laramie rose stiffly; he glanced about at the dead men staring glassily in the lamplight, shuddered, and retched suddenly at the reek of the blood that blackened the planks.

"Let's get out in the open!"

As they emerged into the cool dusk, they were aware that the shooting had ceased. A voice was bawling loudly at the head of the canyon, though the distance made the words unintelligible.

Slim came running back through the dusk.

"They're makin' a parley, Bob!" he reported. "They want to know if they'll be give a fair trial if they surrender."

"I'll talk to 'em. Rest of you keep under cover."

The sheriff worked toward the head of the canyon until he was within earshot of the men in and about the tunnel, and shouted: "Are you *hombres* ready to give in?"

"What's yore terms?" bawled back the spokesman, recognizing the sheriff's voice.

"I ain't makin' terms. You'll all get a fair trial in an honest court. You better make up yore minds. I know they ain't a lot of you left. Harrison's dead and so is Rawley. I got forty men outside this canyon and enough inside, behind you, to wipe you out. Throw yore guns out here where I can see 'em, and come out with yore hands high. I'll give you till I count ten."

And as he began to count, rifles and pistols began clattering on the bare earth, and haggard, blood-stained, powder-blackened men rose from behind rocks with their hands in the air, and came out of the tunnel in the same manner.

"We quits," announced the spokesman. "Four of the boys are layin' back amongst the rocks too shot up to move under their own power. One's got a broke laig where his horse fell on him. Some of the rest of us need to have wounds dressed."

Laramie and Slim and the punchers came out of cover, with guns trained on the weary outlaws, and at a shout from Anders, the men outside came streaming through the tunnel, whooping vengefully.

"No mob-stuff," warned Anders, as the men grabbed the prisoners and bound their hands, none too gently. "Get those four wounded men out of the rocks, and we'll see what we can do for them."

Presently, a curious parade came filing through the tunnel into the outer valley where twilight still lingered. And as Laramie emerged from that dark tunnel, he felt as if his dark and sinister past had fallen from him like a worn-out coat.

One of the four wounded men who had been brought through the tunnel on crude stretchers rigged out of rifles and coats was in a talkative mood. Fear and the pain of his wound had broken his nerve entirely and he was overflowing with information.

"I'll tell you anything you want to know! Put in a good word for me at my trial, and I'll spill the works!" he declaimed, ignoring the sullen glares of his hardier companions.

"How did Harrison get mixed up in this deal?" demanded the sheriff.

"Mixed, hell! He planned the whole thing. He was cashier in the bank when the Laramies robbed it; the real ones, I mean. If it hadn't been for that robbery, old Brown would soon found out that Harrison was stealin' from him. But the Laramies killed Brown and give Harrison a chance to cover his tracks. They got blamed for the dough he'd stole, as well as the money they'd actually taken.

"That give Harrison an idee how to be king of San Leon. The Laramies had acted as scape-goats for him once, and he aimed to use 'em again. But he had to wait till he could get to be president of the bank, and had taken time to round up a gang."

"So he'd ruin the ranchers, give mortgages and finally get their outfits, and then send his coyotes outa the country and be king of San Leon," broke in Laramie. "We know that part of it. Where'd Rawlins come in?"

"Harrison knowed him years ago, on the Rio Grande. When Harrison aimed to raise his gang, he went to Mexico and found Rawlins. Harrison knowed the real Laramies had a secret hide-out, so Rawlins made friends with Luke Laramie, and – "

"We know all about that," interrupted Anders with a quick glance at Buck.

"Yeah? Well, everything was *bueno* till word come from Mexico that Buck Laramie was ridin' up from there. Harrison got skittish. He thought Laramie was comin' to take toll for his brother. So he sent Rawlins to waylay Laramie. Rawlins missed, but later went on to San Leon to try again. He shot you instead, Anders. Word was out to get you, anyway. You'd been prowlin' too close to our hide-out to suit Harrison.

"Harrison seemed to kinda go locoed when first he heard Laramie was headin' this way. He made us pull that fool stunt of a fake bank hold-up to pull wool over folks's eyes more'n ever. Hell, nobody suspected him anyway. Then he risked comin' out here. But he was panicky and wanted us to git ready to make a clean sweep tonight and pull out. When Laramie got away from us this mornin', Harrison decided he'd ride to Mexico with us.

"Well, when the fightin' had started, Harrison and Rawley stayed outa sight. Nothin' they could do, and they hoped we'd be able to break out of the canyon. They didn't want to be seen and recognized. If it should turn out Laramie hadn't told anybody he was head of the gang, Harrison would be able to stay on, then."

Preparations were being made to start back to San Leon with the prisoners, when a sheepish looking delegation headed by Mayor Jim Watkins approached Laramie. Watkins hummed and hawed with embarrassment, and finally blurted out, with typical Western bluntness:

"Look here, Laramie, we owe you somethin' now, and we're just as hot to pay our debts as you are to pay yours. Harrison had a small ranch out a ways from town, which he ain't needin' no more, and he ain't got no heirs, so we can get it easy enough. We thought if you was aimin', maybe, to stay around San Leon, we'd like powerful well to make you a present of that ranch, and kinda help you get a start in the cow business. And we don't want the fifty thousand Waters said you aimed to give us. You've wiped out that debt."

A curious moroseness had settled over Laramie, a futile feeling of anti-climax, and a bitter yearning he did not understand. He felt old and weary, a desire to be alone, and an urge to ride away over the rim of the world and forget – he did not even realize what it was he wanted to forget.

"Thanks," he muttered. "I'm paying that fifty thousand back to the men it belonged to. And I'll be movin' on tomorrow."

"Where to?"

He made a helpless, uncertain gesture.

"You think it over," urged Watkins, turning away. Men were already mounting, moving down the trail. Anders touched Laramie's sleeve.

"Let's go, Buck. You need some attention on them wounds."

"Go ahead, Bob. I'll be along. I wanta kind set here and rest."

Anders glanced sharply at him and then made a hidden gesture to Slim Jones, and turned away. The cavalcade moved down the trail in the growing darkness, armed men riding toward a new era of peace and prosperity; gaunt, haggard bound men riding toward the penitentiary and the gallows.

Laramie sat motionless, his empty hands hanging limp on his knees. A vital chapter in his life had closed, leaving him without a goal. He had kept his vow. Now he had no plan or purpose to take its place.

Slim Jones, standing nearby, not understanding Laramie's mood, but not intruding on it, started to speak. Then both men lifted their heads at the unexpected rumble of wheels.

"A buckboard!" ejaculated Slim.

"No buckboard ever come up that trail," snorted Laramie.

"One's comin' now; and who d'you think? Old Joel, by golly. And look who's drivin'!"

Laramie's heart gave a convulsive leap and then started pounding as he saw the slim, supple figure beside the old rancher. She pulled up near them and handed the lines to Slim, who sprang to help her down.

"Biggest fight ever fit in San Leon County!" roared Waters, "and I didn't git to fire a shot. Cuss a busted laig, anyway!"

"You done a man's part, anyway, Joel," assured Laramie; and then he forgot Joel Waters entirely, in the miracle of seeing Judy Anders standing before him, smiling gently, her hand outstretched and the rising moon melting her soft hair to golden witch-fire.

"I'm sorry for the way I spoke to you today," she said softly. "I've been bitter about things that were none of your fault."

"D-don't apologize, please," he stuttered, inwardly cursing himself because of his confusion. The touch of her slim, firm hand sent shivers through his frame and he knew all at once what that empty, gnawing yearning was; the more poignant now, because so unattainable.

"You saved my neck. Nobody that does that needs to apologize. You was probably right, anyhow. Er – uh – Bob went down the trail with the others. You must have missed him."

"I saw him and talked to him," she said softly. "He said you were behind them. I came on, expecting to meet you."

He was momentarily startled. "You came on to meet *me?* Of, of course. Joel would want to see how bad shot up I was." He achieved a ghastly excuse for a laugh.

"Mr. Waters wanted to see you, of course. But I – Buck, I wanted to see you, too."

She was leaning close to him, looking up at him, and he was dizzy with the fragrance and beauty of her; and in his dizziness said the most inane and idiotic thing he could possibly have said.

"To see me?" he gurgled wildly. "What – what you want to see *me* for?"

She seemed to draw away from him and her voice was a bit too precise.

"I wanted to apologize for my rudeness this morning," she said, a little distantly.

"I said don't apologize to me," he gasped. "You saved my life – and I – I – Judy, dang it, I love you!"

It was out – the amazing statement, blurted out involuntarily. He was frozen by his own audacity, stunned and paralyzed. But she did not seem to mind. Somehow he found she was in his arms, and numbly he heard her saying: "I love you too, Buck. I've loved you ever since I was a little girl, and we went to school together. Only I've tried to force myself not to think of you for the past six years. But I've loved the memory of you – that's why it hurt me so to think that you'd gone bad – as I thought you had. That horse I brought you – it wasn't altogether because you'd helped Bob that I brought it to you. It – it was partly because of my own feeling. Oh, Buck, to learn you're straight and honorable is like having a black shadow lifted from between us. You'll never leave me, Buck?"

"Leave you?" Laramie gasped. "Just long enough to find Watkins and tell him I'm takin' him up on a proposition he made me, and then I'm aimin' on spendin' the rest of my life makin' you happy." The rest was lost in a perfectly natural sound.

"Kissin'!" beamed Joel Waters, sitting in his buckboard and gently manipulating his wounded leg. "Reckon they'll be a marryin' in these parts purty soon, Slim."

"Don't tell me yo're figgerin' on gittin' hitched?" inquired Slim, pretending to misunderstand, but grinning behind his hand.

"You go light on that sarcastic tone. I'm liable to git married any day now. It's just a matter of time till I decide what type of woman would make me the best wife."

John Ringold

There was a land of which he never spoke.
   A girl, perhaps, but no one knew her name,
   And few there were who knew from whence he came
For from his past he never raised the cloak.
No word he spake except to sneer or joke,
   Or, deep in drink, to curse men, life and Fate;
   Often his fierce black eyes, Hell-hot with hate,
Gleamed wolf-like through the shifting powder smoke.

His trail lay through saloon and gambling hall,
   Lone, sombre devil in a barren land.
   Perhaps, when drunk, he dreamed of mansions old,
   Ballrooms and women, proud and fair as gold –
Trail's-end, upon the strangest stage of all,
   The sun, a lone mesquite tree and the sand.

Vultures of Wahpeton

CHAPTER I

Guns in the Dark

The bare plank walls of the Golden Eagle Saloon seemed still to vibrate with the crashing echoes of the guns which had split the sudden darkness with spurts of red. But only a nervous shuffling of booted feet sounded in the tense silence that followed the shots. Then somewhere a match rasped on leather and a yellow flicker sprang up, etching a shaky hand and a pallid face. An instant later an oil lamp with a broken chimney illuminated the saloon, throwing tense bearded faces into bold relief. The big lamp that hung from the ceiling was a smashed ruin; kerosene dripped from it to the floor, making an oily puddle beside a grimmer, darker pool.

Two figures held the center of the room, under the broken lamp. One lay face-down, motionless arms outstretching empty hands. The other was crawling to his feet, blinking and gaping stupidly, like a man whose wits are still muddled by drink. His right arm hung limply by his side, a long-barreled pistol sagging from his fingers.

The rigid line of figures along the bar melted into movement. Men came forward, stooping to stare down at the limp shape. A confused babble of conversation rose. Hurried steps sounded outside, and the crowd divided as a man pushed his way abruptly through. Instantly he dominated the scene. His broad-shouldered, trim-hipped figure was above medium height, and his broad-brimmed white hat, neat boots and cravat contrasted with the rough garb of the others, just as his keen, dark face with its narrow black mustache contrasted with the bearded countenances about him. He held an ivory-butted gun in his right hand, muzzle tilted upward.

187

"What devil's work is this?" he harshly demanded; and then his gaze fell on the man on the floor. His eyes widened.

"Grimes!" he ejaculated. "Jim Grimes, my deputy! Who did this?" There was something tigerish about him as he wheeled toward the uneasy crowd. "Who did this?" he demanded, half crouching, his gun still lifted, but seeming to hover like a live thing ready to swoop.

Feet shuffled as men backed away, but one man spoke up: "We don't know, Middleton. Jackson there was havin' a little fun, shootin' at the ceilin', and the rest of us was at the bar, watchin' him, when Grimes come in and started to arrest him – "

"So Jackson shot him!" snarled Middleton, his gun covering the befuddled one in a baffling blur of motion. Jackson yelped in fear and threw up his hands, and the man who had first spoken interposed.

"No, Sheriff, it couldn't have been Jackson. His gun was empty when the lights went out. I know he slung six bullets into the ceilin' while he was playin' the fool, and I heard him snap the gun three times afterwards, so I know it was empty. But when Grimes went up to him, somebody shot the light out, and a gun banged in the dark, and when we got a light on again, there Grimes was on the floor, and Jackson was just gettin' up."

"I didn't shoot him," muttered Jackson. "I was just havin' a little fun. I was drunk, but I ain't now. I wouldn't have resisted arrest. When the light went out I didn't know what had happened. I heard the gun bang, and Grimes dragged me down with him as he fell. I didn't shoot him. I dunno who did."

"None of us knows," added a bearded miner. "Somebody shot in the dark – "

"More'n one," muttered another. "I heard at least three or four guns speakin'."

Silence followed, in which each man looked sidewise at his neighbor. The men had drawn back to the bar, leaving the middle of the big room clear, where the sheriff stood. Suspicion and fear galvanized the crowd, leaping like an electric spark from man to man. Each man knew that a murderer stood near him, possibly at his elbow. Men refused to look directly into the eyes of their neighbors, fearing to surprise guilty knowledge there –and die for the discovery. They stared at the sheriff who stood facing them, as if expecting to see him fall suddenly before a blast from the same unknown guns that had mowed down his deputy.

Middleton's steely eyes ranged along the silent line of men. Their eyes avoided or gave back his stare. In some he read fear; some were inscrutable; in others flickered a sinister mockery.

"The men who killed Jim Grimes are in this saloon," he said finally. "Some of you are the murderers." He was careful not to let his eyes single out anyone when he spoke; they swept the whole assemblage.

"I've been expecting this. Things have been getting a little too hot for the robbers and murderers who have been terrorizing this camp, so they've started shooting my deputies in the back. I suppose you'll try to kill me, next. Well, I want to tell you sneaking rats, whoever you are, that I'm ready for you, any time."

He fell silent, his rangy frame tense, his eyes burning with watchful alertness. None moved. The men along the bar might have been figures cut from stone.

He relaxed and shoved his gun into its scabbard; a sneer twisted his lips.

"I know your breed. You won't shoot a man unless his back is toward you. Forty men have been murdered in the vicinity of this camp within the last year, and not one had a chance to defend himself.

"Maybe this killing is an ultimatum to me. All right; I've got an answer ready: I've got a new deputy, and you won't find him so easy as Grimes. I'm fighting fire with fire from here on. I'm riding out of the Gulch early in the morning, and when I come back, I'll have a man with me. A gunfighter from Texas!"

He paused to let this information sink in, and laughed grimly at the furtive glances that darted from man to man.

"You'll find him no lamb," he predicted vindictively. "He was too wild for the country where gun-throwing was invented. What he did down there is none of my business. What he'll do here is what counts. And all I ask is that the men who murdered Grimes here, try that same trick on this Texan.

"Another thing, on my own account. I'm meeting this man at Ogalala Spring tomorrow morning. I'll be riding out alone, at dawn. If anybody wants to try to waylay me, let him make his plans now! I'll follow the open trail, and anyone who has any business with me will find me ready."

And turning his trimly-tailored back scornfully on the throng at the bar, the sheriff of Wahpeton strode from the saloon.

Ten miles east of Wahpeton a man squatted on his heels frying strips of deer meat over a tiny fire. The sun was just coming up. A short distance away a rangy mustang nibbled at the wiry grass that grew sparsely between broken rocks. The man had camped there that night, but his saddle and blanket were hidden back in the bushes. That fact showed him to be a man of wary nature. No one following the trail that led past Ogalala Spring could have seen him as he slept among the bushes. Now, in full daylight, he was making no attempt to conceal his presence.

The man was tall, broad-shouldered, deep-chested, lean-hipped, like one who had spent his life in the saddle. His unruly black hair matched a face burned dark by the sun, but his eyes were a burning blue. Low on either hip the black butt of a heavy Colt jutted from a worn black leather scabbard. These guns seemed as much part of the man as his eyes or his hands. He had worn them so constantly and so long that their association was as natural as the use of his limbs.

As he fried his meat and watched his coffee boiling in a battered old pot, his gaze darted continually eastward where the trail crossed a wide open space before it vanished among the thickets of a broken hill country. Westward the trail mounted a gentle slope and quickly disappeared among trees and bushes that crowded up within a few yards of the spring. But it was always eastward that the man looked.

When a rider emerged from the thickets to the east, the man at the spring set aside the skillet with its sizzling meat strips, and picked up his rifle – a long range Sharps .50. His eyes narrowed with satisfaction. He did not rise, but remained on one knee, the rifle resting negligently in his hands, the muzzle tilted upward, not aimed.

The rider came straight on, and the man at the spring watched him from under the brim of his hat. Only when the stranger pulled up a few yards away did the first man lift his head and give the other a full view of his face.

The horseman was a supple youth of medium height, and his hat did not conceal the fact that his hair was yellow and curly. His wide eyes were ingenuous, and an infectious smile curved his lips. There was no rifle under his knee, but an ivory-butted .45 hung low at his right hip.

His expression as he saw the other man's face gave no hint to his reaction, except for a slight, momentary contraction of the muscles that control the eyes – a movement involuntary and all but uncontrollable. Then he grinned broadly, and hailed:

"That meat smells prime, stranger!"

"Light and help me with it," invited the other instantly. "Coffee, too, if you don't mind drinkin' out of the pot."

He laid aside the rifle as the other swung from his saddle. The blond youngster threw his reins over the horse's head, fumbled in his blanket roll and drew out a battered tin cup. Holding this in his right hand he approached the fire with the rolling gait of a man born to a horse.

"I ain't et my breakfast," he admitted. "Camped down the trail a piece last night, and come on up here early to meet a man. Thought you was the *hombre* till you looked up. Kinda startled me," he added frankly. He sat down opposite the taller man, who shoved the skillet and coffee pot toward him. The tall man moved both these utensils with his left hand. His right rested lightly and apparently casually on his right thigh.

The youth filled his tin cup, drank the black, unsweetened coffee with evident enjoyment, and filled the cup again. He picked out pieces of the cooling meat with his fingers – and he was careful to use only his left hand for that part of the breakfast that would leave grease on his fingers. But he used his right hand for pouring coffee and holding the cup to his lips. He did not seem to notice the position of the other's right hand.

"Name's Glanton," he confided. "Billy Glanton. Texas. Guadalupe country. Went up the trail with a herd of mossy horns, went broke buckin' faro in Hayes City, and headed west lookin' for gold. Hell of a prospector I turned out to be! Now I'm lookin' for a job, and the man I was goin' to meet here said he had one for me. If I read your marks right you're a Texan, too?"

The last sentence was more a statement than a question.

"That's my brand," grunted the other. "Name's O'Donnell. Pecos River country, originally."

His statement, like that of Glanton, was indefinite. Both the Pecos and the Guadalupe cover considerable areas of territory. But Glanton grinned boyishly and stuck out his hand.

"Shake!" he cried. "I'm glad to meet an *hombre* from my home state, even if our stampin' grounds down there are a right smart piece apart!"

Their hands met and locked briefly – brown, sinewy hands that had never worn gloves, and that gripped with the abrupt tension of steel springs.

The hand-shake seemed to relax O'Donnell. When he poured out another cup of coffee he held the cup in one hand and the pot in the other, instead of setting the cup on the ground beside him and pouring with his left hand.

"I've been in California," he volunteered. "Drifted back on this side of the mountains a month ago. Been in Wahpeton for the last few weeks, but gold huntin' ain't my style. I'm a *vaquero*. Never should have tried to be anything else. I'm headin' back for Texas."

"Why don't you try Kansas?" asked Glanton. "It's fillin' up with Texas men, bringin' cattle up the trail to stock the ranges. Within a year they'll be drivin' 'em into Wyoming and Montana."

"Maybe I might." O'Donnell lifted the coffee cup absently. He held it in his left hand, and his right lay in his lap, almost touching the big black pistol butt. But the tension was gone out of his frame. He seemed relaxed, absorbed in what Glanton was saying. The use of his left hand and the position of his right seemed mechanical, merely an unconscious habit.

"It's a great country," declared Glanton, lowering his head to conceal the momentary and uncontrollable flicker of triumph in his eyes. "Fine ranges. Towns springin' up wherever the railroad touches.

"Everybody gettin' rich on Texas beef. Talkin' about 'cattle kings'! Wish I could have knowed this beef boom was comin' when I was a kid! I'd have rounded up about fifty thousand of them maverick steers that was roamin' loose all over lower Texas, and put me a brand on 'em, and saved 'em for the market!" He laughed at his own conceit.

"They wasn't worth six-bits a head then," he added, as men in making small talk will state a fact well-known to everyone. "Now twenty dollars a head ain't the top price."

He emptied his cup and set it on the ground near his right hip. His easy flow of speech flowed on – but the natural movement of his hand away from the cup turned into a blur of speed that flicked the heavy gun from its scabbard.

Two shots roared like one long stuttering detonation.

The blond newcomer slumped sidewise, his smoking gun falling from his fingers, a widening spot of crimson suddenly dyeing his shirt, his wide eyes fixed in sardonic self-mockery on the gun in O'Donnell's right hand.

"Corcoran!" he muttered. "I thought I had you fooled – you – "

Self-mocking laughter bubbled to his lips, cynical to the last; he was laughing as he died.

The man whose real name was Corcoran rose and looked down at his victim unemotionally. There was a hole in the side of his shirt, and a seared spot on the skin of his ribs burned like fire. Even with his aim spoiled by ripping lead, Glanton's bullet had passed close.

Reloading the empty chamber of his Colt, Corcoran started toward the horse the dead man had ridden up to the spring. He had taken but one step when a sound brought him around, the heavy Colt jumping back into his hand.

He scowled at the man who stood before him: a tall man, trimly built, and clad in frontier elegance.

"Don't shoot," this man said imperturbably. "I'm John Middleton, sheriff of Wahpeton Gulch."

The warning attitude of the other did not relax.

"This was a private matter," he said.

"I guessed as much. Anyway, it's none of my business. I saw two men at the spring as I rode over a rise in the trail some distance back. I was only expecting one. I can't afford to take any chances. I left my horse a short distance back and came on afoot. I was watching from the bushes and saw the whole thing. He reached for his gun first, but you already had your hand almost on your gun. Your shot was first by a flicker. He fooled me. His move came as an absolute surprise to me."

"He thought it would to me," said Corcoran. "Billy Glanton always wanted the drop on his man. He always tried to get some advantage before he pulled his gun.

"He knew me as soon as he saw me; knew that I knew him. But he thought he was making me think that he didn't know me. I made him think that. He could take chances because he knew I wouldn't shoot him down without warnin' – which is just what he figured on doin' to me. Finally he thought he had me off my guard, and went for his gun. I was foolin' him all along."

Middleton looked at Corcoran with much interest. He was familiar with the two opposite breeds of gunmen. One kind was like Glanton; utterly cynical, courageous enough when courage was necessary, but always preferring to gain an advantage by treachery whenever possible. Corcoran typified the opposite breed; men too direct by nature, or too proud of their skill to resort to trickery when it was possible to meet their enemies in the open and rely on sheer speed and nerve and accuracy. But that Corcoran was a strategist was proved by his tricking Glanton into drawing.

Middleton looked down at Glanton; in death the yellow curls and boyish features gave the youthful gunman an appearance of innocence. But Middleton knew that that mask had covered the heart of a merciless grey wolf.

"A bad man!" he muttered, staring at the rows of niches on the ivory stock of Glanton's Colt.

"Plenty bad," agreed Corcoran. "My folks and his had a feud between 'em down in Texas. He came back from Kansas and killed an uncle of mine – shot him down in cold blood. I was in California when it happened. Got a letter a year after the feud was over. I was headin' for Kansas, where I figured he'd gone back to, when I met a man who told me he was in this part of the country, and was ridin' towards Wahpeton. I cut his trail and camped here last night waitin' for him.

"It'd been years since we'd seen each other, but he knew me – didn't know I knew he knew me, though. That gave me the edge. You're the man he was goin' to meet here?"

"Yes. I need a gun-fighting deputy bad. I'd heard of him. Sent him word."

Middleton's gaze wandered over Corcoran's hard frame, lingering on the guns at his hips.

"You pack two irons," remarked the sheriff. "I know what you can do with your right. But what about the left? I've seen plenty of men who wore two guns, but those who could use both I can count on my fingers."

"Well?"

"Well," smiled the sheriff, "I thought maybe you'd like to show what you can do with your left."

"Why do you think it makes any difference to me whether you believe I can handle both guns or not?" retorted Corcoran without heat.

Middleton seemed to like the reply.

"A tin-horn would be anxious to make me believe he could. You don't have to prove anything to me. I've seen enough to show me that you're the man I need. Corcoran, I came out here to hire Glanton as my deputy. I'll make the same proposition to you. What you were down in Texas, or out in California, makes no difference to me. I know your breed, and I know that you'll shoot square with a man who trusts you, regardless of what you may have been in other parts, or will be again, somewhere else.

"I'm up against a situation in Wahpeton that I can't cope with alone, or with the forces I have.

"For a year the town and the camps up and down the gulch have been terrorized by a gang of outlaws who call themselves the Vultures.

"That describes them perfectly. No man's life or property is safe. Forty or fifty men have been murdered, hundreds robbed. It's next to impossible for a man to pack out any dust, or for a big shipment of gold to get through on the stage. So many men have been shot trying to protect shipments that the stage company has trouble hiring guards anymore.

"Nobody knows who are the leaders of the gang. There are a number of ruffians who are suspected of being members of the Vultures, but we have no proof that would stand up, even in a miners' court. Nobody dares give evidence against any of them. When a man recognizes the men who rob him he doesn't dare reveal his knowledge. I can't get anyone to identify a criminal, though I know that robbers and murderers are walking the streets, and rubbing elbows with me along the bars. It's maddening! And yet I can't blame the poor devils. Any man who dared testify against one of them would be murdered.

"People blame me some, but I can't give adequate protection to the camp with the resources allowed me. You know how a gold camp is; everybody so greedy-blind they don't want to do anything but grab for the yellow dust. My deputies are brave men, but they can't be everywhere, and they're not gun-fighters. If I arrest a man there are a dozen to stand up in a miners' court and swear enough lies to acquit him. Only last night they murdered one of my deputies, Jim Grimes, in cold blood.

"I sent for Billy Glanton when I heard he was in this country, because I need a man of more than usual skill. I need a man who can handle a gun like a streak of forked lightning, and knows all the tricks of trapping and killing a man. I'm tired of arresting criminals to be turned loose! Wild Bill Hickok has the right idea – kill the badmen and save the jails for the petty offenders!"

The Texan scowled slightly at the mention of Hickok, who was not loved by the riders who came up the cattle trails, but he nodded agreement with the sentiment expressed. The fact that he, himself, would fall into Hickok's category of those to be exterminated did not prejudice his viewpoint.

"You're a better man than Glanton," said Middleton abruptly. "The proof is that Glanton lies there dead, and here you stand very much alive. I'll offer you the same terms I meant to offer him."

He named a monthly salary considerably larger than that drawn by the average Eastern city marshal. Gold was the most plentiful commodity in Wahpeton.

"And a monthly bonus," added Middleton. "When I hire talent I expect to pay for it; so do the merchants and miners who look to me for protection."

Corcoran meditated a moment.

"No use in me goin' on to Kansas now," he said finally. "None of my folks in Texas are havin' any feud that I know of. I'd like to see this Wahpeton. I'll take you up."

"Good!" Middleton extended his hand and as Corcoran took it he noticed that it was much browner than the left. No glove had covered that hand for many years.

"Let's get it started right away! But first we'll have to dispose of Glanton's body."

"I'll take along his gun and horse and send 'em to Texas to his folks," said Corcoran.

"But the body?"

"Hell, the buzzards'll 'tend to it."

"No, no!" protested Middleton. "Let's cover it with bushes and rocks, at least."

Corcoran shrugged his shoulders. It was not vindictiveness which prompted his seeming callousness. His hatred of the blond youth did not extend to the lifeless body of the man. It was simply that he saw no use in going to what seemed to him an unnecessary task. He had hated Glanton with the merciless hate of his race, which is more enduring and more relentless than the hate of an Indian or a Spaniard. But toward the body that was no longer animated by the personality he had hated, he was simply indifferent. He expected some day to leave his own corpse stretched on the ground, and the thought of buzzards tearing at his dead flesh moved him no more than the sight of his dead enemy. His creed was pagan and nakedly elemental.

A man's body, once life had left it, was no more than any other carcass, moldering back into the soil which once produced it.

But he helped Middleton drag the body into an opening among the bushes, and build a rude cairn above it. And he waited patiently while Middleton carved the dead youth's name on a rude cross fashioned from broken branches, and thrust up-right among the stones.

Then they rode for Wahpeton, Corcoran leading the riderless roan; over the horn of the empty saddle hung the belt supporting the dead man's gun, the ivory stock of which bore eleven notches, each of which represented a man's life.

CHAPTER II

Golden Madness

The mining town of Wahpeton sprawled in a wide gulch that wandered between sheer rock walls and steep hillsides. Cabins, saloons, and dance halls, backed against the cliffs on the south side of the gulch. The houses facing them were almost on the bank of Wahpeton Creek, which wandered down the gulch, keeping mostly to the center. On both sides of the creek cabins and tents straggled for a mile and a half each way from the main body of the town. Men were washing gold dust out of the creek, and out of its smaller tributaries which meandered into the canyon along tortuous ravines. Some of these ravines opened into the gulch between the houses built against the wall, and the cabins and tents which straggled up them gave the impression that the town had overflowed the main gulch and spilled into its tributaries.

Buildings were of logs, or of bare planks laboriously freighted over the mountains. Squalor and draggled or gaudy elegance rubbed elbows. An intense virility surged through the scene. What other qualities it might have lacked, it overflowed with a superabundance of vitality. Color, action, movement – growth and power! The atmosphere was alive with these elements, stinging and tingling. Here there were no delicate shadings or subtle contrasts. Life painted here in broad, raw colors, in bold, vivid strokes. Men who came here left behind them the delicate nuances, the cultured tranquilities of life. An empire was being built on muscle and guts and audacity, and men dreamed gigantically and wrought terrifically. No dream was too mad, no enterprise too tremendous to be accomplished.

Passions ran raw and turbulent. Boot heels stamped on bare plank floors, in the eddying dust of the street. Voices boomed, tempers exploded in sudden outbursts of primitive violence. Shrill voices of painted harpies mingled with the clank of gold on gambling tables, gusty mirth and vociferous altercation along the bars where raw liquor hissed in a steady stream down hairy, dust-caked throats. It was one of a thousand similar panoramas of the day, when a giant empire was bellowing in lusty infancy.

But a sinister undercurrent was apparent. Corcoran, riding by the sheriff, was aware of this, his senses and intuitions whetted to razor keenness by the life he led. The instincts of a gunfighter were developed to an abnormal alertness, else he had never lived out his first year of gunmanship. But it took no abnormally developed instinct to tell Corcoran that hidden currents ran here, darkly and strongly.

As they threaded their way among trains of pack-mules, rumbling wagons and swarms of men on foot which thronged the straggling street, Corcoran was aware of many eyes following them. Talk ceased suddenly among gesticulating groups as they recognized the sheriff, then the eyes swung to Corcoran, searching and appraising. He did not seem to be aware of their scrutiny.

Middleton murmured: "They know I'm bringing back a gunfighting deputy. Some of those fellows are Vultures, though I can't prove it. Look out for yourself."

Corcoran considered this advice too unnecessary to merit a reply. They were riding past the King of Diamonds gambling hall at the moment, and a group of men clustered in the doorway turned to stare at them. One lifted a hand in greeting to the sheriff.

"Ace Brent, the biggest gambler in the gulch," murmured Middleton as he returned the salute. Corcoran got a glimpse of a slim figure in elegant broadcloth, a keen, inscrutable countenance, and a pair of piercing black eyes.

Middleton did not enlarge upon his description of the man, but rode on in silence.

They traversed the body of the town – the clusters of stores and saloons – and passed on, halting at a cabin apart from the rest. Between it and the town the creek swung out in a wide loop that carried it some distance from the south wall of the gulch, and the cabins and tents straggled after the creek. That left this particular cabin isolated, for it was built with its back wall squarely against the sheer cliff. There was a corral on one side, a clump of trees on the other. Beyond the trees a narrow ravine opened into the gulch, dry and unoccupied.

"This is my cabin," said Middleton. "That cabin back there" – he pointed to one which they had passed, a few hundred yards back up the road – "I use for a sheriff's office. I need only one room. You can bunk in the back room. You can keep your horse in my corral, if you want to. I always keep several there for my deputies. It pays to have a fresh supply of horse-flesh always on hand."

As Corcoran dismounted he glanced back at the cabin he was to occupy. It stood close to a clump of trees, perhaps a hundred yards from the steep wall of the gulch.

There were four men at the sheriff's cabin, one of which Middleton introduced to Corcoran as Colonel Hopkins, formerly of Tennessee. He was a tall, portly man with an iron grey mustache and goatee, as well dressed as Middleton himself.

"Colonel Hopkins owns the rich Elinor A. claim, in partnership with Dick Bisley," said Middleton, "in addition to being one of the most prominent merchants in the Gulch."

"A great deal of good either occupation does me, when I can't get my money out of town," retorted the colonel. "Three times my partner and I have lost big shipments of gold on the stage. Once we sent out a load concealed in wagons loaded with supplies supposed to be intended for the miners at Teton Gulch. Once clear of Wahpeton the drivers were to swing back east through the mountains. But somehow the Vultures learned of our plan; they caught the wagons fifteen miles south of Wahpeton, looted them and murdered the guards and drivers."

"The town's honeycombed with their spies," muttered Middleton.

"Of course. One doesn't know who to trust. It was being whispered in the streets that my men had been killed and robbed, before their bodies had been found. We know that the Vultures knew all about our plan, that they rode straight out from Wahpeton, committed that crime and rode straight back with the gold dust. But we could do nothing. We can't prove anything, or convict anybody."

Middleton introduced Corcoran to the three deputies, Bill McNab, Richardson, and Stark. McNab was as tall as Corcoran and more heavily built, hairy and muscular, with restless eyes that reflected a violent temper. Richardson was more slender, with cold, unblinking eyes, and Corcoran instantly classified him as the most dangerous of the three. Stark was a burly, bearded fellow, not differing in type from hundreds of miners. Corcoran found the appearances of these men incongruous with their protestations of helplessness in the face of the odds against them. They looked like hard men, well able to take care of themselves in any situation.

Middleton, as if sensing his thoughts, said: "These men are not afraid of the devil, and they can throw a gun as quick as the average man, or quicker. But it's hard for a stranger to appreciate just what we're up against here in Wahpeton. If it was a matter of an open fight, it would be different. I wouldn't need any more help. But it's blind going, working in the dark, not knowing who to trust. I don't dare to deputize a man unless I'm sure of his honesty. And who can be sure of who? We know the town is full of spies. We don't know who they are; we don't know who the leader of the Vultures is."

Hopkins' bearded chin jutted stubbornly as he said: "I still believe that gambler, Ace Brent, is mixed up with the gang. Gamblers have been murdered and robbed, but Brent's never been molested. What becomes of all the dust he wins? Many of the miners, despairing of ever getting out of the gulch with their gold, blow it all in the saloons and gambling halls. Brent's won thousands of dollars in dust and nuggets. So have several others. What becomes of it? It doesn't all go back into circulation. I believe they get it out, over the mountains. And if they do, when no one else can, that proves to my mind that they're members of the Vultures."

"Maybe they cache it, like you and the other merchants are doing," suggested Middleton. "I don't know. Brent's intelligent enough to be the chief of the Vultures. But I've never been able to get anything on him."

"You've never been able to get anything definite on anybody, except petty offenders," said Colonel Hopkins bluntly, as he took up his hat. "No offense intended, John. We know what you're up against, and we can't blame you. But it looks like, for the good of the camp, we're going to have to take direct action."

Middleton stared after the broadcloth-clad back as it receded from the cabin.

" 'We,' " he murmured. "That means the vigilantes – or rather the men who have been agitating a vigilante movement. I can understand their feelings, but I consider it an unwise move. In the first place, such an organization is itself outside the law, and would be playing into the hands of the lawless element. Then, what's to prevent outlaws from joining the vigilantes, and diverting it to suit their own ends?"

"Not a damned thing!" broke in McNab heatedly. "Colonel Hopkins and his friends are hot-headed. They expect too much from us. Hell, we're just ordinary workin' men. We do the best we can, but we ain't gun-slingers like this man Corcoran here."

Corcoran found himself mentally questioning the whole truth of this statement; Richardson had all the earmarks of a gunman, if he had ever seen one, and the Texan's experience in such matters ranged from the Pacific to the Gulf.

Middleton picked up his hat. "You boys scatter out through the camp. I'm going to take Corcoran around, when I've sworn him in and given him his badge, and introduce him to the leading men of the camp.

"I don't want any mistake, or any chance of mistake, about his standing. I've put you in a tight spot, Corcoran, I'll admit – boasting about the gun-fighting deputy I was going to get. But I'm confident that you can take care of yourself."

The eyes that had followed their ride down the street focused on the sheriff and his companion as they made their way on foot along the straggling street with its teeming saloons and gambling halls. Gamblers and bartenders were swamped with business, and merchants were getting rich with all commodities selling at unheard-of prices. Wages for day-labor matched prices for groceries, for few men could be found to toil for a prosaic, set salary when their eyes were dazzled by visions of creeks fat with yellow dust and gorges crammed with nuggets. Some of those dreams were not disappointed; millions of dollars in virgin gold was being taken out of the claims up and down the gulch. But the finders frequently found it a golden weight hung to their necks to drag them down to a bloody death. Unseen, unknown, on furtive feet the human wolves stole among them, unerringly marking their prey and striking in the dark.

From saloon to saloon, dance hall to dance hall, where weary girls in tawdry finery allowed themselves to be tussled and hauled about by bear-like males who emptied sacks of gold-dust down the low necks of their dresses, Middleton piloted Corcoran, talking rapidly and incessantly. He pointed out men in the crowd and gave their names and status in the community, and introduced the Texan to the more important citizens of the camp.

All eyes followed Corcoran curiously. The day was still in the future when the northern ranges would be flooded by Texas cattle, driven by wiry Texas riders; but Texans were not unknown, even then, in the mining camps of the Northwest. In the first days of the gold rushes they had drifted in from the camps of California, to which, at a still earlier date, the Southwest had sent some of her staunchest and some of her most turbulent sons. And of late others had drifted in from the Kansas cattle towns along whose streets the lean riders were swaggering and fighting out feuds brought up from the far south country. Many in Wahpeton were familiar with the characteristics of the Texas breed, and all had heard tales of the fighting men bred among the live oaks and mesquites of that hot, turbulent country where racial traits met and clashed, and the traditions of the Old South mingled with those of the untamed West.

Here, then, was a lean grey wolf from that southern pack; some of the men looked their scowling animosity; but most merely looked, in the role of spectators, eager to witness the drama all felt imminent.

"You're primarily to fight the Vultures, of course," Middleton told Corcoran as they walked together down the street. "But that doesn't mean you're to overlook petty offenders. A lot of small-time crooks and bullies are so emboldened by the success of the big robbers that they think they can get away with things, too. If you see a man shooting up a saloon, take his gun away and throw him into jail to sober up. That's the jail, up yonder at the other end of town. Don't let men fight on the street or in saloons. Innocent bystanders get hurt.'

"All right." Corcoran saw no harm in shooting up saloons or fighting in public places. In Texas few innocent bystanders were ever hurt, for there men sent their bullets straight to the mark intended. But he was ready to follow instructions.

"So much for the smaller fry. You know what to do with the really bad men. We're not bringing any more murderers into court to be acquitted through their friends' lies!"

CHAPTER III

Gunman's Trap

Night had fallen over the roaring madness that was Wahpeton Gulch. Light streamed from the open doors of saloons and honky-tonks, and the gusts of noise that rushed out into the street smote the passers-by like the impact of a physical blow.

Corcoran traversed the street with the smooth, easy stride of perfectly poised muscles. He seemed to be looking straight ahead, but his eyes missed nothing on either side of him. As he passed each building in turn he analyzed the sounds that issued from the open door, and knew just how much was rough merriment and horse-play, recognized the elements of anger and menace when they edged some of the voices, and accurately appraised the extent and intensity of those emotions. A real gun-fighter was not merely a man whose eye was truer, whose muscles were quicker than other men; he was a practical psychologist, a student of human nature, whose life depended on the correctness of his conclusions.

It was the Golden Garter dance hall that gave him his first job as a defender of law and order.

As he passed a startling clamor burst forth inside – strident feminine shrieks piercing a din of coarse masculine hilarity. Instantly he was through the door and elbowing a way through the crowd which was clustered about the center of the room. Men cursed and turned belligerently as they felt his elbows in their ribs, twisted their heads to threaten him, and then gave back as they recognized the new deputy.

Corcoran broke through into the open space the crowd ringed, and saw two women fighting like furies. One, a tall, fine blond girl, had bent a shrieking, biting, clawing Mexican girl back over a billiard table, and the crowd was yelling joyful encouragement to one or the other: "Give it to her, Glory!" "Slug her, gal!" "Hell, Conchita, bite her!"

The brown girl heeded this last bit of advice and followed it so energetically that Glory cried out sharply and jerked away her wrist, which dripped blood. In the grip of the hysterical frenzy which seizes women in such moments, she caught up a billiard ball and lifted it to crash it down on the head of her screaming captive.

Corcoran caught that uplifted wrist, and deftly flicked the ivory sphere from her fingers. Instantly she whirled on him like a tigress, her yellow hair falling in disorder over her shoulders, bared by the violence of the struggle, her eyes blazing. She lifted her hands toward his face, her fingers working spasmodically, at which some drunk bawled, with a shout of laughter: "Scratch his eyes out, Glory!"

Corcoran made no move to defend his features; he did not seem to see the white fingers twitching so near his face. He was staring into her furious face, and the candid admiration of his gaze seemed to confuse her, even in her anger. She dropped her hands but fell back on woman's traditional weapon – her tongue.

"You're Middleton's new deputy! I might have expected you to butt in! Where are McNab and the rest? Drunk in some gutter? Is this the way you catch murderers? You lawmen are all alike – better at bullying girls than at catching outlaws!"

Corcoran stepped past her and picked up the hysterical Mexican girl. Conchita seeing that she was more frightened than hurt, scurried toward the back rooms, sobbing in rage and humiliation, and clutching about her the shreds of garments her enemy's tigerish attack had left her.

Corcoran looked again at Glory, who stood clenching and unclenching her white fists. She was still fermenting with anger, and furious at his intervention. No one in the crowd about them spoke; no one laughed, but all seemed to hold their breaths as she launched into another tirade. They knew Corcoran was a dangerous man, but they did not know the code by which he had been reared; did not know that Glory, or any other woman, was safe from violence at his hands, whatever her offense.

"Why don't you call McNab?" she sneered. "Judging from the way Middleton's deputies have been working, it will probably take three or four of you to drag one helpless girl to jail!"

"Who said anything about takin' you to jail?" Corcoran's gaze dwelt in fascination on her ruddy cheeks, the crimson of her full lips in startling contrast against the whiteness of her teeth. She shook her yellow hair back impatiently, as a spirited young animal might shake back its flowing mane.

"You're not arresting me?" She seemed startled, thrown into confusion by this unexpected statement.

"No. I just kept you from killin' that girl. If you'd brained her with that billiard ball I'd have had to arrest you."

"She lied about me!" Her wide eyes flashed, and her breast heaved again.

"That wasn't no excuse for makin' a public show of yourself," he answered without heat. "If ladies have got to fight, they ought to do it in private."

And so saying he turned away. A gusty exhalation of breath seemed to escape the crowd, and the tension vanished, as they turned to the bar. The incident was forgotten, merely a trifling episode in an existence crowded with violent incidents. Jovial masculine voices mingled with the shriller laughter of women, as glasses began to clink along the bar.

Glory hesitated, drawing her torn dress together over her bosom, then darted after Corcoran, who was moving toward the door. When she touched his arm he whipped about as quick as a cat, a hand flashing to a gun. She glimpsed a momentary gleam in his eyes as menacing and predatory as the threat that leaps in a panther's eyes. Then it was gone as he saw whose hand had touched him.

"She lied about me," Glory said, as if defending herself from a charge of misconduct. "She's a dirty little cat."

Corcoran looked her over from head to foot, as if he had not heard her; his blue eyes burned her like a physical fire.

She stammered in confusion. Direct and unveiled admiration was commonplace, but there was an elemental candor about the Texan such as she had never before encountered.

He broke in on her stammerings in a way that showed he had paid no attention to what she was saying.

"Let me buy you a drink. There's a table over there where we can sit down."

"No. I must go and put on another dress. I just wanted to say that I'm glad you kept me from killing Conchita. She's a slut, but I don't want her blood on my hands."

"All right."

She found it hard to make conversation with him, and could not have said why she wished to make conversation.

"McNab arrested me once," she said, irrelevantly, her eyes dilating as if at the memory of an injustice. "I slapped him for something he said. He was going to put me in jail for resisting an officer of the law! Middleton made him turn me loose."

"McNab must be a fool," said Corcoran slowly.

"He's mean; he's got a nasty temper, and he – what's that?"

Down the street sounded a fusillade of shots, a blurry voice yelling gleefully.

"Some fool shooting up a saloon," she murmured, and darted a strange glance at her companion, as if a drunk shooting into the air was an unusual occurrence in that wild mining camp.

"Middleton said that's against the law," he grunted, turning away.

"Wait!" she cried sharply, catching at him. But he was already moving through the door, and Glory stopped short as a hand fell lightly on her shoulder from behind. Turning her head she paled to see the keenly chiselled face of Ace Brent. His hand lay gently on her shoulder, but there was a command and a blood-chilling threat in its touch. She shivered and stood still as a statue, as Corcoran, unaware of the drama being played behind him, disappeared into the street.

The racket was coming from the Blackfoot Chief Saloon, a few doors down, and on the same side of the street as the Golden Garter. With a few long strides Corcoran reached the door. But he did not rush in. He halted and swept his cool gaze deliberately over the interior. In the center of the saloon a roughly dressed man was reeling about, whooping and discharging a pistol into the ceiling, perilously close to the big oil lamp which hung there. The bar was lined with men, all bearded and uncouthly garbed, so it was impossible to tell which were ruffians and which were honest miners. All the men in the room were at the bar, with the exception of the drunken man.

Corcoran paid little heed to him as he came through the door, though he moved straight toward him, and to the tense watchers it seemed the Texan was looking at no one else. In reality, from the corner of his eye he was watching the men at the bar; and as he moved deliberately from the door, across the room, he distinguished the pose of honest curiosity from the tension of intended murder. He saw the three hands that gripped gun butts.

And as he, apparently ignorant of what was going on at the bar, stepped toward the man reeling in the center of the room, a gun jumped from its scabbard and pointed toward the lamp. And even as it moved, Corcoran moved quicker. His turn was a blur of motion too quick for the eye to follow and even as he turned his gun was burning red.

The man who had drawn died on his feet with his gun still pointed toward the ceiling, unfired. Another stood gaping, stunned, a pistol dangling in his fingers, for that fleeting tick of time; then as he woke and whipped the gun up, hot lead ripped through his brain. A third gun spoke once as the owner fired wildly, and then he went to his knees under the blast of ripping lead, slumped over on the floor and lay twitching.

It was over in a flash, action so blurred with speed that not one of the watchers could ever tell just exactly what had happened. One instant Corcoran had been moving toward the man in the center of the room, the next both guns were blazing and three men were falling from the bar, crashing dead on the floor.

For an instant the scene held, Corcoran half crouching, guns held at his hips, facing the men who stood stunned along the bar. Wisps of blue smoke drifted from the muzzles of his guns, forming a misty veil through which his grim face looked, implacable and passionless as that of an image carved from granite. But his eyes blazed.

Shakily, moving like puppets on a string, the men at the bar lifted their hands clear of their waistline. Death hung on the crook of a finger for a shuddering tick of time. Then with a choking gasp the man who had played drunk made a stumbling rush toward the door. With a catlike wheel and stroke Corcoran crashed a gun barrel over his head and stretched him stunned and bleeding on the floor.

The Texan was facing the men at the bar again before any of them could have moved. He had not looked at the men on the floor since they had fallen.

"Well, *amigos!*" His voice was soft, but it was thick with killer's lust. "Why don't you-all keep the *baile* goin'? Ain't these *hombres* got no friends?"

Apparently they had not. No one made a move.

Realizing that the crisis had passed, that there was no more killing to be done just then, Corcoran straightened, shoving his guns back in his scabbards.

"Purty crude," he criticized. "I don't see how anybody could fall for a trick that stale. Man plays drunk and starts shootin' at the roof. Officer comes in to arrest him. When the officer's back's turned, somebody shoots out the light, and the drunk falls on the floor to get out of the line of fire. Three or four men planted along the bar start blazin' away in the dark at the place where they know the law's standin', and out of eighteen or twenty-four shots, some's bound to connect."

With a harsh laugh he stooped, grabbed the "drunk" by the collar and hauled him upright. The man staggered and stared wildly about him, blood dripping from the gash in his scalp.

"You got to come along to jail," said Corcoran unemotionally. "Sheriff says it's against the law to shoot up saloons. I ought to shoot you, but I ain't in the habit of pluggin' men with empty guns. Reckon you'll be more value to the sheriff alive than dead, anyway."

And propelling his dizzy charge, he strode out into the street. A crowd had gathered about the door, and they gave back suddenly. He saw a supple, feminine figure dart into the circle of light, which illumined the white face and golden hair of the girl Glory.

"Oh!" she exclaimed sharply. "Oh!" Her exclamation was almost drowned in a sudden clamor of voices as the men in the street realized what had happened in the Blackfoot Chief.

Corcoran felt her pluck at his sleeve as he passed her, heard her tense whisper.

"I was afraid – I tried to warn you – I'm glad they didn't – "

A shadow of a smile touched his hard lips as he glanced down at her. Then he was gone, striding down the street toward the jail, half pushing, half dragging his bewildered prisoner.

CHAPTER IV

The Madness That Blinds Men

Corcoran locked the door on the man who seemed utterly unable to realize just what had happened, and turned away, heading for the sheriff's office at the other end of town. He kicked on the door of the jailer's shack, a few yards from the jail, and roused that individual out of a slumber he believed was alcoholic and informed him he had a prisoner in his care. The jailer seemed as surprised as the victim was.

No one had followed Corcoran to the jail, and the street was almost deserted as the people jammed morbidly into the Blackfoot Chief to stare at the bodies and listen to conflicting stories as to just what had happened.

Colonel Hopkins came running up, breathlessly, to grab Corcoran's hand and pump it vigorously.

"By gad, sir, you have the real spirit! Guts! Speed! They tell me the loafers at the bar didn't even to have time to dive for cover before it was over! I'll admit I'd ceased to expect much of John's deputies, but you've shown your metal! These fellows were undoubtedly Vultures. That Tom Deal, you've got in jail, I've suspected him for some time. We'll question him – make him tell us who the rest are, and who their leader is. Come in and have a drink, sir!"

"Thanks, but not just now. I'm goin' to find Middleton and report this business. His office ought to be closer to the jail. I don't think much of his jailer. When I get through reportin' I'm going back and guard that fellow myself."

Hopkins emitted more laudations, and then clapped the Texan on the back and darted away to take part in whatever informal inquest was being made, and Corcoran strode on through the emptying street. The fact that so much uproar was being made over the killing of three would-be murderers showed him how rare was a successful resistance to the Vultures. He shrugged his shoulders as he remembered feuds and range wars in his native Southwest: men falling like flies under the unerring drive of bullets on the open range and in the streets of Texas towns. But there all men were frontiersmen, sons and grandsons of frontiersmen; here, in the mining camps, the frontier element was only one of several elements, many drawn from sections where men had forgotten how to defend themselves through generations of law and order.

He saw a light spring up in the sheriff's cabin just before he reached it, and, with his mind on possible gunmen lurking in ambush – for they must have known he would go directly to the cabin from the jail – he swung about and approached the building by a route that would not take him across the bar of light pouring from the window. So it was that the man who came running noisily down the road passed him without seeing the Texan as he kept in the shadows of the cliff. The man was McNab; Corcoran knew him by his powerful build, his slouching carriage. And as he burst through the door, his face was illuminated and Corcoran was amazed to see it contorted in a grimace of passion.

Voices rose inside the cabin, McNab's bull-like roar, thick with fury, and the calmer tones of Middleton. Corcoran hurried forward, and as he approached he heard McNab roar: "Damn you, Middleton, you've got a lot of explainin' to do! Why didn't you warn the boys he was a killer?"

At that moment Corcoran stepped into the cabin and demanded: "What's the trouble, McNab?"

The big deputy whirled with a feline snarl of rage, his eyes glaring with murderous madness as they recognized Corcoran.

"You damned – " A string of filthy expletives gushed from his thick lips as he ripped out his gun. Its muzzle had scarcely cleared leather when a Colt banged in Corcoran's right hand. McNab's gun clattered to the floor and he staggered back, grasping his right arm with his left hand, and cursing like a madman.

"What's the matter with you, you fool?" demanded Corcoran harshly. "Shut up! I did you a favor by not killin' you. If you wasn't a deputy I'd have drilled you through the head. But I will anyway, if you don't shut your dirty trap."

"You killed Breckman, Red Bill and Curly!" raved McNab; he looked like a wounded grizzly as he swayed there, blood trickling down his wrist and dripping off his fingers.

"Was that their names? Well, what about it?"

"Bill's drunk, Corcoran," interposed Middleton. "He goes crazy when he's full of liquor."

McNab's roar of fury shook the cabin. His eyes turned red and he swayed on his feet as if about to plunge at Middleton's throat.

"Drunk?" he bellowed. "You lie, Middleton! Damn you, what's your game? You sent your own men to death! Without warnin'!"

"His own men?" Corcoran's eyes were suddenly glittering slits. He stepped back and made a half turn so that he was facing both men; his hands became claws hovering over his gun-butts.

"Yes, his men!" snarled McNab. "You fool, *he's* the chief of the Vultures!"

An electric silence gripped the cabin. Middleton stood rigid, his empty hands hanging limp, knowing that his life hung on a thread no more substantial than a filament of morning dew. If he moved, if, when he spoke, his tone jarred on Corcoran's suspicious ears, guns would be roaring before a man could snap his fingers.

"Is that so?" Corcoran shot at him.

"Yes," Middleton said calmly, with no inflection in his voice that could be taken as a threat. "I'm chief of the Vultures."

Corcoran glared at him puzzled. "What's your game?" he demanded, his tone thick with the deadly instinct of his breed.

"That's what I want to know!" bawled McNab. "We killed Grimes for you, because he was catchin' on to things. And we set the same trap for this devil. He knew! He must have known! You warned him – told him all about it!"

"He told me nothin'," grated Corcoran. "He didn't have to. Nobody but a fool would have been caught in a trap like that. Middleton, before I blow you to hell, I want to know one thing; what good was it goin' to do you to bring me into Wahpeton, and have me killed the first night I was here?"

"I didn't bring you here for that," answered Middleton.

"Then what'd you bring him here for?" yelled McNab. "You told us – "

"I told you I was bringing a new deputy here, that was a gun-slinging fool," broke in Middleton. "That was the truth. That should have been warning enough."

"But we thought that was just talk, to fool the people," protested McNab bewilderedly. He sensed that he was beginning to be wound in a web he could not break.

"Did I tell you it was just talk?"

"No, but we thought – "

"I gave you no reason to think anything. The night when Grimes was killed I told everyone in the Golden Eagle that I was bringing in a Texas gunfighter as my deputy. I spoke the truth."

"But you wanted him killed, and – "

"I didn't. I didn't say a word about having him killed."

"But – "

"Did I?" Middleton pursued relentlessly. "Did I give you a definite order to kill Corcoran, to molest him in any way?"

Corcoran's eyes were molten steel, burning into McNab's soul. The befuddled giant scowled and floundered, vaguely realizing that he was being put in the wrong, but not understanding how, or why.

"No, you didn't tell us to kill him in so many words; but you didn't tell us to let him alone."

"Do I have to tell you to let people alone to keep you from killing them? There are about three thousand people in this camp I've never given any definite orders about. Are you going out and kill them, and say you thought I meant you to do it, because I didn't tell you not to?"

"Well, I – " McNab began apologetically, then burst out in righteous though bewildered wrath: "Damn it, it was the understandin' that we'd get rid of deputies like that, who wasn't on the inside. We thought you were bringin' in an honest deputy to fool the folks, just like you hired Jim Grimes to fool 'em. We thought you was just makin' a talk to the fools in the Golden Eagle. We thought you'd want him out of the way as quick as possible – "

"You drew your own conclusions and acted without my orders," snapped Middleton. "That's all that it amounts to. Naturally Corcoran defended himself. If I'd had any idea that you fools would try to murder him, I'd have passed the word to let him alone. I thought you understood my motives. I brought Corcoran in here to fool the people, yes. But he's not a man like Jim Grimes. Corcoran is with us. He'll clean out the thieves that are working outside our gang, and we'll accomplish two things with one stroke: get rid of competition and make the miners think we're on the level."

McNab stood glaring at Middleton; three times he opened his mouth, and each time he shut it without speaking. He knew that an injustice had been done him; that a responsibility that was not rightfully his had been dumped on his brawny shoulders. But the subtle play of Middleton's wits was beyond him; he did not know how to defend himself or make a countercharge.

"All right," he snarled. "We'll forget it. But the boys ain't going to forget how Corcoran shot down their pards. I'll talk to 'em, though. Tom Deal's got to be out of that jail before daylight. Hopkins is aimin' to question him about the gang. I'll stage a fake jail-break for him. But first I've got to get this arm dressed." And he slouched out of the cabin and away through the darkness, a baffled giant, burning with murderous rage, but too tangled in a net of subtlety to know where or how or who to smite.

Back in the cabin Middleton faced Corcoran, who still stood with his thumbs hooked in his belt, his fingers near his gun butts. A whimsical smile played on Middleton's thin lips, and Corcoran smiled back; but it was the mirthless grin of a crouching panther.

"You can't tangle me up with words like you did that big ox," Corcoran said. "You let me walk into that trap. You knew your men were ribbin' it up. You let 'em go ahead, when a word from you would have stopped it. You knew they'd think you wanted me killed, like Grimes, if you didn't say nothin'. You let 'em think that, but you played safe by not givin' any definite orders, so if anything went wrong, you could step out from under and shift the blame onto McNab."

Middleton smiled appreciatively, and nodded coolly.

"That's right. All of it. You're no fool, Corcoran."

Corcoran ripped out an oath, and this glimpse of the passionate nature that lurked under his inscrutable exterior was like a momentary glimpse of an enraged cougar, eyes blazing, spitting and snarling.

"Why?" he exclaimed. "Why did you plot all this for me? If you had a grudge against Glanton, I can understand why you'd rib up a trap for him, though you wouldn't have had no more luck with him than you have with me. But you ain't got no feud against me. I never saw you before this mornin'!"

"I have no feud with you; I had none with Glanton. But if Fate hadn't thrown you into my path, it would have been Glanton who would have been ambushed in the Blackfoot Chief. Don't you see, Corcoran? It was a test. I had to be sure you were the man I wanted."

Corcoran scowled, puzzled himself now.

"What do you mean?"

"Sit down!" Middleton himself sat down on a nearby chair, unbuckled his gun-belt and threw it, with the heavy, holstered gun, onto a table, out of easy reach. Corcoran seated himself, but his vigilance did not relax, and his gaze rested on Middleton's left armpit, where a second gun might be hidden.

"In the first place," said Middleton, his voice flowing tranquilly, but pitched too low to be heard outside the cabin, "I'm chief of the Vultures, as that fool said. I organized them, even before I was made sheriff. Killing a robber and murderer, who was working outside my gang, made the people of Wahpeton think I'd make a good sheriff. When they gave me the office, I saw what an advantage it would be to me and my gang.

"Our organization is air-tight. There are about fifty men in the gang. They are scattered throughout these mountains. Some pose as miners; some are gamblers – Ace Brent, for instance. He's my right-hand man. Some work in saloons, some clerk in stores. One of the regular drivers of the stage-line company is a Vulture, and so is a clerk of the company, and one of the men who works in the company's stables, tending the horses.

"With spies scattered all over the camp, I know who's trying to take out gold, and when. It's a cinch. We can't lose."

"I don't see how the camp stands for it," grunted Corcoran.

"Men are too crazy after gold to think about anything else. As long as a man isn't molested himself, he doesn't care much what happens to his neighbors. We are organized; they are not. We know who to trust; they don't. It can't last forever. Sooner or later the more intelligent citizens will organize themselves into a vigilante committee and sweep the gulch clean. But when that happens, I intend to be far away – with one man I can trust."

Corcoran nodded, comprehension beginning to gleam in his eyes.

"Already some men are talking vigilante. Colonel Hopkins, for instance. I encourage him as subtly as I can."

"Why, in the name of Satan?"

"To avert suspicion; and for another reason. The vigilantes will serve my purpose at the end."

"And your purpose is to skip out and leave the gang holdin' the sack!"

"Exactly! Look here!"

Taking the candle from the table, he led the way through a back room, where heavy shutters covered the one window. Shutting the door, he turned to the back wall and drew aside some skins that were hung over it. Setting the candle on a roughly hewed table, he fumbled at the logs, and a section swung outward, revealing a heavy plank door set in the solid rock against which the back wall of the cabin was built. It was braced with iron and showed a ponderous lock. Middleton produced a key, and turned it in the lock, and pushed the door inward. He lifted the candle and revealed a small cave, lined and heaped with canvas and buckskin sacks. One of these sacks had burst open, and a golden stream caught the glints of the candle.

"Gold! Sacks and sacks of it!"

Corcoran caught his breath, and his eyes glittered like a wolf's in the candlelight. No man could visualize the contents of those bags unmoved. And the gold-madness had long ago entered Corcoran's veins, more powerfully than he had dreamed, even though he had followed the lure to California and back over the mountains again. The sight of that glittering heap, of those bulging sacks, sent his pulses pounding in his temples, and his hand unconsciously locked on the butt of a gun.

"There must be a million there!"

"Enough to require a good-sized mule-train to pack it out," answered

Middleton. "You see why I have to have a man to help me the night I pull out. And I need a man like you. You're an outdoor man, hardened by wilderness-travel. You're a frontiersman, a *vaquero*, a trail-driver. These men I lead are mostly rats that grew up in border towns – gamblers, thieves, barroom gladiators, saloon-bred gunmen; a few miners gone wrong. You can stand things that would kill any of them.

"The flight we'll have to make will be hard traveling. We'll have to leave the beaten trails and strike out through the mountains. They'll be sure to follow us, and we'll probably have to fight them off. Then there are Indians – Blackfeet and Crows; we may run into a war-party of them. I knew I had to have a fighting man of the keenest type; not only a fighting man, but a man bred on the frontier. That's why I sent for Glanton. But you're a better man than he was."

Corcoran frowned his suspicion.

"Why didn't you tell me all this at first?"

"Because I wanted to try you out. I wanted to be sure you were the right man. I had to be sure. If you were stupid enough, and slow enough to be caught in such a trap as McNab and the rest would set for you, you weren't the man I wanted."

"You're takin' a lot for granted," snapped Corcoran. "How do you know I'll fall in with you and help you loot the camp and then double-cross your gang? What's to prevent me from blowin' your head off for the trick you played on me? Or spillin' the beans to Hopkins, or to McNab?"

"Half a million in gold!" answered Middleton. "If you do any of those things, you'll miss your chance to share that cache with me."

He shut the door, locked it, pushed the other door to and hung the skins over it. Taking the candle he led the way back into the outer room.

He seated himself at the table and poured whisky from a jug into two glasses.

"Well, what about it?"

Corcoran did not at once reply. His brain was still filled with blinding golden visions. His countenance darkened, became sinister as he meditated, staring into his whisky-glass.

The men of the West lived by their own code. The line between the outlaw and the honest cattleman or *vaquero* was sometimes a hair line, too vague to always be traced with accuracy. Men's personal codes were frequently inconsistent, but rigid as iron. Corcoran would not have stolen one cow, or three cows from a squatter, but he had swept across the border to loot Mexican *rancherios* of hundreds of head. He would not hold up a man and take his money, nor would he murder a man in cold blood; but he felt no compunctions about killing a thief and taking the money the thief had stolen. The gold in that cache was blood-stained, the fruit of crimes to which he would have scorned to stoop. But his code of honesty did not prevent him from looting it from the thieves who had looted it in turn from honest men.

"What's my part in the game?" Corcoran asked abruptly.

Middleton grinned zestfully. "Good! I thought you'd see it my way. No man could look at that gold and refuse a share of it! They trust me more than they do any other member of the gang. That's why I keep it here. They know – or think they know – that I couldn't slip out with it. But that's where we'll fool them.

"Your job will be just what I told McNab: you'll uphold law and order. I'll tell the boys not to pull any more hold-ups inside the town itself, and that'll give you a reputation. People will think you've got the gang too scared to work in close. You'll enforce laws like those against shooting up saloons, fighting on the street, and the like. And you'll catch the thieves that are still working alone. When you kill one we'll make it appear that he was a Vulture. You've put yourself solid with the people tonight, by killing those fools in the Blackfoot Chief. We'll keep up the deception.

"I don't trust Ace Brent. I believe he's secretly trying to usurp my place as chief of the gang. He's too damned smart. But I don't want you to kill him. He has too many friends in the gang. Even if they didn't suspect I put you up to it, even if it looked like a private quarrel, they'd want your scalp. I'll frame him – get somebody outside the gang to kill him, when the time comes.

"When we get ready to skip, I'll set the vigilantes and the Vultures to battling each other – how, I don't know, but I'll find a way – and we'll sneak while they're at it. Then for California – South America and the sharing of the gold!"

"The sharin' of the gold!" echoed Corcoran, his eyes lit with grim laughter.

Their hard hands met across the rough table, and the same enigmatic smile played on the lips of both men.

CHAPTER V

The Wheel Begins to Turn

Corcoran stalked through the milling crowd that swarmed in the street, and headed toward the Golden Garter Dance Hall and Saloon. A man lurching through the door with the wide swing of hilarious intoxication stumbled into him and clutched at him to keep from falling to the floor.

Corcoran righted him, smiling faintly into the bearded, rubicund countenance that peered into his.

"Steve Corcoran, by thunder!" whooped the inebriated one gleefully. "Besh damn' deputy in the Territory! 'S' a honor to get picked up by Steve Corcoran! Come in and have a drink."

"You've had too many now," returned Corcoran.

"Right!" agreed the other. "I'm goin' home now, 'f I can get there. Lasht time I was a little full, I didn't make it, by a quarter of a mile! I went to sleep in a ditch across from your shack. I'd 'a' come in and slept on the floor, only I was 'fraid you'd shoot me for one of them derned Vultures!"

Men about them laughed. The intoxicated man was Joe Willoughby, a prominent merchant in Wahpeton, and extremely popular for his free-hearted and open-handed ways.

"Just knock on the door next time and tell me who it is," grinned Corcoran. "You're welcome to a blanket in the sheriff's office, or a bunk in my room, any time you need it."

"Soul of gener – generoshity!" proclaimed Willoughby boisterously. "Goin' home now before the licker gets down in my legs. S'long, old pard!"

He weaved away down the street, amidst the jovial joshings of the miners, to which he retorted with bibulous good nature.

Corcoran turned again into the dance hall and brushed against another man, at whom he glanced sharply, noting the set jaw, the haggard counte-nance and the bloodshot eyes. This man, a young miner well known to

Corcoran, pushed his way through the crowd and hurried up the street with the manner of a man who goes with a definite purpose. Corcoran hesitated, as though to follow him, then decided against it and entered the dance hall. Half the reason for a gunfighter's continued existence lay in his ability to read and analyze the expressions men wore, to correctly interpret the jut of jaw, the glitter of eye. He knew this young miner was determined on some course of action that might result in violence. But the man was not a criminal, and Corcoran never interfered in private quarrels so long as they did not threaten the public safety.

A girl was singing, in a clear, melodious voice, to the accompaniment of a jangling, banging piano. As Corcoran seated himself at a table, with his back to the wall and a clear view of the whole hall before him, she concluded her number amid a boisterous clamor of applause. Her face lit as she saw him. Coming lightly across the hall, she sat down at his table. She rested her elbows on the table, cupped her chin in her hands, and fixed her wide clear gaze on his brown face.

"Shot any Vultures today, Steve?"

He made no answer as he lifted the glass of beer brought him by a waiter.

"They must be scared of you," she continued, and something of youthful hero-worship glowed in her eyes. "There hasn't been a murder or hold-up in town for the past month, since you've been here. Of course you can't be everywhere. They still kill men and rob them in the camps up the ravines, but they keep out of town.

"And that time you took the stage through to Yankton! It wasn't your fault that they held it up and got the gold on the other side of Yankton. You weren't in it, then. I wish I'd been there and seen the fight, when you fought off the men who tried to hold you up, halfway between here and Yankton."

"There wasn't any fight to it," he said impatiently, restless under praise he knew he did not deserve.

"I know; they were afraid of you. You shot at them and they ran."

Very true; it had been Middleton's idea for Corcoran to take the stage through to the next town east, and beat off a fake attempt at hold-up. Corcoran had never relished the memory; whatever his faults, he had the pride of his profession; a fake gunfight was as repugnant to him as a business hoax to an honest business man.

"Everybody knows that the stage company tried to hire you away from

Middleton, as a regular shotgun-guard. But you told them that your business was to protect life and property here in Wahpeton."

She mediated a moment and then laughed reminiscently.

"You know, when you pulled me off of Conchita that night, I thought you were just another blustering bully like McNab. I was beginning to believe that Middleton was taking pay from the Vultures, and that his deputies were crooked. I know things that some people don't." Her eyes became shadowed as if by an unpleasant memory in which, though her companion could not know it, was limned the handsome, sinister face of Ace Brent. "Or maybe people do. Maybe they guess things, but are afraid to say anything.

"But I was mistaken about you, and since you're square, then Middleton must be, too. I guess it was just too big a job for him and his other deputies. None of them could have wiped out that gang in the Blackfoot Chief that night like you did. It wasn't your fault that Tom Deal got away that night, before he could be questioned. If he hadn't, though, maybe you could have made him tell who the other Vultures were."

"I met Jack McBride comin' out of here," said Corcoran abruptly. "He looked like he was about ready to start gunnin' for somebody. Did he drink much in here?"

"Not much. I know what's the matter with him. He's been gambling too much down at the King of Diamonds. Ace Brent has been winning his money for a week. McBride's nearly broke, and I believe he thinks Brent is crooked. He came in here, drank some whisky, and let fall a remark about having a showdown with Brent."

Corcoran rose abruptly. "Reckon I better drift down toward the King of Diamonds. Somethin' may bust loose there. McBride's quick with a gun, and high-tempered. Brent's deadly. Their private business is none of my affair. But if they want to fight it out, they'll have to get out where innocent people won't get hit by stray slugs."

Glory Bland watched him as his tall, erect figure swung out of the door, and there was a glow in her eyes that had never been awakened there by any other man.

Corcoran had almost reached the King of Diamonds gambling hall, when the ordinary noises of the street were split by the crash of a heavy gun.

Simultaneously men came headlong out of the doors, shouting, shoving, plunging in their haste.

"McBride's killed!" bawled a hairy miner.

"No, it's Brent!" yelped another. The crowd surged and milled, craning their necks to see through the windows, yet crowding back from the door in fear of stray bullets. As Corcoran made for the door he heard a man bawl in answer to an eager question: "McBride accused Brent of usin' marked cards, and offered to prove it to the crowd. Brent said he'd kill him and pulled his gun to do it. But it snapped. I heard the hammer click. Then McBride drilled him before he could try again."

Men gave way as Corcoran pushed through the crowd. Somebody yelped: "Look out, Steve! McBride's on the warpath!"

Corcoran stepped into the gambling hall, which was deserted except for the gambler who lay dead on the floor, with a bullet-hole over his heart, and the killer who half-crouched with his back to the bar, and a smoking gun lifted in his hand.

McBride's lips were twisted hard in a snarl, and he looked like a wolf at bay.

"Get back, Corcoran," he warned. "I ain't got nothin' against you, but I ain't goin' to be murdered like a sheep."

"Who said anything about murderin' you?" demanded Corcoran impatiently.

"Oh, I know you wouldn't. But Brent's got friends. They'll never let me get away with killin' him. I believe he was a Vulture. I believe the Vultures will be after me for this. But if they get me, they've got to get me fightin'."

"Nobody's goin' to hurt you," said Corcoran tranquilly. "You better give me your gun and come along. I'll have to arrest you, but it won't amount to nothin', and you ought to know it. As soon as a miner's court can be got together, you'll be tried and acquitted. I reckon no honest folks will do any grievin' for Ace Brent."

"But if I give up my gun and go to jail," objected McBride, wavering, "I'm afraid the toughs will take me out and lynch me."

"I'm givin' you my word you won't be harmed while you're under arrest," answered Corcoran.

"That's enough for me," said McBride promptly, extending his pistol.

Corcoran took it and thrust it into his waist-band. "It's damned foolishness, takin' an honest man's gun," he grunted. "But accordin' to Middleton that's the law. Give me your word that you won't skip, till you've been properly acquitted, and I won't lock you up."

"I'd rather go to jail," said McBride. "I wouldn't skip. But I'll be safer in jail, with you guardin' me, than I would be walkin' around loose for some of Brent's friends to shoot me in the back. After I've been cleared by due process of law, they won't dare to lynch me, and I ain't afraid of 'em when it comes to gun-fightin', in the open."

"All right." Corcoran stooped and picked up the dead gambler's gun, and thrust it into his belt. The crowd surging about the door gave way as he led his prisoner out.

"There the skunk is!" bawled a rough voice. "He murdered Ace Brent!"

McBride turned pale with anger and glared into the crowd, but Corcoran urged him along, and the miner grinned as other voices rose: "A damned good thing, too!" "Brent was crooked!" "He was a Vulture!" bawled somebody, and for a space a tense silence held. That charge was too sinister to bring openly against even a dead man. Frightened by his own indiscretion the man who had shouted slunk away, hoping none had identified his voice.

"I've been gamblin' too much," growled McBride, as he strode along beside Corcoran. "Afraid to try to take my gold out, though, and didn't know what else to do with it. Brent won thousands of dollars' worth of dust from me; poker, mostly.

"This mornin' I was talkin' to Middleton, and he showed a card he said a gambler dropped in his cabin last night. He showed me it was marked, in a way I'd never have suspected. I recognized it as one of the same brand Brent always uses, though Middleton wouldn't tell me who the gambler was. But later I learned that Brent slept off a drunk in Middleton's cabin. Damned poor business for a gambler to get drunk.

"I went to the King of Diamonds awhile ago, and started playin' poker with Brent and a couple of miners. As soon as he raked in the first pot, I called him – flashed the card I got from Middleton and started to show the boys where it was marked. Then Brent pulled his gun; it snapped, and I killed him before he could cock it again. He knew I had the goods on him. He didn't even give me time to tell where I'd gotten the card."

Corcoran made no reply. He locked McBride in the jail, called the jailer from his nearby shack and told him to furnish the prisoner with food, liquor and anything else he needed, and then hurried to his own cabin. Sitting on his bunk in the room behind the sheriff's office, he ejected the cartridge on which Brent's pistol had snapped. The cap was dented, but had not detonated the powder. Looking closely he saw faint abrasions on both the bullet and brass case. They were such as might have been made by the jaws of iron pinchers and a vise.

Securing a wire cutter with pincher jaws, he began to work at the bullet. It slipped out with unusual ease, and the contents of the case spilled into his hand. He did not need to use a match to prove that it was not powder. He knew what the stuff was at first glance – iron filings, to give the proper weight to the cartridge from which the powder had been removed.

At that moment he heard someone enter the outer room, and recognized the firm, easy tread of Sheriff Middleton. Corcoran went into the office and Middleton turned, hung his white hat on a nail.

"McNab tells me McBride killed Ace Brent!"

"You ought to know!" Corcoran grinned. He tossed the bullet and empty case on the table, dumped the tiny pile of iron dust beside them.

"Brent spent the night with you. You got him drunk, and stole one of his cards to show to McBride. You knew how his cards were marked. You took a cartridge out of Brent's gun and put that one in place. One would be enough. You knew there'd be gunplay between him and McBride, when you showed McBride that marked card, and you wanted to be sure it was Brent who stopped lead."

"That's right," agreed Middleton. "I haven't seen you since early yesterday morning. I was going to tell you about the frame I'd ribbed, as soon as I saw you. I didn't know McBride would go after Brent as quickly as he did.

"Brent got too ambitious. He acted as if he were suspicious of us both, lately. Maybe, though, it was just jealousy as far as you were concerned. He liked Glory Bland, and she could never see him. It gouged him to see her falling for you.

"And he wanted my place as leader of the Vultures. If there was one man in the gang that could have kept us from skipping with the loot, it was Ace Brent.

"But I think I've worked it neatly. No one can accuse me of having him murdered, because McBride isn't in the gang. I have no control over him. But Brent's friends will want revenge."

"A miners' court will acquit McBride on the first ballot."

"That's true. Maybe we'd better let him get shot, trying to escape!"

"We will like hell!" rapped Corcoran. "I swore he wouldn't be harmed while he was under arrest. His part of the deal was on the level. He didn't know Brent had a blank in his gun, any more than Brent did. If Brent's friends want his scalp, let 'em go after McBride, like white men ought to, when he's in a position to defend himself."

"But after he's acquitted," argued Middleton, "they won't dare gang up on him in the street, and he'll be too sharp to give them a chance at him in the hills."

"What the hell do I care?" snarled Corcoran. "What difference does it make to me whether Brent's friends get even or not? Far as I'm concerned, he got what was comin' to him. If they ain't got the guts to give McBride an even break, I sure ain't goin' to fix it so they can murder him without riskin' their own hides. If I catch 'em sneakin' around the jail for a shot at him, I'll fill 'em full of hot lead.

"If I'd thought the miners would be crazy enough to do anything to him for killin' Brent, I'd never arrested him. They won't. They'll acquit him. Until they do, I'm responsible for him, and I've give my word. And anybody that tries to lynch him while's he's in my charge better be damned sure they're quicker with a gun than I am."

"There's nobody of that nature in Wahpeton," admitted Middleton with a wry smile. "All right, if you feel your personal honor is involved. But I'll have to find a way to placate Brent's friends, or they'll be accusing me of being indifferent about what happened to him."

CHAPTER VI

Vultures' Court

Next morning Corcoran was awakened by a wild shouting in the street. He had slept in the jail that night, not trusting Brent's friends, but there had been no attempt at violence. He jerked on his boots, and went out into the street, followed by McBride, to learn what the shouting was about.

Men milled about in the street, even at that early hour – for the sun was not yet up – surging about a man in the garb of a miner. This man was astride a horse whose coat was dark with sweat; the man was wild-eyed, bare-headed, and he held his hat in his hands, holding it down for the shouting, cursing throng to see.

"Look at 'em!" he yelled. "Nuggets as big as hen eggs! I took 'em out in an hour, with a pick, diggin' in the wet sand by the creek! And there's plenty more! It's the richest strike these hills ever seen!"

"Where?" roared a hundred voices.

"Well, I got my claim staked out, all I need," said the man, "so I don't mind tellin' you. It ain't twenty miles from here, in a little canyon everybody's overlooked and passed over – Jackrabbit Gorge! The creek's buttered with dust, and the banks are crammed with pockets of nuggets!"

An exuberant whoop greeted this information, and the crowd broke up suddenly as men raced for their shacks.

"New strike," sighed McBride enviously. "The whole town will be surgin' down Jackrabbit Gorge. Wish I could go."

"Gimme your word you'll come back and stand trial, and you can go," promptly offered Corcoran. McBride stubbornly shook his head.

"No, not till I've been cleared legally. Anyway, only a handful of men will get anything. The rest will be pullin' back in to their claims in Wahpeton Gulch tomorrow. Hell, I've been in plenty of them rushes. Only a few ever get anything."

Colonel Hopkins and his partner Dick Bisley hurried past. Hopkins shouted: "We'll have to postpone your trial until this rush is over, Jack! We were going to hold it today, but in an hour there won't be enough men in Wahpeton to impanel a jury! Sorry you can't make the rush. If we can, Dick and I will stake out a claim for you!"

"Thanks, Colonel!"

"No thanks! The camp owes you something for ridding it of that scoundrel Brent. Corcoran, we'll do the same for you, if you like."

"No, thanks," drawled Corcoran. "Minin's too hard work. I've got a gold mine right here in Wahpeton that don't take so much labor!"

The men burst into laughter at this conceit, and Bisley shouted back as they hurried on: "That's right! Your salary looks like an assay from the Comstock lode! But you earn it, all right!"

Joe Willoughby came rolling by, leading a seedy-looking burro on which illy-hung pick and shovel banged against skillet and kettle. Willoughby grasped a jug in one hand, and that he had already been sampling it was proved by his wide-legged gait.

"H'ray for the new diggin's!" he whooped, brandishing the jug at Corcoran and McBride. "Git along, jackass! I'll be scoopin' out nuggets bigger'n this jug before night – if the licker don't get in my legs before I git there!"

"And if it does, he'll fall into a ravine and wake up in the mornin' with a fifty pound nugget in each hand," said McBride. "He's the luckiest son of a gun in the camp; and the best natured."

"I'm goin' and get some ham-and-eggs," said Corcoran. "You want to come and eat with me, or let Pete Daley fix your breakfast here?"

"I'll eat in the jail," decided McBride. "I want to stay in jail till I'm acquitted. Then nobody can accuse me of tryin' to beat the law in any way."

"All right." With a shout to the jailer, Corcoran swung across the road and headed for the camp's most pretentious restaurant, whose proprietor was growing rich, in spite of the terrific prices he had to pay for vegetables and food of all kinds – prices he passed on to his customers.

While Corcoran was eating, Middleton entered hurriedly, and bending over him, with a hand on his shoulder, spoke softly in his ear.

"I've just got wind that that old miner, Joe Brockman, is trying to sneak his gold out on a pack mule, under the pretense of making this rush. I don't know whether it's so or not, but some of the boys up in the hills think it is, and are planning to waylay him and kill him. If he intends getting away, he'll leave the trail to Jackrabbit Gorge a few miles out of town, and swing back toward Yankton, taking the trail over Grizzly Ridge – you know where the thickets are so close. The boys will be laying for him either on the ridge or just beyond.

"He hasn't enough dust to make it worth our while to take it. If they hold him up they'll have to kill him, and we want as few murders as possible. Vigilante sentiment is growing, in spite of the people's trust in you and me. Get on your horse and ride to Grizzly Ridge and see that the old man gets away safe. Tell the boys Middleton said to lay off. If they won't listen – but they will. They wouldn't buck you, even without my word to back you. I'll follow the old man, and try to catch up with him before he leaves the Jackrabbit Gorge road.

"I've sent McNab up to watch the jail, just as a formality. I know McBride won't try to escape, but we mustn't be accused of carelessness."

"Let McNab be mighty careful with his shootin' irons," warned Corcoran. "No 'shot while attempin' to escape,' Middleton. I don't trust McNab. If he lays a hand on McBride, I'll kill him as sure as I'm sittin' here."

"Don't worry. McNab hated Brent. Better get going. Take the short cut through the hills to Grizzly Ridge."

"Sure." Corcoran rose and hurried out in the street which was all but deserted. Far down toward the other end of the gulch rose the dust of the rearguard of the army which was surging toward the new strike. Wahpeton looked almost like a deserted town in the early morning light, foreshadowing its ultimate destiny.

Corcoran went to the corral beside the sheriff's cabin and saddled a fast horse, glancing cryptically at the powerful pack mules whose numbers were steadily increasing. He smiled grimly as he remembered Middleton telling Colonel Hopkins that pack mules were a good investment. As he led his horse out of the corral his gaze fell on a man sprawling under the trees across the road, lazily whittling. Day and night, in one way or another, the gang kept an eye on the cabin that hid the cache of their gold. Corcoran doubted if they actually suspected Middleton's intentions. But they wanted to be sure that no stranger did any snooping about.

Corcoran rode into a ravine that straggled away from the gulch, and a few minutes later he followed a narrow path to its rim, and headed through the mountains toward the spot, miles away, where a trail crossed Grizzly Ridge, a long, steep backbone, thickly timbered.

He had not left the ravine far behind him when a quick rattle of hoofs brought him around, in time to see a horse slide recklessly down a low bluff amid a shower of shale. He swore at the sight of its rider.

"Glory! What the hell?"

"Steve!" She reined up breathlessly beside him. "Go back! It's a trick! I heard Buck Gorman talking to Conchita; he's sweet on her. He's a friend of Brent's – a Vulture! She twists all his secrets out of him. Her room is next to mine, she thought I was out. I overheard them talking. Gorman said a trick had been played on you to get you out of town. He didn't say how. Said you'd go to Grizzly Ridge on a wild-goose chase. While you're gone, they're going to assemble a 'miners' court,' out of the riff-raff left in town. They're going to appoint a 'judge' and 'jury,' take McBride out of jail, try him for killing Ace Brent – and hang him!"

A lurid oath ripped through Steve Corcoran's lips, and for an instant the tiger flashed into view, eyes blazing, fangs bared. Then his dark face was an inscrutable mask again. He wrenched his horse around.

"Much obliged, Glory. I'll be dustin' back into town. You circle around and come in another way. I don't want folks to know you told me."

"Neither do I!" she shuddered. "I knew Ace Brent was a Vulture. He boasted of it to me, once when he was drunk. But I never dared tell anyone. He told me what he'd do to me if I did. I'm glad he's dead. I didn't know Gorman was a Vulture, but I might have guessed it. He was Brent's closest friend. If they ever find out I told you – "

"They won't," Corcoran assured her. It was natural for a girl to fear such blackhearted rogues as the Vultures, but the thought of them actually harming her never entered his mind. He came from a country where not even the worst of scoundrels would ever dream of hurting a woman.

He drove his horse at a reckless gallop back the way he had come, but not all the way. Before he reached the Gulch he swung wide of the ravine he had followed out, and plunged into another, that would bring him into the Gulch at the end of town where the jail stood. As he rode down it he heard a deep, awesome roar he recognized – the roar of the man-pack, hunting its own kind.

A band of men surged up the dusty street, roaring, cursing. One man waved a rope. Pale faces of bartenders, store clerks and dance-hall girls peered timidly out of doorways as the unsavory mob roared past. Corcoran knew them, by sight or reputation: plug-uglies, barroom loafers, skulkers – many were Vultures, as he knew; others were riff-raff, ready for any sort of deviltry that required neither courage nor intelligence – the scum that gathers in any mining camp.

Dismounting, Corcoran glided through the straggling trees that grew behind the jail, and heard McNab challenge the mob.

"What do you want?"

"We aim to try your prisoner!" shouted the leader. "We come in the due process of law. We've app'inted a jedge and panelled a jury, and we demands that you hand over the prisoner to be tried in miners' court, accordin' to legal precedent!"

"How do I know you're representative of the camp?" parried McNab.

" 'Cause we're the only body of men in camp right now!" yelled someone, and this was greeted by a roar of laughter.

"We come empowered with the proper authority – " began the leader, and broke off suddenly: "Grab him, boys!"

There was the sound of a brief scuffle, McNab swore vigorously, and the leader's voice rose triumphantly: "Let go of him, boys, but don't give him his gun. McNab, you ought to know better'n to try to oppose legal procedure, and you a upholder of law and order!"

Again a roar of sardonic laughter, and McNab growled: "All right; go ahead with the trial. But you do it over my protests. I don't believe this is a representative assembly."

"Yes, it is," averred the leader, and then his voice thickened with blood-lust. "Now, Daley, gimme that key and bring out the prisoner."

The mob surged toward the door of the jail, and at that instant Corcoran stepped around the corner of the cabin and leaped up on the low porch it boasted. There was a hissing intake of breath. Men halted suddenly, digging their heels against the pressure behind them. The surging line wavered backward, leaving two figures isolated – McNab, scowling, disarmed, and a hairy giant whose huge belly was girt with a broad belt bristling with gun butts and knife hilts. He held a noose in one hand, and his bearded lips gaped as he glared at the unexpected apparition.

For a breathless instant Corcoran did not speak. He did not look at McBride's pallid countenance peering through the barred door behind him. He stood facing the mob, his head slightly bent, a somber, immobile figure, sinister with menace.

"Well," he said finally, softly, "what's holdin' up the baile?"

The leader blustered feebly.

"We come here to try a murderer!"

Corcoran lifed his head and the man involuntarily recoiled at the lethal glitter of his eyes.

"Who's your judge?" the Texan inquired softly.

"We appointed Jake Bissett, there," spoke up a man, pointing at the uncomfortable giant on the porch.

"So you're goin' to hold a miners' court," murmured Corcoran. "With a judge and jury picked out of the dives and honky-tonks – scum and dirt of the gutter!" And suddenly uncontrollable fury flamed in his eyes. Bissett, sensing his intention, bellowed in ox-like alarm and grabbed frantically at a gun. His fingers had scarcely touched the checkered butt when smoke and flame roared from Corcoran's right hip. Bisset pitched backward off the porch as if he had been struck by a hammer; the rope tangled about his limbs as he fell, and he lay in the dust that slowly turned crimson, his hairy fingers twitching spasmodically.

Corcoran faced the mob, livid under his sun-burnt bronze. His eyes were coals of blue hell's-fire. There was a gun in each hand, and from the right-hand muzzle a wisp of blue smoke drifted lazily upward.

"I declare this court adjourned!" he roared. "The judge is done impeached, and the jury's discharged! I'll give you thirty seconds to clear the court-room!"

He was one man against nearly a hundred, but he was a grey wolf facing a pack of yapping jackals. Each man knew that if the mob surged on him, they would drag him down at last; but each man knew what an awful toll would first be paid, and each man feared that he himself would be one of those to pay that toll.

They hesitated, stumbled back – gave way suddenly and scattered in all directions. Some backed away, some shamelessly turned their backs and fled. With a snarl Corcoran thrust his guns back in their scabbards and turned toward the door where McBride stood, grasping the bars.

"I thought I was a goner that time, Corcoran," he gasped. The Texan pulled the door open, and pushed McBride's pistol into his hand.

"There's a horse tied behind the jail," said Corcoran. "Get on it and dust out of here. I'll take the full responsibility. If you stay here they'll burn down the jail, or shoot you through the window. You can make it out of town while they're scattered. I'll explain to Middleton and Hopkins. In a month or so, if you want to, come back and stand trial, as a matter of formality. Things will be cleaned up around here by then."

McBride needed no urging. The grisly fate he had just escaped had shaken his nerve. Shaking Corcoran's hand passionately, he ran stumblingly through the trees to the horse Corcoran had left there. A few moments later he was fogging it out of the Gulch.

McNab came up, scowling and grumbling.

"You had no authority to let him go. I tried to stop the mob – "

Corcoran wheeled and faced him, making no attempt to conceal his hatred.

"You did like hell! Don't pull that stuff with me, McNab. You was in on this, and so was Middleton. You put up a bluff of talk, so afterwards you could tell Colonel Hopkins and the others that you tried to stop the lynchin' and was overpowered. I saw the scrap you put up when they grabbed you! Hell! You're a rotten actor."

"You can't talk to me like that!" roared McNab.

The old tigerish light flickered in the blue eyes. Corcoran did not exactly move, yet he seemed to sink into a half crouch, as a cougar does for the killing spring.

"If you don't like my style, McNab," he said softly, thickly, "you're more'n welcome to open the *baile* whenever you get ready!"

For an instant they faced each other, McNab black-browed and scowling, Corcoran's thin lips almost smiling, but blue fire lighting his eyes. Then with a grunt McNab turned and slouched away, his shaggy head swaying from side to side like that of a surly bull.

CHAPTER VII

A Vulture's Wings are Clipped

Middleton pulled up his horse suddenly as Corcoran reined out of the bushes. One glance showed the sheriff that Corcoran's mood was far from placid. They were amidst a grove of alders, perhaps a mile from the Gulch.

"Why, hello, Corcoran," began Middleton, concealing his surprise. "I caught up with Brockman. It was just a wild rumor. He didn't have any gold. That – "

"Drop it!" snapped Corcoran. "I know why you sent me off on that wild-goose chase – same reason you pulled out of town. To give Brent's friends a chance to get even with McBride. If I hadn't turned around and dusted back into Wahpeton, McBride would be kickin' his life out at the end of a rope, right now."

"You came back – ?"

"Yeah! And now Jake Bissett's in hell instead of Jack McBride, and McBride's dusted out – on a horse I gave him. I told you I gave him my word he wouldn't be lynched."

"You killed Bissett?"

"Deader'n hell!"

"He was a Vulture," muttered Middleton, but he did not seem displeased. "Brent, Bissett – the more Vultures die, the easier it will be for us to get away when we go. That's one reason I had Brent killed. But you should have let them hang McBride. Of course I framed this affair; I had to do something to satisfy Brent's friends. Otherwise they might have gotten suspicious.

"If they suspicioned I had anything to do with having him killed, or thought I wasn't anxious to punish the man who killed him, they'd make trouble for me. I can't have a split in the gang now. And even I can't protect you from Brent's friends, after this."

"Have I ever asked you, or any man, for protection?" The quick jealous pride of the gunfighter vibrated in his voice.

"Breckman, Red Bill, Curly, and now Bissett. You've killed too many Vultures. I made them think the killing of the first three was a mistake, all around. Bissett wasn't very popular. But they won't forgive you for stopping them from hanging the man who killed Ace Brent. They won't attack you openly, of course. But you'll have to watch every step you make. They'll kill you if they can, and I won't be able to prevent them."

"If I'd tell 'em just how Ace Brent died, you'd be in the same boat," said Corcoran bitingly. "Of course, I won't. Our final getaway depends on you keepin' their confidence – as well as the confidence of the honest folks. This last killin' ought to put me, and therefore you, ace-high with Hopkins and his crowd."

"They're still talking vigilante. I encourage it. It's coming anyway. Murders in the outlying camps are driving men to a frenzy of fear and rage, even though such crimes have ceased in Wahpeton. Better to fall in line with the inevitable and twist it to a man's own ends, than to try to oppose it. If you can keep Brent's friends from killing you for a few more weeks, we'll be ready to jump. Look out for Buck Gorman. He's the most dangerous man in the gang. He was Brent's friend, and he has his own friends – all dangerous men. Don't kill him unless you have to."

"I'll take care of myself," answered Corcoran somberly. "I looked for Gorman in the mob, but he wasn't there. Too smart. But he's the man behind the mob. Bissett was just a stupid ox; Gorman planned it – or rather, I reckon he helped you plan it."

"I'm wondering how you found out about it," said Middleton. "You wouldn't have come back unless somebody told you. Who was it?"

"None of your business," growled Corcoran. It did not occur to him that Glory Bland would be in any danger from Middleton, even if the sheriff knew about her part in the affair, but he did not relish being questioned, and did not feel obliged to answer anybody's queries.

"That new gold strike sure came in mighty handy for you and Gorman," he said. "Did you frame that, too?"

Middleton nodded.

"Of course. That was one of my men who posed as a miner. He had a hatful of nuggets from the cache. He served his purpose and joined the men who hide up there in the hills. The mob of miners will be back tomorrow, tired and mad and disgusted, and when they hear about what happened, they'll recognize the handiwork of the Vultures; at least some of them will. But they won't connect me with it in any way. Now we'll ride back to town. Things are breaking our way, in spite of your foolish interference with the mob. But let Gorman alone. You can't afford to make any more enemies in the gang."

Buck Gorman leaned on the bar in the Golden Eagle and expressed his opinion of Steve Corcoran in no uncertain terms. The crowd listened sympathetically, for, almost to a man, they were the ruffians and riff-raff of the camp.

"The dog pretends to be a deputy!" roared Gorman, whose blood-shot eyes and damp tangled hair attested to the amount of liquor he had drunk. "But he kills an appointed judge, breaks up a court and drives away the jury – yes, and releases the prisoner, a man charged with murder!"

233

It was the day after the fake gold strike, and the disillusioned miners were drowning their chagrin in the saloons. But few honest miners were in the Golden Eagle.

"Colonel Hopkins and other prominent citizens held an investigation," said some one. "They declared that evidence showed Corcoran to have been justified – denounced the court as a mob, acquitted Corcoran of killing Bissett, and then went ahead and acquitted McBride for killing Brent, even though he wasn't there."

Gorman snarled like a cat, and reached for his whisky glass. His hand did not twitch or quiver, his movements were more catlike than ever. The whisky had inflamed his mind, illumined his brain with a white-hot certainty that was akin to insanity, but it had not affected his nerves or any part of his muscular system. He was more deadly drunk than sober.

"I was Brent's best friend!" he roared. "I was Bissett's friend."

"They say Bissett was a Vulture," whispered a voice. Gorman lifted his tawny head and glared about the room as a lion might glare.

"Who says he was a Vulture? Why don't these slanderers accuse a living man? It's always a dead man they accuse! Well, what if he was? He was my friend! Maybe that makes *me* a Vulture!"

No one laughed or spoke as his flaming gaze swept the room, but each man, as those blazing eyes rested on him in turn, felt the chill breath of Death blowing upon him.

"Bissett a Vulture!" he said, wild enough with drink and fury to commit any folly, as well as any atrocity. He did not heed the eyes fixed on him, some in fear, a few in intense interest. "Who knows who the Vultures are? Who knows who, or what anybody really is? Who really knows anything about this man Corcoran, for instance? I could tell – "

A light step on the threshold brought him about as Corcoran loomed in the door. Gorman froze, snarling, lips writhed back, a tawny-maned incarnation of hate and menace.

"I heard you was makin' a talk about me down here, Gorman," said Corcoran. His face was bleak and emotionless as that of a stone image, but his eyes burned with murderous purpose.

Gorman snarled wordlessly.

"I looked for you in the mob," said Corcoran, tonelessly, his voice as soft and without emphasis as the even strokes of a feather. It seemed almost as if his voice were a thing apart from him; his lips murmuring while all the rest of his being was tense with concentration on the man before him.

"You wasn't there. You sent your coyotes, but you didn't have the guts to come yourself, and – "

The dart of Gorman's hand to his gun was like the blurring stroke of a snake's head, but no eye could follow Corcoran's hand. His gun smashed before anyone knew he had reached for it. Like an echo came the roar of Gorman's shot. But the bullet ploughed splinteringly into the floor, from a hand that was already death-stricken and falling. Gorman pitched over and lay still, the swinging lamp glinting on his upturned spurs and the blue steel of the smoking gun which lay by his hand.

CHAPTER VIII

The Coming of the Vigilantes

Colonel Hopkins looked absently at the liquor in his glass, stirred restlessly, and said abruptly: "Middleton, I might as well come to the point. My friends and I have organized a vigilante committee, just as we should have done months ago. Now, wait a minute. Don't take this as a criticism of your methods. You've done wonders in the last month, ever since you brought Steve Corcoran in here. Not a hold-up in the town, not a killing – that is, not a murder, and only a few shootings among the honest citizens.

"Added to that the ridding of the camp of such scoundrels as Jake Bissett and Buck Gorman. They were both undoubtedly members of the Vultures. I wish Corcoran hadn't killed Gorman just when he did, though. The man was drunk, and about to make some reckless disclosures about the gang. At least that's what a friend of mine thinks, who was in the Golden Eagle that night. But anyway, it couldn't be helped.

"No, we're not criticizing you at all. But obviously you can't stop the murders and robberies that are going on up and down the Gulch, all the time. And you can't stop the outlaws from holding up the stage regularly.

"So that's where we come in. We have sifted the camp, carefully, over a period of months, until we have fifty men we can trust absolutely. It's taken a long time, because we've had to be sure of our men. We didn't want to take in a man who might be a spy for the Vultures. But at last we

235

know where we stand. We're not sure just who is a Vulture, but we know who isn't in as far as our organization is concerned.

"We can work together, John. We have no intention of interfering within your jurisdiction, or trying to take the law out of your hands. We demand a free hand outside the camp; inside the limits of Wahpeton we are willing to act under your orders, or at least according to your advice. Of course, we will work in absolute secrecy until we have proof enough to strike."

"You must remember, Colonel," reminded Middleton, "that all along I've admitted the impossibility of my breaking up the Vultures with the limited means at my disposal. I've never opposed a vigilante committee. All I've demanded was that when it was formed, it should be composed of honest men, and be free of any element that might seek to twist its purpose into the wrong channels."

"That's true. I didn't expect any opposition from you, and I can assure you that we'll always work hand-in-hand with you and your deputies." He hesitated, as if over something unpleasant, and then said: "John, are you sure of all your deputies?"

Middleton's head jerked up and he shot a startled glance at the Colonel, as if the latter had surprised him by putting into words a thought that had already occurred to him.

"Why do you ask?" he parried.

"Well," Hopkins was embarrassed. "I don't know – maybe I'm prejudiced – but – well, damn it, to put it bluntly, I've sometimes wondered about Bill McNab!"

Middleton filled the glasses again before he answered.

"Colonel, I never accuse a man without iron-clad evidence. I'm not always satisfied with McNab's actions, but it may merely be the man's nature. He's a surly brute. But he has his virtues. I'll tell you frankly, the reason I haven't discharged him is that I'm not sure of him. That probably sounds ambiguous."

"Not at all. I appreciate your position. You have as much as said you suspect him of double-dealing, and are keeping him on your force so you can watch him. Your wits are not dull, John. Frankly – and this will probably surprise you – until a month ago some of the men were beginning to whisper some queer things about you – queer suspicions, that is. But your bringing Corcoran in showed us that you were on the level. You'd have never brought him in if you'd been taking pay from the Vultures!"

Middleton halted with his glass at his lips.

"Great heavens!" he ejaculated. "Did they suspect me of *that?*"

"Just a fool idea some of the men had," Hopkins assured him. "Of course I never gave it a thought. The men who thought it are ashamed now. The killing of Bissett, of Gorman, of the men in the Blackfoot Chief, show that Corcoran's on the level. And of course, he's merely taking orders from you. All those men were Vultures, of course. It's a pity Tom Deal got away before we could question him." He rose to go.

"McNab was guarding Deal," said Middleton, and his tone implied more than his words said.

Hopkins shot him a startled glance.

"By heaven, so he was! But he was really wounded – I saw the bullet hole in his arm, where Deal shot him in making his getaway."

"That's true." Middleton rose and reached for his hat. "I'll walk along with you. I want to find Corcoran and tell him what you've just told me."

"It's been a week since he killed Gorman," mused Hopkins. "I've been expecting Gorman's Vulture friends to try to get him, any time."

"So have I!" answered Middleton, with a grimness which his companion missed.

CHAPTER IX

The Vultures Swoop

Down the gulch lights blazed; the windows of cabins were yellow squares in the night, and beyond them the velvet sky reflected the lurid heart of the camp. The intermittent breeze brought faint strains of music and the noises of hilarity. But up the gulch, where a clump of trees straggled near an unlighted cabin, the darkness of the moonless night was a mask that the faint stars did not illuminate.

Figures moved in the deep shadows of the trees, voices whispered, their furtive tones mingling with the rustling of the wind through the leaves.

"We ain't close enough. We ought to lay alongside his cabin and blast him as he goes in."

A second voice joined the first, muttering like a bodyless voice in a conclave of ghosts.

"We've gone all over that. I tell you this is the best way. Get him off guard. You're sure Middleton was playin' cards at the King of Diamonds?"

Another voice answered: "He'll be there till daylight, likely."

"He'll be awful mad," whispered the first speaker.

"Let him. He can't afford to do anything about it. *Listen!* Somebody's comin' up the road!"

They crouched down in the bushes, merging with the blacker shadows. They were so far from the cabin, and it was so dark, that the approaching figure was only a dim blur in the gloom.

"It's him!" a voice hissed fiercely, as the blur merged with the bulkier shadow that was the cabin.

In the stillness a door rasped across a sill. A yellow light sprang up, streaming through the door, blocking out a small window high up in the wall. The man inside did not cross the lighted doorway, and the window was too high to see through into the cabin.

The light went out after a few minutes.

"Come on!" The three men rose and went stealthily toward the cabin. Their bare feet made no sound, for they had discarded their boots. Coats too had been discarded, any garment that might swing loosely and rustle, or catch on projections. Cocked guns were in their hands; they could have been no more wary had they been approaching the lair of a lion. And each man's heart pounded suffocatingly, for the prey they stalked was far more dangerous than any lion.

When one spoke it was so low that his companions hardly heard him with their ears a matter of inches from his bearded lips.

"We'll take our places like we planned, Joel. You'll go to the door and call him, like we told you. He knows Middleton trusts you. He don't know you'd be helpin' Gorman's friends. He'll recognize your voice, and he won't suspect nothin'. When he comes to the door and opens it, step into the shadows and fall flat. We'll do the rest from where we'll be layin'."

His voice shook slightly as he spoke, and the other man shuddered; his face was a pallid oval in the darkness.

"I'll do it, but I bet he kills some of us. I bet he kills me, anyway. I must have been crazy when I said I'd help you fellows."

"You can't back out now!" hissed the other. They stole forward, their guns advanced, their hearts in their mouths. Then the foremost man caught at the arms of his companions.

"Wait! Look there! He's left the door open!"

The open doorway was a blacker shadow in the shadow of the wall.

"He knows we're after him!" There was a catch of hysteria in the babbling whisper. "It's a trap!"

"Don't be a fool! How could he know? He's asleep. I hear him snorin'. We won't wake him. We'll step into the cabin and let him have it! We'll have enough light from the window to locate the bunk, and we'll rake it with lead before he can move. He'll wake up in hell. Come on, and for God's sake, don't make no noise!"

The last advice was unnecessary. Each man, as he set his bare foot down, felt as if he were setting it into the lair of a diamond-backed rattler.

As they glided, one after another, across the threshold, they made less noise than the wind blowing through the black branches. They crouched by the door, straining their eyes across the room, whence came the rhythmic snoring. Enough light sifted through the small window to show them a vague outline that was a bunk, with a shapeless mass upon it.

A man caught his breath in a short, uncontrollable gasp. Then the cabin was shaken by a thunderous volley, three guns roaring together. Lead swept the bunk in a devastating storm, thudding into flesh and bone, smacking into wood. A wild cry broke in a gagging gasp. Limbs thrashed wildly and a heavy body tumbled to the floor. From the darkness on the floor beside the bunk welled up hideous sounds, choking gurgles and a convulsive flopping and thumping. The men crouching near the door poured lead blindly at the sounds. There was fear and panic in the haste and number of their shots. They did not cease jerking their triggers until their guns were empty, and the noises on the floor had ceased.

"Out of here, quick!" gasped one.

"No! Here's the table and a candle on it. I felt it in the dark. I've got to *know* that he's dead before I leave this cabin. I've got to see him lyin' dead if I'm goin' to sleep easy. We've got plenty of time to get away. Folks down the gulch must have heard the shots, but it'll take time for them to get here. No danger. I'm goin' to light the candle!"

There was a rasping sound, and a yellow light sprang up, etching three staring, bearded faces. Wisps of blue smoke blurred the light as the candle-wick ignited from the fumbling match, but the men saw a huddled shape crumpled near the bunk, from which streams of dark crimson radiated in every direction.

"Ahhh!"

They whirled at the sound of running footsteps.

"Oh, God!" shrieked one of the men, falling to his knees, his hands lifted to shut out a terrible sight. The other ruffians staggered with the shock of what they saw. They stood gaping, livid, helpless, empty guns sagging in their hands.

For in the doorway, glaring in dangerous amazement, with a gun in each hand, stood the man whose lifeless body they thought lay over there by the splintered bunk!

"Drop them guns!" Corcoran rasped. They clattered on the floor as the hands of their owner mechanically reached skyward. The man on the floor staggered up, his hands empty; he retched, shaken by the nausea of fear.

"Joel Miller!" said Corcoran evenly; his surprise was passed, as he realized what had happened. "Didn't know you run with Gorman's crowd. Reckon Middleton'll be some surprised, too."

"You're a devil!" gasped Miller. "You can't be killed! We killed you – heard you roll off your bunk and die on the floor, in the dark. We kept shooting after we knew you were dead. But you're alive!"

"You didn't shoot me," grunted Corcoran. "You shot a man you thought was me. I was comin' up the road when I heard the shots. You killed Joe Willoughby! He was drunk and I reckon he staggered in here and fell in my bunk, like he's done before."

The men went whiter yet under their bushy beards, with rage and chagrin and fear.

"Willoughby!" babbled Miller. "The camp will never stand for this! Let us go, Corcoran! Hopkins and his crowd will hang us! It'll mean the end of the Vultures! Your end, too, Corcoran! If they hang us, we'll talk first! They'll find out that you're one of us!"

"In that case," muttered Corcoran, his eyes narrowing, "I'd better kill the three of you. That's the sensible solution. You killed Willoughby, tryin' to get me; I kill you, in self-defense."

"Don't do it, Corcoran!" screamed Miller, frantic with terror.

"Shut up, you dog," growled one of the other men, glaring balefully at their captor. "Corcoran wouldn't shoot down unarmed men."

"No, I wouldn't," said Corcoran. "Not unless you made some kind of a break. I'm peculiar that way, which I see is a handicap in this country. But it's the way I was raised, and I can't get over it. No, I ain't goin' to beef you cold, though you've just tried to get me that way.

"But I'll be damned if I'm goin' to let you sneak off, to come back here and try it again the minute you get your nerve bucked up. I'd about as soon be hanged by the vigilantes as shot in the back by a passle of rats like you all. Vultures, hell! You ain't even got the guts to be good buzzards.

"I'm goin' to take you down the gulch and throw you in jail. It'll be up to Middleton to decide what to do with you. He'll probably work out some scheme that'll swindle everybody except himself; but I warn you – one yap about the Vultures to anybody, and I'll forget my raisin' and send you to hell with your belts empty and your boots on."

The noise in the King of Diamonds was hushed suddenly as a man rushed in and bawled: "The Vultures have murdered Joe Willoughby! Steve Corcoran caught three of 'em, and has just locked 'em up! This time we've got some live Vultures to work on!"

A roar answered him and the gambling hall emptied itself as men rushed yelling into the street. John Middleton laid down his hand of cards, donned his white hat with a hand that was steady as a rock, and strode after them.

Already a crowd was surging and roaring around the jail. The miners were lashed into a murderous frenzy and were restrained from shattering the door and dragging forth the cowering prisoners only by the presence of Corcoran, who faced them on the jail-porch. McNab, Richardson, and Stark were there, also. McNab was pale under his whiskers, and Stark seemed nervous and ill at ease, but Richardson, as always, was cold as ice.

"Hang 'em" roared the mob. "Let us have 'em, Steve! You've done your part! This camp's put up with enough! Let us have 'em!"

Middleton climbed up on the porch, and was greeted by loud cheers, but his efforts to quiet the throng proved futile. Somebody brandished a rope with a noose in it. Resentment, long smoldering, was bursting into flame, fanned by hysterical fear and hate. The mob had no wish to harm either Corcoran or Middleton – did not intend to harm them. But they were determined to drag out the prisoners and string them up.

Colonel Hopkins forced his way through the crowd, mounted the step, and waved his hands until he obtained a certain amount of silence.

"Listen, men!" he roared, "this is the beginning of a new era for Wahpeton! This camp has been terrorized long enough. We're beginning a rule of law and order, right now! But don't spoil it at the very beginning! These men shall hang – I swear it! But let's do it legally, and with the sanction of law. Another thing: if you hang them out of hand, we'll never learn who their companions and leaders are.

"Tomorrow, I promise you, a court of inquiry will sit on their case. They'll be questioned and forced to reveal the men above and behind them. This camp is going to be cleaned up! Let's clean it up lawfully and in order!"

"Colonel's right!" bawled a bearded giant. "Ain't no use to hang the little rats till we find out who's the big 'uns!"

A roar of approbation rose as the temper of the mob changed. It began to break up, as the men scattered to hasten back to the bars and indulge in their passion to discuss the new development.

Hopkins shook Corcoran's hand heartily.

"Congratulations, sir! I've seen poor Joe's body. A terrible sight. The fiends fairly shot the poor fellow to ribbons. Middleton, I told you the vigilantes wouldn't usurp your authority in Wahpeton. I keep my word. We'll leave these murderers in your jail, guarded by your deputies. Tomorrow the vigilante court will sit in session, and I hope we'll come to the bottom of this filthy mess."

And so saying he strode off, followed by a dozen or so steely-eyed men whom Middleton knew formed the nucleus of the Colonel's organization.

When they were out of hearing, Middleton stepped to the door and spoke quickly to the prisoners: "Keep your mouths shut. You fools have gotten us all in a jam, but I'll snake you out of it, somehow." To McNab he spoke: "Watch the jail. Don't let anybody come near it. Corcoran and I have got to talk this over." Lowering his voice so the prisoners could not hear, he added: "If anybody does come, that you can't order off, and these fools start shooting off their heads, close their mouths with lead."

Corcoran followed Middleton into the shadow of the gulch-wall. Out of earshot of the nearest cabin, Middleton turned. "Just what happened?"

"Gorman's friends tried to get me. They killed Joe Willoughby by mistake. I hauled them in. That's all."

"That's not all," muttered Middleton. "There will be hell to pay if they come to trial. Miller's yellow. He'll talk, sure. I've been afraid Gorman's friends would try to kill you – wondering how it would work out. It's worked out just about the worst way it possibly could. You should either have killed them or let them go. Yet I appreciate your attitude. You have scruples against cold-blooded murder; and if you'd turned them loose, they'd have been back potting at you the next night."

"I couldn't have turned them loose if I'd wanted to. Men had heard the shots; they came runnin'; found me there holdin' a gun on those devils, and Joe Willoughby's body layin' on the floor, shot to pieces."

"I know. But we can't keep members of our own gang in jail, and we can't hand them over to the vigilantes. I've got to delay that trial, somehow. If I were ready, we'd jump tonight, and to hell with it. But I'm not ready. After all, perhaps it's as well this happened. It may give us our chance to skip. We're one jump ahead of the vigilantes and the gang, too. We know the vigilantes have formed and are ready to strike, and the rest of the gang don't. I've told no one but you what Hopkins told me early in the evening.

"Listen, Corcoran, we've got to move tomorrow night! I wanted to pull one last job, the biggest of all – the looting of Hopkins and Bisley's private cache. I believe I could have done it, in spite of all their guards and precautions. But we'll have to let that slide. I'll persuade Hopkins to put off the trial another day. I think I know how. Tomorrow night I'll have the vigilantes and the Vultures at each others' throats! We'll load the mules and pull out while they're fighting. Once let us get a good start, and they're welcome to chase us if they want to.

"I'm going to find Hopkins now. You get back to the jail. If McNab talks to Miller or the others, be sure you listen to what's said."

Middleton found Hopkins in the Golden Eagle Saloon.

"I've come to ask a favor of you, Colonel," he began directly. "I want you, if it's possible, to put off the investigating trial until day after tomorrow. I've been talking to Joel Miller. He's cracking. If I can get him away from Barlow and Letcher, and talk to him, I believe he'll tell me everything I want to know. It'll be better to get his confession, signed and sworn to, before we bring the matter into court. Before a judge, with all eyes on him, and his friends in the crowd, he might stiffen and refuse to incriminate anyone. I don't believe the others will talk. But talking to me, alone, I believe Miller will spill the whole works. But it's going to take time to wear him down. I believe that by tomorrow night I'll have a full confession from him."

"That would make our work a great deal easier," admitted Hopkins.

"And another thing: these men ought to be represented by proper counsel. You'll prosecute them, of course; and the only other lawyer within reach is Judge Bixby, at Yankton. We're doing this thing in as close accordance to regular legal procedure as possible. Therefore we can't refuse the prisoner the right to be defended by an attorney. I've sent a man after Bixby. It will be late tomorrow evening before he can get back with the Judge, even if he has no trouble in locating him.

"Considering all these things, I feel it would be better to postpone the trial until we can get Bixby here, and until I can get Miller's confession."

"What will the camp think?"

"Most of them are men of reason. The few hotheads who might want to take matters into their own hands can't do any harm."

"All right," agreed Hopkins. "After all, they're your prisoners, since your deputy captured them, and the attempted murder of an officer of the law is one of the charges for which they'll have to stand trial. We'll set the trial for day after tomorrow. Meanwhile, work on Joel Miller. If we have his signed confession, naming the leaders of the gang, it will expedite matters a great deal at the trial."

CHAPTER X

The Blood on the Gold

Wahpeton learned of the postponement of the trial and reacted in various ways. The air was surcharged with tension. Little work was done that day. Men gathering in heated, gesticulating groups, crowded in at the bars. Voices rose in hot altercation, fists pounded on the bars. Unfamiliar faces were observed, men who were seldom seen in the gulch – miners from claims in distant canyons, or more sinister figures from the hills, whose business was less obvious.

Lines of cleavage were noticed. Here and there clumps of men gathered, keeping to themselves and talking in low tones. In certain dives the ruffian element of the camp gathered, and these saloons were shunned by honest men. But still the great mass of the people milled about, suspicious and uncertain. The status of too many men was still in doubt. Certain men were known to be above suspicion, certain others were known to be ruffians and criminals; but between these two extremes there were possibilities for all shades of distrust and suspicion.

So most men wandered aimlessly to and fro, with their weapons ready to their hands, glancing at their fellows out of the corners of their eyes.

To the surprise of all, Steve Corcoran was noticed at several bars, drinking heavily, though the liquor did not seem to affect him in any way.

The men in the jail were suffering from nerves. Somehow the word had gotten out that the vigilante organization was a reality, and that they were to be tried before a vigilante court. Joel Miller, hysterical, accused Middleton of double-crossing his men.

"Shut up, you fool!" snarled the sheriff, showing the strain under which he was laboring merely by the irascible edge on his voice. "Haven't you seen your friends drifting by the jail? I've gathered the men in from the hills. They're all here. Forty-odd men, every Vulture in the gang, is here in Wahpeton.

"Now, get this: and McNab, listen closely: we'll stage the break just before daylight, when everybody is asleep. Just before dawn is the best time, because that's about the only time in the whole twenty-four hours that the camp isn't going full blast.

"Some of the boys, with masks on, will swoop down and overpower you deputies. There'll be no shots fired until they've gotten the prisoners and started off. Then start yelling and shooting after them – in the air, of course. That'll bring everybody on the run to hear how you were overpowered by a gang of masked riders.

"Miller, you and Letcher and Barlow will put up a fight – "

"Why?"

"Why, you fool, to make it look like it's a mob that's capturing you, instead of friends rescuing you. That'll explain why none of the deputies are hurt. Men wanting to lynch you wouldn't want to hurt the officers.

You'll yell and scream blue murder, and the men in the masks will drag you out, tie you and throw you across horses and ride off. Somebody is bound to see them riding away. It'll look like a capture, not a rescue."

Bearded lips gaped in admiring grins at the strategy.

"All right. Don't make a botch of it. There'll be hell to pay, but I'll convince Hopkins that it was the work of a mob, and we'll search the hills to find your bodies hanging from trees. We won't find any bodies, naturally, but maybe we'll contrive to find a mass of ashes where a log hut had been burned to the ground, and a few hats and belt buckles easy to identify."

Miller shivered at the implication and stared at Middleton with painful intensity.

"Middleton, you ain't planning to have us put out of the way? These men in masks are our friends, not vigilantes you've put up to this?"

"Don't be a fool!" flared Middleton disgustedly. "Do you think the gang would stand for anything like that, even if I was imbecile enough to try it? You'll recognize your friends when they come.

"Miller, I want your name at the foot of a confession I've drawn up, implicating somebody as the leader of the Vultures. There's no use trying to deny you and the others are members of the gang. Hopkins knows you are; instead of trying to play innocent, you'll divert suspicion to someone outside the gang. I haven't filled in the name of the leader, but Dick Lennox is as good as anybody. He's a gambler, has few friends, and never would work with us. I'll write his name in your 'confession' as chief of the Vultures, and Corcoran will kill him 'for resisting arrest,' before he has time to prove that it's a lie. Then, before anybody has time to get suspicious, we'll make our last big haul – the raid on the Hopkins and Bisley cache! – and blow! Be ready to jump, when the gang swoops in.

"Miller, put your signature to this paper. Read it first if you want to. I'll fill in the blanks I left for the 'chief's name later. Where's Corcoran?"

"I saw him in the Golden Eagle an hour ago," growled McNab. "He's drinkin' like a fish."

"Damnation!" Middleton's mask slipped a bit despite himself, then he regained his easy control. "Well, it doesn't matter. We won't need him tonight. Better for him not to be here when the jail break's made. Folks would think it was funny if he didn't kill somebody. I'll drop back later in the night."

Even a man of steel nerves feels the strain of waiting for a crisis. Corcoran was in this case no exception. Middleton's mind was so occupied in planning, scheming and conniving that he had little time for the strain to corrode his will power. But Corcoran had nothing to occupy his attention until the moment came for the jump.

He began to drink, almost without realizing it. His veins seemed on fire, his external senses abnormally alert. Like most men of his breed he was high-strung, his nervous system poised on a hair-trigger balance, in spite of his mask of unemotional coolness. He lived on, and for, violent action. Action kept his mind from turning inward; it kept his brain clear and his hand steady; failing action, he fell back on whisky. Liquor artificially stimulated him to that pitch which his temperament required. It was not fear that made his nerves thrum so intolerably. It was the strain of waiting inertly, the realization of the stakes for which they played. Inaction maddened him. Thought of the gold cached in the cave behind John Middleton's cabin made Corcoran's lips dry, set a nerve to pounding maddeningly in his temples.

So he drank, and drank, and drank again, as the long day wore on.

The noise from the bar was a blurred medley in the back room of the Golden Garter. Glory Bland stared uneasily across the table at her companion. Corcoran's blue eyes seemed lit by dancing fires. Tiny beads of perspiration shone on his dark face. His tongue was not thick; he spoke lucidly and without exaggeration; he had not stumbled when he entered. Nevertheless he was drunk, though to what extent the girl did not guess.

"I never saw you this way before, Steve," she said reproachfully.

"I've never had a hand in a game like this before," he answered, the wild flame flickering bluely in his eyes. He reached across the table and caught her white wrist with an unconscious strength that made her wince. "Glory, I'm pullin' out of here tonight. I want you to go with me!"

"You're leaving Wahpeton? *Tonight?*"

"Yes. For good. Go with me! This joint ain't fit for you. I don't know how you got into this game, and I don't give a damn. But you're different

247

from these other dance hall girls. I'm takin' you with me. I'll make a queen out of you! I'll cover you with diamonds!"

She laughed nervously.

"You're drunker than I thought. I know you've been getting a big salary, but – "

"Salary?" His laugh of contempt startled her. "I'll throw my salary into the street for the beggars to fight over. Once I told that fool Hopkins that I had a gold mine right here in Wahpeton. I told him no lie. I'm rich!"

"What do you mean?" She was slightly pale, frightened by his vehemence.

His fingers unconsciously tightened on her wrist and his eyes gleamed with the hard arrogance of possession and desire.

"You're mine, anyway," he muttered. "I'll kill any man that looks at you. But you're in love with me. I know it. Any fool could see it. I can trust you. You wouldn't dare betray me. I'll tell you. I wouldn't take you along without tellin' you the truth. Tonight Middleton and I are goin' over the mountains with a million dollars' worth of gold tied on pack mules!"

He did not see the growing light of incredulous horror in her eyes.

"A million in gold! It'd make a devil out of a saint! Middleton thinks he'll kill me when we get away safe, and grab the whole load. He's a fool. It'll be him that dies, when the time comes. I've planned while he planned. I didn't ever intend to split the loot with him. I wouldn't be a thief for less than a million."

"Middleton – " she choked.

"Yeah! He's chief of the Vultures, and I'm his right-hand man. If it hadn't been for me, the camp would have caught on long ago."

"But you upheld the law," she panted, as if clutching at straws. "You killed murderers – saved McBride from the mob."

"I killed men who tried to kill me. I shot as square with the camp as I could, without goin' against my own interests. That business of McBride has nothin' to do with it. I'd given him my word. That's all behind us now. Tonight, while the vigilantes and the Vultures kill each other, we'll *vamose!* And you'll go with me!"

With a cry of loathing she wrenched her hand away, and sprang up, her eyes blazing.

"Oh!" It was a cry of bitter disillussionment. "I thought you were straight – honest! I worshiped you because I thought you were honorable.

So many men were dishonest and bestial – I idolized you! And you've just been pretending – playing a part! Betraying the people who trusted you!" The poignant anguish of her enlightenment choked her, then galvanized her with another possibility.

"I suppose you've been pretending with me, too!" she cried wildly. "If you haven't been straight with the camp, you couldn't have been straight with me, either! You've made a fool of me! Laughed at me and shamed me! And now you boast of it in my teeth!"

"Glory!" He was on his feet, groping for her, stunned and bewildered by her grief and rage. She sprang back from him.

"Don't touch me! Don't look at me! Oh, I hate the very sight of you!"

And turning, with an hysterical sob, she ran from the room. He stood swaying slightly, staring stupidly after her. Then fumbling with his hat, he stalked out, moving like an automaton. His thoughts were a confused maelstrom, whirling until he was giddy. All at once the liquor seethed madly in his brain, dulling his perceptions, even his recollections of what had just passed. He had drunk more than he realized.

Not long after dark had settled over Wahpeton, a low call from the darkness brought Colonel Hopkins to the door of his cabin, gun in hand.

"Who is it?" he demanded suspiciously.

"It's Middleton. Let me in, quick!"

The sheriff entered, and Hopkins, shutting the door, stared at him in surprise. Middleton showed more agitation than the Colonel had ever seen him display. His face was pale and drawn. A great actor was lost to the world when John Middleton took the dark road of outlawry.

"Colonel, I don't know what to say. I've been a blind fool. I feel that the lives of murdered men are hung about my neck for all Eternity! All through my blindness and stupidity!"

"What do you mean, John?" ejaculated Colonel Hopkins.

"Colonel, Miller talked at last. He just finished telling me the whole dirty business. I have his confession, written as he dictated."

"He named the chief of the Vultures?" exclaimed Hopkins eagerly.

"He did!" answered Middleton grimly, producing a paper and unfolding it. Joel Miller's unmistakable signature sprawled at the bottom. "Here is the name of the leader, dictated by Miller to me!"

"Good God!" whispered Hopkins. "Bill McNab!"

"Yes! My deputy! The man I trusted next to Corcoran. What a fool – what a blind fool I've been. Even when his actions seemed peculiar, even when you voiced your suspicions of him, I could not bring myself to believe it. But it's all clear now. No wonder the gang always knew my plans as soon as I knew them myself! No wonder my deputies – before Corcoran came – were never able to kill or capture any Vultures. No wonder, for instance, that Tom Deal 'escaped,' before we could question him. That bullet hole in McNab's arm, supposedly made by Deal – Miller told me McNab got that in a quarrel with one of his own gang. It came in handy to help pull the wool over my eyes.

"Colonel Hopkins, I'll turn in my resignation tomorrow. I recommend Corcoran as my successor. I shall be glad to serve as deputy under him."

"Nonsense, John!" Hopkins laid his hand sympathetically on Middleton's shoulder. "It's not your fault. You've played a man's part all the way through. Forget talk about resigning. Wahpeton doesn't need a new sheriff; you just need some new deputies. Just now we've got some planning to do. Where is McNab?"

"At the jail, guarding the prisoners. I couldn't remove him without exciting his suspicion. Of course he doesn't dream that Miller has talked. And I learned something else. They plan a jail-break shortly after midnight."

"We might have expected that!"

"Yes. A band of masked men will approach the jail, pretend to overpower the guards – yes, Stark and Richardson are Vultures, too – and release the prisoners. Now this is my plan. Take fifty men and conceal them in the trees near the jail. You can plant some on one side, some on the other. Corcoran and I will be with you, of course. When the bandits come, we can kill or capture them all at one swoop. We have the advantage of knowing their plans, without their knowing we know them."

"That's a good plan, John!" warmly endorsed Hopkins. "You should have been a general. I'll gather the men at once. Of course, we must use the utmost secrecy."

"Of course. If we work it right, we'll bag prisoners, deputies and rescuers with one stroke. We'll break the back of the Vultures!"

"John, don't ever talk resignation to me again!" exclaimed Hopkins, grabbing his hat and buckling on his gunbelt. "A man like you ought to be in the Senate. Go get Corcoran. I'll gather my men and we'll be in our places before midnight. NcNab and the others in the jail won't hear a sound."

"Good! Corcoran and I will join you before the Vultures reach the jail."

Leaving Hopkins's cabin, Middleton hurried to the bar of the King of Diamonds. As he drank, a rough-looking individual moved casually up beside him. Middleton bent his head over his whisky glass and spoke, hardly moving his lips. None could have heard him a yard away.

"I've just talked to Hopkins. The vigilantes are afraid of a jailbreak. They're going to take the prisoners out just before daylight and hang them out of hand. That talk about legal proceedings was just a bluff. Get all the boys, go to the jail and get the prisoners out within a half hour after midnight. Wear your masks, but let there be no shooting or yelling. I'll tell McNab our plan's been changed. Go silently. Leave your horses at least a quarter of a mile down the gulch and sneak up to the jail on foot, so you won't make so much noise. Corcoran and I will be hiding in the brush to give you a hand in case anything goes wrong."

The other man had not looked toward Middleton; he did not look now. Emptying his glass, he strolled deliberately toward the door. No casual onlooker could have known that any words had passed between them.

When Glory Bland ran from the backroom of the Golden Garter, her soul was in an emotional turmoil that almost amounted to insanity. The shock of her brutal disillusionment vied with passionate shame of her own gullibility and an unreasoning anger. Out of this seething cauldron grew a blind desire to hurt the man who had unwittingly hurt her. Smarting vanity had its part, too, for with characteristic and illogical feminine conceit, she believed that he had practiced an elaborate deception in order to fool her into falling in love with him – or rather with the man she thought he was. If he was false with men, he must be false with women, too. That thought sent her into hysterical fury, blind to all except a desire for revenge. She was a primitive, elemental young animal, like most of her profession of that age and place; her emotions were powerful and easily stirred, her passions stormy. Love could change quickly to hate.

She reached an instant decision. She would find Hopkins and tell him everything Corcoran had told her! In that instant she desired nothing so much as the ruin of the man she had loved.

She ran down the crowded street, ignoring men who pawed at her and called after her. She hardly saw the people who stared after her. She supposed that Hopkins would be at the jail, helping guard the prisoners, and she directed her steps thither. As she ran up on the porch Bill McNab confronted her with a leer, and laid a hand on her arm, laughing when she jerked away.

"Come to see me, Glory? Or are you lookin' for Corcoran?"

She struck his hand away. His words, and the insinuating guffaws of his companions were sparks enough to touch off the explosives seething in her.

"You fool! You're being sold out, and don't know it!"

The leer vanished.

"What do you mean?" he snarled.

"I mean that your boss is fixing to skip out with all the gold you thieves have grabbed!" she blurted, heedless of consequences, in her emotional storm, indeed scarcely aware of what she was saying. "He and Corcoran are going to leave you holding the sack, tonight!"

And not seeing the man she was looking for, she eluded McNab's grasp, jumped down from the porch and darted away in the darkness.

The deputies stared at each other, and the prisoners, having heard everything, began to clamor to be turned out.

"Shut up!" snarled McNab. "She may be lyin'. Might have had a quarrel with Corcoran and took this fool way to get even with him. We can't afford to take no chances. We've got to be sure we know what we're doin' before we move either way. We can't afford to let you out now, on the chance that she might be lyin'. But we'll give you weapons to defend yourselves.

"Here, take these rifles and hide 'em under the bunks. Pete Daley, you stay here and keep folks shooed away from the jail till we get back. Richardson, you and Stark come with me! We'll have a showdown with Middleton right now!"

When Glory left the jail she headed for Hopkins' cabin. But she had not gone far when a reaction shook her. She was like one waking from a nightmare, or a dope-jag. She was still sickened by the discovery of

Corcoran's duplicity in regard to the people of the camp, but she began to apply reason to her suspicions of his motives in regard to herself. She began to realize that she had acted illogically. If Corcoran's attitude toward her was not sincere, he certainly would not have asked her to leave the camp with him. At the expense of her vanity she was forced to admit that his attentions to her had not been necessary in his game of duping the camp. That was something apart; his own private business; it must be so. She had suspected him of trifling with her affections, but she had to admit that she had no proof that he had ever paid the slightest attention to any other woman in Wahpeton. No; whatever his motives or actions in general, his feeling toward her must be sincere and real.

With a shock she remembered her present errand, her reckless words to McNab. Despair seized her, in which she realized that she loved Steve Corcoran in spite of all he might be. Chill fear seized her that McNab and his friends would kill her lover. Her unreasoning fury died out, gave way to frantic terror.

Turning she ran swiftly down the gulch toward Corcoran's cabin. She was hardly aware of it when she passed through the blazing heart of the camp. Lights and bearded faces were like a nightmarish blur, in which nothing was real but the icy terror in her heart.

She did not realize it when the clusters of cabins fell behind her. The patter of her slippered feet in the road terrified her, and the black shadows under the trees seemed pregnant with menace. Ahead of her she saw Corcoran's cabin at last, a light streaming through the open door. She burst in to the office-room, panting – and was confronted by Middleton who wheeled with a gun in his hand.

"What the devil are you doing here?" He spoke without friendliness, though he returned the gun to its scabbard.

"Where's Corcoran?" she panted. Fear took hold of her as she faced the man she now knew was the monster behind the grisly crimes that had made a reign of terror over Wahpeton Gulch. But fear for Corcoran overshadowed her own terror.

"I don't know. I looked for him through the bars a short time ago, and didn't find him. I'm expecting him here any minute. What do you want with him?"

"That's none of your business," she flared.

"It might be." He came toward her, and the mask had fallen from his dark, handsome face. It looked wolfish.

"You were a fool to come here. You pry into things that don't concern you. You know too much. You talk too much. Don't think I'm not wise to you! I know more about you than you suspect."

A chill fear froze her. Her heart seemed to be turning to ice. Middleton was like a stranger to her, a terrible stranger. The mask was off, and the evil spirit of the man was reflected in his dark, sinister face. His eyes burned her like actual coals.

"I didn't pry into secrets," she whispered with dry lips. "I didn't ask any questions. I never before suspected you were the chief of the Vultures – "

The expression of his face told her she had made an awful mistake.

"So you know that!" His voice was soft, almost a whisper, but murder stood stark and naked in his flaming eyes. "I didn't know that. I was talking about something else. Conchita told me it was you who told Corcoran about the plan to lynch McBride. I wouldn't have killed you for that, though it interfered with my plans. But you know too much. After tonight it wouldn't matter. But tonight's not over yet – "

"Oh!" she moaned, staring with dilated eyes as the big pistol slid from its scabbard in a dull gleam of blue steel. She could not move, she could not cry out. She could only cower dumbly until the crash of the shot knocked her to the floor.

As Middleton stood above her, the smoking gun in his hand, he heard a stirring in the room behind him. He quickly upset the long table, so it could hide the body of the girl, and turned, just as the door opened. Corcoran came from the back room, blinking, a gun in his hand. It was evident that he had just awakened from a drunken sleep, but his hands did not shake, his pantherish tread was sure as ever, and his eyes were neither dull nor bloodshot.

Nevertheless Middleton swore.

"Corcoran, are you crazy?"

"You shot?"

"I shot at a snake that crawled across the floor. You must have been mad, to soak up liquor today, of all days!"

"I'm all right," muttered Corcoran, shoving his gun back in its scab-bard.

"Well, come on. I've got the mules in the clump of trees next to my cabin. Nobody will see us load them. Nobody will see us go. We'll go up the ravine beyond my cabin, as we planned. There's nobody watching my cabin tonight. All the Vultures are down in the camp, waiting for the signal to move. I'm hoping none will escape the vigilantes, and that most of the vigilantes themselves are killed in the fight that's sure to come. Come on! We've got thirty mules to load, and that job will take us from now until midnight, at least. We won't pull out until we hear the guns on the other side of the camp."

"Listen!"

It was footsteps, approaching the cabin almost at a run. Both men wheeled and stood motionless as McNab loomed in the door. He lurched into the room, followed by Richardson and Stark. Instantly, the air was supercharged with suspicion, hate, tension. Silence held for a tick of time.

"You fools!" snarled Middleton. "What are you doing away from the jail?"

"We came to talk to you," said McNab. "We've heard that you and Corcoran planned to skip with the gold."

Never was Middleton's superb self-control more evident. Though the shock of that blunt thunderbolt must have been terrific, he showed no emotion that might not have been showed by any honest man, falsely accused.

"Are you utterly mad?" he ejaculated, not in a rage, but as if amazement had submerged whatever anger he might have felt at the charge.

McNab shifted his great bulk uneasily, not sure of his ground. Cor-coran was not looking at him, but at Richardson, in whose cold eyes a lethal glitter was growing. More quickly than Middleton, Corcoran sensed the inevitable struggle in which this situation must culminate.

"I'm just sayin' what we heard. Maybe it's so, maybe it ain't. If it ain't there's no harm done." said McNab slowly. "On the chance that it was so, I sent word for the boys not to wait till midnight. They're goin' to the jail within the next half hour and take Miller and the rest out."

Another breathless silence followed that statement. Middleton did not bother to reply. His eyes began to smolder. Without moving, he yet seemed to crouch, to gather himself for a spring. He had realized what Corcoran had already sensed; that this situation was not to be passed over by words, that a climax of violence was inevitable.

Richardson knew this; Stark seemed merely puzzled. McNab, if he had any thoughts, concealed the fact.

"Say you *was* intendin' to skip," he said, "this might be a good chance, while the boys was takin' Miller and them off up into the hills. I don't know. I ain't accusin' you. I'm just askin' you to clear yourself. You can do it easy. Just come back to the jail with us and help get the boys out."

Middleton's answer was what Richardson, instinctive man-killer, had sensed it would be. He whipped out a gun in a blur of speed. And even as it cleared leather, Richardson's gun was out. But Corcoran had not taken his eyes off the cold-eyed gunman, and his draw was the quicker by a lightning-flicker. Quick as was Middleton, both the other guns spoke before his, like a double detonation. Corcoran's slug blasted Richarson's brains just in time to spoil his shot at Middleton. But the bullet grazed Middleton so close that it caused him to miss McNab with his first shot.

McNab's gun was out and Stark was a split second behind him. Middleton's second shot and McNab's first crashed almost together, but already Corcoran's guns had sent lead ripping through the giant's flesh. His ball merely flicked Middleton's hair in passing, and the chief's slug smashed full into his brawny breast. Middleton fired again and yet again as the giant was falling. Stark was down, dying on the floor, having pulled trigger blindly as he fell, until the gun was empty.

Middleton stared wildly about him, through the floating blue fog of smoke that veiled the room. In that fleeting instant, as he glimpsed Corcoran's image-like face, he felt that only in such a setting as this did the Texan appear fitted. Like a somber figure of Fate he moved implacably against a background of blood and slaughter.

"God!" gasped Middleton. "That was the quickest, bloodiest fight I was ever in!" Even as he talked he was jamming cartridges into his empty gun chambers.

"We've got no time to lose now! I don't know how much McNab told the gang of his suspicions. He must not have told them much, or some of them would have come with him. Anyway, their first move will be to liberate the prisoners. I have an idea they'll go through with that just as we planned, even when McNab doesn't return to lead them. They won't come looking for him, or come after us, until they turn Miller and the others loose.

"It just means the fight will come within the half hour instead of at midnight. The vigilantes will be there by that time. They're probably lying in ambush already. Come on! We've got to sling gold on those mules like devils. We may have to leave some of it; we'll know when the fight's started, by the sound of the guns! One thing, nobody will come up here to investigate the shooting. All attention is focused on the jail!"

Corcoran followed him out of the cabin, then turned back with a muttered: "Left a bottle of whisky in the back room."

"Well, hurry and get it and come on!" Middleton broke into a run toward his cabin, and Corcoran re-entered the smoke-veiled room. He did not glance at the crumpled bodies that lay on the crimson-stained floor, staring glassily up at him. With a stride he reached the back room, groped in his bunk until he found what he wanted, and then strode again toward the outer door, the bottle in his hand.

The sound of a low moan brought him whirling about, a gun in his left hand. Startled, he stared at the figures on the floor. He knew none of them had moaned; all three were past moaning. Yet his ears had not deceived him.

His narrowed eyes swept the cabin suspiciously, and focused on a thin trickle of crimson that stole from under the upset table as it lay on its side near the wall. None of the corpses lay near it.

He pulled aside the table and halted as if shot through the heart, his breath catching in a convulsive gasp. An instant later he was kneeling beside Glory Bland, cradling her golden head in his arm. His hand, as he brought the whisky bottle to her lips, shook queerly.

Her magnificent eyes lifted toward him, glazed with pain. But by some miracle the delirium faded, and she knew him in her last few moments of life.

"Who did this?" he choked. Her white throat was laced by a tiny trickle of crimson from her lips.

"Middleton – " she whispered. "Steve, oh, Steve – I tried – " And with the whisper uncompleted she went limp in his arms. Her golden head lolled back; she seemed like a child, a child just fallen asleep. Dazedly he eased her to the floor.

Corcoran's brain was clear of liquor as he left the cabin, but he staggered like a drunken man. The monstrous, incredible thing that had happened left him stunned, hardly able to credit his own senses. It had never occurred to him that Middleton would kill a woman, that any white man would. Corcoran lived by his own code, and it was wild and rough and hard, violent and incongruous, but it included the conviction that womankind was sacred, immune from the violence that attended the lives of men. This code was as much a vital, living element of the life of the Southwestern frontier as was personal honor, and the resentment of insult. Without pompousness, without pretentiousness, without any of the tawdry glitter and sham of a false chivalry, the people of Corcoran's breed practiced this code in their daily lives. To Corcoran, as to his people, a woman's life and body were inviolate. It had never occurred to him that that code would, or could be violated, or that there could be any other kind.

Cold rage swept the daze from his mind and left him crammed to the brim with murder. His feelings toward Glory Bland had approached the normal love experienced by the average man as closely as was possible for one of his iron nature. But if she had been a stranger, or even a person he had disliked, he would have killed Middleton for outraging a code he had considered absolute.

He entered Middleton's cabin with the soft stride of a stalking panther. Middleton was bringing bulging buckskin sacks from the cave, heaping them on a table in the main room. He staggered with their weight. Already the table was almost covered.

"Get busy!" he exclaimed. Then he halted short at the blaze in Corcoran's eyes. The fat sacks spilled from his arms, thudding on the floor.

"You killed Glory Bland!" It was almost a whisper from the Texan's livid lips.

"Yes." Middleton's voice was even. He did not ask how Corcoran knew, he did not seek to justify himself. He knew the time for argument was past. He did not think of his plans, or of the gold on the table, or that still

258

back there in the cave. A man standing face to face with Eternity sees only the naked elements of life and death.

"*Draw!*" A catamount might have spat the challenge, eyes flaming, teeth flashing.

Middleton's hand was a streak to his gun butt. Even in that flash he knew he was beaten – heard Corcoran's gun roar just as he pulled trigger. He swayed back, falling, and in a blind gust of passion Corcoran emptied both guns into him as he crumpled.

For a long moment that seemed ticking into Eternity the killer stood over his victim, a somber, brooding figure that might have been carved from the iron night of the Fates. Off toward the other end of the camp other guns burst forth suddenly, in salvo after thundering salvo. The fight that was plotted to mask the flight of the Vulture chief had begun. But the figure that stood above the dead man in the lonely cabin did not seem to hear.

Corcoran looked down at his victim, vaguely finding it strange, after all, that all those bloody schemes and terrible ambitions should end like that, in a puddle of oozing blood on a cabin floor. He lifted his head to stare somberly at the bulging sacks on the table. Revulsion gagged him.

A sack had split, spilling a golden stream that glittered evilly in the candle-light. His eyes were no longer blinded by the yellow sheen. For the first time he saw the blood on that gold, it was black with blood; the blood of innocent men; the blood of a woman. The mere thought of touching it nauseated him, made him feel as if the slime that had covered John Middleton's soul would befoul him. Sickly he realized that some of Middleton's guilt was on his own head. He had not pulled the trigger that ripped a woman's life from her body; but he had worked hand-in-glove with the man destined to be her murderer – Corcoran shuddered and a clammy sweat broke out upon his flesh.

Down the gulch the firing had ceased, faint yells came to him, freighted with victory and triumph. Many men must be shouting at once for the sound to carry so far. He knew what it portended; the Vultures had walked into the trap laid for them by the man they trusted as a leader. Since the firing had ceased, it meant the whole band were either dead or captives. Wahpeton's reign of terror had ended.

But he must stir. There would be prisoners, eager to talk. Their speech would weave a noose about his neck.

He did not glance again at the gold, gleaming there where the honest people of Wahpeton would find it. Striding from the cabin he swung on one of the horses that stood saddled and ready among the trees. The lights of the camp, the roar of the distant voices fell away behind him, and before him lay what wild destiny he could not guess. But the night was full of haunting shadows, and within him grew a strange pain, like a revelation; perhaps it was his soul, at last awakening.

Vultures of Wahpeton: Alternate Ending

Editor's Note

When "The Vultures of Wahpeton" was published in Smashing Novels Magazine, December 1936 (under the title "Vultures of Whapeton"), two endings were printed. The shorter of the two is used with the story as presented in this volume. This is the longer, "happy" ending, along with the original editor's notes from Smashing Novels Magazine.

The author has written this story with two endings. In the first, Corcoran, the lone wolf, rides away, leaving his dead love behind him.

In the second ending, he finds she has only been stunned, and they ride away together; the conventional "happy" ending.

The author left it to the editor which ending to use, but the editor passes the buck to the reader. The first is undoubtedly more powerful, dramatically, but it involves frustration. The second will undoubtedly be more pleasing, as it eliminates the tragedy of the girl's death, and the hero who has found himself, starts his new life with his chosen woman at his side.

The second ending follows.

But he must stir. There would be prisoners, eager to talk. Their speech would weave a noose about his neck. The men of Wahpeton must not find him here when they came.

But before he turned his back forever upon Wahpeton Gulch, he had a task to perform. He did not glance again at the gold, gleaming there where the honest people of the camp would find it. Two horses waited, bridled and saddled, among the restless mules tethered under the trees. One was the animal which had borne him into Wahpeton. He mounted it and rode slowly toward the cabin where a woman lay beside dead men. He felt vaguely that it was not right to leave her lying there among those shot-torn rogues.

He braced himself against the sight as he entered the cabin of death. Then he started and went livid under his sun-burnt hue. *Glory was not lying as he had left her!* With a low cry he reached her, lifted her in his arms. He felt life, pulsing strongly under his hands.

"Glory! For God's sake!" Her eyes were open, not so glazed now, though shadowed by pain and bewilderment. Her arms groped toward him. He lifted and carried her into the back room, laid her on the bunk where Joe Willoughby had received his death wounds. His mind was a whirling turmoil, as he felt with practised fingers of the darkly-clotted wound at the edge of her golden hair.

"Steve," she whimpered. "I'm afraid! Middleton – "

"He won't hurt you any more. Don't talk. I'm goin' to wash that wound and dress it."

Working fast and skillfully, he washed the blood away with a rag torn from her petticoat – as being the cleanest material he could find – and soaked in water and whisky. Corcoran had just ceased bandaging her head when she struggled upright, despite his profane objections, and caught at his arm.

"Steve!" Her eyes were wide with fear. "You must go – go quick! I was crazy – I told McNab what you told me – told Middleton, too, that's why he shot me. They'll kill you."

"Not them," he muttered. "Do you feel better now?"

"Oh, don't mind me! Go! Please go! Oh, Steve, I must have been mad! I betrayed you! I was coming here to tell you that I had, to warn you to get away, when I met Middleton. Where is he?"

"In Hell, where he ought to been years ago," grunted Corcoran. "Never mind. But the vigilantes will be headin' this way soon as some of the rats they've caught get to talkin'. I've got to dust out. But I'll take you back to the Golden Garter first."

"Steve, you're mad! You'd run your head into a noose! Get on your horse and ride!"

"Will you go with me?" His hands closed on her, hurting her with their unconscious strength.

"You still want me, after – after what I did?" she gasped.

"I've always wanted you, since I first saw you. I always will. Forgive you? There's nothin' to forgive. Nothin' you could have ever done could

262

be anywhere near as black as what I've been for the past month. I've been like a mad-dog; the gold blinded me. I'm awake now. And I want you."

For answer her arms groped about his neck, clung convulsively; he felt the moisture of her passionate tears on his throat. Lifting her, he carried her out of the cabin, pressing her face against his breast that she might not see the stark figures lying there in their splashes of crimson.

An instant later he was settled in the saddle, holding her before him, cradled like a child in his muscular arms. He had wrapped his coat about her, and the pale oval of her face stared up at his like a white blossom in the night. Her arms still clung to him, as if she feared he might be torn from her.

"How the lights blaze over the camp!" she murmured irrelevantly, as they climbed toward the ravine.

"Take a good look," he said, his voice harsh with suppressed and unfamiliar emotions. "It's our old life we're leavin' behind, and I hope we're headin' for a better one. And as a beginnin', we're goin' to get married the first town we hit."

An incoherent murmur was her only reply as she snuggled closer in his arms; behind them the lights of the camp, the distant roar of voices fell away and grew blurred in the distance. But it seemed to Corcoran that they rode in a blaze of glory, that emanated not from moon nor stars, but from his own breast. And perhaps it was his soul, at last awakened.

Editor's Note

Of course, giving a story two endings is sort of unorthodox. But Smashing Novels, ever since its first issue, hasn't been a particularly orthodox magazine. We've tried, and we are trying, to give you different stories with different slants, and we've been doing our darndest to give you the best stories possible.

Drop us a line, and let us know which of these endings you prefer. Or if you think that we made a mistake in using two endings to one story, write and tell us about it. We want to know what you like.

Cliff Campbell, Editor
Smashing Novels

Vultures' Sanctuary

A vagrant wind stirred tiny dust-eddies where the road to California became, for a few hundred yards, the main street of Capitan town. A few mongrel dogs lazed in the shade of the false-fronted frame buildings. Horses at the hitching rack stamped and switched flies. A child loitered along the warped board walk; except for these signs of life, Capitan might have been a ghost town, deserted to sun and wind. A covered wagon creaked slowly along the road from the east. The horses, gaunt and old, leaned forward with each lurching step. The girl on the seat peered under a shading hand and spoke to the old man beside her.

"There's a town ahead, father."

He nodded. "Capitan. We won't wast time there. A bad town. I've heard of it ever since we crossed the Pecos. No law there. A haunt of renegades and refugees. But we must stop there long enough to buy bacon and coffee."

His tired old voice encouraged the laboring horses; dust of the long, long trail sifted greyly from the wagon bed as they creaked into Capitan.

Capitan, baking under the sun that drew a curtain of shimmering heat waves between it and the bare Guadalupes, rising from the rolling wastelands to the south. Capitan, haunt of the hunted, yet not the last haunt, not the ultimate, irrevocable refuge for the desperate and damned.

But not all who came to Capitan were scarred with the wolf-trail brand. One was standing even then at the bar of the Four Aces saloon, frowning at the man before him. Big Mac, cowpuncher from Texas, broad-shouldered, deep-chested, with thews hardened to the toughness of woven steel by years on the cattle trails that stretch from the live-oaks of the Gulf marshes to the prairies of Canada. A familiar figure wherever cowmen gathered, with his broad brown face, volcanic blue eyes, and unruly thatch of curly black hair. There were no notches in the butt of the big Colt .45 which jutted from the scabbard at his right hip, but that butt was worn smooth from much usage. Big Mac did not notch his gun, but it had blazed in range wars and cow-town feuds from the Sabine to Milk River.

"You're Bill McClanahan, ain't you?" the other man asked with a strange eagerness his casual manner could not conceal. "You remember me?"

"Yeah." A man with many enemies must have a keen memory for faces. "You're the Checotah Kid. I saw you in Hayes City, three years ago."

"Let's drink." At the Kid's gesture, the bartender sent glasses and a bottle sliding down the wet bar. The Kid was Mac's opposite in type. Slender, though hard as steel, smooth-faced, blond, his wide grey eyes seemed guileless at first glance. But a man wise in the ways of men could see cruelty and murderous treachery lurking in their depths.

But something else burned there now, something fearful and hunted. There was a nervous tension underlying the Kid's manner that puzzled Big Mac, who remembered him as a suave, self-possessed young scoundrel of the Kansas trail-towns. Doubtless he was on the dodge; yet that did not explain his nervousness, for there was no law in Capitan, and the Border was less than a hundred miles to the south.

Now the Kid leaned toward him and lowered his voice, though only the bartender and a loafer at a table shared the saloon with them.

"Mac, I need a partner! I've found color in the Guadalupes! Gold, as sure as hell!"

"Never knew you were a prospector," grunted Big Mac.

"A man gets to be lots of things!" The Kid's laugh was mirthless. "But I mean it!"

"Why'n't you stay and work it, then?" demanded the other.

"El Bravo's gang ran me out. Thought I was a sheriff or something!" Again the Kid laughed harshly, almost hysterically. "You've heard of El Bravo, maybe? Heads a gang of outlaws that hang out in the Guadalupes. But with a man to watch and another to work, we could take out plenty! The pocket's in a canyon just in the edge of the hills. What do you say?" Again that flaming intentness. His eyes burned on Big Mac like the eyes of a condemned man, seeking reprieve.

The Texan emptied his glass and shook his head.

"I'm no prospector," he rumbled. "I'm sick of work, anyway. I ain't never had a vacation all my life, except a few days in town at the end of the

265

drive, or before round-up. I quit my job at the Lazy K three weeks ago, and I'm headin' for San Francisco to enjoy life for a spell. I'm tired of cow towns. I want to see what a real city looks like."

"But it's a fortune!" urged the Kid passionately, his grey eyes blazing with a weird light. "You'd be a fool to pass it up!"

Big Mac bristled. He'd never liked Checotah anyway. But he merely replied: "Well, mebbyso, but that's how she stands."

"You won't do it?" It was almost a whisper. Sweat beaded the Kid's forehead.

"No! Looks like to me you could find some other partner easy enough."

Mac turned away, reaching for the bottle.

It was a glimpse of the big mirror behind the bar, caught from the tail of his eye, that saved his life. In that fleeting reflection he saw the Checotah Kid, his face a livid mask of desperation, draw his pistol. Big Mac whirled, knocking the gun aside with the bottle in his hand. The smash of breaking glass mingled with the bang of the shot. The bullet ripped through the slack of the Texan's shirt and thudded into the wall. Almost simultaneously Mac crashed his left fist full into the Kid's face.

The killer staggered backward, the smoking pistol escaping his numbed fingers. Mac was after him like a big catamount. There could be no quarter in such a fight. Mac did not spare his strength, for he knew the Kid was deadly – knew he had killed half a dozen men already, some treacherously. He might have another gun hidden on him somewhere.

But it was a knife he was groping for, as he reeled backward under the sledge-hammer impact of the Texan's fists. He found it, just as a thundering clout on the jaw knocked him headlong backward through the door to fall sprawling in the dusty street. He lay still, stunned, blood trickling from his mouth. Big Mac strode swiftly toward him to learn whether or not he was possuming.

But he never reached him. There was a quick patter of light feet, a swish of skirts, and even as Mac saw the girl spring in front of him, he received a resounding slap on his startled face.

He recoiled, glaring in amazement at the slender figure which confronted him, vibrant with anger.

"Don't you dare touch him again, you big bully!" she panted, her dark eyes blazing. "You coward! You brute! Attacking a boy half your size!"

He found no words to reply. He did not fully realize how savage and formidable he looked, with his fierce eyes and dark, scarred face as he stood there with his mallet-like fists clenched, glaring down at the man he had knocked down. He looked like a giant beside the slender Kid. Checotah looked boyish, innocent; to the girl, ignorant of men's ways, it looked like the brutal attack of a ruffian on an inoffensive boy. Mac realized this vaguely, but he could not find words to defend himself. She had not seen the bowie knife, which had fallen in the dust.

A small crowd was gathering, silent and inscrutable. The loafer who had been in the saloon was among them. An old man, his hands gnarled and his bony shoulders stooped, came from the store that stood next to the saloon, with bundles in his hands. He started toward a dust-stained wagon standing beside a board fence just beyond the store, then saw the crowd and hurried toward it, concern shadowing his eyes.

The girl turned lithely and knelt beside the Kid, who was struggling to a sitting position. He saw the pity in her wet, dark eyes, and understood. Checotah could play his cards as they fell.

"Don't let him kill me, Miss." he groaned. "I wasn't doing anything!"

"He shan't touch you," she assured him, flashing a look of defiance at Big Mac. She wiped the blood from the Kid's mouth, and looked angrily at the taciturn, leather-faced men who stood about.

"You should be ashamed of yourselves!" she stormed, with the ignorant courage of the very young. "Letting a bully like him abuse a boy!"

They made no response; only their lips twisted a little, in grim, sardonic humor she could not understand. Big Mac, his face dark, muttered under his breath and turning on his heel, re-entered the saloon. In there the voices reached him only as an incoherent murmur – the faltering, hypocritical voice of the Kid followed quickly by the soothing, sympathetic tones of the girl.

"Hell's fire!" Big Mac grabbed the whisky bottle.

"Wimmen are shore funny critters," remarked the bartender, scouring the bar. Mac's snarl discouraged conversation. The Texan took the bottle to a table at the back of the saloon. He was smarting mentally. The slap the girl had given him was no more than the tap of a feather. But a deeper sting persisted. He was angry and humiliated. A slip of a girl had abused him, like, as he would have put it, an egg-suckin' dog. Like most men of the wild trails, he was extremely sensitive where women were concerned. Indifferent to the opinions of men, a woman's scorn or anger could hurt him deeply. Like all men of his breed, he held women in high esteem, and desired their good opinion. But this girl had condemned him on the appearance of things. His sense of justice was outraged; his soul harbored a sting not to be soothed by the thought of the thousand-odd dollars in greenbacks in his pocket, nor the anticipation of spending them in that far-away city which he had never seen.

He drank, and drank again. His face grew darker, his blue eyes burned more savagely. As he sat there, huge, dark and brooding, he looked capable of any wild, ferocious deed. So thought the man who after awhile entered furtively and slipped into a chair opposite him. Big Mac scowled at him. He knew him as Slip Ratner, one of the many shady characters which haunted Capitan.

"I was in here when the Kid drawed on you," said Ratner, a faint, evil smile twisting his thin lips. "That girl sure hauled you over the coals, didn't she?"

"Shut up!" snarled Big Mac, grabbing the bottle again.

"Sure, sure!" soothed Ratner. "No offense. Sassy snip she was – you ought to of smacked her face for her. Listen!" He hunched forward and lowered his voice: "How'd you like to get even with that fresh dame?"

Big Mac merely grunted. He was paying little attention to what Ratner was saying. Get even with a woman? The thought never entered his mind. His code, the rigid, iron-bound code of the Texas frontier, did not permit of retaliation against a woman, whatever the provocation. But Ratner was speaking again, hurriedly.

"I don't know why the Kid tried to drill you, but that gold-talk of his was a lie. He's been in the Guadalupes, yes, but not after gold. He was trying to join up with El Bravo. I have ways of knowing things –

"Checotah hit Capitan just a few days ago. He's just a few jumps ahead of the Federal marshals. Besides that, there's reward notices for him stuck up all over Mexico. He's killed and robbed on both sides of the Line till there ain't but one place left for him – El Bravo's hide-out in the Guadalupes. That's where men go when both the United States and Mexico are barred to them.

"But El Bravo don't take in no man free. They have to buy into the gang. You remember Stark Campbell, that robbed the bank at Nogales? He got ten thousand dollars and he had to give every cent of it to El Bravo to join the gang. Tough, but it was that or his life. They say El Bravo's got a regular treasure trove hid away somewhere up in the Guadalupes.

"But Checotah didn't have nothing, and El Bravo wouldn't take him. The Kid's desperate. If he stayed here the law would get him in a few days, and there wasn't no place else for him to go. When I seen him playing up to that fool girl, I figgered he had something up his sleeve. And he did! He begged them to take him out of town with them – said he was afraid you'd murder him if he stayed in Capitan. And you know what they done? Invited him to go on to California with them! They laid him in the wagon, him pretending to be crippled, and pulled out, the girl washing the blood off his face, and his saddle-horse tied to the tail-board.

"Well, when they took him to the wagon, I sneaked up behind that board fence and listened to them talk. The girl told Checotah everything. Their names is Ellis; she's Judith Ellis. The old man's got a thousand dollars he saved up, working on a farm back in Illinois or somewhere, and he aims to use it making first payment on a piece of irrigated land in California.

"Now, I know the Kid. He ain't goin' to California. Why, he don't even dare show himself in the next town, out beyond Scalping Knife. Somewhere along the trail he'll kill old Ellis and head for the Guadalupes with the money and the girl. He'll pay his way into the Bravo gang with them! El Bravo likes women, and she's purty enough for any man.

"Here's where we come in. I don't figure the Kid'll strike till after they've passed Seven Mule Pass. That's nine miles from here. If we get on our horses and ride through the sage-brush, we can get past them and waylay them in the pass. Or we can wait till the Kid kills the old man, and then crack down on him. We kill the Kid, and that evens you up with him. Then we split the loot. I take the money. You take the girl. Nobody'll ever know. Plenty of places in the mountains you can take her, and – "

For an instant Big Mac sat silent, glaring incredulously at the leering face before him, while the monstrous proposal soaked in. Ratner could not properly interpret his stunned silence; Ratner credited all men with his own buzzard-instincts.

"What do you say?" he urged.

"Why, you damned – !" Big Mac's eyes flared red as he heaved up. The table crashed sidewise, bottles smashing on the floor. Ratner, almost pinned beneath it, yelped in fright and fury as he jumped clear. He snatched at a pistol as the berserk cowman towered over him. Mac did not waste lead on him. His movement was like the swipe of a bear's paw as his hand locked on Ratner's wrist. The renegade screamed, and a bone snapped. The pistol flew into the corner, and Big Mac hurled the snarling wretch after it, to lie in a stunned, crumpled heap. Men scattered as Big Mac stormed out of the saloon and made for the hitching rack where stood his big bay gelding.

A few moments later the giant Texan thundered out of town in a whirlwind of dust, and took the road that ran west.

East of Capitan, the road stretched across a dusty level and was visible for miles, which was an advantage to the citizens, for it was from the east that sheriffs and Federal marshals were most likely to come riding. But westward the terrain changed to a broken country in which the road disappeared from view of the town within a mile. Miles away to the southwest rose the grim outlines of the Guadalupes, shimmering under a sky tinted steel-white by the morning sun. Haunt of fierce desert killers they had always been – painted red men once, and later sombreroed *bandidos* – but never had they sheltered more deadly slayers than the gang of the mysterious El Bravo. Big Mac had heard of him, had heard, too, that few knew his real identity, save that he was a white man.

The town disappeared behind him, and after that the Texan passed only one habitation – the adobe hut of a Mexican sheepherder, some five miles west of Capitan. A mile further on the trail dipped down into the broad deep canyon cut by Scalping Knife River, in its southerly course – now only a trickle of water in its shallow bed. Three miles beyond the canyon lay a chain of hills, a spur of the Guadalupes, through which the road threaded by Seven Mule Pass. There it was that Ratner expected to lay ambush. Big Mac expected to overhaul the slow-moving wagon long before it reached the Pass.

But as he rode down the eastern slope of the canyon, he grunted and stiffened at the sight of the form lying limply on the canyon floor. The Kid had not waited to get beyond the Pass. Mac bent over old man Ellis. He had been shot through the left shoulder and was unconscious. He had lost a great deal of blood, but the thrum of his old heart was strong. The wagon was nowhere in sight. Wheel tracks wandered away up the canyon; the tracks of a single horse went down the canyon. Big Mac read the sign easily. Ratner had prophesied unerringly, with the wisdom of a wolf concerning the ways of wolves. Checotah had shot the old man – probably without warning. The team, frightened, had run away with the wagon. The Kid had ridden down the canyon with the girl, and, without doubt, the old man's pitiful savings.

Mac stanched the flow of blood with his bandanna. He lifted the senseless man across the saddle and turned back on his trail, leading the big bay, and cursing as the rocks of the flinty trail turned under his high-heeled boots. Back at the sheepherders hut, a mile from the canyon, he lifted the wounded man down and carried him in, laid him on a bunk. The old Mexican watched inscrutably.

Mac tore a ten dollar bill in two, and handed one half to the peon.

"If he's alive when I get back, you get the other half. If he ain't, I'll make you hard to catch. There's a wagon and team up the canyon. Send a boy to find 'em and bring 'em back here."

"Si, señor." The old man at once gave his attention to the wounded man; more than half Indian, his knowledge of primitive surgery was aboriginal, but effective.

Mac headed back for the canyon. The Kid had not bothered to hide his sign. There was no law in Capitan. There were men there who would not have allowed him to kidnap a girl if they could have prevented it. But they would not attempt to follow him into the outlaw-haunted Guadelupes.

The trail was plain down the canyon. He followed it for three miles, the walls growing steeper and higher as the canyon wound deeper and deeper into the hills. The trail turned aside up a narrow ravine, and Mac, following it, came out upon a benchland, dry and sandy, hemmed in by the slopes of the mountains. At the south edge of the flat buzzards rose and flapped heavily away. They had not feasted; they had been waiting, with grisly patience, for a feast. A few moments later Big Mac looked down on the sprawling form of the Checotah Kid. He had been shot in the open, and a smear of blood on the sand showed how he had wriggled an agonized way to the shade of a big rock.

He had been shot through the body, near the heart. His eyes were glazed, and at each choking gasp bloody bubbles burst on his blue lips.

Big Mac looked down on him with hard, merciless eyes.

"You dirty skunk! I'm sorry somebody beat me to it! Where's the girl?"

"El Bravo took her," panted the Kid. "They saw me riding – with the flag. Came to meet me. I gave him the girl – to pay my way into the gang. Tried to hold out the thousand – I took off the old man. They grabbed me – searched me – El Bravo shot me – for trying to hold out."

"Where'd they take her to?"

"The hideout. I don't know where. Nobody knows but them." The Kid's voice was growing weaker and thicker. "They watch the trails – all the time. Nobody can get – in the Guadalupes – without them knowing it. I carried the signal flag – only reason I got this far." He gestured vaguely toward a cottonwood limb with a shred of white cloth tied to it, which lay near him.

Curiosity prompted Big Mac's next question.

"Why'd you try to shoot me? We never had no trouble in Kansas."

"You were to be my price," gasped the Kid. "That's why I tried to lure you into the hills. El Bravo had rather have you alive. But when you wouldn't come, I thought if I brought him proof I'd downed you, maybe he'd take me in anyway. He's Garth Bissett!"

Garth Bissett! That explained many things. There were reasons why Bissett should hate Big Mac. They first met in a Kansas cow-town, at the end of a cattle-trail from Texas. Bissett was marshal of that town. A hard man, wary as a wolf, quick as summer lightning with the ivory-butted pistols that hung at his hips – and withal as rotten-souled a scoundrel as ever ruled a buzzard-roost trail town. It was Big Mac who broke his dominion. Going to the aid of a young cowboy, framed by one of Bissett's gun-fighting deputies, the big herd-boss had left the deputy dead on a dance-hall floor after a blur of gun-smoke, and in the dead man's pockets were found letters revealing the extent of Bissett's crookedness – proof of theft and murder. A Federal marshal stepped into the game. Bissett might have escaped, but he paused at the cow-camp at the edge of town to even scores with the big trail-driver.

Big Mac came out of the gun-play that followed with a bullet in his breast-muscles, while Bissett, his leg broken by a slug from Mac's .45, was taken by the Federal man. He was tried and sentenced to life imprisonment, but on the way to the penitentiary escaped, and dropped out of sight. Rumor said he had fled to Mexico, and become involved in a revolution.

Big Mac absently noted that the Kid was dead. Without another glance he mounted and rode deeper into the hills, following the faint trail the slayers had left. His face was darker and grimmer, but the shadow of a sardonic smile played about the corners of his hard mouth, and in one hand he carried the make-shift flag the Kid had borne. He had made his plan, a desperate, reckless plan, with one chance in a thousand of success. But it was the only one. He knew that he could not go into the Guadalupes shooting. If he tried to force his way to the bandit hangout, even if he should find it he would be shot from ambush long before he got there. There was but one way to reach the heart of El Bravo's stronghold. He was taking that way.

He did not ask himself why he followed the trail of a girl who meant nothing to him. It was part of him that he should do so – part of the code of the Texas Border, born of half a century of merciless warfare with red men and brown men, to whom the women of the whites were fair prey. A white man went to the aid of a woman in distress, regardless of who she might be. That was all there was to it. And so Big Mac was going to the aid of the girl who had despised him, instead of riding on his way to the far-off city where he expected to squander the wad of greenbacks he carried in his pocket. Only he knew how much hard work and self-denial they represented.

He had left the flat a few miles behind him and was riding through a rugged defile when a harsh voice bawled an order to halt. Instantly he pulled up and elevated his hands. The command came from a cluster of boulders to the right.

"Who're you and what'a you want?" came the crisp question.

"I'm Big Mac," answered the Texan tranquilly. "I'm lookin' for El Bravo."

"What you got for him?" was the next demand – a stock question, evidently.

Big Mac laughed. "Myself!"

"Are you crazy?" There was a snarl in the voice.

"No. Take me to Bissett. If he don't thank you, he'll be crazy."

"Well, he ain't!" growled the bushwhacker. "Get off yore horse! Now unbuckle yore gun-belt and let 'er drop. Now step back away from it – further back, blast you! Keep yore hands up. I got a .45-70 trained on yore heart all the time."

Big Mac did exactly as he was told. He was standing there, unarmed, his hands in the air, when the man came from behind the rocks, a tall man, who walked with the springy tread of a cougar. Mac knew him instantly.

"Stark Campbell!" he said softly. "So this is why they never got you!"

"And they never will, neither!" retorted the outlaw with an oath. "They can't git to us, up here in the Guadalupes. But a man has to pay high to git in." Bitter anger vibrated in his voice as he said that. "What you done, that you want in?"

"Never mind that. You just lead me to Bissett."

"I'll have to take you to the hang-out, if you see him," said Campbell. "He just taken a girl there. He don't let nobody see the hang-out and live, unless they're in his gang. If he don't let you join us, he'll kill you. You can go back, though, if you want to, now. I won't stop you. You ain't no law."

"I want to see Bissett," replied the Texan. Campbell shrugged his shoulders and drew a pistol, laying aside the rifle. He ordered Big Mac to turn around and put his hands behind him, and the outlaw then bound his wrists – awkwardly, with one hand, for he kept the pistol muzzle jammed in Mac's back with the other, but when the Texan's hands were partly confined, he completed the job with both hands. Then Campbell led his own horse, a rangy roan, from behind the rocks, and hung Mac's gun-belt over the roan's saddle-horn.

"Git on yore horse," he growled. "I'll help you up."

They started on, Campbell leading the big bay. For three or four miles they threaded a precarious path through as wild and broken a country as Big Mac had ever seen, until they entered a steep-walled canyon which, apparently, came to a blind in ahead of them, as the walls pinched to-gether. But as they neared it Big Mac saw a cleft in the angle, fifty feet above the canyon floor, and reached by a narrow, winding trail. A man hailed them from above.

"It's me, Campbell!" shouted his captor, and a growling voice bade them advance. "This is the only way into our hang-out," said Campbell. "You see how much chance a posse'd have of gittin' in, even if they found it. One man with plenty of shells could hold that cleft agen a army."

They went up the trail, single file. The horses crowded against the wall, fearful of the narrow footing. Mac knew that Campbell spoke the truth when he said no posse could charge up that trail, raked by fire from above.

As they entered the cleft a black-whiskered man rose from behind a ledge of rock and glared suspiciously at them.

"All right, Wilson. I'm takin' this fellow to Bissett."

"Ain't that Big Mac?" asked Wilson, in whom Mac recognized another "lost outlaw." "What's he got for Bissett? You searched him?"

"You know damn' well I ain't, only for guns," snarled Campbell. "You know the rule, well as me. Nobody takes money off 'em except Bissett." He spat. "Come on, Mac. If you got somethin' Bissett'll accept, I'll take yore ropes off. If you ain't, you won't be carin' anyway, not with a bullet through yore head."

The cleft was like a tunnel in the rock. It ran for forty feet and then widened out into a space that was like a continuation of the canyon they had left. It formed a bowl, its floor higher than the floor of the canyon outside by fifty feet, walled by unbroken cliffs three hundred feet high, and apparently unscalable. Campbell confirmed this.

"Can't nobody git at us from them cliffs," he snarled. "They're steep outside as inside. It's jest like somebody scooped a holler in the middle of a rock mesa. The holler's this bowl. Gwan. Git down."

Big Mac managed it, with his hands bound, and Campbell left the horses standing in the shade of the wall, reins hanging. He drove Big Mac before him toward the adobe hut that stood in the middle of the bowl, surrounded by a square rock wall, breast-high to a tall man.

"Last line of defense, Bissett says," growled Campbell. "Even if a posse was to git into the bowl – which ain't possible – we could fight 'em off indefinite behind that wall. There's a spring inside the stockade, and we got provisions and ca'tridges enough for a year."

The renegade marshal had always been a master of strategy. Big Mac did not believe the outlaw hangout would ever fall by a direct attack, regardless of the numbers assailing it – if it were ever discovered by the lawmen.

A man Campbell addressed as Garrison came from the corral, adjoining the wall, where a dozen horses grazed, and another met them at the heavy plank gate, built to turn bullets.

"Why, hell!" ejaculated the latter. "That's Big Mac! Where'd you catch him?"

"He rode in with a flag of truce, Emmett," answered Campbell. "Bissett in the shack?"

"Yeah; with the girl," grunted Emmett. "By God, I dunno what to make of this!"

Evidently Emmett knew something of Bissett's former life. The three men followed Mac as he strode across the yard toward the hut. Stark Campbell, John Garrison, Red Emmett; Wolf Wilson, back there at the tunnel. He had indeed come into the last haunt of the hunted, last retreat of these, the most desperate of all the Border renegades, to whom all other doors were barred, against whom the hands of all men were raised. Only in this lost canyon of the Guadalupes could they find sanctuary – the refuge of the wolf's lair, for which they had forfeited all their blood-tinged gains.

Theirs could be only a wolf-pack alliance. Bissett dominated them by virtue of keener wits and swifter gun-hand. They hated him for the brutal avarice that stripped from them their last shred of plunder, in return for a chance of bare life; but they feared him too, and recognized his superiority, knew that without his leadership the pack must perish, despite all natural advantages.

Campbell pushed the door open. As Big Mac loomed in the doorway, the man in the room turned with the blurring speed of a wolf, his hand streaking to an ivory-handled gun even in the instant it took him to see the stranger was a captive, with his hands bound behind him.

"You!" It was the ripping snarl of a timber wolf. Bissett was as tall as Big Mac, but not so heavy. He was wiry, rangy; yellow mustaches drooped below a mouth thin as a knife gash. His pale eyes glittered with an icy, blood-chilling fire.

"What the hell!" He seemed stunned with surprise. Big Mac looked past him to the girl who cringed in the corner, her eyes wide with terror.

There was no hope in them when they met his. To her he was but another beast of prey.

Big Mac grinned at Bissett, without mirth.

"Come to join your gang, Garth," he said calmly. "Heard you had to have a gift. Well, I'm it! I've heard you'd bid high for my hide!"

He was gambling on his knowledge of Bissett's nature – on the chance that the outlaw would not instantly shoot him down. They faced each other, the big dark Texan smiling, a trifle grimly, but calm; Bissett snarling, tense, suspicious as a wolf.

"Where'd you get him, Campbell?" he snapped.

"He come in under a flag of truce," growled Campbell. "Same as any man that wants to join up with us. Said you'd be glad to see him."

Bissett turned on Mac, his eyes shining like a wolf's that scents a trap. "Why did you come here?" he ripped out. "You're no fool. You wouldn't put yourself in my power unless you had a damned good reason – some edge – " He whirled on his men, in a frenzy of suspicion.

"Get out to the wall, damn you! Watch the cliffs! Watch everything! This devil wouldn't come in here alone unless he had something up his sleeve – "

"Well, I – " began Campbell, but Bissett's voice cut his sullen drawl like the slash of a whip.

"Shut up, damn you! Get out there! I do the thinking for the gang!"

Mac saw the unveiled hate in Campbell's eyes as he slouched silently out after the others, saw Bissett's eyes dwell burningly on the man. Bad blood there. Campbell feared Bissett less than the others, and was therefore the focus of the wolfish chief's suspicion.

As the men left the building, Bissett picked up a double-barreled shotgun, and cocked it.

"I don't know what your game is," he said between his teeth. "You must have a gang following you, or something. But whatever happens, I aim to get *you!*"

Mac appeared helpless, unarmed, his hands bound; but a wolf-like suspicion of appearances was at once Bissett's strength and his weakness.

"You're no outlaw," he snarled. "You didn't come here to join my gang. You knew I'd skin you alive, or stake you out on an ant-bed. What are you up to?"

Big Mac laughed in his face. A man who followed the herds up the long trail year after year learned to judge men as well as animals. Bissett was reacting exactly as Mac had expected him to. The Texan was playing that knowledge blindly, waiting for some kind of a break. A desperate game, but he was used to games where the Devil dealt for deadly stakes.

"You ain't got a very big gang, Bissett," he said.

"They're not all here," rapped the outlaw. "Some are out on a raid, toward the Border. Never mind. What's your game? If you talk, your finish will be easier."

Mac glanced again at Judith Ellis, cowering in a corner. The stark terror in her wide eyes hurt him. To this girl, unused to violence, her experience was like a nightmare.

"My game, Bissett?" asked Big Mac coolly. "What could it be? Nobody could get past Wilson in the tunnel, could they? Nobody could climb the cliffs, could they? What good would it do if I did have a gang followin' me, like you think?"

"You wouldn't come here without an ace in the hole," Bissett all but whispered.

"*What about your own men?*" Big Mac played his ace.

Bissett blanched. His suspicions crystalized, for the moment – suspisions of Big Mac's coming, suspicions of his own men, which forever gnawed at his brain. His eyes, glaring at Mac over the shotgun's black muzzles, were tinged with madness.

"You're trapped Bissett!" jeered Big Mac, playing his hand from minute to minute, for whater it might be worth. "You own men have sold you out! For the loot you took from them and hid – "

And at that moment the break came. Outside Campbell had turned back toward the adobe, and Mac saw him and yelled: "*Campbell! Help!*" Bissett whirled like a flash, shifting the shotgun to cover his amazed follower. It was an instinctive movement. Even so he would not have pulled the triggers – would have seen through Mac's flimsy scheme, had he had time to think.

But Mac saw and took his desperate chance. He hurled himself head-long against Bissett, and at the impact the shotgun hammers, hung on hair-triggers, fell to the involuntary, convulsive jerk of Bissett's fingers. Both barrels exploded as Bissett went down under Mac's hurtling body, and buckshot blasted Stark Campbell's skull. He died on his feet without knowing why. That was chance; Mac did not, could not have planned his death.

As they went down together, Mac drove his knee savagely into Bissett's belly and rolled clear as the outlaw doubled in gasping agony. Mac heaved up on his feet somehow, roaring: "His knife, quick! Cut these cords!"

The impact of his voice jolted the terrified girl into action. She sprang blindly forward, snatched the knife from Bissett's boot, and sawed at the cords that held Mac's wrists, slicing skin as well as hemp. It had all happened in a stunning instant. Outside, Garrison and Emmett were running toward the house with guns in their hands. Some of the strands parted under the blade, and Mac snapped the others. He stooped and dragged Bissett to his feet. The half-senseless outlaw was clawing dazedly at his pistols. Mac jerked them from him and swung the limp frame around before him.

"Tell your men to get back!" he snarled, jamming a muzzle hard in Bissett's back. "They'll obey you! Tell 'em, quick!"

But the order was never given. The men outside did not know what had happened in the hut. They had only seen Campbell blasted down by a shot through the doorway, and they thought their leader was turning against them. Emmett caught a glimpse of Bissett through the door and fired. Mac felt Bissett's body jerk convulsively in his hands. The bullet had drilled through the outlaw's head.

Mac threw the corpse aside, and fired from the hip. Emmett, struck in the mouth, went down heavily on his back. Garrison, as he saw Emmett fall and Mac loom in the doorway, began to fall back, firing as he went. He was making for the protection of the corral. Once there, he might make a long fight of it. Wilson would be coming up from the tunnel. If it came to a siege, the girl would be endangered by the raking lead.

Mac sprang recklessly into the open, shooting two-handed. He felt hot lead rip through his shirt, burn the skin on his ribs. Garrison snarled, whirled, sprang for the wall. In mid-stride he staggered drunkenly, hard hit. He wheeled and started shooting again, even as he crumpled, holding his sixshooter in both hands. Hit again and yet again, he kept on pulling the trigger, his bullets knocking up the dirt in front of Big Mac's boots.

His pistol snapped on an empty chamber before he lurched to the ground and lay still, in a spreading red puddle.

Mac heard Judith scream, and simultaneously came a report behind him and the impact of a blow that knocked him staggering. He came about in a drunken semi-circle, glimpsing Wilson's black-bearded face. The outlaw was straddling the wall, preparing to leap down inside before he fired again. Mac's last bullet broke his neck and dropped him at the foot of the wall, flopping for a dozen seconds like a beheaded chicken.

In the deafening silence that followed the roar of the guns, Mac turned back toward the hut, blood streaming down his shirt. The pale girl cowered in the door, still uncertain as to her fate. His first words reassured her.

"Don't be scairt, Miss. I come to take you back to your dad."

Then she was clinging to him, weeping in hysterical relief.

"Oh, you're hurt! You're bleeding!"

"Just a slug in my shoulder," he grunted, self-conscious. "Ain't nothin'."

"Let me dress it," she begged, and he followed her into the hut. She avoided looking at Bissett, sprawling in a red pool, as she bound up Mac's shoulder with strips torn from her dress, fumbling and clumsily.

"I – I misjudged you," she faltered. "I'm sorry. The Kid – he was a beast – my father – " She choked on the words.

"Your dad's all right," he assured her. "Just drilled through the shoulder, like me. Some rotten shootin' in these parts. Couple of horses saddled at the mouth of the tunnel. Go on out there and wait for me."

After she had gone, he began a hasty search. And presently he desisted, swearing. Neither the pockets of the dead chief nor a hasty ransacking of the rooms rewarded him with what he sought. The money taken from Ellis had gone to join the rest of Bissett's loot, in whatever crypt he had hidden it. Surely he had planned, some day, a flight to some other continent with his plunder. But whatever it was, it was well hidden; a man might hunt it for years, in vain. And Big Mac had not time for hunting. Bissett might have been lying when he said he had other men, out on a raid, but with the girl, Mac could not take the chance of being caught by returning outlaws. He hurried from the hut.

The girl had already mounted Campbell's roan. A few minutes later they were riding together down the outer canyon.

"I found that thousand Checotah took off your dad," he announced, handing her a wad of dingy greenbacks. "Next time don't tell nobody about it."

"You're a guardian angel," she said faintly. "It was all we had – we'd have starved without it – I don't know how I can ever thank you – "

"Aw, shucks, don't try!"

His shoulder hurt, but another, deeper sting was gone, and Big Mac grinned contentedly, even as he slapped his flat pocket, and reflected on the dusty miles back to the Lazy K in Texas where the job he had quit still awaited him; after all, he reckoned he could get along another year without a vacation.

The Dead Remember

Dodge City, Kansas,
November 3, 1877.

Mr. William L. Gordon,
Antioch, Texas.

Dear Bill:

I am writing you because I have got a feeling I am not long for this world. This may surprise you, because you know I was in good health when I left the herd, and I am not sick now as far as that goes, but just the same I believe I am as good as a dead man.

Before I tell you why I think so, I will tell you the rest of what I have to say, which is that we got to Dodge City all right with the herd, which tallied 3,400 head, and the trail boss, John Elston, got twenty dollars a head from Mr. R. J. Blaine, but Joe Richards, one of the boys, was killed by a steer near the crossing of the Canadian. His sister, Mrs. Dick Westfall, lives near Seguin, and I wish you'd ride over and tell her about her brother. John Elston is sending her his saddle and bridle and gun and money.

Now, Bill, I will try to tell you why I know I'm a goner. You remember last August, just before I left for Kansas with the herd, they found that Old Joel, that used to be Colonel Henry's slave, and his woman dead – the ones that lived in that live-oak thicket down by Zavalla Creek. You know they called his woman Jezebel, and folks said she was a witch. She was a high-yellow gal and a lot younger than Joel. She told fortunes, and even some of the white folks were afraid of her. I took no stock in those stories.

Well, when we was rounding up the cattle for the trail drive, I found myself near Zavalla Creek along toward sundown, and my horse was tired, and I was hungry, and I decided I'd stop in at Joel's and make his woman cook me something to eat. So I rode up to his hut in the middle of the live-oak grove, and Joel was cutting some wood to cook some beef which Jezebel had stewing over an open fire. I remember she had on a red and green checked dress. I won't likely forget that.

They told me to light and I done so, and set down and ate a hearty supper, then Joel brought out a bottle of tequila and we had a drink, and I said I could beat him shooting craps. He asked me if I had any dice, and I said no, and he said he had some dice and would roll me for a five-cent piece.

So we got to shooting craps, and drinking tequila, and I got pretty full and raring to go, but Joel won all my money, which was about five dollars and seventy-five cents. This made me mad, and I told him I'd take another drink and get on my horse and ride. But he said the bottle was empty, and I told him to get some more. He said he didn't have no more, and I got madder, and begun to swear and abuse him, because I was pretty drunk. Jezebel come to the door of the hut and tried to get me to ride on, but I told her I was free, white and twenty-one, and for her to look out, because I didn't have no use for smart high-yellow gals.

Then Joel got mad and said, yes, he had some more tequila in the hut, but he wouldn't give me a drink if I was dying of thirst. So I said: "Why, damn you, you get me drunk and take my money with crooked dice, and now you insult me. I've seen nigras hung for less than that."

He said: "You can't eat my beef and drink my licker and then call my dice crooked. No white man can do that. I'm just as tough as you are."

I said: "Damn your black soul, I'll kick you all over this flat."

He said: "White man, you won't kick nobody." Then he grabbed up the knife he'd been cutting beef with, and ran at me. I pulled my pistol and shot him twice through the belly. He fell down and I shot him again, through the head.

Then Jezebel come running out screaming and cursing, with an old muzzle-loading musket. She pointed it at me and pulled the trigger, but the cap burst without firing the piece, and I yelled for her to get back or I'd kill her. But she run in on me and swung the musket like a club. I dodged and it hit me a glancing lick, tearing the hide on the side of my head, and I clapped my pistol against her bosom and jerked the trigger.

The shot knocked her staggering back several foot, and she reeled and fell down on the ground, with her hand to her bosom and blood running out between her fingers.

I went over to her and stood looking down with the pistol in my hand, swearing and cursing her, and she looked up and said: "You've killed Joel and you've killed me, but by God, you won't live to brag about it. I curse you by the big snake and the black swamp and the white cock. Before this day rolls around again you'll be branding the devil's cows in hell. You'll see, I'll come to you when the time's ripe and ready."

Then the blood gushed out of her mouth and she fell back and I knew she was dead. Then I got scared and sobered up and got on my horse and rode. Nobody seen me, and I told the boys next day I got that bruise on the side of my head from a tree branch my horse had run me against. Nobody ever knew it was me that killed them two, and I wouldn't be telling you now, only I know I have not got long to live.

That curse has been dogging me, and there is no use trying to dodge it. All the way up the trail I could feel something following me. Before we got to Red River I found a rattlesnake coiled up in my boot one morning, and after that I slept with my boots on all the time. Then when we was crossing the Canadian it was up a little, and I was riding point, and the herd got to milling for no reason at all, and caught me in the mill. My horse drowned, and I would have, too, if Steve Kirby hadn't roped me and dragged me out from amongst them crazy cows. Then one of the hands was cleaning a buffalo rifle one night, and it went off in his hands and blowed a hole in my hat. By this time the boys was joking and saying I was a hoodoo.

But after we crossed the Canadian, the cattle stampeded on the clearest, quietest night I ever seen. I was riding night-herd and didn't see nor hear nothing that might have started it, but one of the boys said just before the break he heard a low wailing sound down amongst a grove of cottonwoods, and saw a strange blue light glimmering there. Anyway, the steers broke so sudden and unexpected they nearly caught me and I had to ride for all I was worth. There was steers behind me and on both sides of me, and if I hadn't been riding the fastest horse ever raised in South Texas, they'd have trampled me to a pulp.

Well, I finally pulled out of the fringe of them, and we spent all next day rounding them up out of the breaks. That was when Joe Richards got killed. We was out in the breaks, driving in a bunch of steers, and all at once, without any reason I could see, my horse gave an awful scream and rared and fell backward with me. I jumped off just in time to keep from getting mashed, and a big mossy horn give a bellow and come for me.

There wasn't a tree bigger than a bush anywhere near, so I tried to pull my pistol, and some way the hammer got jammed under my belt, and I couldn't get it loose. That wild steer wasn't more than ten jumps from me when Joe Richards roped it, and the horse, a green one, was jerked down and sideways. As it fell, Joe tried to swing clear, but his spur caught in the back cinch, and the next instant that steer had drove both horns clean through him. It was an awful sight.

By that time I had my pistol out, and I shot the steer, but Joe was dead. He was tore up something terrible. We covered him up where he fell, and put up a wood cross, and John Elston carved on the name and date with his bowie knife.

After that the boys didn't joke any more about me being a hoodoo. They didn't say much of anything to me and I kept to myself, though the Lord knows, it wasn't any fault of mine as I can see.

Well, we got to Dodge City and sold the steers. And last night I dreamt I saw Jezebel, just as plain I see the pistol on my hip. She smiled like the devil himself and said something I couldn't understand, but she pointed at me, and I think I know what that means.

Bill, you'll never see me again. I'm a dead man. I don't know how I'll go out, but I feel I'll never live to see another sunrise. So I'm writing you this letter to let you know about this business and I reckon I've been a fool but it looks like a man just kind of has to go it blind and there is not any blazed trail to follow.

Anyway, whatever takes me will find me on my feet with my pistol drawed. I never knuckled down to anything alive, and I won't even to the dead. I am going out fighting, whatever comes. I keep my scabbard-end tied down, and I clean and oil my pistol every day. And, Bill, sometimes I think I am going crazy, but I reckon it is just thinking and dreaming so much about Jezebel; because I am using an old shirt of yours for cleaning rags, you know that black and white checked shirt you got at San Antonio last Christmas, but sometimes when I am cleaning my pistol with them rags, they don't look black and white any more. They turn to red and green, just the color of the dress Jezebel was wearing when I killed her.

Your brother.

Jim.

STATEMENT OF JOHN ELSTON, NOVEMBER 4, 1877

My name is John Elston. I am the foreman of Mr. J. J. Connolly's ranch in Gonzales County, Texas. I was trail boss of the herd that Jim Gordon was employed on. I was sharing his hotel room with him. The morning of the third of November he seemed moody and wouldn't talk much. He would not go out with me, but said he was going to write a letter.

I did not see him again until that night. I came into the room to get something and he was cleaning his Colt's .45. I laughed and jokingly asked him if he was afraid of Bat Masterson, and he said: "John, what I'm afraid of ain't human, but I'm going out shooting if I can." I laughed and asked him what he was afraid of, and he said: "A high-yeller gal that's been dead four months." I thought he was drunk, and went on out. I don't know what time that was, but it was after dark.

I didn't see him again alive. About midnight I was passing the Big Chief saloon and I heard a shot, and a lot of people ran into the saloon. I heard somebody say a man was shot. I went in with the rest, and went on back into the back room. A man was lying in the doorway, with his legs out in the alley and his body in the door. He was covered with blood, but by his build and clothes I recognized Jim Gordon. He was dead. I did not see him killed, and know nothing beyond what I have already said.

STATEMENT OF MIKE O'DONNELL

My name is Michael Joseph O'Donnell. I am the bartender in the Big Chief saloon on the night-shift. A few minutes before midnight I noticed a cowboy talking to Sam Grimes just outside the saloon. They seemed to be arguing. After awhile the cowboy came on in and took a drink of whiskey at the bar. I noticed him because he wore a pistol, whereas the others had theirs out of sight, and because he looked so wild and pale. He looked like he was drunk, but I don't believe he was. I never saw a man who looked just like him.

I did not pay much attention to him after that because I was very busy tending bar. I suppose he must have gone on into the back room. At about midnight I heard a shot in the back room and Tom Allison ran out saying that a man had been shot. I was the first one to reach him. He was lying partly in the door and partly in the alley. I saw he wore a gun-belt and a Mexican carved holster and believed it to be the same man I had noticed earlier. His right hand was torn practically off, being just a mass of bloody tatters. His head was shattered in a way I had never seen caused by a gunshot. He was dead by the time I got there and it is my opinion he was killed instantly. While we were standing around him a man I knew to be John Elston came through the crowd and said: "My God, it's Jim Gordon!"

STATEMENT OF DEPUTY GRIMES

My name is Sam Grimes. I am a deputy sheriff of Ford County, Kansas. I met the deceased, Jim Gordon, before the Big Chief saloon, at about twenty minutes until twelve, November 3rd. I saw he had his pistol buckled on, so I stopped him and asked him why he was carrying his pistol, and if he did not know it was against the law. He said he was packing it for protection. I told him if he was in danger it was my business to protect him, and he had better take his gun back to his hotel and leave it there till he was ready to leave town, because I saw by his clothes that he was a cowboy from Texas. He laughed and said: "Deputy, not even Wyatt Earp could protect me from my fate!" He went into the saloon.

I believed he was sick and out of his head, so I did not arrest him. I thought maybe he would take a drink and then go and leave his gun at his hotel as I had requested. I kept watching him to see that he did not make any play toward anybody in the saloon, but he noticed no one, took a drink at the bar, and went on into the back room.

A few minutes later a man ran out, shouting that somebody was killed. I went right to the back room, getting there just as Mike O'Donnell was bending over the man, who I believed to be the one I had accosted in the street. He had been killed by the bursting of the pistol in his hand. I don't know who he was shooting at, if anybody. I found nobody in the alley, nor anybody who had seen the killing except Tom Allison. I did find pieces of the pistol that had exploded, together with the end of the barrel, which I turned over to the coroner.

STATEMENT OF TOM ALLISON

My name is Thomas Allison. I am a teamster, employed by McFarlane & Company. On the night of November 3rd, I was in the Big Chief saloon. I did not notice the deceased when he came in. There was a lot of men in the saloon. I had had several drinks but was not drunk. I saw "Grizzly" Gullins, a buffalo hunter, approaching the entrance of the saloon. I had had trouble with him, and knew he was a bad man. He was drunk and I did not want any trouble. I decided to go out the back way.

I went through the back room and saw a man sitting at a table with his head in his hands. I took no notice of him, but went on to the back door, which was bolted on the inside. I lifted the bolt and opened the door and started to step outside.

Then I saw a woman standing in front of me. The light was dim that streamed out into the alley through the open door, but I saw her plain enough to tell she was a Negro woman. I don't know how she was dressed. She was not pure black but a light brown or yellow. I could tell that in the dim light. I was so surprised I stopped short, and she spoke to me and said: "Go tell Jim Gordon I've come for him."

I said: "Who the devil are you and who is Jim Gordon?" She said: "The man in the back room sitting at the table; tell him I've come!"

Something made me turn cold all over, I can't say why. I turned around and went back into the room, and said: "Are you Jim Gordon?" The man at the table looked up and I saw his face was pale and haggard. I said: "Somebody wants to see you." He said: "Who wants to see me, stranger?" I said: "A high-yellow woman there at the back door."

With that he heaved up from the chair, knocking it over along with the table. I thought he was crazy and fell back from him. His eyes were wild. He gave a kind of strangled cry and rushed to the open door. I saw him glare out into the alley and thought I heard a laugh from the darkness.

Then he screamed again and jerked out his pistol and threw down on somebody I couldn't see.

There was a flash that blinded me and a terrible report, and when the smoke cleared a little, I saw the man lying in the door with his head and body covered with blood. His brains were oozing out, and there was blood all over his right hand. I ran to the front of the saloon, shouting for the bartender. I don't know whether he was shooting at the woman or not, or if anybody shot back. I never heard but the one shot, when his pistol burst.

CORONER'S REPORT

We, the coroner's jury, having held inquest over the remains of James A. Gordon, of Antioch, Texas, have reached a verdict of death by accidental gunshot wounds, caused by the bursting of the deceased's pistol, he having apparently failed to remove a cleaning rag from the barrel after cleaning it. Portions of the burnt rag were found in the barrel. They had evidently been a piece of a woman's red and green checked dress.

> Signed:
> J. S. Ordley, Coroner,
> Richard Donovan,
> Ezra Blaine,
> Joseph T. Decker,
> Jack Wiltshaw,
> Alexander V. Williams.

The Ghost of Camp Colorado

> The muffled drum's sad roll has beat
> The soldiers' last tattoo;
> No more on life's parade shall meet
> That brave and fallen few.
> —The Bivouac of the Dead

On the banks of the Jim Ned River in Coleman County, central West Texas, stands a ghost. It is a substantial ghost, built of square cut stone and sturdy timber, but just the same it is a phantom, rising on the ruins of a forgotten past. It is all that is left of the army post known as Camp Colorado in the pioneer days of Texas. This camp, one of a line of posts built in the 1850's to protect the settlers from Indian raids, had a career as brief as it was stirring. When Henry Sackett, whose name is well known in frontier annals, came to Camp Colorado in 1870, he found the post long deserted and the adobe buildings already falling into ruins. From these ruins he built a home and it is to his home and to the community school house on the site of the old post, that the term of Camp Colorado is today applied.

Today the house he built in 1870 is as strong as if erected yesterday, a splendid type of pioneer Texas ranch-house. It stands upon the foundations of the old army commissary and many of its doors and much of its flooring came from the old government buildings, the lumber for which was freighted across the plains three-quarters of a century ago. The doors, strong as iron, show plainly, beneath their paint, the scars of bullets and arrows, mute evidence of the days when the Comanches swept down like a red cloud of war and the waves of slaughter washed about the adobe walls where blue-clad iron men held the frontier.

This post was first begun on the Colorado River in 1856, but was shifted to the Jim Ned River, although it retained the original name. Built in 1857, in the stirring times of westward drift and Indian raid, the old post in its heyday sheltered notable men – Major Van Dorn, Captain Theodore O'Hara, whose poem, "The Bivouac of the Dead" has thrilled the hearts of generations, General James B. Hood, General James P. Major, General Kirby Smith, and the famous General Fitzhugh Lee, nephew of General Robert E. Lee. From Camp Colorado went Major Van Dorn, first commander of the post, to Utah, in the days of the Mormon trouble. And from Camp Colorado went General James P. Major with the force under Van Dorn, and Captain Sol Ross, later Governor of Texas, on the expedition which resulted in the death of Peta Nocona, the last great Comanche war chief, and the capture of his white wife, Cynthia Ann Parker, whose life-long captivity among the Indians forms one of the classics of the Southwest.

When the clouds of Civil War loomed in the East and the boys in blue marched away from the post in 1861, their going did not end Camp Colorado's connection with redskin history. For from the ranch-house and store built on the site of the post, Henry Sackett rode with Captain Maltby's Frontier Battalion Rangers in 1874, on the path of Big Foot and Jape the Comanche, who were leaving a trail of fire and blood across western Texas. On Dove Creek, in Runnels County, which adjoins Coleman County on the west, the Rangers came up with the marauders and it was Henry Sackett's rifle which, with that of Captain Maltby, put an end forever to the careers of Big Foot and Jape the Comanche, and brought to a swift conclusion the last Indian raid in central West Texas.

Of the original buildings of the post, only one remains – the guard house, a small stone room with a slanting roof now connected with the ranch-house. It was the only post building made of stone; the others, adobe-built, have long since crumbled away and vanished. Of the barracks, the officers' quarters, the blacksmith shop, the bakery and the other adjuncts of an army camp, only tumbled heaps of foundation stones remain, in which can be occasionally traced the plan of the building. Some of the old corral still stands, built of heavy stones and strengthened with adobe, but it too is crumbling and falling down.

The old guard house, which, with its single window, now walled up, forms a storeroom on the back of the Sackett house, has a vivid history all its own, apart from the military occupancy of the post. After the camp was deserted by the soldiers, it served as a saloon wherein the civilian settlers of the vicinity quenched their thirst, argued political questions and conceivably converted it into a blockhouse in event of Indian menace. One scene of bloodshed at least, it witnessed, for at its crude bar two men quarreled and just outside its door they shot it out, as was the custom of the frontier, and the loser of that desperate game fell dead there.

Today there remains a deep crevice in one of the walls where two military prisoners, confined there when the building was still serving as a dungeon, made a vain attempt to dig their way to liberty through the thick, solid stone of the wall. Who they were, what their crime was, and what implements they used are forgotten; only the scratches they made remain, mute evidence of their desperation and their failure.

In early days there was another saloon at the post, but of that building no trace today remains. Yet it was in use at least up to the time that Coleman County was created, for it was here that the first sheriff of the county, celebrating the gorgeous occasion of his election, emerged from the saloon, fired his six-shooter into the air and yelled: "Coleman Country, by God, and I'm sheriff of every damn' foot of her! I got the world by the tail on a downhill pull! Yippee!"

A word in regard to the builder of the house that now represents Camp Colorado might not be amiss. The Honorable Henry Sackett was born in Orsett, Essexshire, England, in 1851 and came to America while a youth. Building the house, largely with his own labor, in 1870, he lived there until his death a few years ago, acting as postmaster under seven Presidents, and as store-keeper for the settlers. The south side of the stone house, built into a single great room, was used as post office and general store. Henry Sackett was a pioneer in the truest sense of the word, an upright and universally respected gentleman, a member of the Frontier Battalion of Rangers, and later Representative in the Legislature of Texas, from Brown and Coleman Counties. He married Miss Mary MacNamara, daughter of Captain Michael MacNamara of the United States Army. Mrs. Sackett still lives at Camp Colorado.

The countryside is unusually picturesue – broad, rolling hills, thick with mesquite and scrub oaks, with the river winding its serpentine course through its narrow valley. On the slopes cattle and sheep graze and over all broods a drowsy quiet. But it is easy to resurrect the past in day dreams – to see the adobe walls rise out of dusty oblivion and stand up like ghosts, to hear again the faint and spectral bugle call and see the old corral thronged with lean, wicked-eyed mustangs, the buildings and the drill grounds with blue-clad figures – bronzed, hard-bitten men, with the sun and the wind of the open lands in their eyes – the old Dragoons! Nor is it hard to imagine that yonder chaparral shakes, not to the breeze, but to crawling, stealthy shapes, and that a painted, coppery face glares from the brush, and the sun glints from a tomahawk in a red hand.

But they have long faded into the night – the reckless, roistering cavalry men, the painted Comanches, the settlers in their homespun and buckskins; only the night wind whispers old tales of Camp Colorado.

A half mile perhaps from the Sackett house stands another remnant of the past – a sort of mile-stone, definitely marking the close of one age and the opening of another. It stands on a hillside in a corner of the great Dibrell ranch – a marble monument on which is the inscription:

BREEZE 21ST 31984

HEREFORD COW

BORN 1887   DIED 1903

MOTHER OF THE DIBRELL HERD

DIBRELL

This monument marks the resting place of one of the first registered, short-horn cows of central West Texas. When Breeze was born, west Texas swarmed with half-wild longhorns, descendants of those cattle the Spaniards brought from Andalusia; now one might look far before finding one of those picturesque denizens of the old ranges. Fat, white faced, short horned Herefords of Breeze's breed and kind have replaced them, and in the vast pageant of the west, the longhorn follows buffalo and Indian into oblivion.

The Strange Case of Josiah Wilbarger

Even amid the stark realities of frontier life, the fantastic and unexplainable had its place. There was no event stranger than the case of the man whose scalped and bloody head came thrice to a woman in a dream.

One early morning in autumn, 1833, five men were cooking their breakfast of venison over a campfire on the banks of a stream some miles south of what is now the city of Austin, Texas. They were Josiah Wilbarger, Christian, Maynie, Strother and Standifer. They had been out on a land prospecting trip and were returning to the settlements. Wilbarger's cabin was on the Colorado River, near the present site of Bastrop, and only one family – the Hornsbys – lived above him.

As the party busied themselves over their meal, there came a sudden interruption – common enough in those perilous days.

From the surrounding thickets and trees crashed a volley of shots, a whistling flight of arrows. Unseen, the red-skinned painted warriors had stolen up and trapped their prey. Three of the men dropped, riddled. The other two, miraculously untouched by the missiles whistling about them, sprang to their horses, broke through the ambush and out-ran their attackers. Looking back as they rode, they saw the bodies of their three companions lying motionless in pools of blood. One of these was Wilbarger, and they plainly saw the feathered end of an arrow standing up from his body.

They drove in the spurs and raced madly through the thickets, striving to shut out from their horrified ears the triumphant and fiendish yells of their barbaric attackers.

These had not long pursued the fleeing survivors; they returned to the bodies which lay by the small fire which still burned cheerfully, lighting that scene of horror. They gathered about, those lean, naked men, hideously painted, with shaven heads, and bearing tomahawks in their beaded girdles. They stripped the bodies and then, as a hunter might strip the pelt from a trapped animal, they took the symbols of their victory – the scalps of their victims.

This horrible practice, which the English settlers first introduced to the red man, and which did not originate with him, varied with different tribes. Some only took a small part of the scalp. Some ripped off the entire scalp. The braves who had surprised the land prospectors took the whole scalp.

Josiah Wilbarger, struck once by an arrow and twice by bullets, was not dead, though he lay like a lifeless corpse. He was only semi-conscious, dimly aware of what was going on about him. He felt rude hands ripping the clothing from his body, and he saw, as in a dream, the gory scalps ripped from the heads of his dead companions. Then he felt a lean muscular hand locked in his own hair, pulling back his head at an agonizing angle. It is fantastic that he could have so feigned death as to fool the keen hunters in whose hands he lay.

He realized the horror of his position, but he lay like man struck dumb and paralyzed. He felt the keen edge of the scalping knife slice through his skin, and perhaps he would have cried out, but he could not. He felt the knife circle his head above the ears, though he experienced only a vague stinging. Then his head was almost wrenched from his body as his tormentor ripped the scalp away with ferocious force. Still he felt no unusual agony, numbed as he was by his desperate wounds, but the noise of the scalp leaving his head sounded in his ears like a clap of thunder. And his remaining shred of consciousness was blanked out.

Had he been capable of any distinct thought, as he sank into senselessness, it must have been that this, at last, was death. Yet again he opened his eyes upon the bloody scene and the naked, scalped corpses about the dead ashes of the fire – how much later he had no interest in even speculating about. Now all was silent and deserted; the red slayers had gone as silently and swiftly as they had come.

And in this wounded and mutilated man awoke dimly the instinct to live, so powerful in the men of the raw frontier. He began to crawl, slowly, painfully, toward the direction of the settlements. To seek to depict the agonies of that ghastly journey would be but to display the frailty of the mere written word. Flies hung in clouds over his bloody head and he left red smears on the ground and the rocks. A quarter of a mile he dragged himself, then even his steely frame rebelled, and he reposed unconscious beneath a giant post-oak tree.

Now the occult element enters into the tale. The survivors of the massacre had ridden through the wide-flung settlements, bearing the tale of the crime. They had passed the cabin of the Hornsbys, which was the only cabin on the river above that of Josiah Wilbarger.

The following night, Mrs. Hornsby lay sleeping and she dreamed. The tale of the massacre was in her mind, and it is not strange that she dreamed of her neighbor, Josiah Wilbarger. Not strange, even, that in her dream she saw him naked and scalped, since the survivors had told her he had been killed, and she was familiar with Indian customs. But what was strange is that, in her dream, she saw him, not at the camping place, but beneath a great post-oak tree, some distance from where he was struck down – and alive.

Awakened by the terror of the nightmare, she told her husband, who soothed her and told her to go back to sleep.

Again she slept, again she dreamed and again she saw Wilbarger, naked, wounded and scalped – but living – under the oak tree. Once again she awoke, and again her husband soothed her distress, and again she slept. But when she dreamed the same dream for the third time she refused any longer to doubt. She began assembling things that might be needed to bandage the wounds of a wounded man, and her vehemence convinced her husband, who gathered a party and set out. First they went to the place where the attack had occurred; they saw the two dead men there and the track Wilbarger had made in dragging his wounded body away. And beneath the great post-oak tree, they found Wilbarger, alive – but just barely!

Josiah Wilbarger lived twelve years thereafter, but his wounds never fully healed, and at last he met his death – by a dream. In a nightmare he again experienced the horror of his scalping, and leaping up, struck his head with terrific force against the bedpost. This blow, coupled with his other wounds, finally caused his death.

Marking the spot where Josiah Pugh Wilbarger of Austin's Colony was stabbed and scalped by the Indians, is a marker placed there by the State of Texas, in 1936, which explains that while Wilbarger was attacked and scalped in 1833, he died on April 11, 1845.

A footnote to the story has it that Wilbarger told his rescuers that he had seen, in a vision, his sister Margaret, at the time when he was sure he would bleed to death without help. She urged him not to give up, that help was on the way, and that he would be found – friends would find him. Three months later, it was learned that about the time Wilbarger had this "visitation," and as nearly as they could figure out at the same hour – Margaret died in her home in Missouri.

The chronicles of the Middle Ages can offer no stranger tale, yet its truth is well substantiated, and it is, perhaps the most unexplainable event in Texas history.

Beyond the Brazos River

A student of early Texas history is struck by the fact that some of the most savage battles with the Indians were fought in the territory between the Brazos and Trinity rivers. A look at the country makes one realize why this was so. After leaving the thickly timbered littoral of East Texas, the westward sweeping pioneers drove the red men across the treeless rolling expanse now called the Fort Worth prairie, with comparative ease. But beyond the Trinity a new kind of country was encountered – bare, rugged hills, thickly timbered valleys, rocky soil that yielded scanty harvest, and was scantily watered. Here the Indians turned ferociously at bay and among those wild bare hills many a desperate war was fought out to a red finish. It took nearly forty years to win that country, and late into the '70s it was the scene of swift and bloody raids and forays – leaving their reservations above Red River and riding like fiends the Comanches would strike the cross-timber hills within twenty-four hours. Then it was touch and go! Much as one may hate the red devils one must almost admire their reckless courage – and it took courage to drive a raid across Red River in those days! They staked their lives against stolen horses and white men's scalps. Some times they won, and outracing the avengers, splashed across Red River and gained their tipis, where the fires blazed, the drums boomed and the painted, feathered warriors leaped in grotesque dances celebrating their gains in horses and scalps – some times they did not win and those somber hills could tell many a tale of swift retribution – of buzzards wheeling low and red-skinned bodies lying in silent heaps.

But that was in the later days. In the old times the red-skins held the banks of the Brazos. Sometimes they drove the ever-encroaching settlers back – sometimes the white men crossed the Brazos, only to be hurled back again, sometimes clear back beyond the Trinity. But they came on again – in spite of flood, drouth, starvation and Indian massacre. In that debatable land I was born and spent most of my early childhood. Little wonder these old tales seem so real to me, when every hill and grove and valley was haunted with such wild traditions!

Yes, the region between the Trinity and the Brazos saw many a red drama enacted. I remember an old woman, a Mrs. Crawford, whom I knew as a child, and who was one of the old settlers of the country. A gaunt, somber figure she was behind whose immobile countenance dreamed red memories. I remember the story she used to tell of the fate of her first husband, a Mr. Brown, in the year 1872.

One evening some of the stock failed to come up and Mr. Brown decided to go and look for them. The Browns lived in a big two-storied ranch-house, several miles from the nearest settlement – Black Springs. So Brown left the ranch-house, hearing the tinkling of a horse-bell some-where off among the mesquite. It was a chill dreary day, grey clouds deepening slowly toward the veiled sunset. Mrs. Brown stood on the porch of the ranch-house and watched her husband striding off among the mesquites, while beyond him the bell tinkled incessantly. She was a strange woman who saw visions, and claimed the gift of second-sight. Smitten with premonition, but held by the fatalism of the pioneers, she saw Brown disappear among the mesquites. The tinkling bell seemed slowly to recede until the tiny sound died out entirely. Brown did not reappear, and the clouds hung like a grey shroud, a cold wind shook the bare limbs and shuddered among the dead grasses, and she knew he would never return. She went into the house, and with her servants – a negro woman and boy – she barred the doors and shuttered the windows. She put buckets of water where they would be handy in case of fire, she armed the terrified blacks, and led them into the second story of the ranch-house, there to make their last stand. She herself went out upon the balcony of the second story and waited silently. And soon again she heard the tinkle of a horse-bell; and with it many bells. Cow-bells jangled a devil's tune as the mesquite bent and swayed and the riders swept in view – naked, painted men, riding hard, with cow-horns on their heads and cow-tails swinging grotesquely from their girdles. They drove with them a swarm of horses, some of which Mrs. Brown recognized as her own property, and at their saddle-bows swung fresh crimson scalps – one of these had a grim familiarity and she shuddered, but stood unmoving, starkly impassive. Inside the house the blacks were groveling and whimpering with terror. The Comanches swept around the house, racing at full speed. They loosed their arrows at the statue-like figure on the upper balcony and one of the shafts tore a lock of hair from her head. She did not move, did not shift the long rifle she held across her arm. She knew that unless maddened by the death or wounding of one of their number, they would not attack the house. That one arrow flight had been in barbaric defiance or contempt. They were riding hard, spurred on by the thought of avengers hot on their trail, light-eyed fighters, as ferocious as themselves. They were after horses – the Comanche's everlasting need – they had lured the rancher to his doom with a tinkling horse-bell. They would not waste time and blood storming the ranch-house. They did not care to come to grips with that silent impassive figure who stood so statue-like on the upper balcony, terrible with potentialities of ferocity, and ready to spring and die like a wounded tigress among the embers of her home. Aye, they would have paid high for that scalp – there would have been no futile screams of terror, no vain pleas for mercy where no mercy ever existed, no gleeful slitting of a helpless soft throat; there would have been the billowing of rifle-smoke, the whine of flying lead, the emptying of saddles, riderless horses racing through the mesquite and red forms lying crumpled. Aye, and the drinking of knives, the crunching of axes, and hot blood hissing in the flames, before they ripped the scalp from that frontier woman's head.

Silent she stood and saw them round up all the horses on the ranch, except one in a stable they overlooked – and ride away like a whirlwind, to vanish as they had come – as the Comanches always rode. They came like a sudden wind of destruction, they struck, they passed on like the wind, leaving desolation behind them. Taking the one horse that remained to her, she went into the mesquites and some half a mile from the house she found her husband. He lay among the dead grasses, with a dozen arrows still protruding from him, his scalped head in a great pool of congealed blood. With the aid of the blacks who had followed her, wailing a wordless dirge of death, she lifted the corpse across the horse and carried it to the ranch-house. Then she put the black boy on the horse and sent him flying toward Black Springs, whence he soon returned with a strong force of settlers. They saw the dead man and the tracks of the marauders; the wind blew cold and night had come down over the hills, and they feared for their own families. Mrs. Brown bade them go to their respective homes and leave her as a guard in case of the return of the slayers, only Captain McAdams, with whom, she said, she would feel as safe as with an army. So this was done, but the Comanches did not return. They swept in a wide half circle like a prairie fire, driving all the horses they found before them, and outracing the avengers, crossed Red River and gained their reservations and the protection of a benevolent Federal government.

Mrs. Brown was Mrs. Crawford when I knew her. A strange woman, and one whom the countryside looked on as a "medium"; a seer of visions and a communer with the dead. After she married Crawford, he went forth one day to look for his horses, just as her former husband had. Again it was a cold drear day, gloomed with grey clouds. Crawford rode away awhile before sundown and she heard his horse's hoofs dwindle away on the hard barren ground. The sun sank and the air grew cold and brittle. On the wings of a howling blue blizzard night shut down and Crawford did not come. Mrs. Crawford retired after awhile, and as she lay in the darkness, with the wild wind screaming outside, suddenly a strange feeling came over her which she recognized as the forerunner of a vision. The room filled suddenly with a weird blue light, the walls melted away, distance lost its meaning and she was looking through the hills, the long stretches of mesquite, the swirling blue distances and the night, upon the open reaches of prairie. Over the prairie blew an unearthly wind, and out of the wind came a luminous cloud and out of the cloud a horseman, riding hard. She recognized her husband, face set grimly, rifle in his grasp, and on him a blue army coat such as she had never seen before. He rode in utter silence; she did not hear the thunder of his ride, but beneath his horse's hoofs that spurned the hard earth, the dead prairie grass bent and the flints spat fire. Whether he rode alone she could not tell, for the luminous cloud closed in before and behind and he rode in the heart of the cloud. Then as a mist fades the vision faded and she was alone in the dark room with the wind screaming about the house and the wolves howling along the gale. Three days later Crawford came home, riding slowly on a weary horse. The blizzard had blown itself out; the cold sunlight warmed the shivering prairies and Crawford wore no coat, as when he had ridden away. He had not found his horses, but he had found the tracks of the raiders who had taken them, and while examining them, a band of settlers had swept past on the trail, shouting for him to follow. And he had followed and in the teeth of the freezing blizzard they had harried the marauders to the very banks of Red River, emptying more than one saddle in that long running fight. She asked about the coat, the blue army coat she had seen in the vision, and he replied with surprize that he had stopped at a settler's house long enough to borrow the coat, and had returned it as he rode back by, returning from the chase.

Many a time, as a child have I listened to her telling strange tales of old times when white men and red men locked in a last struggle for supremacy. I wandered around her old ranch-house in awe. It was not the memories of Indian forays that made me shiver – it was the strange tales the country folk told – of doors in the old ranch-house that opened and closed without human agency, of an old chair rocking to and fro in the night in an empty room. In this chair Crawford had spent his last days. Men swore that the chair rocked at night, as he had rocked, and his old spittoon clinked regularly, as it had clinked in his life-time when he rocked, chewing tobacco, and from time to time spat. Mrs. Crawford was a true pioneer woman. No higher tribute could be paid her. I liked and admired her, as I admire her memory. But to me as a child, she was endowed with a certain awesomeness, not only as far as I was concerned, but to the country-folk in general.

Billy the Kid and
the Lincoln County War

How few people give any thought to the history of even their own locality!
Why, it was from the Concho River, only about a hundred miles from here
that John Chisum started to New Mexico in 1868, with his herd of ten
thousand cattle, his caravan of waggons and his army of hard-bit Texas
cowpunchers, yet his name is hardly known in this country. John Chisum
was born in Tennessee and grew up in East Texas. He was an empire
builder if one ever lived. To read New Mexican history of the '70s it would
seem that he supported the territory – people either worked for John
Chisum or stole cattle from him! In the days of his greatest power his
herd numbered more than a hundred thousand head. The Long-rail and
the Jingle-bob were known from Border to Border. He always kept open
house; there any man could stay and eat his fill as long as he wished and
no questions were asked him. Breakfast, dinner and supper places were
set for twenty-six at the table in his big adobe house and generally all
places were full. He was a figure of really heroic proportions, a builder of
empires, yet he was by instinct merely a hard headed business man.
Nothing dramatic about John Chisum, and maybe that's why history has
slighted him in favor of fruitless but flashing characters who blazed vain
trails of blood and slaughter across the West. John Chisum never even
buckled a gun on his hip in his life; he was a builder, not a destroyer. He
did not even take the war-path in that feud known as the bloody Lincoln
County war. Have you ever read of it? There's drama! There's epic and
saga and the red tides of slaughter! Heroism, reckless courage, brute
ferocity, blind idealism and bestial greed. And the peak of red drama was
touched that bloody night in the shuddering little mountain town of
Lincoln, when Murphy's henchmen crouched like tigers in the night
behind the flaming walls of McSween's 'dobe dwelling. Let me try to

draw that picture as it has been told and re-told in song and story in the fierce annals of the Southwest – the greatest fight of them all.

The night is forked with leaping tongues of crimson flame; the bullet-riddled 'dobe walls have crumbled; the fire has devoured the west wing, the front part of the building, and now licks greedily at the last room remaining of the east wing. The walls are beginning to crumble, the roof is falling. Hidden behind wall and stable, eager and blood-maddened, crouch the Murphy men, rifles at the ready. For three days and nights they have waged a fruitless battle with the defenders; now since treachery has fired the adobe house, their turn has come at last. They keep their eyes and rifle muzzles fixed hard on the single door. Before that door, in the red glare of the climbing flames lie McSween, Harvey Morris, Semora, Romero and Salazar in pools of their own blood, where the bullets struck them down as they rushed from the burning house; four dead, one – Salazar – badly wounded. O'Folliard, Skurlock, Gonzalez and Chavez have made the dash and somehow raced through that rain of lead and escaped in the darkness. Now is the peak of red drama, for in that blazing snare still lurks one man. The watchers grip their rifles until their knuckles show white. McSween's right hand man has yet to dare that lead tipped gantlet – Billy the Kid, that slim nineteen year-old boy, with the steel grey eyes, the gay smile, the soft voice and the deadliness of a rattler. The flames roar and toss; soon he must leap through that door if he would not be burned like a rat in a trap. Bob Beckwith, whose bullet struck down McSween, curses between his teeth and trembles like a tensed hunting hound in his eagerness. He and his comrades, hidden by wall and semi-darkness, are comparatively safe – but no foe of the Kid's is safe within gun-shot range. Scarce ten yards away the soaring flames will etch their prey mercilessly in their rifle sights – how can the best marksmen of the Southwest miss at that range? Bob Beckwith curses and his eyes dance with madness. He killed McSween; now to his everlasting glory he must kill Billy the Kid, and wipe out the stain of Murphy blood – Morton, Baker – victims of the Kid's unerring eye and steady hand. A shower of sparks – the roof falls in with a roar; as if the happening hurled him from the building, a figure leaps through the door into the red glare. A mad rattle of rifle-fire volleys and the air is filled with singing lead. Through that howling hail of death the Kid races and his own guns are spurting jets of fire. Bob Beckwith falls across the wall, stone dead. Two more of the posse bellow as the Kid's bullets mark them for life. Slugs rip through the Kid's hat and clothes; death sings in the air about him – but he clears the wall and vanishes in the darkness. His time is not yet come and there still remain further red chapters to write in that red life. The Murphy men come from their coverts to roar their triumph, and while fiddles are brought and set going, the victors drink and shout and dance among the corpses in the light of the flaming embers, in a wild debauch of primitive exultation. But the Kid is fleeing unharmed through the night and he wastes no time in cursing his luck; plans for swift and gory vengeance occupy his full thoughts.

Truly the bloody Lincoln County war is the saga of the Southwest; glory and shame and murder and courage and cruelty and hate flaming into raw, red primitive drama, while through all stalked the gigantic shadow-shape of Billy the Kid, dominating all – as if that crimson feud were but the stage set for his brief stellar role – his star that flamed suddenly up and was as suddenly extinguished.

★ ★ ★

The Lincoln County war began in a cattle row. Thieves were stealing John Chisum's cows and being acquitted in the courts. Dolan, Reilly and Murphy were merchants in the town of Lincoln and all-powerful. Murphy ordered his lawyer, McSween, to defend certain rustlers against the charge brought against them by Chisum. McSween refused and Murphy fired him. McSween was engaged by Chisum, prosecuted the rustlers and sent them up the river. Then McSween, Chisum and an Englishman named Tunstall went into partnership and McSween opened a big general store in Lincoln. He grabbed most of the trade and Murphy saw he was being ruined. McSween won a suit against him and for reasons too complicated and lengthy to narrate here, Murphy got out a writ of attachment against McSween's store and Tunstall's ranch – the last an obviously illegal movement, since Tunstall owned his ranch apart from the partnership and had nothing to do with the law suit. A posse of some twenty men rode over to attach Tunstall's ranch. They overtook him in the mountains, shot him down in cold blood, beat out his brains with a jagged rock and left him lying beside his dead horse. That was the beginning of the Bloody Lincoln County War.

Billy the Kid was working for Tunstall as a cowboy. The Kid's real name was William Bonney; he was born in the slums of New York, the son of Irish emigrants. He was brought west when a very young baby and raised in Kansas and New Mexico – mainly the latter. Pancho Villa killed his first man when he was fourteen; Billy went him one better; he was only twelve when he stabbed a big blacksmith to death in Silver City, New Mexico. That started him on the wild life. When he drifted into the Lincoln County country, he already had eleven or twelve killings to his name, though only nineteen years old – that isn't counting Mexicans and Indians. No white man of that age who had any pretensions to gun-fame counted any but the regal warriors of his own race and color. The Kid had probably killed ten or fifteen men of brown and red skins, but he never considered them worthy of mention, though he was considerably proud of his white record.

The Kid was a small man – five feet eight inches, 140 pounds, perhaps – but he was very strong. But it was in his quickness of eye and hand, his perfect co-ordination that made him terrible. There was never a man more perfectly fitted for his trade.

The Kid had been living by gambling and rustling until he started working for Tunstall. At the time of the latter's brutal murder, he was making an honest living as top-hand on the Rio Feliz rancho. Had the Englishman lived, the redder phase of the Kid's life might well have never been written, for Billy liked Tunstall almost well enough to go straight for him.

But the murder of his friend drove him on the red trail of vengeance. McSween organized a posse to arrest the murderers, and had Dick Brewer, foreman of the murdered Englishman, sworn in as a special constable. They rode out after the killers and caught two of them in the Pecos Valley – Morton and Baker – former friends of the Kid. On the way back to Lincoln the Kid killed both of them, supposedly when they tried to escape. One of the posse, an old buffalo hunter named McCloskey, was killed by Frank McNab when he tried to protect the victims.

The next victim was a Murphy man named "Buckshot" Roberts, a Texas man whom it had once taken twenty-five Rangers to arrest. He was so full of lead that he couldn't lift his rifle shoulder high, but shot from the hip. Thirteen McSween men cornered him at Blazer's Mill on the Tularosa river, led by Dick Brewer and the Kid. Bowdre, the Kid's closest friend, shot Roberts through and through, but before the old Texan fell he wounded Bowdre, John Middleton and George Coe, and as he lay dying he shot off the top of Dick Brewer's skull.

The next episode took place in the town of Lincoln. Judge Bristol dared not open the regular session of court there and sent word for Sheriff Brady – a Murphy man – to open court and adjourn it as a matter of routine. On his way down the street to the courthouse, the Sheriff and his deputies were ambushed from an adobe wall by the Kid, Bowdre, O'Folliard – a Texas man – , Jim French, Frank McNab and Fred Wayte; and Sheriff Brady and Deputy Sheriff Hindman were killed. McSween was enraged by this cold blooded murder and threatened to prosecute Billy, which he probably would have done had events allowed. A very religious man was McSween and no more fitted for the role in which Fate had cast him, than a rabbit is fit to lead a pack of wolves. However, he felt that he was in the right, and did his best. Following the murder of the Sheriff, he elected – by force of his gunmen – a fellow named Copeland to the office. Murphy appealed to Governor Axtell, who removed Copeland and appointed George Peppin in his place.

Peppin immediately organized a posse and rode out after McSween's men, killing Frank McNab. Then followed the famous battle of the McSween House. The clans met in Lincoln and in the fighting that followed, Morris, Romero, Semora, and McSween were killed on the McSween side, and Salazar and Gonzalez were wounded, while on the Murphy side, Crawford was killed by Fernando Herrera, and Lacio Montoya was wounded by the same man. Bob Beckwith was killed by the Kid who also wounded two others.

That was the end of the Lincoln County war, proper. Murphy had died, a broken man, a crownless monarch, and the rest were ready to throw down their guns and call it a draw. All except the Kid and his immediate followers. But from that point, Billy's career was not that of an avenger, fighting a blood-feud. He reverted to his earlier days and became simply a gunman and an outlaw, subsisting by cattle-rustling. There was one other incident of the war, after peace had been declared; one George Chapman, a lawyer from Las Vegas, hired by Mrs. McSween, was murdered wantonly and in cold blood by a Murphy man, one Richardson, a Texan.

Emigration to that part of New Mexico had just about ceased. The tale of the Kid's reign of terror spread clear back east of the Mississippi. President Hayes took the governorship away from Axtell and gave it to Wallace – who, by the way, while writing "Ben Hur" had to keep his shutters close drawn lest a bullet from the Kid's six-shooter put a sudden termination to both book and author. John Chisum, the Kid's former friend, and others got together and elected Pat Garrett Sheriff. Garrett was a friend of the Kid's and knew his gang and his ways. He, himself, was Alabama born, Texas raised – a man of grim determination and cold steel nerves.

Meanwhile the Kid went his ways, rustling cattle and horses. One Joe Bernstein, clerk at the Mescalero agency, made the mistake of arguing with the Kid over some horses Billy was about to drive off. A Jew can be very offensive in dispute. Billy shot him down in cold blood, remarking casually that the fellow was only a Jew.

Several times Garrett and his man-hunters thought they had their hands on Billy but he eluded them. Once they cornered him at a roadhouse, but he killed Deputy Sheriff Jim Carlisle – again in cold blood – and escaped. At Fort Sumner he killed one Joe Grant, a Texas bad man who was after the reward offered for the Kid.

But Garrett was on his trail unceasingly. The Kid's best friends were Bowdre and O'Folliard. At Fort Sumner Garrett killed O'Folliard and at Tivan Arroyo, or Stinking Spring, he killed Bowdre and captured the Kid. Billy was tried in Mesilla and sentenced to be hanged for the murder of Brady and Hindman. He was confined in Lincoln and kept chained, watched day and night by Deputy Sheriffs Bell and Ollinger. He killed them both and got clean away. But love for a Mexican girl drew him back to Fort Sumner when he might have gotten clean away into Old Mexico –

I think the very night must have ceased to breathe as the Kid came from Saval Gutierrez's house through the shadows. Surely the nightwind ceased to rustle the pinon leaves and a breathless stillness, pregnant with doom lay over the shadowy mountains and the dim deserts beneath the stars. Surely the quivering mesquites, the sleeping lizards, the blind cactus, the winds whispering down the canyons and the 'dobe walls that glimmered in the starlight, surely they sensed the passing of a figure already legendary and heroic. Aye, surely the night was hushed and brooding as the Southwest's most famous son went blind to his doom.

He crossed the yard, came onto the porch of Pete Maxwell's house. He was going after beef, for Celsa Gutierrez to cook for a midnight supper. His butcher knife was in his hand, his gun in his scabbard. Pete Maxwell was his friend; he expected no foes. On the porch he met one of Garrett's deputies, but neither recognized the other. The Kid, wary as a wolf, flashed his gun, though, and backed into Pete's room which opened on the porch. There he halted short – in the shadows he made out vaguely a dim form that should not be there – someone he knew instinctively was neither Pete nor one of Pete's servants. Where was that steel trap will of the Kid's that had gotten him out of so many desperate places? Why did he hold his fire then, he who was so quick to shoot at the least hint of suspicion? Azrael's hand was on him and his hour was come. He made his last mistake, leaping back into the doorway where he was clearly limned against the sky. He snapped a fierce enquiry – and then Death bellowed in the dark from the jaws of Pat Garrett's six-shooter. They carried the Kid into a vacant carpenter shop and laid him on a bench, while the Mexican women screamed and tore their long black hair and flung their white arms wildly against the night, and the Mexican men gathered in scowling, fiercely muttering groups.

The Kid was twenty-one when he was killed, and he had killed twenty-one white men. He was left handed and used, mainly, a forty-one caliber Colt double action six shooter, though he was a crack shot with a rifle, too. That he was a cold blooded murderer there is no doubt, but he was loyal to his friends, honest in his way, truthful, possessed of a refinement in thought and conversation rare even in these days, and no man ever lived who was braver than he. He belonged in an older, wilder age of blood-feud and rapine and war.

* * *

Of Lincoln Walter Noble Burns, author of "The Saga of Billy the Kid" has said: "The village went to sleep at the close of the Lincoln County war and has never awakened again. If a railroad never comes to link it with the far-away world, it may slumber on for a thousand years. You will find Lincoln now just as it was when Murphy and McSween and Billy the Kid knew it. The village is an anachronism; a sort of mummy town. . . . "

I can offer no better description. A mummy town. Nowhere have I ever come face to face with the past more vividly; nowhere has that past become so realistic, so understandable. It was like stepping out of my own age, into the fragment of an elder age, that had somehow survived. In Lincoln I felt the Past, not as dusty, meaningless names, and the out-worn repetition of moldy heroisms, but as a living, breathing reality; it was as if a mythical giant, thought dead and forgotten, had suddenly reared his awesome head and titan shoulders above the surrounding mountains and looked at us with living eyes.

Lincoln is a haunted place; it is a dead town; yet it lives with a life that died fifty years ago.

It stands on a lap of land jutting from the base of the mountains that form the right wall of the Bonito Valley. To the left the Rio Bonito ripples along the canyon floor. The ground slopes down from the site of the town, to the river bed. Down that slope Billy the Kid dropped, with his guns blazing death, on that red summer night in 1878, when the flames of McSween's burning house shone crimson on the bodies of its owner and his friends where they had fallen before the bullet-raked door.

The houses, adobe mostly, straggle on either side of the long, crooked street. Our entrance into the town was peculiarly undramatic. Straggling clumps of trees hid it from our view until we had entered the eastern end of the street. We drove on, slowly, past the reconstructed torreon – the ancient round tower where the early settlers fought off the Apaches – past the old Montana House dance hall – adorned by a sign which stated that "Billy the Kid Cut His Initials on This House" – past the garage which is Lincoln's one reflection of modernity – past the stores where descendants of the Kid's friends and enemies lounged in the growing heat of the day – past the tavern which stands where the McSween house stood – we were both looking for one thing – the old courthouse whence Billy made the most dramatic escape ever made in the Southwest. We rounded a crook in the meandering street and it burst upon us like the impact of a physical blow. There was no mistaking it. We did not – at least I did not – need the sight of the sign upon it to identify it. I had seen its picture – how many times I do not know. I do not know how many times, and in what myriad different ways and occasions I have heard the tale of Billy's escape. It is the most often repeated, the most dramatic of all the tales of South-western folk-lore. When you hear a story long enough and often enough, it becomes like a legend. Yet I will not say that the sight of that old house was like meeting a legend face to face; there was nothing fabulous or legendary about the actuality. The realism was too potent, too indisputable to admit any feeling of mythology. If the Kid himself had stepped out of that old house, it would not have surprised me at all.

We explored the exterior, found it locked, and went across the street to the La Paloma saloon, which bears a sign that claims existence in the Kid's day. The owner is one Ramon Maes, grandson of Lucio Montoya, "Murphy's sharpshooter" as he told us with pride – a supple, well-built man, tall for a Mexican and broad-shouldered, with a thin-nostrilled Mountain Indian look about his face. The name of Montoya is woven into the Kid's saga. He took part in the three-day fight in which McSween was killed; he lay on the mountain that commanded the Montana House, with Crawford, firing from behind a boulder. Fernando Herrera, firing from the Montana House with a buffalo gun, killed Crawford, and broke Montoya's leg. The range was nine hundred yards, but Herrera was a crack shot. All day Montoya lay in the glare of the sun, with his splintered leg, until, when night fell, his friends dared a sortie to get him. I did not speak of this to his grandson. To him the feud seemed like something that happened yesterday. He was very courteous and eager to point out interesting spots, and answer our questions, but when he spoke of the fighting and the killing, a red flame came into his eyes. The descendants of old enemies live peacefully side by side in the little village; yet I found myself wondering if the old feud were really dead, or if the embers only smoldered, and might be blown to flame by a careless breath. Maes gave us the key to the old courthouse, which once was Murphy's store. It is used as a storeplace for junk now, and there is talk, we were told, of tearing it down to build a community hall. It should be preserved. When it is torn down one of the landmarks of Southwestern history will be gone. We wandered about the old building, entered the room where the Kid was confined – they knew no jail would hold him, so they kept him imprisoned in the courthouse itself. Strange how familiar everything seemed to me, though I had never been within one hundred miles of Lincoln before. Yet it seemed to me that I was going over territory traversed a hundred times before. We tried to re-create the situation that April morning in 1881 when the Kid, tricking his captor, J. Bell, off-guard by a game of monte, snatched his pistol and fought his way to liberty. We followed the route through the rooms and hallway by which Billy marched his prisoner, intending to lock him into the armory. We saw the stair where Bell made his desperate break, and the hole in the wall at the foot where the Kid's bullet had lodged, after tearing its way through Bell's heart. Bell was a Texas man, by the way – Dallas County. We stood at the window from which the Kid watched Bob Ollinger run across the street at the sound of the shot; the same window from which he poured eighteen buckshot into Ollinger's breast from the man's own shotgun. Then we went out onto the balcony from which Billy hurled the fragments of the gun with a curse at the corpse of his victim – and I could close my eyes and imagine that scene, the livid, snarling, flame-eyed figure of the killer, tense with the hate that then broke its bounds of iron control for the first and only time in his whole life – the crumpled corpse sprawled in the dust at the corner of the house, the stiffening fingers spread like claws and digging into the earth with their last convulsion – the men on the porch of the saloon and of the hotel, standing frozen, silent and motionless as statues, like spectators watching a play. Something, too, like men watching a blood-mad tiger and fearful to draw a deep breath lest the dripping fangs and talons strike in their direction. Presently, glancing away along the dusty road, it would not have seemed at all strange had we seen a lithe, pantherish figure on a mustang, in the garb of other days, with fetters still on his ankles and a rifle in each hand, riding westward toward Bacca Canyon – so close-linked in Lincoln seem Yesterday and Today.

From the old courthouse we went to the inn, which stands on the site of the old McSween house. There everything is changed. I could not recreate in my mind the climax of that three-day battle. The only thing that is as it was then is the slope of the land from the edge of the yard down to the river – and on that slope the thickets which sheltered the Kid as he ran are gone. But we learned that the bodies of McSween and most of his companions lie close to where they fell; behind a stable now, unmarked, trampled over by burros and cattle.

I have never felt anywhere the exact sensations Lincoln aroused in me – a sort of horror predominating. If there is a haunted spot on this hemisphere, then Lincoln is haunted. I felt that if I slept the night there, the ghosts of the slain would stalk through my dreams. The town itself seemed like a bleached, grinning skull. There was a feel of skeletons in the earth underfoot. And that, I understand, is no flight of fancy. Every now and then somebody ploughs up a human skull. So many men died in Lincoln. Stand with me a moment on the balcony of the old courthouse. Yonder, to the east, stands the old tower about which, in the past, waves of painted braves washed like a red tide. Their bodies littered the earth like bright-colored leaves when that tide broke. Not once but many times. Yonder in the dusty street men fell when the Horrels rode from Ruidoso one night – Texas men, with a ruthless hate for all Latins impelling them – there, before that squat-built store, Constable Martinez died beneath their bullets, and with him his deputies Gillam and Warner. There, too, fell Bill Horrel. And in that adobe house that was a dance hall then, guns blazed when the Horrels came again, the death of their brother rankling, to stretch four men and a woman dead on the floor. That was before the Kid's time. Come down the years a little. Behind us stands the stair at the foot of which Bell tumbled, with the Kid's bullet through his heart. There at the corner of the house Bob Ollinger fell, with his breast mangled. Yonder, to the east, you can see among the shade trees, the roof of the building which stands where the McSween store stood. A few feet beyond that point Sheriff Brady and his deputy Hindman were struck down by the bullets that rained upon them from the ambush the Kid and his warriors had planned. Brady fell dead there, but when the Kid took his guns from his body, he put another bullet through his head just to make sure. Hindman, shot in the back, lay in the street for half an hour, moaning for water. None dared fetch it to him. It might be construed by the killers as an act of hostility. Peaceable people kept within their doors, clenching their teeth against the agony-edged groans of the dying man. At last Port Stockton, himself a desperado, tending bar at the time, unbuckled his gun-belt and laid his weapons on the bar, filled his sombrero with water and stalked forth, his jaw set stubbornly. The skin must have crawled between his shoulders as he felt the eyes of Billy the Kid on him, opaque, passionless eyes, faintly questioning, weighing his action without emotion, without mercy. Stockton bent and set the brim of his hat to the dying man's lips, while his life hung on the crook of the Kid's trigger finger. But Billy did not fire; Hindman drank and fell back dead. And

Stockton went his way unmolested along the trail that led ultimately to his bloody death in Durango. The dusty street stretches still and sleepy in the hot sunshine before us; there is a bird singing in a cottonwood, and a woman calls her child in petulant Spanish. But once that street was a stage for violent and bloody drama. Turn your head now and look at the mountain that rises behind the town. There on the bare, rock-littered slope Crawford and Montoya crouched that hot summer day so long ago. There Crawford died, pitching headlong from the ledge where he crouched, to roll down the long slope like a rag doll. Perhaps he did not die instantly. Men say death came slowly to him, all through the long, hot day as he lay groaning with the agony of a broken back. On the ledge above his comrade Montoya lay with his broken leg. Turn again to the dusty street of Lincoln and look at the inn, which stands where the McSween house stood. Men died in the backyard there – Harvey Morris, Francisco Semora, Vincente Romero, McSween himself, Bob Beckwith. And yonder in the road before the site of the old house George Chapman, the Las Vegas lawyer, was killed by Bill Campbell, one of Murphy's Texan gunmen. No one dared go forth at the sound of the shot; they peered from their windows and saw the body of a man lying in the street, but until daylight came none knew who it was.

Lincoln is a haunted town – yet it is not merely the fact of knowing so many men died there that makes it haunted, to me. I have visited many spots where death was dealt whole-sale: the Alamo, for instance; the battle-field of Goliad; La Bahia, where Fannin's men were massacred; Fort Griffin; Fort McKavett; the hanging-tree in the courthouse yard at Goliad where so many men kicked out their lives. But none of those places ever affected me just as Lincoln did. My conception of them was not tinged with a definite horror as with Lincoln. I think I know why. Burns, in his splendid book that narrates the feud, missed one dominant element entirely; and this is the geographical, or perhaps I should say topographical effect on the inhabitants. I think geography is the reason for the unusually savage and bloodthirsty manner in which the feud was fought out, a savagery that has impressed everyone who has ever made an intelligent study of the feud and the psychology behind it. The valley in which Lincoln lies is isolated from the rest of the world. Vast expanses of desert and mountains separate it from the rest of humanity – deserts too barren to support human life. The people in Lincoln lost touch with the world. Isolated as they were, their own affairs, their relationship with one another, took on an importance and significance out of proportion to their actual meaning. Thrown together too much, jealousies and resentments rankled and grew, feeding upon themselves, until they reached monstrous proportions and culminated in those bloody atrocities which startled even the tough West of that day. Visualize that narrow valley, hidden away among the barren hills, isolated from the world, where its inhabitants inescapably dwelt side by side, hating and being hated, and at last killing and being killed. In such restricted, isolated spots, human passions smolder and burn, feeding on the impulses which give them birth, until they reached a point that can hardly be conceived by dwellers in more fortunte spots. It was with a horror I frankly confess that I visualized the reign of terror that stalked that blood-drenched valley; day and night was a tense waiting, waiting, until the thunder of the sudden guns broke the tension for a moment and men died like flies – and then silence followed, and the tension shut down again. No man who valued his life dared speak; when a shot rang out at night and a human being cried out in agony, no one dared open the door and see who had fallen. I visualized people caught together like rats, fighting in terror and agony and bloodshed; going about their work by day with a shut mouth and an averted eye, momentarily expecting a bullet in the back; and at night lying shuddering behind locked doors, trembling in expectation of the stealthy footstep, the hand on the bolt, the sudden blast of lead through the windows. Feuds in Texas were generally fought out in the open, over wide expanses of country. But the nature of the Bonito Valley determined the nature of the feud – narrow, concentrated, horrible. I have heard of people going mad in isolated places; I believe the Lincoln County War was tinged with madness.

The Ballad of Buckshot Roberts

Buckshot Roberts was a Texas man;
(Blue smoke drifting from the pinyons on the hill.)
Exiled from the plains where his rugged life began
(Buzzards circling low over old Blazer Mill.)

On the floor of 'dobe, dying, he lay,
Holding thirteen men at bay.
Thirteen men of the desert's best,
True-born sons of the stark Southwest.
Men from granite and iron hewed –
Riding the trail of the Lincoln feud.

Fighters of iron nerve and will –
But they saw John Middleton lying still
In the thick dust clotted dark and brown,
Where Roberts' bullet cut him down;
So they crouched in cover, on belly or knee,
Warily firing from bush and tree.

Even Billy the Kid held hard his hate,
Waiting his chance as a wolf might wait,
His cold gaze fixed on the brooding Mill
Where the black muzzle gleamed on the window sill.

There on the floor Bill Roberts lay,
His life in a red stream ebbing away:

The Ballad of Buckshot Roberts

Weather beaten and gnarled and scarred,
Grown old in a land where life was hard,
Soldier, ranger and pioneer,
Rawhide son of the Last Frontier.

Indian forays and border wars
Had left their mark in his many scars.
He had coursed with Death – and the pace was fast:
But he knew he had reached the end at last.
Shot through and through and nearly done –
Close he huddled his buffalo gun,
Propped the barrel on the window sill –
The firing ceased, and the land was still.

They knew he had taken his mortal wound,
And they waited like silent wolves around,
All but Dick Brewer who led the band:
His fury burned him like a brand;
Reckless he rose in his savage ire,
Stood in the open to aim and fire.

Roberts laughed in a ghastly croak,
His finger crooked, and the old gun spoke.
Blue smoke spat, and the whistling lead
Tore off the top of Brewer's head.

Roberts laughed, and the red tide welled
Up to his lips – the echoes belled
Clear and far – then faint and far,
Like a haunting call from a twilight star.

The gnarled hands slid from the worn old gun;
A lark flashed up in the golden sun;
A mountain breeze went quivering past –
So he came to the long trail's end at last.

Buckshot Roberts was a Texas man
(Nightwinds sighing over Ruidosa way) –
Heart and blood and marrow of a fighting clan!
(So the Tularosa whispers in the dawning of the day.)

SOURCE ACKNOWLEDGMENTS

"Golden Hope" Christmas: *The Tattler*, December 22, 1922

Drums of the Sunset: *Cross Plains Review*, November 1928–January 1929 (in 9 parts), and copy of incomplete original typescript provided by Glenn Lord

The Extermination of Yellow Donory: Copy of original typescript provided by Glenn Lord

The Judgment of the Desert: The Vultures (Lakemont GA: Fictioneer Books Ltd., 1973, as "Showdown at Hell's Canyon")

Gunman's Debt: Copy of original typescript provided by Glenn Lord

The Man on the Ground: *Weird Tales*, July 1933

The Sand-Hills' Crest: Transcript provided by Glenn Lord

The Devil's Joker: *Cross Plains* no. 6 (1975)

Knife, Bullet and Noose: *The Howard Collector* no. 6 (Spring 1965)

Law-Shooters of Cowtown: Copy of original typescript provided by Cross Plains Public Library, Texas

The Last Ride: *Western Aces*, October 1935 (as "Boot-Hill Payoff")

John Ringold: *The Howard Collector* no. 5 (Summer 1964)

Vultures of Wahpeton: *Smashing Novels Magazine*, December 1936 (as "Vultures of Whapeton"; letters and files of Howard's agent show that original spelling was "Wahpeton")

Vultures of Wahpeton Alternate Ending: *Smashing Novels Magazine*, December 1936

Vultures' Sanctuary: Copy of carbon of original typescript provided by Glenn Lord

The Dead Remember: *Argosy*, August 15, 1936

The Ghost of Camp Colorado: *Texaco Star*, April 1931

The Strange Case of Josiah Wilbarger: *The West*, September 1967 (as "Apparition of Josiah Wilbarger")

Beyond the Brazos River: Excerpts from letters to H. P. Lovecraft, August 1931 and October 1931, selected, arranged and titled by the editor, from copies of original letters provided by Glenn Lord

Source Acknowledgments

Billy the Kid and the Lincoln County War: Excerpts from letters to H. P. Lovecraft, January 1931, February 1931, and July 1935, selected, arranged and titled by the editor, from copies of original letters provided by Glenn Lord

The Ballad of Buckshot Roberts: *Rhymes of Death* (Memphis TN: Dennis McHaney, 1975)

THE WORKS OF ROBERT E. HOWARD

Boxing Stories
Edited and with an introduction by Chris Gruber

The Black Stranger and Other American Tales
Edited and with an introduction by Steven Tompkins

The End of the Trail: Western Stories
Edited and with an introduction by Rusty Burke

Lord of Samarcand and Other Adventure Tales of the Old Orient
Edited by Rusty Burke
Introduction by Patrice Louinet

The Riot at Bucksnort and Other Western Tales
Edited and with an introduction by David Gentzel